W9-BKF-981

The HYPNOTIST

Also by M. J. Rose

Fiction

THE VENUS FIX
LYING IN BED
THE DELILAH COMPLEX
THE HALO EFFECT
SHEET MUSIC
FLESH TONES
IN FIDELITY
LIP SERVICE

The Reincarnationist series

THE REINCARNATIONIST
THE MEMORIST
THE HYPNOTIST

Nonfiction

BUZZ YOUR BOOK
(with Douglas Clegg)
HOW TO PUBLISH AND PROMOTE ONLINE
(with Angela Adair-Hoy)

M.J. ROSE

The HYPNOTIST

MOUNTAIN VIEW
PUBLIC LIBRARY
Mountain View, CA

MIRA®

MIRA®

Recycling programs
for this product may
not exist in your area.

ISBN-13: 978-0-7783-2675-5

THE HYPNOTIST

Copyright © 2010 by Melisse Shapiro.

All rights reserved. Except for use in any review, the reproduction or
utilization of this work in whole or in part in any form by any electronic,
mechanical or other means, now known or hereafter invented, including
xerography, photocopying and recording, or in any information storage or
retrieval system, is forbidden without the written permission of the publisher,
MIRA Books, 225 Duncan Mill Road, Don Mills, Ontario, Canada M3B 3K9.

This is a work of fiction. Names, characters, places and incidents are
either the product of the author's imagination or are used fictitiously, and
any resemblance to actual persons, living or dead, business establishments,
events or locales is entirely coincidental.

For questions and comments about the quality of this book please contact us at
Customer_eCare@Harlequin.ca.

MIRA and the Star Colophon are trademarks used under license and registered
in Australia, New Zealand, Philippines, United States Patent and Trademark
Office and in other countries.

www.MIRABooks.com

Printed in U.S.A.

To Mad Max Perkins,
for your faith

❧ ❧ ❧

Please visit Reincarnationist.org
to subscribe to my free newsletter
and get exclusive access to special materials,
lost chapters, screen savers and more.

"Often, in the cosseted quarters of a museum, we forget that every work of ancient art is a survivor, a representative of untold numbers of similar artworks that perished. This triumphant exhibition makes us remember, while demonstrating that every survivor saves much more than just itself: long strands of culture, identity and history waiting to be woven back together."

—Roberta Smith, writing in the New York Times about the exhibit Silent Survivors of Afghanistan's 4,000 Tumultuous Years

Chapter

ONE

"Were I called on to define, very briefly, the term Art, I should call it the reproduction of what the Senses perceive in Nature through the veil of the soul."

—Edgar Allan Poe

Twenty Years Ago

Time played tricks on him whenever he stood in front of the easel. Hypnotized by the rhythm of the brush on the canvas, by one color merging into another, the two shades creating a third, the third melting into a fourth, he was lulled into a state of single-minded consciousness focused only on the image emerging. Immersed in the act of painting, he forgot obligations, missed classes, didn't remember to eat or to drink or look at the clock. This was why, at 5:25 that Friday evening, Lucian Glass was rushing down the urine-stinking steps to the gloomy subway platform when he should have already been uptown where Solange Jacobs was waiting for him at her father's framing gallery. Together, they planned to walk over to an exhibit a block away, at the Metropolitan Museum of Art.

When he reached the store, the shade was drawn and the Closed sign faced out, but the front door wasn't locked. Inside, none of the lamps were lit, but there was enough ambient twilight coming through the windows for him to see that Solange wasn't there, only dozens and dozens of empty frames, encasing nothing but pale yellow walls, crowded shoulder-to-shoulder, waiting to be filled like lost souls looking for mates.

As he hurried toward the workroom in the back, the commingled smells of glue and sawdust grew stronger and, except for his own voice calling out, the silence louder.

"Solange?"

Stopping on the threshold, he looked around but saw only more empty frames. *Where was she? And why was she here alone?* Lucian was walking toward the worktable, wondering if there was another room back there, when he saw her. Solange was sprawled on the floor, thrown against a large, ornate frame as if she were its masterpiece, her blood splattered on its broken gold arms, a still life in terror. There were cuts on her face and hands and more blood pooled beneath her.

Kneeling, he touched her shoulder. "Solange?"

Her eyes stayed closed but she offered a ghost of a smile.

While he was thinking of what to do first—help her or call 911—she opened her eyes and lifted her hand to her cheek. Her fingertips came away red with blood.

"Cut?" she asked, as if she had no idea what had happened. He nodded.

"Promise," she whispered, "you won't paint me like this…" Solange had a crescent-shaped scar on her forehead and was forever making sure her bangs covered it. Then, catching herself, she'd laugh at her vanity. That laugh now came out as a moan.

When her eyes fluttered closed, Lucian put his head on her chest. He couldn't hear a heartbeat. Putting his mouth over hers, he attempted resuscitation, frantically mimicking what he'd seen people do in movies, not sure he was doing it right.

He thought he saw her hand move and had a moment of elation that she was going to be all right before realizing it was only his reflection moving in the frame. His head back on her chest, he listened but heard nothing. As he lay there, Solange's blood seeping out of her wound, soaking his hair and shirt, he felt a short, fierce burst of wind.

Lucian was tall but thin…just a skinny kid studying to be a painter. He didn't know how to defend himself, didn't know how to deflect the knife that came down, ripping through his shirt and flesh and muscle. Again. And then again. So many times that finally he wasn't feeling the pain; he was the pain, had become the agony. Making an effort to stay focused, as if somehow that would matter, he tried to memorize all the colors of the scene around him: his attacker's shirtsleeve was ochre, Solange's skin was titanium white…he was drifting…

There were voices next, very far-off and indistinct. Lucian tried to grasp what they were saying.

"…extensive blood loss…"

"…multiple stab wounds…"

He was traveling away from the words. Or were they traveling away from him? Were the people leaving him alone here? Didn't they realize he was hurt? No, they weren't leaving him…they were lifting him. Moving him. He felt cool air on his face. Heard traffic.

Their voices were becoming more indistinct.

"…can't get a pulse…"

"We're losing him…quick, quick. We're losing him…"

The distance between where he was and where they were increased with every second. The words were just faint whispers now, as soft as a wisp of Solange's hair.

"Too late…he's gone."

The last thing he heard was one paramedic telling the other the time was 6:59 p.m. A silence entered Lucian, filling him up and giving him, at last, respite from the pain.

Chapter
TWO

The Present

The building on Fortieth Street and Third Avenue was a series of cantilevered glass boxes. Upstairs on the sixteenth floor, in an opulent office inconsistent with the modern structure, three men were on a conference call with a fourth via a secure phone line. It was an unnecessary precaution. When the mission of Iran to the UN had rented this space, they'd torn down the walls so they could properly insulate against long-range distance microphones. But one could never be too cautious, especially on foreign soil.

A fog of smoke hung over the windowless conference room table and the odor of heavy tobacco overwhelmed Ali Samimi. He hated the stink of the Cuban cigars but he wasn't in charge here and couldn't complain. He coughed. Coughed again. It was so like his boss to blow the smoke in his direction, despite knowing he was sensitive to it. *Farid Taghinia was one mean motherfucking son of a bitch.* Samimi stifled the smile that just thinking the American curse words brought to his lips.

"We have no trouble working with the British, the French or the Austrians. Only with the Americans do complications and conflict continue to arise. Haven't I been generous in offering to allow the museum to keep the sculpture for the opening of their new wing? Haven't they seen the documents we provided proving the sculpture was stolen? Why are they still hesitating?" Even though his voice was traveling six thousand miles, from Tehran to Manhattan, Hicham Nassir's puzzlement was perceptible.

"Because I haven't shown them the documents," said Vartan Reza, a craggy-faced, Iranian-born American lawyer who specialized in cultural heritage cases. It had been almost two years since the mission had hired Reza to orchestrate the return of a piece of sculpture currently owned by the Metropolitan Museum of Art on the basis that it had been illegally taken out of Iran over a hundred years before. The lawyer had hesitated in accepting the case until Taghinia had made it clear that a generous fee would not be the lawyer's only recompense. The members of Reza's family still living in Tehran would be well provided for, too.

If Samimi had respected Taghinia at all, he would have been impressed by his boss's cunning—offering a generous bonus wrapped around a threat. Instead it made him all the more nervous about watching his own back.

"Didn't show them the papers? Why is that?" demanded Taghinia from the opposite end of the table as he put the Cuban up to his mouth and inhaled again.

"I have some questions about their authenticity," Reza explained. "And I don't want to turn anything over to the museum's attorneys that might prove embarrassing and hurt our case."

Taghinia picked a piece of tobacco off his thick lips, blinked his lizard-brown eyes and started tapping his foot on the carpet. "Questions?" *Tap, tap.* "Questions at this point are not a good thing, Mr. Reza." *Tap, tap.* "Our government is losing patience."

"Regardless, it's not in your best interest to have me proceed rashly."

Taghinia glared at Samimi as if this was somehow the underling's fault. The only real civility and cooperation between Iran and America was in the cultural arena, and if this issue dragged on and became an international incident it wouldn't help either country's already strained diplomatic efforts.

"Were you aware of this?" he asked.

"I don't care if Samimi knew about it or not. I want to know what's wrong with the documents." Nassir's voice drew everyone's attention back to the squawk box in the middle of the highly polished ebony table.

"I don't believe they're authentic," Reza said.

"What?" Taghinia's face flushed with an emotion that read as outrage but that Samimi suspected was guilt.

"That's impossible," said Nassir. "Reza, do you understand? That's impossible."

Samimi had never heard the minister of culture so upset. Nassir had studied art history at Oxford and had published two books on Islamic art that had each been translated into more than twenty languages. Nassir had once said that he believed every piece in Iran's museum was a member of his family and it was up to him to safeguard them all.

"The partage agreement that details the fate of the objects found at the Susa excavations is dated 1885," Reza said.

"Yes?" Nassir asked.

"The paper it's written on was manufactured in 1910," Reza explained.

"Impossible."

"I'm afraid not. I've had two experts test it."

"But there are corroborating records," the minister argued.

"None that mention this piece by name or description, Mr.

Nassir. For the past eighteen months, we've been operating on the assumption that these papers were authentic. We've built our whole case on them. This is a serious setback."

At the heart of Iran's request was an eight-foot-tall chryselephantine statue of the Greek god Hypnos, the god of sleep, which neither Samimi nor anyone else on the phone call had ever seen. According to art historians, some of the best chryselephantine sculpture came from the city of Delphi, which had been looted by the Phokians in the mid-fourth century BCE. The Phokians had sold some of the treasures to raise money and pay troops; others they melted to make coins. It was believed that a Persian satrap or king in Susa had bought Hypnos when the Phokians reached the east and that, at some point after that, the statue had been buried. It might have been hidden during an attack to save it from more looters because of the amount of gold, ivory and precious stones that decorated it, or stolen again and hidden by the thief. No one knew, but the result was that it had survived practically intact until the 1880s.

"What about the treaty?" Nassir asked.

Samimi had also given Reza a copy of a treaty dated April 12, 1885, that granted France the exclusive right to excavate the area of Shush, which was on the ancient site of Susa. "That's authentic, but since we have no proof of when Hypnos was found, only when it was shipped out of the country, it's useless."

"It was discovered prior to April. The American collector bought looted art," Taghinia insisted. He turned and looked at Samimi, then blew out more of the toxic smoke.

Samimi knew he couldn't logically be blamed for this latest snafu. Nassir had sent the documents in question to America via the diplomatic pouch. But Taghinia was going to need someone to blame and the case had been Samimi's responsibility for the past year and a half. He knew more about the history of the hypnotist than anyone here but Reza.

When the American collector who'd bought the sculpture died in 1888 he left it, along with the rest of his vast collection, to the Metropolitan Museum of Art. At that time New York's fledgling museum, which had recently moved from Fourteenth Street up to Eighty-First Street and Fifth Avenue, had already outgrown its new space, and its director, General Luigi Palma di Cesnola, was using all available funds for expansions. When he saw how much conservation Hypnos needed he put the sculpture in storage in the cavernous tunnel under Central Park until he had the money to tend to it. In 1908 a young curator mislabeled it and for almost an entire century after that, it remained lost. Then, in the winter of 2007, another curator, searching for a Roman bronze, discovered the mislabeled crate. A few months later, the Met announced its find. Hypnos, they said, would be getting the conservation it needed before being installed in a special exhibition space linking the Greek and Roman wings with the new Islamic wing when it opened in 2011.

Five months later, Vartan Reza formally made a request on behalf of the Iranian government that Hypnos be returned, claiming it had been illegally smuggled out of the country by a French archaeologist.

Once the international press reported the story, the Greek government filed a similar claim, requesting that the sculpture be returned to them since, even though the piece had been found in the Middle East, it was clearly of Greek origin and a national treasure.

It was no surprise that the single surviving piece of chryselephantine sculpture in the world was a prize to fight over, but the Met refused to even get into the ring.

In a *New York Times* op-ed, the museum director wrote about the cultural heritage issue at the heart of the battle:

> There is no case here. Frederick L. Lennox, who bequeathed the sculpture to us, did not engage in buying contraband. Partage was a common and legitimate system in the nineteenth century, and this treasure was part of that fair exchange—expertise traded for a percentage of what was found. It wasn't illegal activity then and can't be looked at as illegal activity now.
>
> Hypnos has been at the Met for over one hundred and twenty years. This is his home, and with us he is safe in a way that he might not be in his homeland. We'll continue to protect him and prepare him to be shown unless and until we have irrefutable proof that he's here illegally.

All over the world, museums engaged in similar battles were watching what happened in New York. When accused of harboring looted treasures, most of them took it upon themselves to do the research necessary to prove the legality of their ownership. Not the Met. The director insisted the burden of that proof was on the claimant. The Metropolitan, he said, was under no obligation to prove the opposite. The last will and testament of Frederick L. Lennox had been verified when it was executed over a hundred years before.

Reza had countered by getting a subpoena requiring the museum to turn over Lennox's bequest and any other pertinent paperwork. When that request was refused, Reza filed with the Manhattan district attorney, asking to be allowed to review the Met's documents and study the detailed history of the object's journey to the museum in order to prove it was there illegally. The district attorney was quoted as saying, "A museum must recognize its obligation to return looted objects of art to their country of origin. That's in the public interest." But, stopping short of penalizing the Metropolitan, he added, "It is, though, incumbent on Iran to first present some proof that the sculpture was removed illegally."

A new fit of coughing overtook Samimi, who hated giving his boss the satisfaction of knowing he was affecting him.

"This situation is taking far too long to resolve," Nassir said. "I'm afraid that this isn't acceptable."

"Cultural heritage issues are never resolved quickly. The result is what matters here, not how long it takes to achieve it," Reza argued.

"But will we ever achieve it? We've been involved in tiresome negotiations for more than a year and a half and have managed only to engage a rival country in our battle. We could wind up doing all the work, only to have the Greeks get custody."

"The sculpture was created there. It's difficult to imagine that the Greeks wouldn't stake a claim once it was reported that—" Reza started.

"You should have anticipated that and found a way to keep our request out of the press," Nassir interrupted, something else he'd never done before today.

Samimi paid strict attention to the volley, looking from the squawk box to the lawyer and then to his boss, who was staring at the burning ember of his cigar.

"Keeping something out of the press is simply not possible in America," Reza countered.

"Really? Don't they say anything is possible in America?" Nassir asked.

"Mr. Nassir, we're arguing about something that happened over a year ago," the lawyer said. "We have a new problem now and need to deal with that. I can't take a chance—"

"Thank you, Mr. Reza," Nassir cut him off again. "Let me look into what you've told me and find out where this phony document originated and where the real one is. Because there is a real one, I assure you. Someone is trying to embarrass us. Can you give the papers back to Samimi… Samimi, are you there?"

"Yes, Minister." He sat up straighter in his chair as if the speakerphone had eyes that had suddenly been turned on him.

"Please show Mr. Reza out and then come back. We have other issues we need to discuss that don't relate to Hypnos."

Reza stood and walked to the door without waiting for Samimi, who rushed to catch up and then escorted the lawyer into the reception area. The mission didn't allow visitors to roam through the offices unescorted.

In the lobby, two uniformed security guards stepped aside to let the men through to the outer hallway where the elevators were.

"I hope you can explain to your boss that we can't untangle in so short a time what it has taken centuries to tangle."

"I will, Mr. Reza. At least, I will try," Samimi said diffidently as he looked up at the lawyer, who had a good three inches on him. "We appreciate your efforts and so does the minister, even if he seemed impatient today." He pressed the elevator button.

"Seemed?"

For the first time since Samimi had met him, Reza looked worried. Trying to be reassuring, the junior attaché smiled. "It was just the shock of finding this out on the heels of discovering how unsympathetic the museum's new director is to our cause." He shrugged. "If I were Tyler Weil, a cultural disaster wouldn't be the way I'd want to begin my tenure."

"Or it would be exactly how you'd want to begin it. By making a strong statement cementing your position."

"Yes, I see your point," Samimi said. He hadn't thought of it that way.

The elevator arrived. Reza stepped inside, put his hand out to hold the door open and said, "Let me know as soon as you have any news."

Samimi noticed the high polish on Reza's oxfords as the door slid shut and then looked down at his own shining shoes. He'd been paying close attention to everything about the lawyer. It was all part of what he called "the education of Ali Samimi," a self-styled course designed to help him fit in the way Reza did, despite the man's skin color and dark hair. Samimi wasn't just impressed with the American Iranian, he was envious of him: Reza was a US citizen who called New York home and didn't worry about being shipped back to Iran on someone's whim.

Returning to the stinking conference room and the call still in progress, Samimi didn't wonder what he'd missed. He'd find out later when he played back the clandestine recording he hoped his boss had no idea he was making.

The only way to play with wolves, his grandfather had taught him, was to be a wolf. And he was certainly playing with wolves. The minute he'd met Taghinia, Samimi had known that he couldn't trust him. Taghinia, with his flatulence and his teeth yellowed from the constant cigars, who flaunted his superiority over Samimi and tried to humiliate the younger man at every opportunity. He'd piled more and more work on him, so that now Samimi was doing the lion's share of his boss's job as well as his own. The only thing that kept him from complaining was his long-term goal, to find a way to stay in America.

At thirty-five, he'd arrived in New York and felt true passion for the first time in his life. He loved everything about his adopted city: its restaurants, culture, nightlife, energetic pace, its architecture and especially its women. Samimi felt as if he'd merely been alive before; now he was living. Complaining would only ensure his return to Tehran, so he put up with this

fifty-two-year-old man who, among his other sins, was immune
to the temptations of his adopted home. *How was that possible?*
Taghinia lived three blocks away from the office and never
strayed from the neighborhood for anything other than neces-
sities, actually boasting that he'd never seen Central Park,
Broadway at night, the Upper East Side or the inside of a restaurant other than Ravagh, the Persian eatery less than ten
blocks away. Taghinia often said that he would gladly die for
his country and living in New York was halfway to dying. De-
spising the city for its excesses, he focused on the day when his
homeland's recognition as a superpower would be restored. He
repeatedly told Samimi that on the day Islam's universal domi-
nance was reestablished he would rest, but not before.

Not me, Samimi thought as he sat back down at the
conference-room table. *Not me.* Dying for a principle was a
lofty ideal, but not when there was so much to live for—Laurie
Yardley being a perfect example of how much. He'd left her
apartment that morning while she was still lying naked in her
bed, a wanton look on her face as she listed what would be
waiting for him when he returned that night. And she was just
one of the women Samimi was seeing. He sat down, just in time
to hide the bulge in his pants.

"The longer you let this go the more damage can be done.
These antique rugs need to be mended as soon as they start to
unravel," Nassir was saying over the speakerphone. "Do you
understand? The time to take care of this is now."

Samimi glanced down at his polished shoes on the brilliant
sapphire-and-ruby rug. There were five other Persians of this
quality in the office. Each was worth more than most people,
even in America, made in a year. It was a travesty. These rugs
belonged in museums, or at least hanging on the walls. Nonetheless, the minister's suggestion didn't make sense. Regardless

of how much traffic the rugs bore, or how much ash his boss dropped on the seventeenth-century masterpieces, none of them needed repairs. Taghinia and the minister were talking in a code Samimi didn't officially know about but one he'd deciphered months ago.

"We'll stay on top of it," Taghinia said.

"I think it's time to let Samimi be responsible for the rugs," the minister said.

Taghinia looked over at Samimi, his thick eyebrows raised as if to suggest he was impressed. "Yes, of course, Minister."

A shiver fishtailed down the younger man's spine.

"Samimi, are you there?"

"Yes, Minister."

"I'm counting on you."

"Yes, Minister."

"Taghinia will explain."

Samimi tried to quash the panic down deep in his gut. "Yes, Minister," he said, hoping that Nassir couldn't hear how dry his voice had suddenly become.

"Excellent," he said, and hung up.

"Repairs? What is he talking about?" Samimi asked.

Taghinia waved off the question. "We're not talking about rugs, you fool."

"It was a code?" Samimi hoped his acting would pass muster.

"Of course it was a code. The minister was telling me he wants us to get Hypnos home."

"We have Reza working on that for us."

"There is too much bureaucracy in this country. Too many regulatory commissions. Too many layers to deal with. We can do it much more quickly bypassing those formalities. We have to move the sculpture out ourselves."

"We can't take Hypnos out of the Met illegally."

"We have men in place in the museum, don't we?"

"Just two."

"What's to stop us from putting in a few more? Get five or six in there."

"We put them inside the museum to protect the sculpture." Taghinia said nothing.

"You said it was security," Samimi insisted.

"And it was, but it can become something else."

Samimi hadn't heard anything about this on the tapes. What had he missed? He felt stupid and then sick as something occurred to him. Twice during the past eight months, Samimi had delivered small objets d'art to the associate curator of the museum's Islamic art department from a wealthy Iranian who Taghinia had said wished to remain anonymous.

"What about the pieces I've given to Deborah Mitchell…is she part of this plan?"

"More insurance." Taghinia nodded.

"Are the pieces bugged?"

"No." Taghinia laughed. "They are quite legitimate. I wanted you to get to know someone inside the museum who was familiar with the Islamic art collection."

Samimi looked down at his fingers, splayed on the table. He had thought he'd outsmarted his boss, but he'd missed some important communiqués. "The Met is one of the most secure institutions in the world."

"Your point?"

"It's impenetrable."

"You sound in awe of this museum. Are you? This Deborah Mitchell…does she mean something to you?"

From the first day that Samimi had walked into the great front hall of the Metropolitan Museum he'd been captivated by the marble and stone, the cool air perfumed by the gigantic arrangements of flowers tucked into alcoves, by the classical Beaux Arts architecture and the endless galleries leading to more endless galleries that offered up the artistic accomplishments of one great culture after another. It was hard for him to separate Deborah from where she worked. Of all the women he'd met in New York and was attracted to, she was the only one he'd refrained from trying to seduce. She was part of the Metropolitan Museum of Art.

"Of course not, but…what you are suggesting…it's insane, Farid. You do realize that we are discussing an eight-foot-tall piece of sculpture. I know it's an important artifact but…"

"Don't be a fool. We're talking about more than just a piece of sculpture." He puffed on his cigar and his reptilian eyes narrowed. "In researching the records for Reza, our minister found a set of documents that he hasn't shared with the lawyer, or anyone else. It appears that Hypnos could be a map of sorts that holds the secret to how man can access his inner realms and higher consciousness, making visions, clairvoyance, precognition and out-of-body experiences all possible. If tapped, this power would allow man to use his imagination to affect reality. You'd just imagine murdering someone and your imagination would make it happen."

"You can't believe that."

"For all the time you've spent in America you still haven't learned her lessons, have you? Is there anything more valuable than potential, Ali? Than possibility? Than a promise or a threat? Hypnos and his secrets are rightfully ours. We want them back." He flicked a half inch of dead ash into a crystal ashtray. "Whatever the cost."

Chapter
THREE

The lanky man ambled down the narrow Viennese street with the lazy insouciance of someone who never worried and who'd never been weighed down with tragedy or illness. He walked as if the stone pavers beneath his feet had been laid for him; as if the sun were shining and it were morning. But it was night and it was windy and wet, with the kind of cold, pelting rain that one expects in April, not May.

He'd been in this city for only six days but had seen enough to dislike it. Vienna felt tired to him, as if the weight of its secrets burdened its people with a heaviness they couldn't shrug off and was too much for them to bear.

Or maybe he didn't like it because he'd failed here.

He'd come to arrest Dr. Malachai Samuels for stealing ancient stones from an archaeological dig in Rome the year before. Samuels, a preeminent past-life therapist and amateur magician, had made all the evidence disappear, and to date neither Interpol nor the FBI had been able to connect him to the crime. But instead of taking the reincarnationist into custody, the agent had been involved in a bizarre incident at the Musikverein. Along with almost a thousand other people, he'd experienced a hallucination while listening to a performance of Beethoven's *Eroica* Symphony. To date, none of the investigators had offered a satisfactory explanation of what had occurred. Music could excite you or lull you into a state of extreme relaxation—but catapult you into a hyperreal fantasy of another time and place? Of another life lived and lost?

The press, both here and abroad, was still reporting the rumors that the occurrence was the result of a sonic anomaly that had caused a mass hypnotic past-life regression. Because he was a rationalist, the agent hoped the authorities testing the air in the music hall would discover there'd been a chemical attack. He preferred a black-and-white explanation and refused to accept that what he'd experienced during the concert was a memory of an earlier existence. Clearly his subconscious had manufactured a story in which people from the present played roles in an imagined past. There were hundreds of painkillers that caused delirium and delusions; his doctors had prescribed several of them for him when he was younger. Under the influence of narcotics, anything was possible.

A middle-aged man, carrying a string bag in one hand and a maroon umbrella in the other, hurried past, giving the agent only a cursory glance. Good. Everything about his demeanor and wardrobe was designed to disguise his involvement with law enforcement. The black shirt, jeans and leather jacket, the hair that fell over his collar—it was basically how he'd looked in college. The clothes just cost more now.

Stopping at number 122, an artless building identified as the Toller Archäologiegesellschaft—the Toller Archaeology Society—he rang the bell. Seconds later he was buzzed into a lobby where a middle-aged woman, wearing a wrinkled and shapeless navy dress, waited for him. Dr. Erika Alderman greeted him solemnly, then opened a second door that would have been invisible from the street and ushered him deeper inside the building.

He'd met the doctor yesterday at the funeral for the man Malachai had traveled to Vienna to visit. Her grief had been palpable and the agent had refrained from asking her about the events of the past few days. It wasn't the right time or place. Besides, was there really anything left to discover? Malachai had been watched from the minute he'd arrived in Vienna, and although he'd visited here three times, there was no indication he'd had anything to do with his colleague's death. So the agent was surprised when, after the ceremony, Dr. Alderman had approached him and, in a hoarse whisper that sounded as if she'd been crying too hard for too long, requested that he come by before he left for America. She had something to show him.

As he followed her through the archway, under the carved letters on the frieze that revealed the brotherhood's true designation, the change from ordinary exterior to extravagant interior was drastic. Leading him into the inner sanctum, she offered up some background. "The Memorist Society was secretly founded in 1809 to study the work of Austrian Orientalist Joseph von Hammer-Purgstall, one of the men responsible for the greatest dissemination of Eastern knowledge in late-eighteenth-century Europe. Did you know that already?"

"I came across some information about the society in preparation for this trip, but I'm hardly an expert."

"When we met you said you worked for the FBI, but you didn't say you worked with art crimes."

"No, I didn't." He wasn't surprised she knew. His name and job description had appeared in far too many articles about the incident at the music hall. There were only eleven FBI agents in the Art Crime Team—ACT—and they made every effort to stay out of the press both overtly and in their covert identities.

A photo of one of them could blow a persona that had taken years to cultivate.

"Can you tell me about your unit?"

"We investigate the theft of objects from museums and residences, auction fraud and consignment fraud between galleries or dealers. We also help out with international requests to find works stolen abroad or artifacts looted from archaeological sites."

"Which one of those brought you to Vienna?"

"I'm not at liberty to discuss that."

She nodded and went back to describing the architecture. "This is all original—the building and the decor. We've done some restoration, of course, but everything is as it was."

They passed columns that stood like sentries and an Egyptian mural that covered an entire wall. Beneath their feet was a gem-toned carpet and above their heads was a cupola painted the cobalt of a night sky where stars—tiny mirrors that caught and reflected light from below—twinkled. Every corner was crammed with too many gleaming objects and artifacts for him to take them all in.

Alderman didn't stop to introduce him to any of the society's members, but he was aware that they were looking at him curiously, even suspiciously, and he pressed his upper arm against the gun in his shoulder holster. *His talisman.* Long ago he had given up looking for reassurance from the people in his life and had come to rely only on this inanimate object.

"Of specific interest to the society's founders," Alderman continued, "was reincarnation—a belief common to the newly discovered Hindu Shruti scriptures, teachings of the Kabbalah, mystery schools of ancient Egypt, Greek philosophers and Christian doctrine prior to the fifth century ACE. And this is our library," she said as she reached the threshold, her timing perfect.

This room was smaller than the public spaces and, like them, was windowless. Wall sconces illuminated four walls of bookshelves crammed with volumes that gave off a slightly musty scent.

Shutting the door behind her, Dr. Alderman locked it with a key hanging from a gold chain around her neck. The tumblers clicked efficiently. When she tried the knob to make sure it was secured, he wondered if her paranoia was justified or an over-reaction to recent events.

"Have a seat, please," she said, gesturing to a grouping of worn leather club chairs. "Can I get you something to drink?"

"Water would be fine."

The bar was ornately carved and well stocked with crystal decanters and heavy glasses that gleamed in the room's soft lights. She filled a tall glass with water and then poured herself an inch of amber liquid. "I'd like to thank you for seeing me so late in the day," Alderman said as she sat down opposite him. "I've just taken over as the head of the society, and there's a lot to deal with rather quickly."

He nodded and waited for her to continue, choosing not to tell her yet that he wanted to talk to her, too.

Reaching into her pocket, she pulled out a pack of cigarettes, took one, and then offered them to him. So many people in Vienna smoked it had made him rethink his abstinence. "I quit, but allow me…" he said as he reached into his pocket.

She lit her cigarette from the steady orange flame he offered. "If you quit, why carry the lighter?"

"To prove I'm the one in control of the habit, not the other way around."

She smiled.

"So, how can I help you, Doctor?" he asked.

"Is it true the US is the world's largest bazaar for stolen art?"

"One of them, yes."

The combination of a largely unregulated marketplace, so many buyers anxious for a deal and so many unscrupulous sellers had created a four- to six-billion-dollar global industry that now fueled everything from terrorism to drug running.

"Since the 9/11 terrorist attacks, art crime has become the third largest worldwide crime, following the drug trade and illicit arms deals," he told her. "Dealers, collectors and academics who are less than stringent are, in effect, helping the terrorists now. At ACT we try as best we can to alert everyone, but…"

He hadn't meant to lecture her, but it was precisely because people didn't recognize the link between the removal and transport of cultural objects and the funding of terrorism that the crimes continued to increase at such alarming rates.

Raising awareness would help, but the last important article on the subject had been a 2006 op-ed in the *New York Times* written by Matthew Bogdanos, a colonel in the marine reserves who described how, during an Iraqi raid on terrorists in underground bunkers, marines had found automatic weapons, stockpiles of ammunition, ski masks, night-vision goggles and a cache of precious artifacts including vases, seals and statues. In the past ten years the trail of terrorists had led more and more to looted artwork. Antiquities were as valuable as drugs and often easier to transport and trade.

"You have a reputation for being very successful at recovery," Dr. Alderman said as she put out her cigarette. "One of the most successful." She stopped and sipped her drink as if she needed fortification. "That's why I would like to hire you."

"Thank you. But I'm already employed."

"I am well aware of that. I'm not proposing to you that you quit your job. It is in fact precisely because of your FBI affiliation, as well as how closely you work with Interpol, that I am making this proposition."

"I appreciate that, but I don't freelance, either."

"Perhaps, then, our needs will overlap and by doing your job you'll be able to help me do mine?"

"A much more likely scenario."

She leaned forward and spoke sotto voce. "An ancient copper booklet that dates back to approximately 2000 BCE has been in the society's possession for hundreds of years."

He saw she was searching his face for a reaction. Not finding one, she continued. "Recently our historian came to believe it was a list of deep meditation aids that could help people access past-life memories."

"Do you mean a list of Memory Tools?" He kept all intonation out of his voice and fought the urge to push her. The Malachai Samuels case he'd been working on for the past eighteen months, which had cost the bureau hundreds of thousands of dollars and had brought him to Vienna, centered on a cache of precious stones thought to be Memory Tools.

"Yes, we believe so. No one had ever been able to figure out what language it was written in or translate it until two years ago when our historian read an article about an archaeologist named Harshul Parva, who'd found the key to Harappan, a language used in the Indus Valley. Apparently, despite a large cache of writing samples from the Harappa mature period, which lasted from 2600 BCE to 1900 BCE, there'd never been any developments in breaking the language."

"Did Parva translate the list?"

"No, our historian wouldn't let anyone else see it. But he did get help from Parva."

"Was the list translated properly?"

"I don't know." Alderman paused to take another drink. "But

let's assume it was. If you knew what was on the list and one of those items came on the market, you'd be in a position to identify it and let us know it had surfaced, yes?"

"Are you in possession of the list?"

Again he watched Alderman search his face, trying to gauge his interest. It was part of an agent's training to learn how to hide emotions, but the last woman he'd lived with complained he'd learned too well. Gilly had told him once that all she ever saw reflected in his eyes were the room's lights. *You've got a cat's unblinking gaze,* she'd said. *Not a real cat, though: a small jade animal I once saw in a museum. Cold, precise, perfect—but a facsimile.* Her comment had stung because he feared it was the truth.

"Last night, after the funeral, I discovered that the booklet is missing from the vault," Alderman said. "I'm hoping our historian secreted it away someplace even more secure and we'll find it."

"In case it's been stolen, I'd like a detailed description so I can log it in with Interpol if you haven't already reported it missing."

She nodded. "I have the translation of the list, though. That wasn't in the vault. Would you like to see it?" While Alderman opened her leather agenda, the library took on the immutable silence of a tomb. Pulling out a single sheet of paper, she put it on the table between them and then rested her right hand on top of it as if she were keeping it from blowing away even though the room was windowless.

"I never believed Memory Tools existed, even after a colleague of mine in New York, a well-respected reincarnationist, claimed to have found one of them," she said. "But I do now and am prepared to offer you anything you want to help us find these."

"Have you shown this to anyone?" *Like the reincarnationist from New York you just mentioned,* he wanted to ask but didn't.

"No one. I'm fairly certain the only other living person who knows there even is a list is in jail and will be for a long time."

"Dr. Alderman, if the tools listed here belonged to the society and have been stolen, both the FBI and Interpol need to know about it."

"They haven't been stolen because, as far as I know, they haven't been found. At least, most of them haven't."

The list could be critically important to his investigation, he thought. It could mean the difference between going back to New York having failed and succeeding. His fingers inched forward. "May I see that?"

It was ordinary typewriter paper. Each item was numbered and handwritten in both English and German in blue ink. He started to read down.

1. Pot of fragrant wax
2. Colored orb
3. Reflection sphere
4. Bone flute

He never finished because of two things that happened so close together he couldn't distinguish which came first: a slight gust of wind blew into the room and the doctor gasped. Instinctively, he let the paper fall as he reached for his gun, but just as his fingers touched the comforting metal something came down hard on the back of his head.

The pain was instantaneous and intense. Sharp, jagged and overwhelming. He was seeing darkness and then titanium-white brightness, and even as he fought to breathe through the pain, he wondered how someone could have gotten into the room, because he'd seen Dr. Alderman lock the door from the inside.

The second blow came almost immediately. He'd suffered

pain like this a long time ago, and that was what he was remembering when the third strike hit. From far away he heard moaning but didn't realize it was coming from his own lips. Before he lost consciousness, Special Agent Lucian Glass was thinking that he didn't really care very much if he died—as long as this time he stayed dead.

Chapter

FOUR

The boy was only sixteen years old, but he stood over the fallen soldier with a look of total control and calm. The soldier writhed and moaned, a coward's crying. Around them the battlefield was still; there were bodies everywhere. It seemed that these two were the last men left alive, except the boy wasn't alive in the same way the soldier was.

The undead can't be.

"Please," the soldier begged. "I was only following orders."

The look in the pale boy's eyes said that had been the wrong answer. "All this..." He spread his hand out over the devastation. "And you didn't even believe in the reason you were fighting?"

The wounded soldier stared up at him.

"You could have at least died a hero," the boy said almost wistfully.

"There are no heroes anymore..." The bloodied fighter managed a disgusted snort.

The expression on the boy's face was both an answer and a promise. "There will be, there have to be," he whispered. And then the zombie turned and walked into the encroaching darkness.

For a few seconds there was total silence.

"And that's a wrap!" Darius Shabaz's deep voice boomed out, his French accent very much evident. "Bravo!"

The director watched the actors break character, the grips shut down the lights and the set become flat and two-dimensional again. This transitional time when fantasy became reality again always left him depressed.

Making the rounds, he thanked the cast and crew for all their hard work and invited everyone to the final wrap party later that evening.

"Masterful job, Mitch. Thank you, once again," Shabaz said when he reached his director of photography.

"It's your vision, Darius. We've got another winner here."

At six-and-a-half feet tall and only 160 pounds, Shabaz towered over everyone and moved faster than any of them. He exuded so much energy one of his assistants once joked that she used to wait for the thunder to follow his lightning.

It took the better part of an hour to talk to everyone. It had been a long day—they'd started filming outdoors at six that morning to catch the early light—but Shabaz wasn't tired. At fifty-three, he ran fifteen miles a week, lifted weights, never drank and was fanatical about what he ate. The silver threads in his thick black hair were the only outward signs of his age. Shabaz had been brought up to revere his body. "We are all we own," his grandfather had always told him.

Outside the shooting stage, the sun was just starting to drop down and the orange groves that stretched out almost a mile in every direction were suffused with a warm glow. Glancing at his watch, he calculated that his driver would be getting back from Santa Barbara in twenty minutes and paced himself accordingly as he set off on his end-of-the-workday walk.

Shabaz had come to America to attend film school when he was seventeen, and while he retained his French citizenship, he'd never gone home again. He was directing by the time he was twenty-two and was responsible for one of the highest grossing horror pictures of all time by the age of thirty. Five years after that he started his own studio. He focused on supernatural plots about the dead coming back to life—vampires, zombies and mummies—but always for noble purposes.

While critics labeled him as a B movie director with messianic delusions, filmgoers ignored the negative reviews. Word of mouth kept people standing in line even in the dead of winter without complaining when a new Shabaz movie debuted. It was often remarked that fans preferred to see his films in theaters as opposed to renting them. It wasn't just because his grand and gory visions were better suited to the big screen, but because seeing them in a roomful of people who collectively gasped was exhilarating.

Passing the main gatepost, Shabaz circled the compound, which included four soundstages, a theater, an editing studio, an employees' gym, a day-care center, a medical building, a commissary and a dozen bungalows. His architect had relied on natural woods and stone so all the structures seemed to have sprung out of the earth and looked as indigenous to the landscape as the orange and eucalyptus trees.

Shabaz's loop ended at the southwest corner where bungalow number six sat on the edge of a small pond. His office was here, along with a private screening room and a bedroom suite for when he stayed over. His olive-drab Range Rover was parked in the driveway, his driver leaning on the car, having a smoke.

"Hey, Mr. Shabaz," the driver said, tipping his Shabaz Films baseball cap with its distinctive emerald-green lightning bolt.

"How badly did they soak us this time, Mike?"

"Not too bad. Everything was under warranty but the new tires. These were a couple of hundred dollars more, but they should last seventy-five thousand miles instead of twenty, which was all we got out of the last set."

"Which means these will get us about forty-five?"

"If we're lucky." The driver grinned. "Are you going to be needing me tonight?"

Shabaz shook his head. "No, I'm working late, so either I'll drive myself home or stay over. See you tomorrow."

The driver doffed his cap for the second time and walked off toward the main parking lot while Shabaz inspected the new wheels. Or so it would have looked to anyone watching. In reality, he was checking to ensure no one was around. Even though there was nothing suspicious about a man taking a package out of his own car, he didn't want an audience.

Inside the bungalow, he greeted the night guard on duty and proceeded to the screening room. With the door locked behind him, Shabaz walked down the aisle past the dozen black leather lounge chairs. The floor and walls were covered with industrial carpet in a subtle pattern of squares in different shades of gray, and in the low light it was impossible to tell that one of the panels was actually a door.

The room on the other side was paneled in similar modular squares, but these were constructed from a blend of concrete and additives engineered for maximum crush resistance. Each was only three inches thick but ten times as strong as an eighteen-inch-thick panel of regular formula cement. They were both fireproof and watertight; nothing but a full-out nuclear attack would destroy them.

There were three identical vaults on the lot, all with the same specs: twenty-five-hundred square feet and designed to withstand an earthquake—or as close to it as engineering could come. Shabaz had never corrected his architect's assumption that film negative would be stored here as well as in the other two vaults. And since no one but the movie director had ever been in this room once it had been completed, the contents of this vault remained a secret.

Tonight, Shabaz didn't focus on any of the precious art objects that lined the shelves. It was the easels set up in a semi-circle that commanded all of his attention. Four of the five had paintings resting on them—paintings that Shabaz, who had a connoisseur's eye, believed were among the finest examples of each artist's oeuvre.

View of the Sea at Scheveningen, by Vincent Van Gogh, was a gray-green, stormy painting: a turbulent emotional reaction to a cloudy, raw day at the beach resort near The Hague. Since the artist was known to paint *en plein,* it was not surprising that there were actual grains of sand mixed in with the paint that Shabaz had felt with his fingertips the few times he dared touch the impasto canvas.

Beach at Pourville, by Claude Monet, was as peaceful as the Van Gogh was violent. It had a lushness that made Shabaz feel as if he were breathing in the salty air. The lavender blue sky, the green sea and sandy shore were painted with a loose brush, but the overall impression was more transportive than a photograph could have been.

Gustav Klimt's *Portrait of a Lady* was an evocative, mysterious painting. There was yearning in the dark-haired woman's almond-shaped eyes and a certain petulance in her full lips. The deep green-blue background hinted at the forest, and in her light yellow dress, she might have been an unexpected and glorious wildflower.

The fourth painting, the smallest, was a jewel. The Renoir was only ten inches by twelve inches, but the bouquet of pink roses was so exuberant and lush, Shabaz had been fooled more than once into thinking their scent was perfuming the room.

Now there was a fifth painting to join the others.

Carefully Shabaz stripped away the butcher paper and multiple layers of Bubble Wrap, finally revealing a cacophony of colors. As if he were handling butterfly wings, he lifted the canvas and placed it on the only empty easel.

Stepping back, he took his first full look at the Matisse masterwork, *View of St. Tropez*.

The exuberant brushstrokes, which appeared so primitive up close, created a luminous beach scene when viewed from a few feet away. It was brighter and louder than the Monet—there was more joy in this painting, less contemplation. It might be the best of the lot.

His hands trembled, and he felt slightly nauseated. It had taken him over two years and had cost six million dollars to assemble this particular group of paintings. Step one of his plan was finally complete. His eyes drifted from one masterpiece to the next. Which one was he going to choose? Maybe the Renoir—perhaps the still life might be less intimidating.

It wasn't the money that bothered him but the act he was about to commit. The cost was certainly substantial, but he'd paid far less for all of the paintings together than what any one of them was worth; fencing stolen paintings of this caliber was difficult. None ever sold for close to their real value. The Renoir was worth eight million, but he'd paid only a million. The Matisse would cost thirty-five million with a clean provenance, but he'd paid only two and a half.

Which one? Which one should he choose? Of all the paintings the Van Gogh was the most valuable, so he'd hold that one out as a carrot. The Klimt would be the least devastating loss.

A Williams-Sonoma shopping bag had been sitting in a corner of the vault for the past month. Inside was a single item, a Shun

Kaji Paring knife that he'd purchased for $134.95 in cash. The time had come. Was it going to be the Monet or the Matisse?

Shabaz walked up to the Monet, then over to the Matisse. He paced between them slowly for the next ninety seconds.

Finally, he came to a decision. With the point of the knife mere inches from the canvas, Shabaz noticed the serene blues and greens mirrored on the blade. How on earth could he do this? Even the reflection was a masterpiece.

Chapter
FIVE

"He saw all these forms and faces in a thousand relationships become newly born. Each one was mortal, a passionate, painful example of all that is transitory. Yet none of them died, they only changed, were always reborn, continually had a new face: only time stood between one face and another."
—Hermann Hesse, *Siddhartha*

Lucian tore the page off the pad. Even before it landed on the pile of previously discarded drawings, his pencil was streaking across a new sheet with grace, authority and an economy of motion. The human face that emerged looked out at him, terror in her eyes. It had taken him less than fifteen minutes to bring the stranger to life, and although the portrait was more than competent, he wasn't satisfied. Ripping the page off, he started again on a clean sheet.

It was the hour before first light when New York City was still gravely quiet—especially downtown, where he lived in an old, refurbished factory on Sullivan Street. The large loft had a separate sleeping area and bathroom but otherwise was wide open, with oversize windows facing north that offered a sliver of skyline, beautiful in the abstract, not hinting of the danger that was always lying in wait.

He stopped drawing, lifted his head up and listened to a car roar down the street, curious that such an ordinary sound could take on such ominous overtones. It was the hour when other-worldly visitations seemed possible even to someone who'd never believed in ghosts. Or in life after death. Or in God. Or in anything that he couldn't prove. Lucian was a disciple of logic, of action and reaction. Long ago he'd trained himself never to waste any time looking backward, but that had changed in the two weeks since a still unknown assailant had discovered the hidden entranceway into the Memorist Society's library and had lain in wait until Dr. Erika Alderman handed Lucian the paper that detailed a partial list of Memory Tools.

The list was gone, and Alderman had died of sustained injuries. Lucian had spent a week in the hospital with a concussion that caused dizziness and constant headaches. The symptoms the doctors feared most never manifested; he had no loss of memory, muscle weakness or paralysis—any of which would have suggested progressive brain damage. Arming him with powerful painkillers and telling him the headaches might take several weeks or months to completely resolve, the doctors had released him and cleared him to travel as long as he promised to rest when he got home.

Yesterday he'd tried to go back to work, but his boss, Doug Comley, had kicked him out, insisting that Lucian heed the doctors' orders and spend at least another week recuperating.

His hand moved in long sweeps across the sheet of paper as he filled in the lines of the woman's jaw, her neck, her collarbone. There was no conscious thought involved in the action; his hand was moving on its own. He was thinking about what else Comley had told him.

When Malachai Samuels was well enough to be interrogated about the list of Memory Tools that had been stolen from the

Memorist Society during the murder of Dr. Erika Alderman, Matt Richmond was going be the agent to interview him, not Lucian.

Matt was the optimistic, energetic dynamo on their team. Lucian trusted him implicitly, but this wasn't Matt's case.

"That should be my interview, Doug."

"How many reasons do you want why you're wrong? Let's start with the fact that you helped save the man's life in Vienna. He knows that. You know that. Think there's objectivity there? Next, you're still recovering from injuries inflicted during the crime in question. You're one of the victims, Lucian."

"It's still my case."

"What happened in Vienna is the department's case, Agent Glass."

When Comley started addressing agents formally, it was time to back off, but Lucian couldn't. "Are you removing me entirely?"

"No. You're not off the case, but I don't want you near Malachai Samuels." He handed Lucian a file. "This is where we are. It's everything we have. If you want my advice don't even open it. Go home, Lucian. Sleep. Go to the movies. Read a book. Eat some good food. Call Gilly and talk to her, see if you can patch things up—"

"Because suddenly she won't care that as soon as you let me I'll be back working as hard as I ever did? Thanks, Doug," Lucian interrupted. He put the folder under his arm and stood up.

"I want my agents to be committed, but at some point this stopped being your job and became your mission. And obsessions can be unhealthy."

Lucian wished he appreciated his boss's paternal efforts, but Comley wanted him married with two kids. On the other hand, he knew Lucian well enough to know how much he needed to review the file. It was disturbingly lacking in substantive evidence. While the Austrian police had been thorough, they had no suspects. The Memorist Society's locked library had been violated via a tunnel running beneath the structure. Apparently Vienna had a complex underground: layers of ancient communities going back to Roman times that included burial sites, sewers and tunnels, making it possible to cross from one part of the city to another without going aboveground.

The file included hand-drawn maps showing a series of passageways that snaked through thirteenth-century Christian catacombs under the Karmeliterkirche—a baroque church in the Leopoldstadt area—and miles later wound up in the subbasement of the Memorist Society. From there, a staircase that was part of the original eighteenth-century structure led to a secret entrance to the library. The police had found evidence confirming that was how the perpetrator of the attack on Dr. Erika Alderman and Lucian Glass had gotten into and out of the locked room. Now, as he continued to draw, Lucian turned over the same litany of questions that had been plaguing him since he'd regained consciousness in the hospital. Who had attacked him? A member of the Memorist Society? Someone working for Malachai Samuels? Or someone working for Dr. Alderman in a convoluted plot of her own invention?

Ripping the sketch off the pad, he let it, too, fall on the floor and started again. Maybe this time he'd get the woman's expression right. He could see her so clearly in his mind's eye.

Although Lucian had stopped painting and quit art school after Solange's death, he'd never stopped sketching. In his capacity as an FBI agent he drew suspects the way other agents took notes. But this was something new. Ever since the attack he had felt the need to draw these faces…was driven to it.

Once he'd come back to New York he'd sought out a neurologist, who looked at his X-rays and concurred with the doctors in Vienna: his injury wasn't severe, he'd recover fully and the headaches would eventually subside. The neurologist didn't think the early-morning sketching sessions were a side effect—he'd never encountered anything like it before but would investigate, and if he discovered any similar cases he would let Lucian know. He also suggested, because of Lucian's medical history, that he visit a psychologist. Since he'd been violently attacked before, he might be suffering from PTSD. Lucian hadn't followed up.

The face looking up at him now was suffused with fear but still not what he saw in his head. She might have been his tenth or his twentieth attempt—he'd stopped counting. There was always some elusive quality missing to his predawn sketches. Except he wasn't drawing these women from life, so how did he know there was something absent? He'd never seen her or any of the others, so why did he feel as if he'd spent months looking at her?

Lucian had never been someone to feel fear, but in the days since his return from Austria, he woke up afraid, bathed in sweat, with his heart pounding. He'd lie in his bed feeling where his legs and torso and shoulders and spine met the sheets, aware of his naked body as if it were new to him—as if, while he'd been sleeping, he'd traveled off without it, left it behind, and was slipping back into it. He was relieved by its suppleness. He'd try to fall asleep again, but his need to draw was too strong, even though it was unreasonable. So he'd give in.

But it wasn't quite giving in, because he'd come to crave the frenzied sketching the way some people craved sex. Even though he knew the process of rendering the faces wouldn't end in orgiastic ecstasy but in despair, he was still addicted. While he couldn't recollect the details of the nightmares that woke him, the faces of the women he saw during those dreams remained with him, their eyes filled with anger, sadness or fear, and the time he spent committing their pain to paper was wrenching. It was as if by exposing the darkness of these lost souls he was exposing his own darkness and forcing himself to look into an abyss that he had long since abandoned as unfathomable.

Of all the dozen people whose portraits he'd drawn over and over, two women reappeared more often than the others. He knew the texture of their hair and the exact arches of their brows. He knew how the shadows fell across their faces and the structures of their bones. And he knew they were accusing him. But of what?

As the dark sky gave way to the first rays of light, Lucian put down the pencil. The pile of discarded drawings was on the floor. He looked at them and then kicked them away.

Chapter

SIX

"It is again a strong proof of men knowing most things before birth, that when mere children they grasp innumerable facts with such speed as to show that they are not then taking them in for the first time, but are remembering and recalling them."
—Marcus Tullius Cicero

Twilight was settling over the city, casting it in a grayish haze. Dr. Malachai Samuels always loved this time of day, the hour lost between darkness and light, when everything became indistinct. Slowly he eased himself out of the chauffeur-driven Mercedes and stood for a moment to catch his breath. He was still sore. He'd been shot—by accident—in Vienna three and a half weeks ago. The bullet had missed his vital organs, but he'd suffered a severe loss of blood. There was little satisfaction that the man who had inflicted this wound on him had been arrested and would spend years in jail. Malachai had lost what he had almost, finally, found—an intact Memory Tool—and that loss was proving to be a wound that refused to heal.

The lugubrious strains of Beethoven's *Moonlight Sonata* followed him out of the car, the appropriate accompaniment to the dusk. Standing under the shadows of the linden trees with all their bright new green leaves, he inspected the Queen Anne–style villa he'd last seen on April 27, when he'd departed for what he'd hoped was going to be a short but successful trip. Warm light glowed through the glass sunburst above the door, but all the windows downstairs, where the offices were, and upstairs, where his aunt lived, were dark. At least no one would be here to witness his ignominious return.

It was demoralizing to return without a Memory Tool, but emotion was a weakness to be conquered, not indulged in, so he buttoned his suit, squared his shoulders and proceeded toward the front door. Although an average-looking man of medium height with unremarkable features and a receding hairline, he was impeccably groomed, wore expensive clothing and carried himself like an old-world aristocrat. His father— his detested, distant father, who'd favored his firstborn, now de- ceased son—had always berated Malachai for putting on airs and pretending to be a Brit, even though his mother had been English and he'd grown up in the UK after their divorce. It was there, as a lonely and insecure little boy, that Malachai had dis- covered the study of magic. Mastering tricks had taken patience, a virtue which served him well even today in his work with children. But taking it slow and steady wasn't an option any longer. His father was an old man. Malachai was going to have to prove what he'd always suspected about his own past life soon if he wanted his father to spend his last days suffering and regretting the indifference he'd shown his second-born son.

Before tackling the steps to the front door, Malachai paused to catch his breath. Even in this murkiness, the elaborate build- ing with its gables, scrolled wrought-iron railing and dozens of gargoyles tucked under the eaves was an impressive sight. It was a symbol of power and wealth that had been standing on this spot since 1847, when Malachai's ancestor, Trevor Talmage, had founded the Phoenix Club along with Henry David Thoreau, Walt Whitman, Bronson Alcott and other well-known transcendentalists. Their mission, the search for intellectual and spiritual enlightenment, had been narrowed to reincarnation research and practice when in 1876 Talmage's brother became obsessed with protecting his wealth for his future lives.

With a burst of energy that promised full recovery, Malachai hurried up the last two steps, opened the front door, with its bas-relief coat of arms of a giant phoenix rising from a pyre, and stepped inside.

Yes, it was good to return and to do it standing on his own, unassisted. It was important to concentrate on the positive instead of being consumed by the all-pervasive negative truth— that for the second time he'd failed at obtaining a Memory Tool. Next time, he *would* succeed. And next time might be fairly soon if all had gone according to plan and the instrument he needed to begin a new search was here waiting for him.

The foyer's priceless Tiffany chandelier cast soft light on the gleaming wood paneling and the polished black-and-white marble floor. This was where the present and the past came together and created an oasis out of time devoted to an ageless belief system which he'd dedicated his life to proving.

"Hello, Dr. Samuels."

Malachai was surprised to find the receptionist at her desk. "Good evening, Frances. It's late. You shouldn't still be here."

He'd planned his arrival for when all the employees would be gone for the day and his aunt would be tucked upstairs in her apartment.

"You have an appointment."

"I don't believe I do."

She nodded to the waiting area where an anxious-looking

man sat at the child-size table beside a little girl of about seven who was busy playing with a wooden puzzle.

"Dr. Talmage asked if you would see her new patient," she said, lowering her voice, "if she didn't get back in time from the doctor."

"Is something wrong?" His aunt, who was the co-director of the foundation, had MS but had been doing well for the past six months.

"Nothing too serious. Just some back pain she didn't want to ignore, and she couldn't get away during regular office hours today. She's lucky to have a doctor who will stay late for her."

"Yes, she is. Please just give me five minutes," he said, and started to walk away.

"Dr. Samuels…"

Malachai turned.

"I wanted to tell you…" She was having a hard time. "We're all glad you're back," she blurted out.

"I appreciate that very much, Frances."

"We were all very concerned."

"Thank you."

It was a short but tiring walk down the hall to his office, which once had been the manse's library. Opening the door, Malachai heard the familiar ticking of the ormolu clock on the marble mantel. *Back. At last.* Easing into his leather chair, he winced, but there was no time now for pain. On top of his desk were two large cordovan leather boxes that contained the mail that had accumulated in his absence. This was why he'd disobeyed his doctor's orders and come back to work two days early: to see if the package from the bookshop on the Left Bank in Paris had come. During his recuperation its whereabouts had been on his mind, but there'd been no way to inquire without calling undue attention to it.

There it was. But before he could open it, there was a knock on the door.

"Come in," Malachai called out as he moved the leather boxes to the side of his desk.

Frances introduced Robert Keyes and his daughter, Veronica, who examined Malachai with troubled deep blue eyes.

The children mattered to him. Their problems came first, and so, as he crossed the room, he wasn't thinking about the parcel from Paris, but what was upsetting this little girl. Acute past-life memories manifested themselves in different ways in different children—some relished each remembrance; others were frightened by what they glimpsed. Malachai, like his aunt, believed he had a duty to offer unconditional understanding, to suspend all disbelief no matter how unbelievable the children's tales and to try to help them navigate through the cloudy memories to find meaning and closure.

"I'm Malachai," he said, extending his hand to Veronica.

She cocked her head slightly and then frowned as if confused by something. "Can't you take some medicine?"

"What do you mean?" Malachai asked.

"You have the hurt face. My son used to have it all the time."

Malachai glanced over at the girl's father, who was frowning.

"In one of the other times before this one," Veronica continued, explaining as if expecting him to be confused. But he wasn't.

Malachai nodded. "Why don't we all sit down so we can talk about it," he said, and indicated the couch.

Robert sat beside his daughter and put his arm around her little shoulders.

Malachai pulled up a chair, trying not to wince with the effort. "I think I know what you mean," he said to Veronica conspiratorially. "You remember a time before now when you had a son and he used to have bad pain."

"They're more like dreams. But most of them are scary. Grandma Nina thinks they're incarnation memories."

Nina Keyes? Was this her granddaughter? Malachai had met the philanthropist several times. Not only was she one of his aunt's acquaintances, she also donated yearly to the foundation. He wished Frances had given him some background.

"Reincarnation memories?"

She nodded.

"A lot of people have them," Malachai said.

"My grandma says that if I talk about the incarnations here then maybe I'll get them out of my system. I don't really know what my system is, though."

"She means get them out of your mind," Robert offered, leaning over and kissing his daughter on her forehead.

"Do they bother you, Veronica?" Malachai asked.

She nodded.

"Can you tell me?"

She leaned toward him. "They're scary," she whispered.

Her father's anxious face told the rest of the story. "For the past few months Veronica has been having really bad dreams and hasn't wanted us to leave her alone. She needs one of us—her mom or me or her grandmother—with her all the time. It's been a problem at school."

"Being alone can be very scary," Malachai said, commiserating with her.

"That's not what's scary."

Her father looked confused. "But, honey, that's what you've been saying."

"What's scary, Veronica?" Malachai asked.

"I don't want everyone else to be alone."

"Why?"

"Something bad could happen."

"Do you know what that something is?"

"No."

"Well, maybe I can help you figure it out so you can stop being scared. Are you willing to try?"

"Yes, Grandma said if I tried I could have hot dogs and hot chocolate and we could go to the store and get anything I wanted."

"The toy store?"

"No. The store at the museum."

"You like the museum?" It had to be the same Nina Keyes; she'd donated an entire wing to the Metropolitan Museum.

"More than anyplace." She sighed. "Except…"

"Yes?"

She didn't answer.

"Veronica has always loved the museum, but a few times lately she's had…" He struggled to find the word.

"What happens at the museum, Veronica?"

She pursed her lips together. "I don't know. But it doesn't happen every time."

"What doesn't happen?"

She shrugged. "I don't know."

"That's okay," Malachai said. "Do you like looking at old things in the museum?"

Veronica nodded vigorously.

Fishing in his pocket, Malachai pulled out a coin. "Why don't I show you something that could be in a museum? It's an ancient Roman coin." He handed it to her. She inspected it with real curiosity and then gave it back.

"Now watch," Malachai said as he rolled it through his fingers, making it appear and disappear. "Do you know where the coin is?"

She shook her head.

Holding out first his right, empty hand and then the other, Malachai proceeded to find the coin behind Veronica's right ear, making her squeal.

"I want you to watch the coin. Follow the sweep that it makes in the air, and let it fill up your eyes."

The child was riveted to the moving golden orb he shifted back and forth in front of her in an even, measured motion. After thirty seconds she had the fixed, unblinking gaze of someone under hypnosis.

Malachai's father had thought his son's desire to learn magic tricks was pointless, but the knowledge helped immeasurably with the children. In minutes, instead of the hours it would otherwise take, he was able to relax them and help them open up.

"Now let's try to remember," Malachai said. "Can you find yourself in another time…the time of one of the bad dreams?"

For a few seconds Veronica was quiet and then, suddenly, startling both Malachai and her father, she jerked back in her chair, put her hand out as if reaching for someone and screamed out, "No!"

"What is it? Where are you?"

"No, please." It was a plaintive whimper, full of fear.

"What's happening?"

Veronica moaned, her eyes fixed on a faraway spot. She wasn't there in the room anymore, but lost in the memory she was seeing in her mind. She started to cry.

Robert Keyes made a move to comfort his daughter, but Malachai put an arm out to stop him. *It's okay*, he mouthed.

"Veronica, listen to me. You're all right. You're safe. What you're seeing is something that happened a long time ago. You don't have to stay there if you want to leave. All right?"

Veronica's voice was hard to understand through her sobbing, but Malachai could just make out the words. *It's my fault*, she'd said.

"What is?"

Her only answer was continued sobs.

"Veronica? You don't have to stay there anymore. Come back to your father. Come back now."

Veronica opened her eyes. There were still fat tears sliding down her cheeks, but she wasn't crying anymore. Malachai asked her if she remembered anything. Scrunching up her face, she tried to think. "No." She sounded frustrated.

Malachai picked up a copy of *Curious George,* which he kept handy for this kind of situation. "It's like this book," he said to Veronica, and showed her the cover.

She smiled a little. "I have that," she said.

"Have you read it?"

She nodded.

"So you probably know we have to start here, on the first page, if we're going to understand the whole story." He flipped to the middle. "It wouldn't make much sense if we started here, would it? We'd miss everything that came first and never understand what was going on afterward, right?"

Veronica nodded.

"We just haven't found the first page of your story yet. That can take a little time. Are you willing to try again another day?"

She nodded and hiccuped a last small sob.

The session was over, and Malachai led them to the door.

Richard Keyes put his arm lovingly around his daughter's shoulders, offering her the kind of support and comfort only a father can, and Malachai watched them walk away.

Chapter
SEVEN

The book of Baudelaire's poetry had cost thirty-five dollars. Its edges were worn, its cover stained and torn. It lay on the black laminate worktable in the foundation's library, surrounded by conservation tools, pads of paper, jugs of pencils and a dozen other books from the mid-1800s about different methods of inducing past-life regressions—books Malachai had been studying the last time he'd been here, before the Viennese trip. Tonight only the Baudelaire held his interest.

He used a razor blade to cut along the edges of the red-and-gold marbleized endpaper, then peeled it back to find a folded sheet of plain white paper that had cost one woman's life and one hundred thousand dollars. Whether or not it would prove to have been a worthwhile investment was yet to be determined. All he knew was that he was finally in possession of the only known list—even if it was only a partial list—of Memory Tools. The real trick now would be figuring out how to find them.

He started to read:

1. Pot of fragrant wax
2. Colored orb

3. Reflection sphere
4. Bone flute
5. Word holder

Malachai heard keys jangling and looked away from the paper he hadn't finished reading and over to the door just as it swung inward. Beryl never came down here. With her MS it wasn't easy to navigate the steep steps—but now he watched the tip of her ebony cane precede her.

Over the past year she'd never wavered in her support of his claim of innocence, but she blamed him for bringing scandal to their front door. The fact that the police had investigated the co-director for more than eighteen months in a robbery and murder case had tarnished the foundation's reputation, a reputation Beryl had nurtured for years. She worked to gain respect from the scientific community, not derision. It was one thing to see patients in a therapeutic situation; quite another, she said, to go off in search of ancient treasures with mystic properties.

She had a dim view of her nephew's obsession with the Memory Tools and had been angry when he'd gone to Vienna looking for yet another one. It would be better if she didn't find out about his decision to take up the quest again.

Malachai withdrew a deck of antique cards from his jacket pocket and started shuffling. Their gilt edges gleamed. He had more than three dozen packs in his collection and he always carried one with him. They were excellent distractions.

"Beryl, how are you? Frances said you were at the doctor, and—"

His aunt wasn't alone; a man followed a few steps behind her. He had close-cropped russet hair and a broad nose that looked as if it had been broken once. His gray slacks and navy blazer were store-bought and made of inferior cloth.

"This gentleman was waiting outside when I got home," Beryl said in a voice tinged with frustration.

"I'm Agent Matt Richmond from the FBI." The man flashed his credentials.

"Good evening, Agent Richmond." Malachai smiled sociably, as if he were welcoming a guest into his home. "It's late for a visit, isn't it?" There was a very slight mocking tone to the question.

"I'd like to talk to you about your recent trip to Vienna."

"Tonight?"

"Is that a problem?"

"Well, I just returned to work for the first time in quite a few weeks. I'd prefer to schedule something for later in the week."

"We'd prefer to do it now."

Malachai smiled again. "If that's the case, I'd be happy to submit to your inquisition. Would you like to sit down? There are some extremely comfortable chairs in the reading room."

"I'm fine standing."

"Beryl, are you planning on staying?" Malachai asked his aunt. "Would you like me to get you a chair?"

"I'll stand, too." Her face was impassive, but her voice was sharp.

"Very well," Malachai said. "Agent Richmond, the proverbial floor is yours."

"Were you in Vienna on Saturday, May third?"

"Obviously you know I was, or you wouldn't be here."

"Where exactly were you on that Saturday?"

"In the hospital, as you must also know. Recovering from a gunshot wound."

"On that evening there was a robbery, and a woman was killed. Did you hear about it?"

"No. I'm afraid I was floating on a sea of narcotics. What was stolen? Who was killed?" Malachai was aware that his heartbeat was quickening and concentrated on slowing it down.

"Dr. Alderman, the director of the Memorist Society. Did you know her?"

"No. I knew the previous director. I'm sorry to hear that, though. Can you tell me what was stolen?"

"A piece of ephemera. Are you familiar with the term, Mr. Samuels?" Richmond asked.

"Dr. Samuels," Malachai corrected him as he held out the playing cards he was still holding. "I collect ephemera. These are nineteenth-century, from England. Purchased at Sotheby's." As he offered them, they slipped from his grip. Gold, red, white and black cards spilled across the table, landing at haphazard angles and creating a random but not unpleasant design. "What kind of ephemera was stolen in Vienna?" Malachai asked as he set about picking them up.

"An ordinary piece of paper with a list of items on it written in blue ink."

Malachai looked up. "Not much detail."

Richmond didn't answer as he moved closer to the table. "We'd like to know if by any chance anyone has contacted you offering to sell you that sheet of paper while you were in Vienna or since your return."

As Malachai continued his cleanup effort, moving books and papers out of the way to find the errant cards, he shook his head slowly. "No. What was on it?"

"I'm not at liberty—"

"To say? How can I help you if I don't know what it's a list of?"

"Either someone contacted you or they didn't," Richmond said.

"No one has contacted me." Done, Malachai shuffled the cards back into a pack, cut them and shuffled them again. The sharp slapping noise they made was the only sound in the room.

"What's down here?" Richmond asked after a few seconds.

"Our library. We have several thousand volumes, many of them rare books. It's the most complete library on reincarnation in the world. Would you like to look around? Just dial me upstairs at extension twelve forty-three when you're done and I'll come down to let you out."

"I don't think that will be necessary. You're certain you don't know anything about the list we're looking for?"

"No," Malachai said. "I don't. And if that's all you were here to discuss, allow me to see you out now." He walked over to the door, opened it and held it open. "After you," he said.

Beryl went first and the two men followed. Even though he'd expected the climb to be difficult, Malachai was still surprised by the amount of pain the simple effort generated. He was moving more slowly than his aunt.

On the main floor, he escorted the agent down the hall and through the foyer. "Good night," he said as he opened the door for Richmond, but the agent remained where he was.

"The cards." He nodded at the deck. "You do tricks?"

"I do. Yes, since childhood. Is that a crime now?"

"Not at all. It's just something I'm interested in."

"Have you studied, Agent Richmond?"

"Just for fun."

Malachai held out the deck. "Care to show off?"

Richmond shook his head. "I'd embarrass myself."

"Then indulge me." He held out the deck. "Pick a card."

The agent did.

"Now look at it but don't let me see it."

Richmond carefully lifted a corner and glanced at it.

Malachai fanned the cards out in his hand. "Now slip it back. Anywhere in the deck."

After Richmond had replaced the card, Malachai shuffled the deck.

* * *

"That man's a master at obfuscation," Lucian said from his vantage point across the street, standing at the window in a fourth-floor studio apartment. The room was sparsely decorated with a battered card table and four chairs but overwhelmed with equipment. Doug Comley was sitting at one of those chairs nursing a diet soda. Using a state-of-the-art ultra-directional microphone trained on the foundation, the agents had been listening since Richmond had gone into the building, but he'd been out of range for most of the visit.

ACT had set up surveillance in this apartment during the memory stone case, when Malachai Samuels had first come under suspicion. When no evidence had surfaced after almost a year, Comley had been ready to close down the operation and let go of the apartment. Then they found out that Malachai was on his way to Vienna in search of a new Memory Tool—and then Lucian had been attacked.

The case was reopened, the apartment was operational again, and there was yet another capital offense to add to the list of unresolved crimes that all connected, tangentially, to the reincarnationist.

"Malachai never lets his guard down," Lucian said, impressed and irritated at the same time.

"Richmond doesn't, either."

"No, but I'll bet even Matt is surprised by how smooth Malachai is." Using binoculars, Lucian watched the reincarnationist cut the deck and shuffle the cards again. "He's hiding things we're not going to find out from talking to him or from going in with a warrant. We've got to get deep inside that place. Malachai's not just dangerous—he's desperate."

"I told you, there's no way you're going in there."

"I didn't say anything about me going in there."

"You didn't have to. I know you, and I'm telling you no in advance."

"What if James Ryan, an art appraiser who works for Sotheby's, had a reason to visit a reincarnationist?"

"No. Two little letters. *N-O*. That simple enough for you? I don't want you in there as Lucian Glass or as James Ryan or as my aunt Edith. You understand?"

"I understand why Lucian Glass can't go in, but what's wrong with Ryan going?"

Doug shook his head.

"You afraid of a little revenge energy?"

"You're not capable of being objective about this. I don't blame you. No one would be."

"Objectivity is overrated. Passion is much more productive."

Across the street, Malachai cut the deck once more, removing the top card from the bottom half. Then, smiling at Richmond, he revealed what it was. Based on Richmond's reaction, it must have been the card he'd chosen.

Lucian was about to continue to argue his case for going into the foundation undercover when Malachai's mellifluous voice filled the room.

"Do you believe in reincarnation, Agent Richmond?"

"Nope, I was raised a Catholic."

"I ask everyone. It's an occupational hazard."

"Do you believe?" Richmond asked.

"I do believe, with all of my being. I believe that we return over and over to experience all the different facets of human behavior, learn from them and become complete in the process."

"And you're searching for a way to prove that, aren't you?"

"Yes."

"You'd probably do anything to prove it, wouldn't you?"

Malachai's sarcastic laugh filled the room. "Now, you don't expect me to fall for that, do you?"

"I wasn't trying to trap you. I wasn't even asking. I was just realizing it. You *would* do anything to prove it. I know that now in a way I didn't before. Good night, Dr. Samuels."

Even though Lucian wished he were the one across the street instead of holed up here doing surveillance, he admired his partner's aplomb. "He did great," he said to Comley as Richmond turned, walked down the steps and headed east, away from the Phoenix Foundation.

"When there's a will…" Comley said, using Richmond's own signature line. The agent repeated it so often he never bothered with "there's a way" anymore.

Lucian kept the binoculars trained on the man who was still standing on the stone steps of the brownstone, watching Richmond walk away, the laughter on his face metamorphosing into…worry? Or was it determination?

Chapter
EIGHT

Before he left for his morning run, Vartan Reza stopped in his daughter's room and kissed the still-sleeping six-year-old on the forehead. She was a miniature of his wife. Both had strawberry-blond hair, high foreheads and finely arched brows. It was lucky that Gala was such a perfect reproduction of her mother. Better to have inherited her delicate looks instead of his swarthy skin and heavy features. Since 2001, the geopolitical situation had worsened, and he didn't want his little one to suffer for her heritage.

Out in the hall, he rang for the elevator and stretched while he waited for it to arrive. When the doors opened Reza stepped into the perfectly polished wood-paneled cage and said good morning to the elevator man. Living in a luxury Park Avenue building was proof of Reza's achievement, the visible reward of relentless effort. Early in his career he'd started taking on the tough cases that no one else had wanted, knowing they'd deliver the highest visibility if he won them. To date, he'd lost only two, but he feared he might be facing his third loss with Hypnos. The sculpture wasn't going home unless he could figure out a new approach. Discovering that the bill of sale was forged had made him suspect every other piece of evidence the Iranian government had given him, and despite Hicham Nassir's insistence that they were all legitimate, Reza was in the process of testing every document now.

Reaching the lobby, Reza thanked the operator and strode off across the black marble tiled floor. No, he wasn't going to spoil his morning run by thinking about this now—he had Central Park to look forward to.

Reza stepped out onto the still, dark street into a steady rain. Not even a downpour would make him skip his run. He was too addicted to the high. Leaning on the streetlamp, he finished his stretches and then set off, jogging west across Park Avenue, to Madison, then to Fifth Avenue; then he turned north and ran the five blocks to the park's Ninetieth Street entrance.

The path was empty, as it often was this time of day. That was one of the reasons Reza ran before six—he liked the solitude. No one needed him here; no one interrupted him. Nothing bothered him.

Before he knew it he'd passed the 102 Street Transverse on his left, and the Lasker Pool and Rink on his right. The rain wasn't affecting his pace at all. Two miles farther in, he reached the north end of the park and took West Drive. After about 3.75 miles he came to the Seventy-Second Street Transverse and, running in place, peered through the downpour to see if the road was clear.

Going over seventy miles an hour, the vehicle hit the lawyer and flipped his body eight feet up into the air. His eyes were open when the paramedics found him; one of them thought the dead man looked as if he were staring up into the overcast sky, trying to ask a last question.

A husband and wife who'd also been out jogging had witnessed the accident, but the rain was too heavy and they were too far away to identify the make of the car or even be sure what color it was. *Dark* was all they could offer. Black? Navy? Deep green? They just didn't know for sure. Neither of them remembered any numbers or letters from the license plate.

The driver slowed down as soon as he exited the park on Eighty-Fourth and Fifth and drove carefully east to Lexington and south to Seventy-Eighth Street, where he parked in front of a fire hydrant, left the keys in the ignition and walked into the Starbucks on the corner, where he ordered an espresso.

Sitting uncomfortably at one of the small wooden tables, sipping the bitter coffee, Farid Taghinia watched as a slight, dark-haired man carrying a briefcase got into the charcoal-gray Mercedes, turned the key in the ignition and drove off.

Only then did Taghinia allow himself to relax, proud of how well the operation had gone. The driver would leave the car, per his instructions, in a garage near Lake Placid, where it would be cleaned and painted and the plates would be changed.

Taghinia was absolutely sure no one would ever discover that it had been used as a murder weapon—so sure that he hadn't noticed that even though it was late May and seventy-two degrees out, Ali Samimi had been wearing leather gloves when he got into the car.

Chapter
NINE

The square, silver-framed glasses squeezed the bridge of his nose, and the mustache and wig of short-cropped hair—both prematurely gray, since he'd told the therapist he was just thirty-five years old—itched. It had been six weeks since Lucian had worn his James Ryan disguise, but usually he slipped into it with more ease than he had on this Monday morning. He lifted Ryan's black briefcase with gold-embossed initials—JR, mostly rubbed away—onto the table in front of the couch.

"I'd never seen any of these women—or the one man—before I started drawing them," Lucian said as he pulled out a sheaf of drawings and arranged five sketches on the parquet floor, and then watched Dr. Iris Bellmer inspect his work.

She had an aqualine nose, prominent cheekbones and fox-brown, chin-length hair that kept falling forward as she looked down no matter how often she pushed it back behind her ears. A silver disc hanging from a black cord slipped out from under her white blouse and swung in the air, catching the overhead light and winking at him.

"I didn't know you were an artist," she said without looking up.

When he'd called, he'd identified himself as an art appraiser for Sotheby's and explained that he was suffering symptoms no traditional doctors could diagnose.

"A hobby."

She glanced up at him again. There were tiny lines crossing her forehead, and her hazel eyes were as intent and direct as her question. "You said you've never seen these women, yet you're terribly upset that you're not capturing them exactly. You're describing an impossible challenge. Do you see that?"

He didn't answer right away. Everything about being here was suddenly surreal. Standing the way he was, with his back to the windows, he had the peculiar sensation that he was both here and across the street in the studio apartment where he, Richmond and Comley had spent so much time spying on this very building. Where one of them was right now, watching and listening.

Over the past few days Lucian had relentlessly pursued Comley to allow him to pose as a patient and infiltrate the Phoenix Foundation. Ultimately, he'd won because there just weren't any other agents available and they couldn't afford to wait—there were secrets hidden in this building that could only be discovered from the inside. As a patient, Lucian's access would be limited, but it might be enough for him to plant listening devices in the areas directional mikes couldn't reach. Would that help? They had to try. Too many people connected to this place had died. If Malachai Samuels had orchestrated the robbery at the Memorist Society in Vienna last month and stolen the list of Memory Tools, he certainly wasn't going to stop there. He'd do whatever was necessary—legal or illegal—to find and acquire the tools. Hadn't he proved that already, evidence or no?

"James, how can you know something is missing from the drawings if you've never seen these women before?"

"I don't know." It was the truth, but James Ryan speaking Lucian Glass's frustrating truth was as perplexing as being inside this building, on this side of the door he'd watched for so long.

Dr. Bellmer returned to studying his sketches as if she'd find better answers in the crosshatched and shaded lines than she was getting from him.

To justify seeking out a past-life regression therapist, Lucian's alter ego, James Ryan, had needed a problem. For expediency's sake, Lucian had chosen his own. Although he didn't believe in reincarnation, he could imagine someone wondering if there was a past-life connection to these drawings. But this was the first time Lucian had borrowed any part of his real self for James, and it was uncomfortable blurring the line of demarcation. *Too bad.* He'd have to get used to it. He'd appropriated his own dreams to get an appointment, and it had worked. And as difficult as it was to be here baring part of his soul, it was also exhilarating to be one of the shadows he used to watch moving behind these windows. Having stepped over the threshold, he was now deep inside the magic kingdom.

Like the entranceway and hallway, Bellmer's office was perfectly restored. Ornate molding capped high ceilings and framed the autumnal-colored, foliage-inspired Art Nouveau wallpaper. A jewel-toned stained-glass chandelier cast soft light on the drawings on the floor. But it was the doctor's extensive collections of snow globes, various crystal rock formations and carved dragons and the scent of burnt orange that gave the room its eccentric personality and hinted at some of the complexities of the woman who was still inspecting his drawings.

"On the phone you said your dreams wake you up, is that right?"

"Yes."

"Tell me about the dream that inspired this drawing." She pointed to a sketch. Like the others, it was done in pencil, carefully and realistically rendered, and showed a woman caught in a precise moment of fear and terror.

"I don't remember the dreams."

"Can you tell me how you feel when you wake up?"

"I usually have a terrible headache."

"And you're furious."

She'd said it as a statement, not a question. "How do you know that?" he asked.

"Just listening to you, watching your face, paying attention to your reactions. Nothing weird, no black magic or tarot cards, don't worry."

"That's reassuring. I think."

"Do you know why the drawings frighten you?"

"I don't think they do." *How the hell did she know that?*

"What makes you want to draw the women?"

"It's not that I want to draw them…it feels like they need me to draw them. To commit them to paper. As if that act will alleviate their suffering."

"Their suffering? Are you sure?"

"As opposed to what?"

"As opposed to your suffering?"

He didn't answer.

"Dreams can be tricky," she said. "Are you a religious man?"

"Not at all."

"Did you have any religious training? Even if you turned your back on it?"

"None. My father was Protestant and my mother is Jewish, but neither of them practiced." He was telling her about himself again, but he needed to give her answers and in all the years he'd posed as the appraiser, he'd never invented this part of Ryan's backstory.

"Do you believe in life after death?"

He answered almost before she finished asking. "No. Do you?"

In traditional therapy he knew it would be unusual for a therapist to answer, but this was anything but traditional.

"I don't believe in the Christian view of heaven or hell, but I do believe in the soul living on after our bodies die. You must, too, a little, or you wouldn't have sought me out."

"I've tried everything else."

"The last resort." She laughed. "I'm used to that. But back to you. Have you lost many people you were close to, James?"

"I never thought much about reincarnation before." If she noticed he'd ignored her question, she didn't show it.

"Are you in some kind of personal hell? Professional hell?"

"Other than what's going on with these drawings? No."

"Are you married? Living with anyone?"

He shook his head. "Not married. I lived with a woman for the past few years, but we broke up a few months ago, and I'm okay with it. No one I care about is ill or in any kind of trouble."

"Do you get any relief from the intensity of your feelings or the headaches once a drawing is done?"

"Yes, the headaches are usually gone."

"For how long?"

"Two hours. Sometimes longer."

"Do you take meds for the pain?"

"Yes."

"Do they offer relief?"

"Usually, at least for a few hours."

"This is a very obvious question, but have you looked into the possibility that you're having a reaction to your pain meds?"

"I wish. But no, we checked that out already."

As she wrote in her notebook, Lucian studied her. She reminded him of the women pre-Raphaelite painters favored, and he understood why painters like Rossetti and Burne-Jones had been attracted to this type of woman. She could carry bigger themes, grander emotions.

Dr. Bellmer looked up and, self-conscious that he'd been caught staring, Lucian pointed to the framed drawing on the wall right behind her. "That looks like an authentic William Blake. Is it yours?"

"No, it belongs to the foundation. One of the directors, Dr. Malachai Samuels, is an avid collector."

"I recognize his name."

She nodded. "He gets his fair share of press."

"Does he only collect Blake?"

"No. He collects all kinds of things, from playing cards to antique pistols." She capped her pen. "James, I'd like to talk to you about hypnosis. It can be a shortcut to the kinds of uncon-scious memories that are very often at the root of our problems. Have you had any experience with hypnosis?"

"Yes, with pain management self-hypnosis."

"Where did you learn it?"

Again, the truth was easier and harmless.

"Here in the city—at the NYU pain center."

"For your headaches?"

"No. It was a while ago."

"When?"

"I was hurt when I was a kid."

"Can you tell me about it?"

He could remember every moment of that evening twenty years ago and relive it without making any effort. "I don't remember much. I was in an accident, lost six pints of blood and died in the ambulance on the way to the hospital."

"You're talking about dying pretty casually. It's an extremely traumatic experience to go through. I'm so sorry you had to experience that."

"It was a long time ago…it feels like it happened to someone else."

"An event like that could change the trajectory of your life."

"I don't think it did in my case," he lied.

"How long did it take for them to revive you?"

"Approximately ninety seconds."

"Did you remember anything about that minute and a half?"

Her voice was like smoke, curling around him, tempting him to let go, give in. He was sorry now that he'd come. He'd never discussed this with anyone. Lucian lifted his hands as if he were throwing the question up in the air and getting rid of it.

He shrugged. "I'm sure you've heard it all before."

"Even if I have, it's fine if I hear it again." She smiled. "It could help explain some of what you are going through now."

"I was aware of a warm light that seemed to be illuminating a path…" He felt himself slipping into the memory and fought back. "In art school," he said evenly and without emotion, "you learn that white light is made up of other colors—red, green and blue—I could see all the different colors streaking by as if the light was fracturing. There was a sound, like a beating heart…it's all such a cliché, isn't it?"

"Go on."

"Everyone says they want to stay in the light. Well, I didn't. It was the last place I wanted to go."

"Because?"

"It was punishment." *Where the hell had that come from? Punishment?*

Dr. Bellmer nodded. "Thank you."

He shrugged.

"Have you discussed this with a doctor before?"

"No."

"A friend? Family member? Girlfriend?"

"No. I haven't."

"Are you ashamed of what happened?"

"Do you really need to know this stuff?"

She smiled. "It helps. Honest."

"Okay. No. I'm not ashamed."

"When you hypnotize yourself, what kind of imagery do you use?"

Briefly, he described a process that must have been familiar to her because she nodded as she listened.

"I use a similar method. Would you be willing to let me hypnotize you and see if we can get somewhere? If you need some time to think about it…"

She was offering him exactly what he was paying her for: the opportunity to return to the heart of Malachai Samuels's lair. He knew enough about hypnosis to fake it.

"Do you have any open appointments later this week?"

Chapter

TEN

Tyler Weil herded the second-graders through the double glass doors of the Egyptian wing of the Metropolitan Museum of Art. The children immediately responded to the hangar-size space and broke ranks. Some ran toward the sloping north wall where the thirty-foot-tall floor-to-ceiling windows looked out into the park; others wanted to see the shallow moat where copper and silver coins sparkled underwater. But the majority of them clambered up the stone steps to the eighty-two-foot-long Temple of Dendur.

When their teacher started to protest and tried to rein them in, Weil shook his head and said, "There's no better way to interest them in art than to let them play around it and in it."

The Met's new director always looked forward to Tuesday mornings, when he left his fourth-floor office and gave these guided tours to schoolchildren. He felt that he was discovering the museum through their eyes in a way that would help him steward it.

Today's group was special because among the children was Veronica Keyes, the granddaughter of a director of the museum's board and one of its most generous benefactors. Nina and Veronica were regulars at the Trustees Dining Room for Sunday brunch.

The little girl was standing in front of the fifteen-foot-tall temple—not running around it, playing in it or ignoring it like some of the other kids, but surveying it. Nina had called him earlier that morning to ask him to keep an eye out for Veronica. As much as she loved the museum, she'd become distraught the past few times she'd visited, panicking when she walked into the main lobby, shrieking and wailing as if she were being chased or hunted. When Tyler had met the class at the school entrance earlier he'd been on alert, but Veronica had been fine.

Tyler found her by the moat, looking up at the temple, very contemplative for a seven-year-old.

"Do you like the temple?" he asked.

She nodded. "It came a far way."

"Yes, all the way from Egypt. Do you want to see on the map?"

"Don't you think I know where Egypt is?" she said, so indignant that Tyler had to swallow a smile. "It should have more trees around it," she added.

"Why?"

"So the people who pray and make sacrifices here have somewhere cool to rest afterward."

Nina often regaled the board of directors with Veronica's precociousness. She read at a fourth-grade level already and devoured history books. "As if she's on a quest to find out," Nina had said.

"I'll let the head gardener know and see if we can fit in a few more trees."

"Can we go see the rocodial now?"

Weil smiled at the way she pronounced the word. "Yes, we can."

Together they walked over to the moat surrounding the temple, where two boys were pointing to the stone sculpture of a small crocodile and making faces at the red granite, first-century-BCE crocodile.

"Have any of you ever seen a real crocodile?" Weil asked.

The taller of the two boys, whose shirt was pulled out of his pants and whose shoelaces were undone, shook his head without taking his eyes off the sculpture. The other, who had a bruise on his chin, said, "I did. In Florida. It had ginormous teeth. Can we see this crocodile's teeth?"

Weil explained how it was a sculpture and static. "Just like in Florida, they had crocodiles in ancient Egypt, too. They lived on the banks of the Nile and were extremely dangerous—some even say the most dangerous creatures the Egyptians had to deal with."

"Didn't they have bears?" asked the child with the bruise.

"Don't be silly, of course not," Veronica said.

"Well, maybe they did," the boy countered.

Before Weil could intervene, he felt the vibration of his cell phone against his hip.

It was his assistant saying it was urgent Weil meet Nicolas Olshling in the shipping department.

Weil had been director of the MMA for five months and this was his first potential crisis. A knot formed in the pit of his stomach as he searched the light-filled room for one of the teachers to let them know he needed to cut the tour short.

Five minutes later he was standing in the windowless shipping room of New York's greatest museum looking at the contents of an unpacked crate, at what he could only describe as a tragedy, staring hypnotically into a lemon-yellow sun shining over a watery azure sea. The bright orb—or what was left of it—burned his eyes. He felt as if someone had just knifed right through his soul, even though it was the Matisse seascape that was no longer intact.

The painting that lay like a corpse on the stainless steel table had been slashed into ragged ribbons, the irregular strips of canvas attached only at the top to the stained wooden stretcher.

Chapter
ELEVEN

Nicolas Olshling, the head of security, was holding a crowbar as if he needed a weapon against this violence. It was probably what he'd used to open the crate that lay in pieces on the floor.

"Why would anyone do this?" Weil asked. He didn't really expect a response and wasn't surprised when he didn't get one.

To Olshling and the other employees in the room, it appeared as if the square-jawed man was completely in control, taking in the situation, assessing the damaged painting and making a decision about how to proceed. What no one could see was that the current head of New York City's great and glorious museum, who was in charge of a six-hundred-person security force and over one thousand employees, was crying.

"Can someone ask Marie Grimshaw to come down?" he said, without turning around. Weil wanted the curator of the European art department here to identify the painting. "Tell her it's urgent."

As Weil returned his attention to the canvas he was vaguely aware of Olshling making a first and then a second call, this last to the FBI Art Crime Team. *Exactly right,* Weil thought, pleased Olshling was being proactive and not waiting for orders. There was a protocol to follow. The authorities needed to be brought in on this right away.

Weil thought of the Met like a great fortress protected by an army of soldiers with Olshling as their general. His was a job that required constant ingenuity, secrecy and cooperation, and he'd been doing it for over fifteen years without incident. This was one area of the museum Weil had felt confident he could let run without his interference while he got up to speed, and so far he'd been right. The Met's security department operated as a fully functional independent entity.

Inside each of the entrances, uniformed men and women inspected the briefcases, pocketbooks and shopping bags of the four million people who visited the cultural Mecca yearly. Hundreds more guards patrolled the high-ceilinged exhibition rooms, keeping watch over the treasures and softly warning visitors to step back when they ventured too close to an object. There was also a phalanx of plainclothes men and women disguised as museumgoers, all trained to be on the lookout for any suspicious activity and avert any potential disasters. Behind the scenes there were hundreds more employees who protected the art in other ways, from conservation to temperature control to running security systems. And since September 11, there were more of these vigilant soldiers employed than there had been before. But nothing criminal or suspect had ever occurred at the Met to make headlines. For such a large institution, one that served so many, the museum remained a calm shelter in the storm of one of the most frenetic cities in the world.

Until today.

Even though Weil was sure this violence to the Matisse had been done off-site and the Met was simply the recipient of the atrocity, he felt as if he'd failed. The museum had been violated on his watch. His new watch. Weil thought he'd been prepared for how difficult it was going to be to follow in Philippe de Montebello's footsteps, but he'd been wrong. After three decades that man and the institution he ran had merged, and the museum was still in shock at having a new leader—especially one with such a controversial background and conflict of interest.

No one had expected the trustees to agree on the president of Sotheby's as the Met's next director. Dissenters complained that Weil didn't have the scholarship needed, while those lobbying for him successfully argued that a twenty-first-century museum was not only about the wall hangings. Managing endowments and understanding legal issues—especially those concerning cultural heritage conflicts—were areas in which Weil had extensive knowledge. Overseeing and guiding educational programs, publications, community development and fundraising were all of equal importance, especially in the economic downturn the country was experiencing. There, too, Weil excelled. Sotheby's was a for-profit corporation, and Weil had been credited with its considerable success under his aegis. On behalf of his choice, the president of the Met's board argued that while scholarship had flourished under the previous director, income building had languished and the museum's corporate mission had lost focus.

In the end, Weil had been elected by a small majority. Now, the very last thing he wanted, while he and the Met were still getting acclimated, was a trial by fire, and he feared this urgent situation was about to escalate into one.

"My God." Marie Grimshaw had arrived and was trying to absorb the monstrosity. The much-beloved elder statesperson of the staff, she was an indomitable scholar who'd authored half-a-dozen books on nineteenth- and early twentieth-century artists. Usually she was the one who helped everyone else through their crises, but now the seventy-two-year-old woman looked pale. Weil guessed that this time she was going to be in need of some support.

"I'm sorry, Marie," he said. "I should have asked them to warn you."

She waved away his concern. "I'll survive. This hasn't."

"I wanted you to see it right away."

She turned her gaze on him. "Do you know what you have here, Tyler?"

"It's obviously a Matisse, or done in his style. With all that damage, it's not easy to be certain."

"But which Matisse?"

"I don't recognize it. He did hundreds of seascapes, Marie." Tyler resented the inquisition.

Like a schoolteacher, she shook her head, admonishing him, and Weil guessed she was pleased with the opportunity to lecture him. Unhappy, like many of the Met's old guard, that the reins of the museum hadn't gone to someone who was more of a scholar, she'd been vocal about her concerns over his appointment.

"It's Matisse's *View of St. Tropez*."

She was watching him with her light blue, inscrutable eyes, waiting, he thought, for some sign of recognition, but the title of the painting didn't mean anything to him.

"I'd like to know what I'm facing before the FBI shows up. That's why I asked you to come down here. Would you fill me in on the painting's background? What's its significance to us?"

"This Matisse was bequeathed to us in the late 1960s by its owner, who died in 2003. We weren't able to take possession because it was stolen before its owner died. The robbery was in the news for weeks all around the world, Tyler."

He wasn't going to give her the satisfaction of reacting to the dig. "Thank you, Marie."

"How did it get here?" Grimshaw asked.

"I haven't been briefed yet." Weil turned to Olshling. "Who unpacked this?" he asked, not accusatory but inquisitive. "Do we know who sent it?"

"Joe McBurney, here, unpacked it." Olshling nodded at a young man in a white smock who shuffled nervously from foot to foot under the director's scrutiny. "And yes," he said, pointing to an ordinary white envelope taped to the inside of the crate, "there's a letter. It's addressed to you, Mr. Weil."

Weil bent over and read his name, typed, with no other identifying marks. He reached out for it.

"Mr. Weil, could you just wait a moment?" Olshling reached behind him, pulled a pair of nitrile gloves out of a dispenser and offered them to the director.

Like most professionals who worked around artwork, Weil knew he should wear gloves while examining a work of art to protect the precious objects from the oils on his skin—and in a situation like this, to protect himself from any hazardous materials—but he'd forgotten. From the look in the chief of security's eyes, Weil knew that Philippe de Montebello wouldn't have needed to be reminded not to contaminate the evidence.

Hands encased in synthetic rubber, Weil slit open the envelope and pulled out a sheet of paper folded around four photographs. He examined each one slowly and carefully before handing the pile to Marie, who had also donned gloves. "I'm guessing these have something in common with the Matisse."

"You're right," she said in a low voice as she looked through the photos a second time. "Every one of these belongs to the museum. All were bequeathed to us, by different donors. And each one was stolen before we were able to take possession." She handed the pile back to Weil. "What's going on?" Her voice trembled like a crystal chandelier reacting to a door being slammed shut.

Chapter

TWELVE

Lucian pulled his 1988 Mustang into a restricted spot on East Seventy-Ninth Street and, because of his government plates, ignored the meter. He'd bought the car at a police auction, and had restored it to pristine condition. Forgoing an umbrella despite the drizzle, he hurried west. A strong wind blew young leaves off tree branches, and a sheet of the *Daily News* plastered Lucian's leg. Pulling it off, he glimpsed the headline, CENTRAL PARK HIT-AND-RUN, and hurried on toward his destination, the New York Society Library.

The library had been housed in this classic limestone building designed by Trowbridge and Livingston since 1937 but had originally opened its doors in 1754 at old City Hall, on Wall Street facing Broad Street. For more than one hundred and fifty years it had been known as the "city library" until the public library system was founded and it became a treasured landmark.

Lucian had passed the building often, but this was his first time inside. He was struck by the quiet after the noisy street. Standing in the entryway for a moment, he looked around, feeling the same grace he experienced whenever he stepped inside a museum. Once he'd read that one of the ways a society's humanity could be measured was by how well it treasured its artwork, literature and music, how much it revered the work of the soul. In a place like this, he thought, you could almost be optimistic. He'd have to share that insight with Matt; his partner would appreciate it.

Following instructions from the elderly woman at the front desk, Lucian climbed a wide marble staircase, took a right, then a left, and found the director's office.

William Hawkes, a venerable man whose skin was so thin Lucian could read his veins like a map, greeted him in a surprisingly youthful voice, gave him a firm handshake and offered him a seat.

The office was richly decorated with a fine Louis XIV partners desk, a large bay window enclosed by ruby damask curtains, an Oriental carpet and three walls of carved walnut shelves with rows of leather-bound, gilt-edged books. The ceiling was paneled, and the crossbeams were feathered with gold inlay.

"It's not often that I get a visit from my friends at the bureau. So how can I help you, Agent Glass?" Hawkes asked after they'd exchanged pleasantries.

"It's about Dr. Malachai Samuels. I know you're close to his aunt, so you might be aware we've had him under suspicion for quite some time."

"Yes, I am."

"He's still the prime suspect in several crimes, including a recent robbery that resulted in a brutal death."

Hawkes put both his hands on his desk and used them to propel himself up. He clasped them behind his back, walked over to the window and looked down to the street below. With his back still to Lucian he said, "Beryl is convinced of her nephew's innocence. She has MS, do you know that?"

"Yes, I do."

"Stress is terrible for her," Hawkes said and turned back to face Lucian. "And the past eighteen months have been very stressful." He shook his head, and a lock of his thick white hair fell across his forehead.

"We have a lot of circumstantial evidence but no hard proof. That's why I'm here, to ask for your help."

"At my age there are so many people I've cared about whom I've lost to age, illness, accidents… I know the toll that loss takes on the spirit, and I just can't imagine what something like this will do to my dear friend Beryl." The news had shaken him, and as he walked back to his desk he seemed more feeble and fragile. "Have you ever lost anyone you cared about, Detective?"

Lucian had come to in the hospital days after Solange's death, too doped up with painkillers to miss her or mourn her. In the months following, when he should have confronted the pain of her death, he focused instead on the physical pain of learning to work the muscles the knife had cut through and the doctors had sewn back together. Loss? It was a tight, impossible knot inside of him that he'd long since given up hoping to unravel.

"I've known Malachai since he was a graduate student…an incredibly bright man. Did you know he studied at Oxford?" Hawkes asked.

Lucian nodded.

"He's a scientist and a well-respected therapist. He works with children, Agent Glass." He shook his head. "He works with *children*." The *shame on you* was unsaid but implicit.

"Yes, I know, but none of those things preclude him from being a suspect."

Hawkes splayed his hands on his desk and looked down at the age-spotted skin as if he'd find an answer to his dilemma there. "You're putting me in a difficult position. I've known

Beryl Talmage longer than I've known your boss. You're asking me to choose between two people I care about. I'm sorry, I don't know how to do that."

Lucian wasn't ready to give up. Comley had told him about this man who'd won a Purple Heart, taught history at Harvard, had twenty-three honorary degrees, had written several books—including two volumes on the life of Albert Einstein—and had then become the director of the Library of Congress. He'd retired six years ago to travel with his wife, but after she died he'd agreed to take on the directorship of this small private library. What would convince him?

"Do you pay attention to coincidences?" Lucian asked.

"Einstein said, 'Coincidence is God's way of remaining anonymous.' But he didn't really believe in God. He said coincidence was unthinkable in physics, once calling it a weakness of the theory. I'm sorry, you didn't come here for a lecture. What does this have to do with Malachai Samuels?"

"I am trained to pay attention to coincidences. And they're piled up around this case like a major accident on the FDR Drive. Can I tell you about some of them before I leave?"

"Certainly."

Outside, either the clouds had become denser or the rain had intensified, because there was now noticeably less light coming through the sheer curtains, and the atmosphere in the room was suddenly oppressive. "Last year when the ancient stones believed to be Memory Tools were stolen, Dr. Samuels was in Rome."

"I know that. But you couldn't find any evidence tying him to the crime. One would have to read the news without glasses not to have been aware of that."

Lucian nodded. "Last week, while Dr. Samuels was in Vienna, a document was stolen from a library he had—"

"What library?"

"The private library at the Memorist Society, an organization that dates back to the early 1800s."

"What kind of document?"

"It was a partial list of ancient Memory Tools. A coincidence? Two robberies less than twelve months apart but both dealing with the Memory Tools. Two robberies occurring in cities Malachai Samuels just happened to be visiting."

Hawkes took a deep breath. It was a few moments before he responded. "What does this have to do with me?"

"Yesterday, Dr. Samuels called and asked you to recommend a librarian he could hire part-time to help him do some research."

"How do you know that?"

"I regret I'm not at liberty to say."

The elderly man's hands knotted into fists on his desk. "Do you have just cause to invade my privacy like this?"

"Not your privacy, Malachai Samuels's. People have been killed, Dr. Hawkes. You were on the other end of a call, and we're sorry about that, but that call has put you in a position to help us."

ACT was anxious to break the case before Malachai could do any more harm. Lucian's appointments with Dr. Bellmer might or might not yield the kind of infiltration the FBI needed, but this solution could.

"How can I do that?"

"We want you to allow us to supply you with the name of the librarian to suggest to Dr. Samuels."

"And that man will be an agent?"

"He'll be a librarian. I'd be happy to show you his CV. I don't want to impose on you to recommend someone you don't feel comfortable with."

"I'm sorry, but I don't think I can accommodate you, Agent Glass."

"Several people have died. We're afraid more will die if we can't put this man in jail. Will you at least give it some serious thought?"

"Yes, that I will do."

"There's one other coincidence."

"What's that?"

"During his call, Malachai told you he's anxious to hire a librarian because he recently obtained new information suggesting that his foundation's own library might contain clues to the location of other Memory Tools, isn't that correct? What information do you think that is? Where did he get it? Vienna?"

Dr. Hawkes glared at Lucian. "I don't like how you do business, Agent Glass."

"I don't always like it, either. But I like murder less."

As Lucian rose to leave he felt his cell phone vibrate for the third time since he'd been there. Once outside the office he finally pulled it out, looked down at the caller ID and checked the two previous calls. All three were from Nicolas Olshling at the Metropolitan Museum. Lucian hit Reply and listened to the phone ringing as he walked out of the library and into the unremitting rain and buffeting wind.

Chapter

THIRTEEN

Driving past the monumental, seventeen-foot-tall sculpture by Noguchi that stood like a sentry on Fifth Avenue and Eightieth Street, Lucian pulled into the underground parking garage abutting the Metropolitan. Locking the doors, he walked through the dark, cavernous space to the museum entrance—an ironically unceremonious access to the structure that was the largest and most comprehensive art museum in the western hemisphere.

The brass-framed glass doors opened into the entryway to the children's museum. The only artwork here was an eight-foot-long, four-foot-wide and three-foot-tall reproduction of the Parthenon. Lucian looked at the kids crowded around it, ogling the colorful statues on the frieze and peering in through the columns to the elaborate miniature of Athena. He could still remember coming here on school trips and always looking at that magical model.

For Lucian, the Met wasn't just filled with artwork; it was a treasure trove of memories. He'd taken his first painting classes here when he was only six. He had come with his parents every Christmas for the tree lighting and to see the Neapolitan

Baroque crèche, a fantastic diorama perfect in every detail down to sparkling streams, goats and barking dogs. He'd taught himself anatomy in high school by sketching the Met's great classical sculptures and had ultimately been admitted to The Cooper Union with a portfolio of those drawings. And he'd brought Solange here the first time they'd gone out together. Walking through the galleries that day, they'd each passed a test they hadn't known they were taking. Their zeal for art was the first thread woven into the fabric of their passion for each other.

While she'd looked at paintings, he'd stolen looks at her lovely face—perfect, he'd thought, except for the strange, pale crescent-moon-shaped mark above her right eyebrow that she covered with bangs. She had been self-conscious about the scar and made up different stories about how she'd gotten it. From a vicious babysitter with a knife when she was five. From a French poodle that had leaped up and taken a bite out of her when she was still a baby. From an incident with a hammer when she was trying to hang her first painting at school. From the devil, signaling she'd sold him her soul so she could paint better.

He'd never found out the truth.

One afternoon she'd taken him to see her favorite painting, Martin Johnson Heade's *Approaching Thunderstorm*. It was a foreboding landscape with blackening clouds over an even darker body of water and a lone boy on the shore staring out into the tense sky. "All I want to do," Solange had said fiercely, "is to be able to paint with this much authority and purity. That's what every artist I respect does—synthesizes a moment or emotion down to its essence. No frivolity."

Lucian didn't often dwell on his memories of her—it had happened a long time ago—but Hawkes had asked him if he'd ever lost anyone he loved, and now he was here, where they'd spent so much time together.

Solange still stood out from the other women he'd known. How could she not? Their relationship had been cut short, never having the time to sour or turn. Their year together was like a living thing trapped in amber, protected for eternity by its method of destruction.

Walking up the simple, unadorned marble staircase from the downstairs level to the first floor, he remembered that, after seeing the Heade that day, they'd gone back to his dorm room. It was their first time, and after she'd undressed, she stood in front of him naked. Before he could reach for her, she asked him to draw her. As his hand streaked across the page he forgot how much he wanted her and became consumed with creating his version of the lithe body standing before him. She'd laughed with delight at his skill in orchestrating the charcoal's movement. The sketch wound up being more assured and alive than anything he'd ever done.

It was a lesson that caused him to look at every piece of art differently from then on. What made something matter on paper or canvas was the intensity of the rage or obsession, the ardor or the excitement of its creator. The urgency to take the moment in, process it and give it back to the world transformed by a singular vision—that was what elevated effort into art.

On his way to meeting Olshling, Lucian walked by centuries-old naked warriors and athletes, immortalized in gleaming marble. Each was a living history of the artists and the models and the journeys of the pieces themselves. Even if their stories had been lost, like his with Solange would be when he was no longer alive to recount it, anyone moved by this art was being touched by the lives of the people who had created it, posed for it, bought it, sold it and treasured it—and even those who had stolen it.

* * *

Tyler Weil, Nicolas Olshling and a half-dozen other museum personnel blocked Lucian's view, but whatever they were looking at had drained all the energy out of the room. He felt as if he'd walked in on a wake.

"Agent Glass, thanks for coming." Olshling came over to greet him and left enough of a gap for Lucian to see a riot of colors—bright lemon, sharp green, cool blue. He stepped closer and stared down at the serrated streamers and threads of canvas. He was doing his job, listening to Olshling explain, while examining a brutally vandalized painting.

"It's a Matisse."

Lucian glanced up. The speaker was a woman in her seventies who had her arms crossed across her chest and was regarding him with hostility. Usually people's reactions to him didn't matter, but this woman was making him uneasy. He turned back to the painting.

Yes, even in ruins, the artist's hand, palette and brushstrokes weren't just recognizable—they were unmistakable.

"The painting has quite a history," Tyler Weil said. "It's entitled *View of St. Tropez,* and it's been in the FBI's national stolen art file for about twenty years."

Lucian had seen this painting only in photographs. Finally looking at it, staring at it, despite everything it symbolized for him, he didn't react. All he could think of was that the photographs he'd seen had not done the painting justice, even in this damaged state.

Then, suddenly, bile rose in his throat and his stomach spasmed. Lucian didn't exhibit any outward sign of his inner turmoil. What was that Einstein quote William Hawkes had told him? *Coincidence is God's way of remaining anonymous.* But Lucian didn't believe in God, either.

Everyone in this room might be aware that this painting had disappeared twenty years ago, but Lucian was the only one who knew the day and the hour. He knew it almost to the minute, because this was the masterpiece that had been stolen by an unknown assailant who had tricked his way inside a well-protected framing gallery, brutally stabbed two teenagers and fled the scene. Solange had died that day because she'd still been at the store waiting for Lucian while he'd been in his studio, playing so hard at being an artist he'd forgotten what time it was.

Chapter

FOURTEEN

Robert Keyes made sure the oversize black umbrella shielded his daughter as they walked west on Eighty-Third Street. Last night Veronica's nightmare had been vicious. He'd heard her wrenching screams and run into her room, finding her thrashing in her bed, twisted up in the sheets, fighting off an invisible evil she couldn't name. Her hair was plastered to her forehead and tears wet her flushed cheeks. Except for telling him that everything was dark in the dream, she couldn't recall who or what was scaring her. The night terror didn't seem to be bothering her now though, as the seven-year-old continued telling him about her class trip to the Metropolitan Museum earlier that day.

"And then Mr. Weil's phone rang, and then he talked to someone, and then he got really quiet for a loooong time and then he had to leave," she complained. "Right when we were looking at the rocodial."

Robert stopped worrying to try to figure out the word. "Crocodile?"

"Uh-huh."

As they approached the Phoenix Foundation with its turret,

stained-glass windows and fancy ironwork railing, Robert spied dozens of gargoyles.

"Look, Veronica." He pointed.

"Monster spouts!" she shouted out, and then laughed.

Robert smiled. Veronica renamed everything using more descriptive terms: their dog was a "furry four-legger" and grilled-cheese sandwiches—her favorites—were "melted cheese toasts." Only the nightmares didn't have names.

Once Frances buzzed the father and daughter inside, Veronica started hopping from black marble square to black marble square up and down the hall, avoiding the whites in some game of her own devising.

"You're early," Frances said after she greeted them.

"I picked Veronica up at school and planned on walking here, but the rain was too heavy. Is it a problem?"

"No." Frances indicated the seating area set up with its child-size seats, a plastic castle and several toy chests overflowing with games, books and puzzles. "There's lots for Veronica to do. I just wanted you to know that Dr. Samuels is out but he'll be back in time for your appointment."

Deep inside Central Park, just west of the Dairy on West Sixty-Fifth Street, Malachai Samuels sat at a stone table inside the otherwise empty Chess and Checkers House. He'd set up the ivory and black pieces over a half hour ago. Since then he'd been playing both sides and checking his watch every few minutes, like any man annoyed that his partner was late—which was exactly how he wanted it to look, even though no one else was there or anywhere near enough to watch.

Malachai had his office swept for bugs every week, but he knew there could be directional mikes aimed at the foundation, and he preferred to have certain conversations out of doors. Frances believed he was at a physical therapy appointment.

A clean-cut man in his mid-thirties wearing chinos, loafers and a blue button-down shirt walked inside the gaming house.

Malachai swept the chess pieces into a wooden box and stood up as Reed Winston approached.

"I'm sorry I'm late." Reed smiled sheepishly.

"So am I, since I have to leave. But I played a good game without you," Malachai said, continuing the charade.

Winston followed his employer outside. The rain was just letting up, and neither of them needed to open an umbrella. Once they were out of earshot of the Chess House, Malachai asked if Winston had any news.

"There hasn't been any activity in Vienna. No one at the society has made any attempt to reach out to any art experts, archaeologists or historians."

"What about linguists?"

Winston shook his head. "Everyone is still pretty shaken up over Alderman's death. They haven't appointed a new director yet, and no one seems focused on the missing list."

"What about the Austrian police?"

"They haven't made any headway." He grinned.

Malachai thought his spy's smile was unseemly but refrained from mentioning it. They'd reached a fork in the path, and the logical way to proceed was to turn right onto the main path and head for Central Park West. Instead, Malachai took a left and Winston followed him into the shadows under a stone arch.

Malachai knew that habits made you easier to track, so he tried to change his often. And he knew it was better to hire a half-dozen men who knew nothing about each other's jobs than to have one with enough information to piece it all together, but he'd made an exception with Winston. Knowing everything allowed the ex-Interpol agent to monitor all aspects of the investigation. If there were connections, he'd be able to recognize them. Malachai couldn't play it as safe as he wished he could. Even if the Memory Tools catalogued on the list had survived, they could be hidden from view or in plain sight, buried in a ruin, on display in a museum, sitting in an antique store or in someone's grandmother's curio cabinet. His search could take years, but his father might not have that long. And Malachai wanted to know about his own past lives. If what he guessed was true, he wanted to shove it in the old man's face.

"I'm going to be hiring a librarian to go through the archived correspondence at the foundation," Malachai said, "to see if we can find any information about the whereabouts of the missing tools. We have documents that go back to the mid-1800s, when we were financing digs all over the Middle East and the Mediterranean. I came across information in those papers about the tools we found in Rome. Maybe there's more information about these others."

"What do you need me to do?"

"Make sure the candidates are clean."

Avoiding a puddle, Malachai checked his watch. "I need to get back to the foundation. One more thing. Have you found out anything else about the Agent Glass who was hurt in the robbery? Is he working on this case now that he's back in New York?"

"I'm not sure."

Malachai stopped, forcing Winston to stop also. "What do you mean?"

"He's been trained in all the surveillance techniques I've been trained in. I can't track him as if he were an ordinary citizen."

"I need to know what he knows and what he's doing about finding out what he doesn't know." Malachai spoke in a level voice, as if he were requesting lemon, not cream, with his tea.

Two elderly, white-haired women walked by. Were they in disguise and really there to watch him? Was the man walking the gray French poodle? Or the woman pushing a baby carriage? Paranoia was annoying, but, perversely, it made him feel safe.

"I'm doing my best to get better information for you."

"I'm going to need better than your best."

Chapter

FIFTEEN

Charlie Danzinger lifted a thin sheet of gold leaf with a sable brush and applied the fourteen-karat foil to a band girding the sculpture's ankle. Sweeping away the extra, he stepped back and inspected his work, pleased at how the precious metal transformed an ordinary sandal strap into something magisterial.

Made of what appeared to be wood, with ivory hands, feet and face, the eight-foot Greek god was more than impressive—he was commanding. The few people allowed to visit the restorer's studio in the Metropolitan's south wing and see this secret project had been awed by its size and majesty. But no one was as interested in Hypnos as the venerated curator Marie Grimshaw, who was sitting on a stool in the corner, watching Danzinger work.

She had come twice a day every day for the past five months, spending fifteen or twenty minutes at a time. Usually she arrived at around ten-thirty in the morning and then between three and four in the afternoon, always bringing coffee for both of them. She'd asked him that first day how he took it and had smiled when he said black with one sugar. "That will be easy to remember," she'd said. "That's how I take it."

Marie had never given Danzinger a reason why she visited so often. Clearly, she was fascinated by the sculpture he was working on, but he sensed she didn't know why. He didn't ask; it wasn't his business. Besides, he liked having her company, especially when she regaled him with tales about the museum. He was shy and found it difficult to get to know people. He'd been working at the Met for more than eighteen years but had few friends among his colleagues. So when Marie had sought him out, Danzinger had been flattered. And still was.

He applied more gold to the left sandal. Out of the corner of his eye, he noticed the curator cross and then re-cross her legs. She'd never been this agitated before, and she'd missed her morning visit. Rising off her stool, she walked past a bank of steel cabinets over to the shelves filled with the tools of his trade: stains and paints, brushes and pens, files and rasps, etching plates, rolls of canvas and trays of wood, glass and stone fragments.

"Charlie, do you know a lot about mythology?"

"I'm a restorer, not a historian," he joked.

"They called your Hypnos the conqueror of the gods because he could put all of the others to sleep. Thanatos, the god of death, was his brother. Nyx, the goddess of night, was his mother and Morpheus, the god of dreams, was his father. Some family, wasn't it? Hypnos lived in the land of eternal darkness, just a short distance beyond the gates of the rising sun in a land called Erebus. Plutarch said his job was to lull and rest men's souls…" She didn't quite put an end to the sentence, and the sound of her last word—*souls*—hung in the air.

Not sure what to make of her soliloquy, he remained quiet.

"Do you believe we have souls?" she finally asked.

He cleared his throat. "Yes." He thought about what he'd said, and then amended it. "Yes, I guess I do."

"You seem surprised by your answer."

"I'm a lapsed Catholic and didn't think I believed in much anymore." He bit his bottom lip as he concentrated on applying a new sheet of gold leaf. Then brushing out a small wrinkle, he continued. "Working on all these valuable objects, I've come to believe that something of every artist's soul is in their work, and that's what I'm really preserving and restoring." He looked up from Hypnos to Marie, whose eyes had filled with tears. She was the strongest woman he knew, as much of a treasure at the Met as one of the pieces of artwork. He never would have guessed he'd see her cry.

"What's wrong?" He spoke softly, wanting her to confide in him if she needed to but still a little in awe of her. "Is there something I can do?"

"An important painting that was bequeathed to the museum years ago was delivered to us this morning."

"That's wonderful, isn't it?"

"It's been completely destroyed."

"How?"

"Someone slashed it with a knife." She whispered the last few words as if they were too terrible to say out loud.

Danzinger recoiled. "Beyond restoration?"

"Someone in your department will have to tell us."

"What's your opinion?"

A tear escaped and slid down her cheek, but she didn't seem to notice. "Even if we can put it back together again, it won't ever be the same."

"Why would anyone do that?"

"To prove he could." Her voice quivered with anger. "The monster who did it said he has four more paintings of equal value, each donated to us, but all stolen before we could take possession. It's blackmail. He says he'll destroy one each week that we delay giving him what he wants."

"What does he want?"

Before she had a chance to tell him, the studio door opened. Tyler Weil walked into the room accompanied by another man Danzinger didn't recognize.

A visit from the director was unusual enough, but then Weil introduced Special Agent Lucian Glass.

The restorer hoped his hand wasn't sweating when he reached out to shake the agent's.

"Mr. Danzinger, can you show Agent Glass what you're working on and explain a bit about how it's progressing?"

"Sure," he said confidently. Talking about his work was one thing he knew he could do.

They clustered in the center of the studio where, dominating the space, were two colossal sculptures, both eight feet tall, identical in shape and subject matter, but not condition. The one on the right was the statue of the ancient Greek god Hypnos that Danzinger had been working on. Young and handsome, with sensitive eyes, sensuous lips and a finely wrought nose, his bone structure was elegant and the expression on his face was both sultry and serene…as if he was slipping into a dream himself.

This polychromatic god was seated, leaning on his arm, in a languid pose. His eyes were obsidian orbs partially veneered with more ivory and inlaid with moss-green chalcedony to give them a lifelike appearance.

The throne he was seated on was a hollow armature made from the same insect- and rot-resistant wood. His tunic was gilded and well decorated. In his left hand he held a silver horn of what legend said was sleep-inducing opium; in his right he held a bronze branch dripping water, symbolized by a drop of lapis lazuli, from the river of forgetfulness, Lethe.

In the back of the sculpture was a three-foot-wide and four-foot-high wooden panel that opened like a door, exposing the sculpture's hollow guts and structural skeleton. One afternoon Danzinger had come back from a meeting to find Marie standing inside Hypnos, her hands outstretched, her fingertips running up and down the inside skin of the god, staring up into his hollowed body as if she were in a trance. Danzinger had called out to her three times before she responded, and then she seemed nonplussed, as if she'd woken to find she'd been sleepwalking. During the past six months, he'd been inside of the structure a few times himself but hadn't noticed anything worthy of her intense interest.

Beside this piece sat a second version of the same god, identical in size and shape but not in condition. This Hypnos was not nearly as glorious. He was the original, two thousand years older and looking his age. Ancient and worn, he was seriously damaged and discolored. One of his silver wings was missing, as were both of his hands. His right foot was gone; his left had only two toes. His tunic was stripped of its gold. One of his eyes was intact, the other was dead black, with both the green pupil and the white sclera missing. The body of the sculpture was badly damaged. What there was of surface space was a mass of scars.

Compared to the almost completed copy, which the museum was going to put on display to show museumgoers what the sculpture had looked like when it was first created, the original was unimposing.

Over the next ten minutes the restorer described the process of making casts of the original, filling the molds with a wood composite he chased with tools so it appeared carved, or with a polymer that resembled the original's ivory. He detailed the stages of painting the sculpture, gilding it and ornamenting it with stones.

The agent took notes and made sketches—Danzinger noticed—in a small Moleskine notebook, the kind used by artists.

"Is the gold on the original thin sheets or leaf?" Glass asked.

"Leaf," Danzinger answered confidently.

"What about the silver?"

"Very thin sheets."

"The stones? What are they? What are they worth?"

"Most are semiprecious, but there are some emeralds, rubies and amethysts. Mostly you're looking at lapis lazuli, amber, garnets, carnelians, banded agates, sardonyx, chalcedony and rock crystal. None of them of exceptional quality."

The FBI agent turned to the director. "What's the value of the sculpture?"

"It's the most complete chryselephantine sculpture to have survived… I think it would go for five to six million."

"Compared to a painting by Matisse or Monet or Van Gogh— it's really small change, isn't it?"

"Yes," Marie answered before the director could. "The paintings are worth so much more."

"Which brings us back to the question none of us can help you with, Agent Glass," Weil said. "Why would anyone want to exchange paintings worth over a hundred and fifty million dollars for our Hypnos?"

Chapter

SIXTEEN

Malachai swung the shiny gold disc slowly, back and forth, until the child's eyes grew heavy and closed.

"Where are you, Veronica?" Malachai asked the little girl sitting opposite him.

"It's so dark…" she whimpered.

"Where are you?"

Nothing.

"Do you recognize this dark place?"

"Yes…" Her voice was quivering.

"Tell me."

She shook her head, *no*, and then again *no*. "Don't go." She sounded frantic, almost hysterical. "Don't go."

Robert Keyes inched forward on the couch. Malachai knew he wanted to stop the hypnosis, but he shook his head at Veronica's father and mouthed, *She's fine*.

"Has someone left you in the dark?" Malachai asked.

"No." Her little voice broke.

"What's happening?" Malachai asked.

She was half panting, half crying.

"Can you step back from where you are? Try to see what's happening, like a picture in a book."

The little girl's panting intensified.

"They're here."

"Can you tell me where you are?"

"Inside."

"Inside your house?"

She nodded.

"Where is your house? Where do you live?"

"Shush," Veronica said. "I live in the ghetto."

"Do you know what year it is?"

"1885."

Malachai had been a reincarnationist for over thirty years and by now knew about almost every culture and country. Shush was in Persia, which at the end of the nineteenth century was a very difficult place for Jews. They weren't allowed to travel outside the ghetto's gates or to wear most colors. They needed to be easily identifiable.

"What is happening to you?"

She was oblivious to his question, reenacting a scene in her mind that had happened over one hundred and thirty years ago. "Don't go," she whimpered, her lower lip trembling, and then she reached out with her little hands to grab at someone who wasn't there, whom Malachai couldn't see.

SEVENTEEN

Farid Taghinia had left work at six o'clock. The rest of the employees departed quickly after he did, so by six-fifteen the mission was empty, but Samimi had decided to wait a bit longer before venturing out of his office. Now that it was seven, it was certainly safe, but he was nervous nonetheless. He was always nervous lately. If his actions were discovered, he'd be sent back to Iran and killed. He had no doubt.

To make it look as if he'd gotten up without premeditation, Samimi left an unfinished document open on his computer, picked up a sheaf of papers, walked down the hall to his boss's office and, using a key he wasn't supposed to have, opened the door.

After laying the papers on Taghinia's desk, Samimi pulled on gloves and then picked up the phone. He always held his breath during this part of the operation. If Taghinia had found the bug he'd be cagey enough to set a trap for whoever had placed it there.

The device was where Samimi had put it last week.

His hands shook as he removed it and slipped it into his pocket. No matter how many times he'd performed the ritual of putting the bug in and taking it out, his fear never lessened. And he'd been at it now for almost six months. Once every ten days, the night before the offices were swept for listening devices, Samimi retrieved his pet and took it home with him, only returning it to its nest the evening after the inspections. That meant that every fortnight he missed twenty-four hours' worth of Taghinia's phone calls. It bothered him, but what could he do? So far he'd been able to pick up where he'd left off in most of the conversations without too much confusion. *But was he missing anything critical?*

At his boss's door, he listened before he walked out. Nothing but street noises and the whir of office equipment. About to leave, he remembered the papers, his excuse if he was caught. *I just came in to leave these here,* he'd say. And if Taghinia questioned him about the locked door? *It wasn't locked.* He'd rehearsed it all in front of the mirror at home a dozen times. *I didn't know you locked your door at night, Farid. Why do you do that?*

Back in his own office, Samimi extracted the day's phone tape from the hiding place he'd constructed in his bookshelf and left the mission for the night.

An hour later he sat sipping Scotch and playing the tapes in the kitchen area of his small Queens studio, which was decorated with clean, modern furniture and not a single Persian rug. He was halfway through his drink and so far none of the calls were important or relevant to the Hypnos rescue.

Since Vartan Reza had discovered the forgery, plans had been speeding up. The statue had first been a symbol of power but now, with the possibility it was a legendary map to unleashing unconscious powers, it was valuable as much more than an artifact. If his country had been determined to reclaim it before, now they were desperate. Something like this could not belong to anyone else. Could not be discovered by anyone else. Hypnos had to come home and be examined.

That was why Samimi was being so careful now and why he'd bought himself such an expensive insurance policy last Friday.

Following Taghinia's instructions, Samimi had driven a gray Mercedes up to the garage in Lake Placid. But not the same Mercedes that had been used in the murder of Vartan Reza. Samimi had put that car into a storage space he'd rented in the Bronx and had driven a replacement he'd bought up to the garage. It had cost him almost half his savings, but how could he put a price on having evidence against Taghinia for vehicular manslaughter and leaving the scene of a crime?

What to do with that evidence weighed on his mind, though. He was afraid to send it to anyone, but he'd written a letter explaining what he'd done, which he kept folded up behind his credit cards in his wallet. If anything happened to him, someone *would* find it.

"My boys loved the last set of American movies you sent, Farid. Thank you," Nassir was saying on the most recent tape. "That young actor—what was his name? Jon Heder. Very funny."

This was it. The minister who was the mastermind of the plan to bring Hypnos home, was employing the code. Ready with a pencil and pad of paper, Samimi wrote down every word the two men said for the next four minutes. When the call ended, he worked on the translation for half an hour. By the time he had it all deciphered and read it through, he needed a second drink.

In code, Nassir told Taghinia he was arranging for a delivery of five pounds of Semtex, the Czech-made plastic explosive. Specifying pre-1991 Semtex, which had no commercial tracing chemicals in it, so it was virtually undetectable. It would arrive via the diplomatic pouch and be delivered to the warehouse the mission owned on the west side of Manhattan. More than enough explosives, Nassir said, to blow up a stone building six stories high.

Hypnos was in the Met. The Met was built of stone…Samimi considered its size. Were they talking about the museum? *What was going on?* He drained the second drink in less time than it had taken him to pour it.

Chapter
EIGHTEEN

"I'm here to see Andre Jacobs," Lucian said as he offered his badge to the uniformed doorman. While the man inspected the agent's credentials, Lucian studied the lobby. It looked the same as it had twenty years ago when he'd camped out upstairs in Solange's parents' Fifth Avenue apartment while they were traveling.

For years after the accident, he had avoided this block. Once he'd been in a taxi that stopped at a light on the corner, instinctively glanced over, counted up ten floors and stared at the darkened rectangle of glass that had been her bedroom window. And suddenly, there in the car, Lucian could smell Solange's lily-of-the-valley scent and feel her body pressed up against his. Unwilling to luxuriate in the agony of missing her in the back of a lousy cab, he'd pushed the memory away.

After that if he came down Fifth either on foot or in a car he avoided looking left; he'd just keep moving.

The doorman hung up the house phone. "You can go on up, Agent Glass. Mr. Jacobs's housekeeper is expecting you. When you get off the elevator it's to your right. Apartment—"

"Ten B," Lucian said, walking to the elevator.

Upstairs, he faced the familiar forest green door, rang the bell and waited. The hallway was small—there were just two apartments per floor—and quiet except for the whir of the elevator as it descended. Lucian examined the brown marble tiles shot through with gold veins, the tan, gold and white wallpaper with its slightly Oriental design, and the gilt-framed mirror hanging over the narrow table centered between the two doorways. In a cut-glass vase was an arrangement of dried flowers that looked as if someone had put them there, fresh, years ago and then forgotten about them.

Finally Lucian heard footsteps, but it wasn't a housekeeper who opened the door. The wasted, worn-out man was a shadow of the person he'd once been. In Andre Jacobs's watery eyes and ravaged face was the evidence of two decades of sorrow.

Lucian started to introduce himself when Jacobs interrupted.

"I didn't call the police," he snarled, as if he'd dismissed the idea that the law could ever be of any value to him a long time ago.

Jacobs hadn't recognized him, but Lucian wasn't surprised. They'd only met a couple of times, and that had been two decades ago, when he'd been nineteen years old, not yet grown into his features, just one of a group of Solange's friends. No, Jacobs hadn't recognized him, but surely he would remember the name that had appeared alongside his daughter's for months in reports of the crime the press had dubbed "the art theft of the decade."

"I'm from the FBI, Agent Lu—"

"The FBI? Well, I certainly didn't call the FBI."

Lucian forced himself not to react to the stink of gin that accompanied the words. It was only three in the afternoon.

"I'm here because we need your help. Can I come in, Mr. Jacobs?" He was going to have to tell the man his name, but now that he'd seen his physical state, he thought Jacobs should be seated in case it came as a shock.

"Is this about art? Because I'm not in the art business any-more. I can't help you with information about any stolen paint-ings." Jacobs spat out the words.

"This time it's about a painting that has been found." Lucian took a step forward, hoping that if he invaded Jacobs's per-sonal space it would force the man to step farther back and let him in.

"That's been found?" There was a flicker of interest in the old man's eyes, but then it faded. "No, I'm not in the business anymore. I can't help you."

Looking past Jacobs, Lucian could see into the foyer. The decor hadn't changed in all these years. "I only need a few minutes of your time."

"Ask me what you want to ask me, and then leave me in peace."

"Twenty years ago, one of your clients gave you a painting to reframe…"

Jacobs leaned more of his weight on the door.

Lucian noticed and continued. "It was a Matisse…"

Jacobs slumped; he was holding on to the door for support now.

"…entitled *View*…"

Jacobs flinched.

"…*of St. Tropez.*"

Jacobs recoiled viscerally.

"The painting was stolen from your shop, on May sixteenth." Lucian's voice was almost a whisper now. "You remember that day, don't you?"

Jacobs barely nodded, as if his head was too heavy to move. This was more difficult than Lucian had anticipated and he was angry with himself for not passing this part of the job on to Matt Richmond as Doug Comley had suggested. But time had brought the past full circle. This was his case and he needed to see it through.

"Mr. Jacobs, we believe the painting found yesterday is that Matisse, but there's no way to confirm—"

"Absolutely not," he interrupted even before he heard the full request. He shook his head as if the movement would put up a wall between the past and the present.

"Please let me just exp—"

"You..." Jacobs was staring at him. "I know who you are!" He was shouting again, as all the pieces of the puzzle came together for him at once.

"What's wrong?" The door blocked the speaker but her voice was clear. Even laced with anxiety it had a lightness to it, as if it were being played in the upper octaves of a fine, well-tuned piano.

Lucian watched the woman as she came into view. She had alabaster skin and pale blond hair that dipped over her forehead, skimmed her shoulders and shone as if it were polished metal. She was dressed in a sleeveless cream-colored shift and wore gold ballet slippers. Everything about her seemed to glow. Later, Lucian would realize that it was sun from the living-room windows sidelighting her, but in that first moment it appeared as if she had a nimbus surrounding her.

"Are you all right?" the woman asked Jacobs as she reached his side and hooked her arm in his in a graceful gesture, offering support.

He fixed his rheumy gaze on her and tried to smile, but all he managed was the remembrance of a smile. Jacobs looked like someone who'd just seen a ghost.

And Lucian was that ghost.

"Are you all right?" the woman asked again. Her voice was both soft and hoarse at the same time, the way velvet felt different depending on which way you brushed the nap.

Jacobs nodded, but she didn't seem reassured. Lucian didn't blame her. She had probably heard the shouting and all she had to do was look at Jacobs to know he wasn't well. Dissatisfied, she turned to Lucian. Her eyes were a fiery amber color, like honey made by electrified bees.

"I'm from the FBI—" Lucian started to say.

"He isn't well," she interrupted. "Is this really necessary?"

"It is. I'm sorry."

She frowned. "Can I at least help him to a chair first?"

"Sure, absolutely."

"I'm not sick. I can get to a chair myself," Jacobs interjected, but he continued to lean on her as they walked across the foyer.

Lucian followed her inside and looked around, reacquainting himself with the apartment. On the left was the dining room with celadon walls, ivy-covered latticework covering the windows and collection of still lifes worthy of a small museum. On the right was the living room, where afternoon light spilled in from the large windows overlooking the park. Two late-period Matisse watercolors and two Degas ballet dancer pastels hung on the walls, and an Art Deco black-and-green rug covered the floor. Everything was the same. Suddenly he could smell lilies of the valley mixed with turpentine and linseed oil—the perfume and art supplies that made up Solange's one-of-a-kind scent. Was her bedroom still intact? When he'd last seen it, it was a collage of leaves painted in every shade of green and affixed to the walls in a way that at first seemed haphazard but then succeeded in making you believe you were in a thicket deep in a primeval forest.

"Are you sure you're all right, Dad?" the woman asked as she helped Jacobs into a chair at the antique card table by the window.

Lucian had been remembering Solange's scent, remembering her in this apartment, thinking about her bedroom. That had to be why he thought he'd heard this woman call Jacobs *Dad*. Twenty years ago Andre Jacobs had had only one daughter, a *nineteen-*

year-old who'd been murdered during the robbery of a Matisse painting from his framing store. Even if he and his wife had had another child right after Solange's death, she'd be only nineteen now. This woman was in her late twenties or early thirties.

"Now, what is this about? What do you want with my father?" she asked without preamble when she returned to Lucian, who was still in the foyer.

He held out his badge. "I'm FBI, Art Crime Team. Special Agent Lucian Glass, and I—"

Her gaze intensified as she reacted to his name. "No wonder my father's so upset. You were in the papers a few weeks ago when they reported on that mass hypnosis session in the Viennese music hall. The reincarnation concert, they called it, right? It was terrible for him seeing your name…remembering…"

"Emeline?" Jacobs called out feebly.

"I'll be right back," she said to Lucian as she ran out.

So Jacobs had seen the press. Although Lucian had refused to answer any questions about what had happened during that performance of Beethoven's *Eroica,* it hadn't stopped the reporters from writing about his presence there. Forensics still hadn't found any evidence of a chemical attack that might have caused a drug-induced delirium. Had reincarnation been proven in the Austrian concert hall? The possibility was so provocative, the story wouldn't die. In newspapers, magazines and Internet sites and on TV and radio talk shows, reincarnation had itself been reincarnated into a hot topic that no one seemed to tire of.

"My father was upset for days just reading about you in the paper," the woman said when she returned. "The past isn't ever very far from his thoughts, and seeing your name in print brought it that much closer." She paused as if it had been difficult for her, as well. "Now that I know who you are, I think it would be better if you'd go." They were standing two feet apart, but her tone put an even greater distance between them.

Lucian couldn't force Andre Jacobs to talk to him. The man wasn't a suspect.

She opened the door and he stepped out into the hallway. He turned, about to ring for the elevator, then turned back. She was about to shut the door. The light from the chandelier shimmered on her hair. Nothing about her looked familiar, and yet he felt as if they knew each other well.

"There's one thing…"

She stopped.

"We need your…your father to identify a painting. The Matisse stolen from his store."

"That would be torture for him," she whispered in a voice that reminded Lucian of the smoke that wafts up after a candle is extinguished.

"I am aware of that." *It's also torture for me.*

"Then why him?" There was nothing aggressive about the soft-spoken words themselves, but in his ears each one snapped like an expletive.

"Before the Matisse was stolen it had been in a private collection for over forty years. The owners, the original dealer, even the adjuster who insured it—have all passed away. Your father is the only person left who can identify it."

"He's not an art historian. Doesn't the museum have people to do that?"

"We found some uncharacteristic markings on the canvas that a framer might have seen and noted. We'd like Mr. Jacobs to come to the Met and take a look. Believe me, there is an enormous amount at stake or I wouldn't be asking. The man who sent this painting might be able to lead us to whoever stole it. And then we'd know, after all this time, who killed Solange."

Emeline was staring at him. He noticed her fingers were gripping the edge of the door so hard her knuckles were white.

"Will you ask your father if he'll help?"

"It's been a long time. It would be better for him to leave the past in the past."

As it would be for me, too.

Her cat's eyes fixed on him. "As it would be for you, too."

Chapter

NINETEEN

The sounds of hammers, electric drills, saws and sanders accompanied a very angry Henry Phillips as he walked through the Met's unfinished Islamic art wing inspecting his firm's work, accompanied by the job's foreman, Victor Keither.

There was of course no art on display, nothing to look at except for the work Keither's crew was doing. As far as Phillips was concerned there was nothing artistic about that.

"All of these inconsistencies in workmanship are not up to our standards," he said.

"You don't have to tell me," Keither agreed. "But I wanted you to see for yourself. I need better men, Henry."

They'd stopped in front of an exposed stone wall with an oculus in its center. The round opening must have once displayed a piece of art, then been closed up and forgotten until Keither had discovered it a few months ago. When you dealt with such an old building there were always surprises. Having the original architectural drawings helped, but alterations over the years weren't always annotated. The committee from the museum that was overseeing the construction had checked this out weeks ago and none of them felt this anomaly was architecturally significant or worth preserving.

"This should have been closed up by now, and the wall should have been plastered over."

Keither took off his helmet and ran his hand through his orange hair. His fair skin, sprinkled with freckles, reddened. "There's been too much turnover, Henry." A competitor, Manhattan Construction, was recruiting Phillips's men and overpaying them by fifteen percent to move. "We'll get back on track if you'll approve additional men."

Since taking the job with Phillips in 1985, Keither had worked on every museum job the firm had handled—six of them, almost back-to-back. He'd started out a member of the crew and now was in charge of the whole operation. Except for the days his children had been born, two bouts of the flu and an appendicitis attack, he'd never missed a day of work, even showing up during two blizzards only to discover that the museum was closed.

"That would take us over budget," Phillips said.

"Over budget or late? Take your pick. The replacements aren't as good as the guys we lost. Can't you keep them?"

"Manhattan Construction is playing an expensive game."

"What do you know about Manhattan?" Keither asked.

"Other than the fact that they're poachers?" Phillips shook his head. "How about if I pull some men off the hotel job and move them here for a few weeks temporarily? We haven't lost anyone on that crew."

"You haven't?" Keither asked. "Not a single man?"

"No. Everyone they've stolen has been from this job. Everyone knows you train them the best."

"I wish that was the reason."

"Me, too. Any ideas?"

"Not yet, but I'm going to work on it."

Chapter
TWENTY

The blinds were drawn, but Dr. Iris Bellmer dialed down the rheostat so that the room was shrouded in darkness. "I'd like you to sit back on the couch, James, and make sure you're comfortable. Put your arms by your sides, uncross your feet and close your eyes. Relax."

Relax at four in the afternoon with two cases weighing on him? Two cases—the Malachai Samuels investigation and the vandalism and extortion situation at the Metropolitan—both of which were fraught with tension and personal conflict. It was hardly ideal, but even if ACT hadn't been understaffed, Lucian—aka James—was too committed and involved to consider withdrawing from either one.

"The concept of what we're doing starts out identical to the process you said you learned from your pain specialist. Once you achieve a deep state of relaxation I'll make a few suggestions that your subconscious will hear and work on, and hopefully we'll make some discoveries. Any questions?"

"Let's do it." He was certain he knew enough about the process to fight her efforts and stay alert. Despite having another upsetting dream this morning that had forced him out of bed to once again draw the young girl whose eyes were filled with fear, he was here as an investigator, not as a patient. Certainly, part of him wanted to understand, but whatever was causing his delusions, it had nothing to do with past lives. The stories Bellmer's patients told her under hypnosis were just that— stories. If humans could manufacture entire fantasies at will—dreaming while sleeping and daydreaming while awake—certainly the mind could create narratives at the suggestion and urging of a trained therapist.

"All right, James, I'd like you to take four deep breaths… slowly…one…two…three…four…now picture a staircase in your mind…as you walk down the steps, count them backward from twenty…nineteen, eighteen, one step after another…one foot after another…counting until you reach the bottom…" She paused, waited and then resumed in the same low, modulated voice. "When you reach the last step you'll see that you've reached a place you know well…the same underground grotto you told me about from your pain therapy…it's comforting here…easy here…"

Lucian's headache was abating. That didn't surprise him. Hypnosis was a well-known remedy for pain. As he'd told Dr. Bellmer, he'd used it himself.

"You're in the grotto now…the lights are low…"

He'd slept little the night before, and he was so tired. Her voice was so soothing.

"There's a pool with turquoise water that's warm and waiting for you…"

Lucian focused on the street noises outside the office instead of on what she was saying. No matter how tempting, he couldn't enter this imaginary oasis, not even if he found respite there from the melancholy that had overwhelmed him since visiting the Jacobs apartment yesterday. He was here as a federal agent investigating a potential suspect, not as a patient.

"You're walking into the pool…slipping into the water. Its warmth embraces you and feels wonderful."

And it did, but it was a luxury he couldn't afford.

"Warm, welcoming water. You're lying on your back now…floating on the surface…comforted by the warm water…by the soft sound of water dripping from the rocks into the pool. You are very comfortable…there's no worry and no stress…no one needs anything from you…you're completely at ease. Now…slowly…look up…up toward the roof of the grotto. It's a mirror, and you can see yourself floating. You can see how relaxed you are…you feel relaxed…in every part of your body…your feet…your ankles…calves…knees…hips…your shoulders and neck are relaxed…your hands…your arms… your diaphragm…you're completely relaxed."

For the next fifteen seconds Iris Bellmer watched James Ryan's breathing, checking its evenness, assessing his state of relaxation, imagining he was slipping back through the layers of time. Some people were afraid of hypnosis, fearing they'd become suggestible and do things against their better judgment. But it was not magic or mind control. You were never more connected to your core being than when under hypnosis. Iris knew that firsthand. Two years ago she'd been working in a psychiatric hospital when one of her patients, who had exhibited no violent tendencies before, attacked her and started to rape her. A guard stepped in and prevented a full assault, but Iris was traumatized and sought out therapy. The doctor used hypnosis to file down the edges of her anxiety. During one session, Iris had a spontaneous past-life memory. Frightened by the intensity of the experience but fascinated, she sought out Dr. Beryl

Talmage. Their meeting led to Iris becoming the first full-time therapist to work with adults in the Phoenix Foundation's history.

"The water that's all around you and supporting you is time, and you're floating through it easily and without effort, able to remember things you thought you'd forgotten, able to see them in your mind's eye. I want you to remember something that happened to you when you were a little boy…something that was fun and that made you happy."

She watched his face and saw the first hint of a smile. "Tell me what you're remembering. Where are you?"

"The bookstore. My mother is with me in the bookstore."

"How old are you?"

"Nine."

"Do you like it there?"

"Yeah, my mom lets me buy as many books as I want."

"Wow, that's great. You're really lucky."

He nodded so enthusiastically that a lock of his hair fell into his eyes, but he was oblivious to it.

Despite her years of experience, when someone first slipped into the past and started to recount events as if they were still occurring, she was amazed anew at the power of the human brain to keep so many memories stored in such precise detail and how the right conditions made them so accessible.

"How many books are you going to buy?"

"So far I've only picked out one—*The Secret Garden*."

Bellmer allowed Ryan to enjoy the memory a few moments longer. She wanted to regress him slowly from one age to the next so the slide from his present past to a deeper past, to the life before this one, was a gentle passage. Step by step she took him back to when he was an even younger child, then a toddler, and finally to when he was an infant.

"Now, I'd like you to think about another time, a time before you were James…before your mother was your mother and your father was your father…to a different lifetime. Will you try to do that?"

He didn't respond.

"I'm right here, James, and I'm staying right here with you. If you are willing to try what I'm asking, we might be able to find out what's compelling you to keep drawing these portraits."

He didn't respond.

"Let the water take you back to where you knew the woman with the dark hair who you drew this morning. Picture her in the place where you knew her."

Iris watched her patient's face muscles relax and then tighten. She was no longer sitting opposite James Ryan but someone from his past who was angry and uncomfortable.

"Hello," Dr. Bellmer said softly.

"Who are you?" he asked aggressively.

"I'm a doctor. I'm here to help you. What's your name?"

"Telamon."

"Do you mind if I ask how old you are?"

"I'm thirteen," he said proudly.

"And where do you live?"

"Delphi."

"What year is this?"

"The first year of the games, of course."

"What games?"

"The Pythian games." He sounded surprised that she didn't know.

This wasn't the first time she'd run into the problem of dating a period when the soul had lived in a time before Christ. Many ancient civilizations didn't keep numbered calendars and the only way to pinpoint the year in ancient Greece was to find out what was happening historically.

"Who is your ruler?"

"Kleisthenes."

The name sounded vaguely familiar and she made a note of it.

"Do you go to school?"

He looked slightly confused. "I'm not a priest. I'm apprentice to the sculptor, Vangelis."

"How long have you been his apprentice?"

"Since my father died. He was a builder of temples and I was going to be apprenticed to him." There was pride in his voice.

"What happened to him?"

Telamon, for Iris had already begun to think of him that way, shrugged as if to make light of what he was going to say, but his voice was now thick with emotion.

"My father could lift heavier stones than any of the men who worked for him until he got sick and couldn't eat and became very weak. He went to the healers at the sleep temple, but they couldn't help. My mother acted as if everything would be all right, except at night I would hear her crying. When she thought none of us would know how bad—"

Telamon broke off. Sensing that the boy was struggling for control and that once he found it he'd continue, Iris waited.

"Afterward…a builder took over my father's workshop, but he had his own apprentices and there was no room for me, so I came here, to Delphi. My cousin Vangelis is a sculptor here, and he accepted me as an apprentice. I wanted to stay with my mother." His voice had lowered to a whisper. "I miss her."

"Is that a secret?"

"Yes."

"Why?"

"Because whenever I get homesick, Zenobia makes fun of me

and tells me I am too young to be an apprentice to anything but my mother's teat." He stopped and swallowed hard.

"Who is Zenobia?"

"The senior apprentice."

"How many of you are there?"

"Four, and I'm the youngest—except, of course, for Iantha."

"Is she another apprentice?"

"A woman? No! She helps out, bringing us food and wine, and tends to the hearth. She's Vangelis's daughter."

"So she is your cousin?"

"No, his daughter from before he married into my family." Telamon's face shifted again, and his mouth lifted into a small smile.

"How old is she?"

"Almost as old as me."

"What does she look like?"

"I could sculpt a likeness of her for you. I did once." He sounded bereft.

"Did you?"

He nodded. "Vangelis had thrown out a block of marble because it had a dark vein that spoiled it for him, so I used it to sculpt a bust of Iantha. I worked the flaw into her hair. Vangelis found me carving one day, and I thought he was going to be angry because I was making a likeness of his daughter. Instead he showed me where my mistakes were… She has beautiful wide eyes, but I'd set them back too far so she looked worried. There was nothing Vangelis could do to fix that, but he gave her cheekbones more definition and fixed her mouth."

"What was wrong with her mouth?"

"She has full lips and always wore a little smile. I hadn't caught that."

Iris looked down at the floor at one of the drawings James

had brought, of a young woman with full lips, high cheek-bones and eyes wide in terror.

"Did you give the sculpture to Iantha?"

"Zenobia saw Vangelis helping me with it. He was always jealous when the master spent extra time with any of us, but I never guessed what he'd do. The next morning when I went to the workshop there were dozens of pieces of shattered marble at my station. At first I didn't realize what I was seeing, then I recognized a fragment of her nose and then one of her mouth. He'd destroyed it. And then I heard laughing behind me. He was gloating."

"What did you do?"

"I tried to hit him, but he was so much bigger than me. He shoved me against a huge block of marble, trapped me there and hit me over and over until my eyes started to swell shut and my nose was bleeding and my stomach ached. I was at his mercy, but he had no mercy.

"And then I saw a mallet someone had left on the ground, so I pretended I was losing consciousness and slipped down to the floor. He believed that he'd knocked me out and that gave me just enough time to grab the mallet, lift it and swing it at him. The flat surface connected with Zenobia's shoulder and there was a loud thud and then he started screaming. I took off, but even in all that pain he came after me, yelling that I was going to be sorry. I hid from him on the far side of a stone so big it had taken all of us to bring it inside and waited to see if he was really going to come after me. When he did I jumped out and wrestled him to the ground. Because of the pain in his arm he was weakened enough for me to get on top of him and then he was at my mercy—and I had the mallet. I was sitting on his stomach and he had blood coming out of his nose and his eyes were watering and he had to be in terrible pain, but he wasn't scared of me. That was the worst part. He still wasn't scared of me.

"'You stupid fool,' he hissed. 'I'm the senior apprentice and the master's favorite. Don't you know what he'll do to you if you hurt me? All I'll have to do is tell Vangelis about the walks you take with Iantha and tell him what the two of you do with each other. He won't stand for it and you'll be out on the streets.'

"He was older and stronger than me, but he was the one on the ground, and I had the advantage—except I was scared, and he knew. He started laughing at me again, and, like a great animal, rose up and pushed me off him. Iantha was there, and she tried to stop him…"

Iris was suffering alongside the sweating, panting boy—yes, boy, because that was who James Ryan was now.

"He was shouting, 'You bug, you insect.' His spit sprayed my face. Then he punched me in the stomach. I was scared for Iantha, worried he was going to hurt her, too, but all his attention was on beating me up, and even after my nose and mouth were bleeding and my head was pounding he still kept coming at me. He kept punching me in the face, and then everything went black. The pain was excruciating. I couldn't open my eyes. I couldn't see. Was I blind? How would I sculpt?"

Her patient had stopped speaking. The room was quiet enough so that Iris could hear cars honking in the street and the drone of the ubiquitous white noise machine in the corner that therapists used to prevent anyone from overhearing a session. His face was twisted with the pain; he'd had enough.

"James, I'm going to start counting, and when I reach ten you're going to wake up. You'll remember what you've told me, but you won't feel any distress or pain. You'll be in control and at peace."

When he opened his eyes he was speaking the same three

words over and over, and despite her instructions there was pain woven into them—deep and long-lasting pain.

"Iantha, I'm sorry. Iantha, I'm sorry. Iantha, I'm sorry."

Chapter
TWENTY-ONE

Even though Samimi had only been called into his boss's office to go over plans for his afternoon appointment at the Met, he was anxious. Since he had learned about the Semtex shipment, everything made him anxious.

"Is the meeting set, Ali?"

"All set. I confirmed an hour ago."

Taghinia smiled as he opened his humidor, extracted a Cuban, rolled it in his fingers, listened to its music, cut off the tip and set about lighting the stinking weed.

Samimi, who was sitting opposite him on the couch, wished he could get out of the office before the stench infiltrated his clothes. He hated his boss's indulgence but was doing his best to keep his revulsion in check, along with his nerves.

"Your mission today is very important," Taghinia said.

"So you've said."

"Be careful, be vigilant." Taghinia inhaled, held the smoke and then blew it out, not caring that it wafted right toward his underling.

Standing, Samimi walked over to the window.

"This is a critical part of our planning," Taghinia continued with a slight edge of aggravation in his voice that Samimi knew he'd provoked by getting up. His boss didn't approve of his employee's disapproval.

"Yes, you've said that before, but it's difficult for me to do my job as well as possible without knowing the details of our plans," Samimi said. "What exactly does Deborah Mitchell have to do with us getting the sculpture back?"

"You know as much as you need to right now." Taghinia took another long pull on the cigar and then let the smoke out achingly slowly.

"I know nothing. If I just understood—"

Taghinia cut him off. "All right, all right." And then, as if he were trying to teach a poor student a basic equation, he continued on in an exasperated voice. "We will need access to an event at the museum over the next few weeks. Deborah Mitchell will afford us that access. Bringing her yet one more little treasure will ensure it. Your job is to make her understand how much you enjoy spending time at the museum and how happy it would make you to be invited to their events, parties and openings. When you need to know more than that, I'll inform you."

Samimi nodded impatiently, as was expected of someone frustrated to be left out of the loop.

"My only fear," Taghinia said, "is that this next step depends on you being charming, and that's not something you excel at."

Samimi was used to his boss's passive-aggressive swipes, but cringed anyway—all part of the act. He was doing what was expected of him, behaving as he'd always behaved, being the same man he'd been for the past three years. Except he wasn't that sorry little man anymore. He had taken control of his own destiny. He was going to shape his future, not let this slob shape it for him.

"Here you are." Taghinia handed Samimi a package. "It arrived via the diplomatic pouch yesterday, and the associate director of the museum in Tehran is standing by on the phone waiting to talk to you about it."

The container was the size and shape of a shoe box and covered in brown leather that was soft to Samimi's touch. Opening the double brass hinge, he found a silk pouch that contained an antique cup made of gold. With one glance, he knew it was both very beautiful and very rare.

"I expect it will be more than impressive and certainly will make up for your deficiencies," Taghinia said.

Samimi winced at the barb as he replaced the object, put the box under his arm and rose.

"One more thing."

Samimi was halfway to the door.

"Yes?"

"Tomorrow, I'd like you to go straight to the warehouse in the morning instead of coming here."

"The warehouse?" Samimi's heart was beating so hard he wondered if his boss could see it.

"We're expecting a delivery. I want you to pay for it."

"What kind of delivery?"

"It's not necessary for you to know."

Samimi frowned. "I think it is, Farid."

"It's not your job to think about whether my decisions are right or wrong. When you need to know, you'll know." He spat out the words as if they were little pieces of tobacco stuck on his tongue.

"What do you want me to do with this delivery?"

"Wait until the courier has left, then call me. I'll give you instructions."

So the Semtex had arrived in the same pouch as the artifact. Samimi shivered as he walked out of Taghinia's office.

* * *

The skinny woman who greeted Samimi had short blond hair and oversize square black glasses. As she gave him a visitor's badge, Laura Freedman introduced herself and then asked him to follow her. Leading him through the museum's grand lobby with its soaring ceiling and enormous bouquets of apple blossom branches in niches carved out of the stone walls, she was quiet. She remained so as they walked through the medieval wing, made a left, went through a few galleries of European furnishings and stopped at an elevator bank near the twentieth-century modern art exhibition space.

Samimi was too worried to give the treasures they passed their due. Why was he meeting with Laura instead of the curator?

Exiting the elevator on the fourth floor, they passed by a receptionist at an ornate desk, walked down a richly carpeted hallway and stopped at the first office on the right. The door was open.

"Thanks, Laura," Deborah Mitchell said as she got up and came around from behind her desk to greet Samimi.

Today she was wearing a long-sleeved ruby dress that set off her dark coloring and chestnut eyes. Her long ebony hair was woven into a braid, and as he shook her hand, Samimi couldn't help imagining that hair loose and spread out on a pillow. His thought must have somehow translated to her because she blushed. Which made him smile. Which just made her blush deepen. Wouldn't Taghinia be surprised?

"Welcome back to the museum," she said.

He thanked her as he put the shopping bag on her desk.

She looked at it and then back at him. "Would you like some coffee? We have cappuccino—or tea, if I remember correctly."

"Yes, tea." He smiled.

"And sugar, right?"

"Yes, please."

There was something pleasantly old-fashioned about the ritual, especially when Deborah went to get it herself. He'd expected her to have her assistant bring the tea.

Sitting in on the visitor's side of her clean modern desk with its computer and assortment of papers, catalogues, pens and photographs, Samimi noticed the poster on the wall. It was different from the one that had been hanging there the last time he'd visited. This was a green, cobalt and turquoise tile blown up to bleed off the edges of the paper with silver type outlined in black that read, EARLY PERSIAN TILEWORK, THE MEDIEVAL FLOWERING OF KASHI and, beneath that, the dates of the exhibition that had opened in January and would run through June.

"Here you are," she said, returning with two navy mugs that had the MMA insignia on them.

He sipped the steaming beverage. "Too many people make tea that isn't hot enough, but this is perfect," he said. "Thank you."

Deborah nodded at the unadorned shopping bag and said, "You've certainly aroused my curiosity with your call, Mr. Samimi. After the last treasure you brought us, I can't wait to see this one."

"Please call me Ali," he said. Reaching inside, he pulled out the leather box, put it on the desk and made a show of opening it to reveal the blue silk pouch embroidered with white flowers with green leaves. Withdrawing it, he offered it to her.

She nodded, almost shyly, which Samimi had found fascinating the last time he'd met her, too. Here was a well-respected art historian working at one of the world's finest museums, but she was still reserved. If he were to ever marry, he'd probably look for a wife more like Deborah than the women he'd been sleeping with—a wife with both feet planted firmly in America but who still sometimes dreamt about the ancient desert.

"The man who owns this would very much like to offer it to the museum if you think it worthy of your collection."

Deborah loosened the tie, reached inside and pulled out an egg-shaped golden cup decorated with the heads of two men, each wearing a crown of leaves. Turning it slowly, she examined it.

"What do you make of it?" He couldn't be certain but he thought she was impressed.

"It's exquisite," she whispered.

"One similar to this, also beaten out of a single sheet of gold, sold in London for over a million dollars last year."

"I know," she said, but something in her voice intimated that an object's value wasn't just what it sold for.

Using a jeweler's loupe, she examined the cup more closely. "It's Achaemenid gold, I think. Everything about the goldsmithing suggests it. Third or fourth century BCE."

What she said was consistent with what Samimi had been told about the cup from the curator of the Tehran museum.

"The workmanship is extraordinary," she offered finally, still staring at the vessel, unable to look away from it. "Does your client—"

"Not a client. The mission is simply helping one of our citizens."

"And he's offering this to us?"

"He's an Iranian American who wants to do his part to help forge a stronger bond between the country of his birth and the country of his children's birth."

She nodded, understanding the sentiment as he'd hoped she would. Farid Taghinia might have come up with the plan, but this explanation was his contribution and he was proud it had worked.

"What's his name?"

"He wants to remain anonymous for now. Will that present a problem?"

"As long as you can show us papers proving he owns the cup outright and there's no controversy surrounding its provenance."

"I can assure you there isn't. We're all aware of how careful you have to be these days. The last thing we'd want to do is add to the conflict your museum and our government are already engaged in. Messy business." He lowered his voice and leaned forward. "Unofficially, I'm embarrassed by how aggressive we are being. A lot of us are. My friend who owns the cup is." Samimi hadn't planned those last few sentences but she'd given him the perfect opening and he wanted to plant the idea that he sympathized with her museum.

She seemed about to say something and then held back.

"The only thing the donor of the cup insists on is that it be displayed. He doesn't want it going into storage. Also, if you do decide to take it, he will go public with who he is. It's important to him that people know of his gesture toward peace."

"It's way too early to give you any promises. First we need to examine the cup, determine its authenticity and clear its history—but I understand the conditions. If we accept this generous offer, we'll certainly put it on display."

Samimi nodded. "How long will the process take?"

"Depending on the paperwork you can provide, the earliest would be four or five weeks. Will that be all right?"

"Yes, fine." According to what he'd heard on the tapes and what Taghinia had told him, those few weeks were what this charade was all about.

"I just need to prepare a receipt." Deborah pushed some clutter out of the way and placed the cup in the center of her desk. "I'll get a few shots to make sure we cover its condition…" She stopped speaking while she photographed the artifact from different angles, including the inside and underside. "If you don't mind waiting, I'll print these out and you can initial them. We'll each have a copy, and you'll have a receipt."

"Not at all." He looked right at her and held her gaze. He hoped he wasn't moving too fast, but he had a feeling—and he was usually right when it came to women—that she didn't get enough attention and she'd preen.

And she did, offering him another shy smile.

While she printed out the photos, Samimi drank more of his tea, even though it was lukewarm now, and inspected the poster again. The glorious green, cobalt and turquoise tile was so indicative of the art of his homeland it made him homesick for a moment—not for the political landscape but for the country of his great-grandparents that he had seen remnants of and heard stories about, and that was lost now, probably forever.

"Here you go, Mr. Samimi." She handed him a stack of photos, a release form and a pen.

"Ali," he said. As he scrawled his initials on each shot, he breathed in air that was slightly perfumed by the scent she wore. Clean and floral, very pleasant. Handing her back the pen, he looked into her warm brown eyes. "Would it be appropriate," he asked formally, guessing by her demeanor that this would be the right approach, "if I called and invited you to dinner one night to celebrate?"

Chapter

TWENTY-TWO

Lucian finished reading about Vartan Reza's hit-and-run accident, looked up from his computer screen and stared out of his window at his sliver of a view. The Art Crime Team offices were crammed into FBI headquarters downtown at 26 Federal Plaza. Between the two buildings across the street, he could see a small park with its curving wood benches, exaggerated lights and glass mounds emitting fog plumes. It was an amusement in the midst of the serious courthouses, government agencies, financial buildings and the destroyed World Trade Towers.

He stood and carried his mug of coffee over to the cork wall facing his desk, where there was a patchwork map of his current case. He always organized it the same way. Dead center was a single photo that was key to the core puzzle: the missing or stolen work of art. Overlapping and radiating out from there were photos, sketches and notes about the locations, players and props that related to the crime.

For more than a year this wall had been devoted to the memory stone theft in Rome and so included photos of Malachai Samuels, the Phoenix Foundation, the stones themselves, where they'd been found and hundreds of other related illustrations, diagrams and images. Recently items associated with the theft in the Memorist Society in Vienna had been added to what others saw as an unorganized mess, but which Lucian had carefully arranged.

In the past thirty-six hours, as he'd amassed a dossier on the sculpture at the heart of his newest case, another section of his wall was filling up with photos of Hypnos and the hostage paintings. Bits and pieces of all three crimes arbitrarily overlapped. Now, noticing it, Lucian wondered whether Malachai's name would surface in the Hypnos crisis.

"How long have you been here?" Doug Comley stood in the door, holding a cardboard cup in one hand and his briefcase in the other.

"A few hours."

"Still can't sleep? You okay?"

"Never better. Listen, there's something curious about the legal battle over the sculpture," Lucian said. He explained what he'd discovered about the law firm that had been hired to replace Reza. "It's owned by Tyler Weil's father."

"The Met's director's father is handling the Iranians' lawsuit? That sounds like a pretty serious conflict of interest. What do you know about the accident?"

"It was early, raining, the park was empty, and there were no witnesses. The NYPD is investigating but have no leads."

"I want you to follow through on this."

"No problem," Lucian said, and then put his hand up to his temple and massaged his forehead. He'd woken up with a headache that had lifted while he'd been drawing. This was the first sign of its return.

"You all right?" Comley asked.

"Like I said, never better."

"You're sure you're not pushing yourself working on both of these cases? Why don't you let Richmond—"

"Are you ordering me off?" Lucian asked, jumping six steps ahead.

Comley threw up his hands. "Ordering you? No. Suggesting. If I ordered you off the memory flute case and you kept working on it, then I'd have to fire you, and I don't have the budget to hire a replacement."

"I can handle it."

"Malachai Samuels is tricky, even for us, Lucian. He proved that last year when—"

Comley was interrupted by the receptionist ringing through on the intercom.

"Agent Glass. Someone's here to see you. She doesn't have an appointment."

"Who is it?"

"Her name is Emeline Jacobs."

She was sitting in one of the blue leatherette chairs, staring straight ahead at a poster of a black-and-white WPA-era photo of New York City's skyline taken by Stieglitz.

"Miss Jacobs?"

She turned, saw Lucian and stood up. Her hair was as gold and her skin as pale as he remembered. Her clothes were mono-chromatic: cream pants, a cream silk round-necked blouse and a cream sweater tied around her shoulders. No rings, no brace-lets, not even a watch. Just a thin gold chain around her neck that bore a tiny gold paintbrush charm with a red tip.

Lucian tried not to stare but failed as a memory rushed him like a hurricane-force wind.

One cold February day, two weeks before Solange's birthday, he'd walked from his dorm uptown to Forty-Seventh Street and

Fifth Avenue to New York's famed Diamond District, where hundreds of individual jewelers rented booths in the arcade buildings that lined the street. For over an hour, he had scanned their offerings, searching for something to give her that he thought she'd like and that he could afford. Everything was either too expensive or too impersonal. And then, in the fourth building, in the back, where there was less noise and foot traffic and the displays were more pedestrian, he passed a case of hundreds of tiny charms, all exquisitely made, and that was where he'd bought the one now hanging around Emeline Jacobs's neck.

He gestured toward his office. Inside, he invited her to sit. "How can I help you?" She didn't answer right away. The way she held his glance felt familiar somehow, an odd combination of curiosity and innocence. Was he wrong or had Solange always paused just so, regarding him almost exactly this way before she spoke? It was the artist in her observing her surroundings. The raw, involuntary sadness he suddenly felt after so long surprised him.

"My father's been very upset since your visit," Emeline said finally. Her soft but raspy voice was a relief and broke through his crazy, meandering thoughts.

"I'm sorry about that…"

"If you still need him to, he'll look at the painting."

It would save Lucian hours of work if Jacobs could identify the mark on the back of the Matisse. "That would be an enormous help."

"He's not doing it to help you. He needs to know if it's the same painting for his own peace of mind…" She hesitated and shook her head as if she were still having an argument with someone who wasn't there. "I don't believe in closure. Therapists don't show any respect for their patients when they suggest there can be an end to missing someone. Seeing this painting could threaten the little emotional stability he has left. He dwells in hell, Agent Glass. I see it in his eyes every time I look at him."

Emeline's voice communicated pathos and pain and was rife with emotion, but she didn't twist her hands in her lap or exhibit any of the signs of distress that Lucian would expect to see in someone talking about such a difficult situation. He didn't doubt that she was telling him the truth, but she was exhibiting amazing self-control.

"'Parting is all we know of heaven, and all we need of hell,'" he said, surprised that the quote had come back to him.

"Emily Dickinson," Emeline said. "I have a book of poetry with that poem in it. The page corner is turned down."

Lucian didn't need to ask whose book it was. Emeline must have all of Solange's books. And what else? Her drawings? Journals? Were there letters from him that she'd found? Had she inherited all the remnants of Solange's life? How much had she learned about him?

"We'll do what we can to make it as painless as possible for your father."

Her laugh was too bitter for someone so young, full of the disappointments of someone who'd lived much longer and suffered much more. Lucian had such a strong, sudden sense of being with Solange that he was swept under, submerged in murky confusion.

Was this a hallucination, a reaction to whatever he'd been exposed to in Vienna? Or did this have to do with his headaches? He wanted to break Emeline Jacobs open and see if the other woman was inside her, to find out where Solange was hiding.

"There's nothing you can do to make it less painful. He's never had a single day of real joy or happiness since…" She broke off, took a deep breath, then continued. "He just has days that are slightly less awful than others. Do you have any idea how difficult it is to see your father like that, for your whole life? To try to do everything you can to make it better? Make him really smile? My father's never recovered." She clasped her hands together.

She's closing up, Lucian thought. And then, as if completing the act, Emeline crossed her legs. Bare legs, he noticed. He glanced back at her face, but her eyes revealed nothing. They were a stranger's eyes. Whatever he'd seen there before must have been in his imagination.

"I'm curious about something. When I knew Solange twenty years ago she was an only child. I didn't know she had a sister."

"When I was eight years old my mother, my father, my brother and I were in a car accident. They were all killed. It was touch and go for me…I don't remember anything about it…but I was in a coma for six weeks. My aunt and uncle, Solange's parents, were there every day. She'd died five months before and they were still grieving, but I was all that was left of their family. When I recovered they adopted me. I don't think they wanted to at first, but once they decided to, I think they hoped I'd fill up some of the space that she'd left."

"Did you?"

"I only made it worse. I was a constant reminder to them of what they'd lost. My aunt never really recovered, and when I went off to college she finally gave in to her depression and committed suicide. Andre has been drinking himself into a state of numbness every day since then. He blames himself for all of it—for leaving Solange in the store the night it was robbed, for trusting his assistant to lock up, for not being able to save his wife from her sorrow." She shrugged as if the burden of the story she'd just shared had settled on her shoulders and was too heavy.

"I'm sorry," he offered compassionately. "They're inadequate words, I know, but there *are* no adequate words, are there?"

"Too many people try to assuage pain that can never be eradicated. All you can do is salute the grief, acknowledge that you carry it, too, and that even though we all travel that path alone we are not alone in traveling it." Emeline said the words as if she'd said them many times before. Was this what she'd learned from her adopted father or mother?

Whatever pleasure Lucian had in life came from solving mysteries. When there was something he didn't understand he forced himself to keep looking until he found a solid, logical and comprehensible solution. But he knew there was no explanation for what was happening—one minute she was a stranger; the next he felt as if he'd always known her. He had to get back to working the case. To getting out of his head.

"Could you and your father come and see the painting at the Met this afternoon?"

"I think it would be better if you could bring it to the apartment. About five?"

The painting had been tested for fingerprints and any residual evidence that might help in the search for the person who had destroyed it, so there was no reason it couldn't be moved, but Lucian didn't think it was a good idea. "It will be horrible no matter where your father sees the Matisse, but it might be emotionally easier for him to see it in a neutral environment."

"Or the opposite. At home my father will have the comfort of his surroundings. That's really all he has left—some artwork and some memories."

"And you. He has you."

Emeline didn't react except to reach for her pocketbook. Lucian knew the meeting was over. He felt disappointed and wasn't sure why. He waited for her to stand, but she didn't. She just sat there looking down at the black leather satchel.

"Do you have a few more minutes?" she asked without glancing up.

"Yes, of course."

Opening the bag, Emeline reached inside and pulled out a few sheets of paper. She unfolded them, laid them on her lap and smoothed down the center crease with her forefinger. Still staring down at the type that Lucian couldn't read upside down, she said, "I printed these e-mails out. My e-mail address at work is easy enough for anyone to find—it's right on the store's Web site."

"What store?"

"My father's framing store."

"You work there?" Maybe he shouldn't have been surprised, but he was. He was stunned.

"I grew up there… At some point Andre was too sick to run it anymore. I have a graduate degree in art history. It just made sense." She was still running her finger back and forth on the paper as if she were trying to iron out the fold mark.

"What are those?"

"About six months after they brought me home, my adopted parents took me to see the same reincarnationist who was in the news with you last month."

"Malachai Samuels?"

"Yes. I saw both him and another doctor at the foundation, Beryl Talmage."

"Why?" As soon as he asked, he was sorry.

"My aunt and uncle thought I might know things."

Lucian felt the hair on the back of his neck rise. "Know things? How?"

"And they both wanted to believe it so badly," Emeline said. "It started in the hospital when they saw this…"

She brushed the hair off her forehead and Lucian stared at the small, white crescent-shaped scar above her right eyebrow.

He felt as if someone had punched him in the solar plexus.

"A birthmark?" he asked.

"Not a birthmark. I got it in the car accident. It's the same scar in the same place as hers. You recognize it, don't you?"

"I'm sorry. I don't understand. How could you have the same scar?"

"Have you ever heard of walk-ins?"

"In what context?"

"Reincarnation."

"No."

She started running her finger up and down the crease of the page again. Lucian strained to read what she was trying so hard to wear away.

"There's a theory," she said, "that in order to accomplish its mission, an advanced soul can walk into another physical body that has been or is about to be abandoned. Like the body of someone about to commit suicide."

"Or the body of a child in a coma?"

She nodded. "My adopted parents desperately wanted to believe that was what had happened to me instead of the more logical explanation. Our families had spent a lot of time together. I'd loved Solange, I'd looked up to her. She was like an older sister to me. And she was an artist. That was the most amazing thing. She used to pose me, then show me drawings she did of me. I thought she was making magic. Every kid picks up mannerisms and remembers things about the people they are in awe of. But my aunt and uncle were convinced that Solange's soul, her spirit, had walked into my body when I was in a coma. That she was still alive in me."

"How long did you go to the Phoenix Foundation?"

"A few months. The doctors said it could have been a case of reincarnation, but I wasn't a good subject for hypnosis, I couldn't concentrate deeply enough, and we never got very far. I was scared of the whole process, but I knew how much my aunt and uncle wanted me to somehow be her, and I didn't want to disappoint them. I knew how desperate they were for the police to find the man who'd killed Solange, but there were no suspects. There were no witnesses. I thought if I could help solve the case they'd be happy, and then we could all be happy. That was all I wanted."

The office was too warm. Lucian took off his jacket. There *was* one witness, but he hadn't seen anything that could help. He'd never felt so useless, so impotent as he did in the weeks after the robbery. The police had interviewed him a dozen times or more, but all Lucian remembered was a brown sleeve, a man's hand and the glitter of a knife. "I'm confused. Why did they think hypnotizing you would help the police solve the case?" he asked.

"If I was Solange reincarnated, then I had seen who broke in that night. I'd seen the killer's face."

"You're kidding."

"Not if you believe in reincarnation."

"Do you?"

Emeline looked down at her hands for a moment. "I wanted to."

Lucian thought she sounded younger just then. As if she was suddenly remembering too much and it was more painful than she'd expected. It was time to come back to the present problem.

"What does all of this have to do with those e-mails?" he asked.

"I was in the news, Agent Glass. My uncle was distraught. He was telling everyone he met how determined he was to catch his daughter's killer and that he believed I was going to help him. It was a sensational crime, and the interviews he gave provided the press with all the fodder they needed to keep the story alive." She paused and looked down at what she was holding. "When all that crazy stuff happened last month in Vienna at the concert and Malachai Samuels was shot, newspapers and all sorts of blogs dug up everything about him and the foundation. Some of them ran lists of anyone with any notoriety he'd ever treated."

Emeline's hand trembled slightly as she held out the papers. Lucian took them and, with a sense of dread, read the first note.

The two lines of type seemed larger on the page than they actually were, as if their toxic meaning gave them billboard stature. He read the second and third printouts even though all of them contained exactly the same message.

Tell anyone what I look like and I'll kill you before they find me. I did it once. I'll do it again. I'll kill you and your father, too.

Chapter

TWENTY-THREE

"During the renovation," Malachai Samuels said, "I had a choice about leaving this staircase in or taking it out." He stopped his descent, his hand on the rail. "I thought it would be appropriate to enter the present on steps that are over a hundred and fifty years old...steps that Walt Whitman, Frederick Law Olmsted, Frederick L. Lennox, Bronson Alcott and so many more traversed."

"I agree." Elgin Barindra, who wore black-framed eyeglasses, had already been looking down, treading carefully on the too-narrow steps. Now he regarded them with more interest. History was his métier, and he relished anecdotes like this one. "Were they all members of the original Phoenix Club?"

"All of them and more. We have the correspondence to show for it, correspondence that is waiting for you." Malachai shook his head. "I've been remiss. We've needed a full-time librarian for years. Then I thought I'd found someone who was right for the job, but..." His voice drifted off.

"What happened?"

"He died," Malachai said with a grimness that put an end to that part of the conversation.

"How far down are we?" Elgin asked as they reached the landing.

"You aren't claustrophobic, are you?"

"Not at all. Just curious."

"We're a little more than a floor below street level in a suite that's both fireproof and airtight. There's only one egress other than this staircase, but it can no longer be accessed from within or without."

Elgin wondered if Agents Richmond and Glass had guessed right about how far down this library was. Would the special electronic tracking device built into his cell phone transmit from so deep underground?

Malachai punched a numerical code into the black panel beside the oversize door, and a red light beam flashed. Based on Elgin's résumé he'd be expected to know about high-tech security, so he didn't question Malachai about the orbital scanner he'd noticed.

A series of four mechanical clicks sounded, and as the reincarnationist opened the door, he boasted about the state-of-the-art lock and the rest of the security systems.

As Elgin crossed the threshold, the slightly stale and cool air reached out for him in an uncomfortable embrace. Thinking about Edgar Allan Poe's poem about Annabel Lee, he followed Malachai inside and found himself in a pearl-gray chamber with a steel-and-glass desk, leather chairs and wall-to-wall bookcases. The gothic interior decorations of the upstairs had given way to a pristine modern environment.

"Our library consists of five rooms housing more than thirty thousand items. It's unquestionably the world's largest and most private library on the subject of reincarnation, and less than five percent of it all has been catalogued."

"Who started the collection?"

"My great-great-great-uncle, Trevor Talmage, in 1847. He

was quite a Renaissance man—an Egyptologist, a philosopher and a passionate believer in reincarnation. He started collecting books and materials related to the subject when he was in college, but the library didn't become a formal part of the foundation until 1999, when I renovated the building and hired a specialist to build this modest bibliotheca." He waved his arms, embracing the space. "Let me show you the rest."

As they walked into each room, motion-activated halogen ceiling spots came on, and Malachai continued describing the cutting-edge environment. "The temperature never falls below sixty-five or goes above seventy. We have high-efficiency filters on the air-handling systems, and the humidity is tested constantly to maintain a forty-five to fifty-five percent level."

Elgin nodded. "That's certainly impressive. Many people with private libraries take care of the temperature, but few are as religious as they should be about the humidity, and it's critical. If there's too much moisture in the air it can lead to mildew, mold and foxing of book pages."

Malachai smiled and moved his job applicant into what he called the reading room, which had a quartet of oversize leather chairs, each with its own individual lighting system. From there they passed through three rare-book rooms where the materials were stored in locking glass-front cases. Elgin noticed the metal shelving coated with baked enamel and again complimented Malachai. "Everything is first-rate—as advanced as any library I've ever seen."

"And this is where you'd be working," the reincarnationist said as he led Elgin into a room that had floor-to-ceiling open shelves filled with custom-made, acid-free boxes for the most fragile of the books and the ephemera that couldn't be shelved. "This is where the private journals, papers and correspondence that make up the bulk of our collection are housed."

Elgin's fingers tingled at the thought of what was secreted away down here. "No one has ever gone through these?"

"No. The only time they've been touched was when I had them transferred into these cases."

Walking up to the closest shelf, Elgin reached out and touched one of the boxes and then looked over at Malachai. "May I?"

"Does that mean you are accepting the job?"

Elgin nodded. "If you're offering it, I certainly am."

There had been no question he was going to take the job if it was offered—and Agent Glass had assured him it would be, because of the glowing letter of recommendation the director of the New York Society Library had written. He'd detailed the time Elgin had worked for him at the Library of Congress, praising his professionalism and ability. And just in case that wasn't enough and Malachai dug deeper, the FBI had planted records at the Library of Congress showing five years of straight commendations and raises even though, in truth, Elgin Barindra hadn't set foot in our nation's library since he'd been in graduate school. He'd certainly never worked there.

"I hope you'll give our receptionist, who also functions as our caretaker, a list of the foods and beverages you prefer. We keep the kitchen upstairs stocked and are happy to have our employees use it. There's also a dining room she'll show you where you should feel free to have your lunch or dinner if you are working late. Occasionally we entertain there, but on those days she'll be sure to tell you if the room will be in use. This afternoon we're having a group of scientists in from Yale University for a meeting on junk DNA and the possibility that it holds the secret to reincarnation memories."

"That certainly sounds fascinating. I'd be interested in reading some of that research, if possible."

Malachai looked at him with a combination of surprise and

chagrin. "It's so very unlike me, but I forgot to ask you, Elgin. What do you think about reincarnation? Do you believe?"

Of everything he'd been briefed on, this was the one thing neither Richmond nor Glass had discussed with him. "Is it a prerequisite for the job?"

"Not at all. I need a man with credentials, not credulity, but I am curious."

There was nothing to do but fall back on what he'd learned on his first job: it's always easier to tell the truth. "Reincarnation is in my blood," Elgin said, and smiled. "I was born in America, as were my parents, but we're Anglo-Indians and practicing Hindus."

"Believers." Malachai rolled the word around in his mouth as if it were a delectable morsel of food.

"From the most simple concepts to soul migration. My father used to tell me a bedtime story that his mother had told him about a soul that stole into the body of a man named Mr. Star during a bad illness. The man, who'd always been mean and nasty, tried to fight the migration but was too ill to throw the soul out and so he took up residence. When Mr. Star recovered it was as a new man, suddenly kind and compassionate to all. After the new soul had accomplished what it needed to and moved on, Mr. Star suddenly went back to being his miserable self. Everyone who'd come to love and care about him abandoned him. For the first time, he understood what kind of man he'd been and vowed to change for good. When I was a kid anyone who was mean to me or my sister became Mr. Star or Miss Star, and we'd pray for a kind soul to come in and take over." Elgin chuckled at the memory.

"Actually, the migrating soul doesn't always take over. Sometimes the visiting soul integrates in a very comfortable way that the host allows without any fight and the two coexist peacefully."

"Not as dramatic as my father's story."

"No. Few experiences are. Most people don't come back as Cleopatra or Napoleon, and not many souls stage hostile takeovers." Malachai smiled sardonically. "So let's discuss how you're going to catalogue over a century and a half of correspondence and diaries."

Doing historical research in such a rarified environment with a salary like the one he'd just been offered was closer to what Elgin Barindra had once imagined he'd be doing with his career than his present job. He'd been at George Washington University, finishing up his library science thesis on the relationship between the Library of Congress and post–Cold War defense research when one of his professors had recommended him for an opening with the bureau. Like so many boys, Elgin had watched the FBI television show every Sunday night with his dad, but he'd never dreamed of becoming an agent. The show was just one of many escapes for a shy boy who never quite fit in. He had a stammer and childhood asthma and wore glasses that were too thick. Libraries were his true refuge. Books not only educated and entertained, they enveloped and comforted. And nothing could have appealed more to the man who'd once been a frail, sickly boy than the idea of working at the FBI library at Quantico.

He'd been sure he wouldn't get the job because he didn't think he could physically handle the rigorous training, but it turned out he only needed to pass the FBI's background check and learn some basic security skills.

For the next five years he was more than satisfied with his job. After 9/11, when he heard the bureau was looking for an agent with library skills to go undercover at a university library, Elgin applied for the position. Since then he'd accepted two other field assignments and while he always started off with a bad case of nerves, once he was on-site, he settled down and did the job he had to do.

Now, sitting across from Malachai Samuels, Elgin concentrated on what his new boss was saying about archiving these vast stores of material. His fingers itched to begin the work. What unknown history would he stumble on? What discoveries would he make?

"There are a few key words for you to be on the lookout for, especially in the letters and journals from the early days of the club." From his inner jacket pocket, Malachai brought out a sheet of writing paper and laid it down between them.

Elgin evaluated the handwritten list of six items without exhibiting any outward signs of the astonishment he was experiencing.

1. Pot of fragrant wax
2. Colored orb
3. Reflection sphere
4. Bone flute
5. Word holder
6. Fire and water beads

This looked like the list Agents Glass and Richmond had briefed him on. Was it possible that this was what Glass had been looking at when he'd been attacked and the Viennese doctor had been killed?

"We have extensive correspondence among half-a-dozen important industrialists from the mid-nineteenth century who financed extensive archaeological digs on behalf of the club. Their largesse was the basis for the foundation's endowment, which still finances excavations. Thanks to them we've dug all over the Middle East and Europe. Much of what we've found we've donated to the governments of those nations."

"What do you keep?"

"These days we don't technically keep anything. With laws changing so fast and so much controversy over whom antiquity belongs to, we turn everything over to the authorities and request to borrow any items that we think will aid us in the study of reincarnation. That's where this list comes in."

"Do you mind if I make some notes?" Elgin asked as he pulled out a worn spiral-bound notebook from his jacket. There were creases on the shiny blue cover, and the corners of the lined paper were turned back and thumbed through. He was aware that Malachai was watching him as he extracted the pencil he kept tucked into the silver spiral, an ordinary yellow pencil with teeth marks running up and down its length.

"What we're looking for are references to ancient tools that aid in deep meditation. We call them Memory Tools," Malachai explained.

Elgin looked up from his notes. "Wasn't there something in the news about Memory Tools recently?"

"Yes, it's believed that four to six thousand years ago, in the Indus Valley, mystics created meditation aids to help people go into deep states of relaxation during which they would have access to past-life memories. There were twelve tools—twelve being a mystical number that we see repeated all through various religions and in nature. I think, and other experts agree, that it's quite possible that two of them have been found in the past fourteen months. The first was a cache of precious stones, and the second was an ancient flute made of human bone. Depending on which newspaper you read, what happened to those tools differs, but one thing I can assure you, both have been lost to research and there's nothing we can learn from either of them for now. It's a travesty."

"How were they lost?"

"Red tape. Ridiculous protocols. Accidents. Fate. But what's past is past. I…we…have lost two chances to find out if there are tools to help us pull memories through the membrane of time. We can't afford to let a third chance slip through our fingers. That's why you're here." He paused for a moment, and when he resumed his voice had taken on more gravitas. "I think it's a real possibility that there were members of the society who heard about the tools, or in some cases may have seen them or even owned them and wrote to my great-great-great-uncle about their discoveries. Clues, Mr. Barindra. I think there are clues hiding here." Malachai spread his arms wide as if embracing all of the thousands of volumes and tens of thousands of papers in the library. There was an expression of naked need on his face, and Elgin glanced back down at his notes, uncomfortable seeing it. Malachai might as well have stripped off his clothes and shown his newest employee the scars on his aging skin.

"The most important part of your job, other than organizing our archives, of course, is to find references to those searches and objects. We can't find what we don't know we are looking for."

"You don't know what the tools are exactly?"

"Only for certain about the two I mentioned—the cache of stones and the flute. The rest?" He smoothed down the sheet of writing paper with the pads of his carefully manicured fingers. "We believe this is a list of others." He sighed. "A list that is as much guesswork as science, since linguists have only recently cracked the code to the Harappan language. But this is what we have, and so this is what I want you to work with. You're looking for mentions of objects that could fit any of these descriptions."

Malachai pushed the list toward Elgin, who followed along as the reincarnationist read each word out loud. "A pot of fragrant wax. Reflection orbs—which could be anything with a mirrorlike or reflective surface. A word holder, which I can't even guess about. Ornamented picture coins. Engraved pillars, and fire and water beads."

"You said there were a dozen and two have been found—but you only mentioned six items."

"The list is incomplete."

"Why?"

"There were four items the translator wasn't able to decipher."

Normal curiosity was fine but too much could make Malachai suspicious. Elgin could risk one or two more questions.

"How did you get the list?"

"I was good friends with the man who translated it from the original. He sent me a copy before he died. If he hadn't I don't think I'd even know it existed."

A perfect answer, Elgin thought—and one that was going to frustrate the hell out of Agent Glass. There'd never be any way to prove or disprove what the reincarnationist claimed if the man who'd translated it and sent it to him had died.

"It's all pretty fascinating," Elgin said, not feigning his interest. He was hooked.

In the overhead lights, Malachai's small dark eyes took on almost maniacal glee. "Fascinating and highly confidential."

Malachai had mentioned the secrecy of the job upstairs in his office, too. Elgin nodded solemnly. "I understand."

"Bill Hawkes said that when you worked with him at the Library of Congress you were involved in several projects that required you to have security clearance."

"That's true."

"I don't suppose you'd enlighten me as to what those jobs were?"

"No, I'm still under a nondisclosure agreement."

Malachai nodded, satisfied, even though it had been an easy setup. Both men knew it, and Elgin guessed that while the co-director of the institute was predisposed to be suspicious, he didn't want to doubt his newest employee. He wanted to get his investigation underway so desperately that Elgin could see it and hear it. That was something else Elgin would be sure to report back to Agents Glass and Richmond.

"How soon do you think you'd be able to start?"

"Monday?"

"There's no way you can start sooner?"

"Tomorrow's Friday." Elgin could feel the other man's impatience. "I could start tomorrow."

"That's terrific." Malachai held out his hand. "Welcome to the Phoenix Foundation, Elgin." The black eyes sparkled. *Charismatic,* Elgin thought. *Yes, definitely, but devilishly so.*

Chapter

TWENTY-FOUR

"I'm sorry, I got caught in traffic." Lucian told Dr. Bellmer his first lie of the hour as he sat down on her couch. He was ten minutes late for James Ryan's two-o'clock appointment, but not at all because of traffic. He'd taken Emeline Jacobs to NYPD headquarters to meet with Chief Eric Broderick and report the menacing e-mails she'd received. She'd agreed to let the department inspect the store's computer but when the chief agreed to Lucian's suggestion that patrol officers check on her a few times a day until they had more information, Emeline objected. Lucian made it clear no one was asking her permission. This was now an open case, he'd said. And then, even though she'd insisted she could get back to work on her own, Lucian dropped her off on Madison Avenue and Eighty-Third without getting out of the car or going into the store, or allowing his thoughts to travel back to what had happened there twenty years before. Once she'd disappeared inside, he sped across town.

"How are you feeling?" Dr. Bellmer asked.

"I'm okay. Thanks."

"How are the headaches?"

"Still there."

"Now?"

"Yes."

"Did you draw this morning?"

He didn't need to invent answers to these questions and so he told her about the episode that had occurred before day-break. "I woke up around four. It was the same woman today, the dark-haired Mediterranean."

"Do you remember what woke you up?"

"Nothing that I can remember. I just woke up needing to draw. It never makes any sense."

"I'd like to hypnotize you again. All right?"

"Yes."

Bellmer used the same set of instructions she'd used the last time, and Lucian steeled himself against her voice and the temptation to relax.

"It's not working, is it?" she asked, surprising him.

"I'm not sure why." A lie.

"Let's try something else today," she said. Reaching out, she pressed her finger on the spot between his eyebrows. "Feel that?"

He nodded.

She let her finger rest there for another moment and then dropped her hand and sat back in her seat. "It's said that in ancient Egypt, in order to gain true knowledge at the esoteric schools of mysticism, you had to first go through a rigorous training that included a forty-day fast, learning to breathe, to become aware and to be attentive. Only then, when you could feel things—as opposed to intellectualizing them—you were taught what they called the fifth technique. *Attention between eyebrows, let mind be before thought. Let form fill with breath essence to the top of the head and then shower of light.*

"Every ancient culture believed that we have a third eye deep in our brains, right behind that spot between your eyebrows, and there are dozens of superstitions and metaphysical theories surrounding this mysterious eye's function. Some believed it to be a dormant organ that could be awakened to enable telepathic communication and initiate supernatural powers. Others felt it controlled memories, or could enable astral projections. We know today that's the seat of the pineal gland, which produces melatonin, the hormone that affects the modulation of wake/sleep patterns and seasonal functions, but ancient mystics had a more elegant explanation of its purpose. They believed when you concentrate on your third eye, it opens, and through that portal you enter an intensely aware state of deep consciousness. The Buddha said that there, in the realm of the third eye, dream and reality are one. For our purposes, it's believed the action of awakening the third eye is the way to enter into hypnosis."

Iris had been watching his face as she explained and imagined she saw his intellect fighting his curiosity. He wore an expression she'd seen before on other patients, but it seemed exaggerated in James. She saw something else, too. Was he being seduced by the possibility of what she was saying? Or maybe it was a flash of recognition, as if he already knew what she was telling him but until now had forgotten it.

"I'd like you to try entering a hypnotic state via your third eye. Touch the spot between your eyebrows with your forefinger and then, while your finger is still there, close your eyes. Now, with both eyes still closed, pull them toward that spot. You'll experience a sensation inside of you as your third eye comes awake." She waited…knew he would feel it because she'd never had a patient who hadn't. Yes…she could see a moment of surprise suffuse his face. As she kept talking, she saw him resist, then relax, and then, finally, saw the slack look that followed as the unending pull and promise of deep relaxation overcame him and he slipped into a hypnotic trance.

"James, I'd like you to travel back to Greece again today, and find the time when you were a young sculptor named Telamon." She stopped, letting him slide backward and slip through this life to one that had occurred far in the past.

"Are you in Delphi now with—"

"Iantha!" he shouted, interrupting.

"What is it?"

"Iantha!"

"Telamon, step away from what you're seeing. Go back further to a time before, when everything was all right."

Iris watched as James's visage calmed and the pained expression was replaced by a benign, placid countenance.

"Tell me where you are."

"In my studio."

"It's yours now?"

"Yes, Vangelis died. Four months ago. Iantha and I were with him, and it was a sad but peaceful passing."

"Tell me about Iantha."

Telamon smiled. "She is my wife and helps me run the studio. We're trying to finish the commissions that fell behind when Vangelis took ill."

"It sounds as if your business is thriving."

"It would be if it wasn't for Zenobia. When Vangelis threw him out two years ago he started his own studio and now uses whatever nefarious means he can think of to take work from us."

Iris was fascinated by how easily patients in regression fell into storytelling mode. "Does he succeed?"

"Yes, since he's not only clever but ruthless. Iantha says she isn't frightened of him, but I know she is. He tells whatever lies he can think of to destroy my reputation. All still to get back at me for being the sculptor that Vangelis chose to succeed him."

"And for being the man Iantha chose."

Telamon smiled.

"How bad is Zenobia's gossip?"

"Very bad. Not even the trial went our way."

"What trial?"

"Just three weeks after Vangelis died, while we were still in mourning, Zenobia broke into the studio during the night and destroyed one of our most important works in progress. I saw him as he was running away and ran after him, but he had too much of a head start. The next day he presented himself to the nobleman who'd ordered the piece and told him that someone had destroyed the sculpture during the night and that with all of our backlog we'd never manage to get the job done, but he could. He stole the commission away from us. When I complained to the court officials, they gave me a trial—a joke of a trial, as it turned out. As litigants each of us argued our cases. Zenobia claimed he was innocent and had not even been in Delphi on the night of the vandalism but was traveling back from Opus, where he'd been working on a frieze for a temple for many days.

"I explained to the jurors that he'd returned the night before the sabotage, because Iantha had seen him following her home from the market. He's followed her before." Telamon shook his head and clenched his hands in his lap. "But Iantha had no proof, and the jurors voted to exonerate him. Most probably he bribed them." Telamon's face was angry now, and sweat had broken out on his brow and upper lip.

Iris felt his fury well up inside her. "Can you move ahead in time to the next period of conflict for you and Iantha?"

Telamon's breathing became labored. The anger on his face morphed into sadness.

"What is it?"

No response except for furrows that creased his forehead.

"Telamon?"

"Iantha." The one word was a wail.

"Telamon, what is it?"

"Iantha," he repeated in the same tortured voice.

"What's happened to Iantha?"

"She's gone."

"Where?"

"It's all my fault."

"Is she dead?"

"It's all my fault."

Iris held her breath, trying not to breathe in his anguish.

"All…my…fault."

Each word was so suffused with suffering it sounded as if every syllable was stabbing him. "Move the pain away. Move it away from you. You are not the pain. You can acknowledge it without feeling it. Step back from it."

She saw the stressed expression on his face relax slightly. "Can you try to tell me what's happened? Does this have to do with a commission? Does it have to do with Zenobia?"

He nodded.

"Try to tell me what happened."

"Pythagoras was exiled from Italy and decided to build a school here in Delphi, where it's safe. A circle of rocks surrounds us and protects us and we're so high on the hill we can see whoever approaches. A priest from the philosopher's cult in Croton arrived first to get the work on the school started, and while he was here he held a competition for a chryselephantine sculpture that would be the central figure in the compound's sleep temple. I was awarded the commission over Zenobia. He was furious."

"When was the decision made?" Iris asked.

"Two weeks ago. Since then he's been drunk most of the time and ranting to everyone who will listen that I'm not qualified to execute such an important commission. Zenobia can be violent when he's had too much wine, and I was worried about both Iantha and the treasures."

"What treasures?"

"Once we won the competition, the priest gave us a casket of precious materials to use on the sculpture. Ivory for the statue's face, hands and feet. Sheets of silver and gold and dozens of stones, especially those with properties associated with the god we were going to carve. Deep green malachite because it soothes and helps bring sleep and meditation. Fine lapis with deep gold veins because it stimulates mystical thinking. To eliminate worry there's creamy brown jasper with lavender swirls. Large chunks of amethyst that help people dream inspirations. So many stones… There was also a sacred object the philosopher wanted hidden inside the statue. The priest was concerned that it be invisible, and I assured him chryselephantine works are large and elaborate enough to hide many such treasures and secrets."

Telamon paused, squared his shoulders, expelled a deep breath and continued with his story. "Huge crowds of people make pilgrimages here to visit our oracle. Greek and foreign dignitaries, heads of state and plebeians all descend during the four days a year the sanctuary is open to the public. They jam our roads and camp in our woods, and the wealthy ones pay large sums of money to bypass the crowds. We're very vigilant about watching for invaders, but two days ago a group from Athens came in disguised as pilgrims and staged an attack at the sanctuary. I had no choice. All of us were needed to go and fight, so I took two of my apprentices with me and left one behind to protect Iantha and the treasures the priest had left with us. I had no choice. As a citizen my duty is to my city first. I couldn't stay behind."

His voice broke and panic gripped Iris. She thought about ending the regression but instead tried to soothe him. "I know you couldn't. And it's not your fault. Will you tell me what happened?"

He sat very still and silent for a moment, but the dread came off his body like tsunami-size waves that broke over her. If she was picking up this much terror from him, she could imagine how much more he was experiencing. It was critical for him to get through this event, though, if he was to figure out the meaning of the drawings that his unconscious demanded he create night after night.

"It's all right, Telamon," she whispered. "What happened?"

"Zenobia came to the studio while I was gone. He stabbed my apprentice and left him to bleed to death. He stole the box of treasures from Pythagoras's priest and destroyed the work we'd already started on the armature. He used our own tools to do it! And he didn't stop with the new work. He scratched angry lines into the marble faces and torsos of other works. He created a funeral pyre outside the studio and set fire to ivory hands, feet and faces, and then…but worse than that…much worse than that…he…he…Iantha was…"

Iris knew what Telamon was going to say before he said it, as if she heard it roaring inside of him as a thought before he managed to spew the word out. "He raped my wife. He took her in my bed. And I was not here to defend her. I don't deserve to live."

"How could you have known?"

"It's not for that infraction that I should be punished."

"For what, then?"

His voice dropped down to the ground and crawled toward her. "For what happened next."

Iris let him take his time.

"He'd soiled her." Telamon's voice was thick with disgust. "He'd touched Iantha and made her unclean. Zenobia had always hated me, always tried to ruin what I had, and had finally succeeded. Iantha wasn't mine anymore. She was his. Even though he had taken her by force, by terrible force, his seed was inside of her and the thought of it made me retch." His voice dropped impossibly lower as he continued his confession. "And when she touched me…I threw her off."

"How did she react? What happened?"

"Iantha…" he started, stopped and then started again. "Iantha thought it was the destruction of my studio that was causing my depression and decided to do something about it. Without telling me, yesterday, she bribed one of Zenobia's servants to tell her when he left the house and then went there to steal back the cache of treasures. For me, so I could sculpt the god, so I could fulfill the commission. She was there in his studio, filling her pockets with the smallest stones to lighten the load of the casket so she could carry it back to our studio…so she could cure my melancholy and help me get back to work…when he came back and found her. He beat her for her transgression, then stripped off her robes and raped her again, over and over. He tore into her with his cock and ruptured her insides, and when he was covered with her blood and finished with his pleasure he picked up her poor naked body and carried her through the streets, her beautiful long black hair dragging in the dirt, her blood leaving a trail from his studio to mine. Then he stood outside, in front of our door, and yelled, *'Telamon, your wife is back, your sweet thieving whore wife is home.'*"

A car horn blasted on the street below, and the sound wrenched Iris out of the past. She'd left this office and this city and this time and had been living in Telamon's world, thousands of years before.

"What happened to Iantha?" she whispered as she wiped tears off her cheeks with the back of her hand.

"The doctors couldn't stop her bleeding. My wife died because…because I couldn't protect her…from my own pride."

Chapter
TWENTY-FIVE

It was just past six o'clock on Thursday night, but there was still a receptionist waiting for Ali Samimi and Farid Taghinia when they got off the elevator and stepped into the wood-paneled hallway. She was wearing a blue shirt and black slacks that showed off her figure in a way that Samimi knew would be immodest in his homeland. As she escorted the two men down the hushed hallway of Weil, Weston and Young, their footsteps fell silently on a rug that Samimi noticed was an expensive copy of a Persian. He smiled to himself at how pervasive they were in America.

It was late for a meeting, but Lou White had suggested the evening summit because of an all-day meeting out of town. As the two men came in he thanked them for accommodating his schedule. "Welcome to my humble abode," he said, gesturing toward his office.

White's irony was well placed. Everything here was impressive, from the massive mahogany desk to the wide windows that afforded a bird's-eye view of Central Park to the wall of undergraduate and graduate degrees and finely carved wooden shelves filled with leather-bound books. The lawyer was equally impressive; he was one of those Superman-looking Americans Samimi envied. Tall with strong features, he had sandy-colored hair and was tanned and athletic.

It was all so random—where you were born determined your fate. No one could call Lou White at a moment's notice and drag him back to a country where he didn't belong anymore, to endure a life he could no longer abide. That was all Samimi wanted—to know he could stay here for as long as he wished.

"Would you like some coffee? Tea? I have something stronger if you don't abstain," White offered, and gestured to the bar set up on the top of the console behind him.

Since Taghinia was devout, Samimi didn't drink when they were together, but he looked at the bottle of whiskey longingly. The thought of the Scotch not only made his mouth water but intensified his ire. He wanted to live an authentic life, not this hypocrisy. Hearing his boss ask for tea with sugar, he said he'd have the same. While White called the request in to his assistant, Samimi studied what the lawyer was wearing as if he'd be tested on it later: navy suit, powder-blue shirt and blue-and-gray-striped tie. His dress, manner and surroundings were all designed to instill trust.

"On the phone you said you had news? Might it be good news?" Taghinia asked.

His boss was too brusque, Samimi thought. Taghinia refused to engage in the social niceties that building business relationships required, and as a result he never inspired anyone to go the extra distance for him.

"It is good news," White said, but instead of telling them right away, he plucked a folder off the corner of his desk, opened it, searched through the first few pages, didn't find what he was looking for, closed the folder, picked up a second and looked inside that one.

Samimi wondered if White was deliberately delaying as a power move. The lawyer was a partner in one of the most prestigious law firms in New York City; you didn't hurry him.

"Yes, here it is," White said as he scanned the sheet of paper he was holding. "We've been able to find out that in the process of removing the statue in question from Persia in the nineteenth century, the archaeologist involved was responsible for the murder of two people. Did you know that?"

"No," Taghinia barked. "But what difference does it make?"

"A great deal. Let me take you through it. The husband and wife who lived in the house above the crypt where the statue was found were killed during the excavation."

"There was a cave-in?" Taghinia asked, again impatiently.

Samimi thought he could detect annoyance in the lawyer's glance but couldn't hear anything but the correct inflection in his voice as he explained.

"No, they were trying to stop the archaeologist from re-moving anything. The contents of the crypt had been in the family for almost three hundred years."

"How does that help us?" Taghinia asked.

Now, White did frown, and then continued. "Based on property laws at the time, despite the partage system, the Persian government didn't have the right to the contents of the crypt."

White's assistant, the winsome young woman wearing the blue shirt and black slacks, entered carrying a silver tray. White thanked her and, as she walked out, offered each man a cup.

"If the artwork was looted, the Metropolitan Museum can't claim the industrialist Frederick L. Lennox left them a piece of sculpture that was free and clear of previous claims, right?" Samimi asked, unsure what answer he hoped to hear. Every-thing would certainly be much simpler if this were true. Iran would get Hypnos back, and he and Taghinia would be re-

warded for jobs well done—even possibly be given promo-
tions, which could result in job shuffling. Success might mean
he'd have to go home. The alternative was a covert, complicated
operation that made his palms sweat but might offer him a way
to stay in America for good.

"Yes, that's right," White said.

"That is indeed good news," Taghinia said.

"Not exactly," the lawyer amended.

"Why?" Samimi asked.

"Starting in the sixteenth century, harsh treatment was the
rule in Persia for the Jews, a situation that didn't change until
early in the twentieth century. The government forced them to
wear identifying headgear and a yellow badge and forbade them
from relations with Jews outside the country. All over the world,
Jews lived in ghettos, but in Iran, those ghettos were high-
security prisons."

"What does this have to do with the sculpture?" Taghinia
interrupted, yet again.

White spoke even more slowly when he resumed explaining.
"At issue to our case are family property laws. During the time
in question, the law of the land stated that if a Jew converted
to Islam he became the sole inheritor of the family's property,
and all other relatives were excluded from the will. The husband and wife who died trying to save the sculpture and the
other artifacts in the crypt were a couple named Bibi and Hosh
Frangi, who had four sons. If all of them had remained obser-
vant Jews they would have all inherited the treasures had they
not been stolen. Each would have had an equal share in them.
But one son, Yoseph, converted to Islam days after the death of
his parents—probably to take advantage of that very law—and
the house and all its contents became his. Which means if the
sculpture hadn't been stolen it would have been his."

"Where is this going?" Taghinia was tapping his foot on the carpet, making a slight but annoying sound that set Samimi's nerves on edge.

White continued as if he had not been interrupted, but the cadence of his words slowed down yet another fraction. Samimi was sure Taghinia didn't notice it—which was so typical of the overweight, bombastic man. *God, he wished he could get away from him.*

"We've done some research. Yoseph Frangi's great-grandson lives in Iran today and works for the government as a health inspector. If you were to get him to agree to donate the sculpture to the government of Iran, you would have much more viable grounds to demand that the Metropolitan Museum return Hypnos to you." White sat back in his chair.

"How long would all this take?" Taghinia asked.

"How long will it take you to convince Ilham Frangi to sign over the sculpture to the government?"

"We don't even know the man…" Taghinia pursed his lips, and his tapping became faster.

Samimi knew his boss was reaching the end of his patience, and interrupted. "But let's say we can take care of that part in days. How long would it take your firm to get us back the sculpture?"

"One and a half to two years instead of the three to four we're looking at without Frangi. But what's critical to understand now is that if the Metropolitan does their research as well as my firm has, they could find out what we've found out and get to Frangi with a better offer. They're a wealthy institution."

"Even one more year of this is not acceptable to our government." Taghinia stood. "We'll get to Frangi, but you'll have to move faster."

"The law can't be rushed," White responded in his slow, measured voice.

"It most certainly can."

"Before you go, there's another matter we haven't even discussed," White said, ignoring the comment.

"And what is that?"

"These archaic laws and the ways that your country treated the Jews won't win any sympathy with the court system if they are brought to the forefront of the case, and if the Metropolitan gets to Frangi first, then they might be."

Taghinia pulled out a cigar and stuck it in his mouth. Samimi thought he detected a slight look of disgust in White's eyes, but the lawyer didn't say anything. "I want you to stay here and work this out," Taghinia said to his second in command. "I have a phone call with the minister I can't be late for. And when you're done, come back to the office. We're obviously working late tonight."

Samimi nodded. Working late tonight was code they'd arranged before arriving at the law firm. It meant Samimi was to stay and agree to pursue whatever path the lawyer suggested, but only for show. It also meant calling Deborah Mitchell in the Islamic department of the Metropolitan, setting up another dinner. Taghinia had said it would now be critical for Samimi to be present at the next few museum events.

Samimi wondered if he'd be too nervous to even enjoy her company in the days and weeks ahead as she unknowingly helped him stage a dangerous and delicate mission that could make him a hero in Iran—or perhaps afford him something he wanted even more.

Chapter
TWENTY-SIX

The harsh afternoon light spilled through the windows, casting everyone in a hyperrealistic glow and drawing attention to every line in Andre Jacobs's worn and creased face. He stood in his living room on Fifth Avenue and Seventy-Ninth Street surrounded by expensive furnishings and a lifetime of memories and confronted the Matisse Marie Grimshaw was unwrapping as if it were a rifle and he were a demoralized soldier about to be executed. As she pulled off the final layer of covering, Jacobs groaned.

"Mr. Jacobs? Are you all right?" Lucian asked.

Ignoring the question, the old man walked to the painting, gripped it with his arthritic hands, turned it around and, without being told where to look, bent down to examine the lower left corner, where there was a red circular mark no one at the Met had been able to explain.

The museum could run all the follow-up tests it wanted. The combined look of wonder and horror in Jacobs's eyes told Lucian what he needed to know. This had to be the painting stolen from Jacobs's workshop that day so long ago; the painting Solange had been killed over.

Jacobs leaned the canvas against the wall, then he stood back and stared at the beach scene, or what was left of it.

"A fitting memorial…" he said softly.

Only Lucian and Emeline were close enough to have heard him.

"A fitting memorial…for my Solange."

Lucian saw his shoulders slump and anticipated the collapse, so that he was there to catch Jacobs as he fell. Olshling ran over to help.

"I'll call an ambulance," Tyler Weil said, punching in 911 on his cell.

Emeline knelt down beside her father. His eyes fluttered open. "Emeline?"

"It's all right—you're all right," she reassured him, and his eyes closed again. Emeline looked up at Lucian and Olshling. "Can you help me get him into his bed?"

"Are you sure we should move him?" Olshling asked.

"Yes, this has happened before. He'll be okay."

Together the two men lifted Jacobs, who was far too light to be healthy, and followed Emeline into the master bedroom.

Sixty seconds after they had lowered him onto the bed, Jacobs came to again. With glassy, bloodshot eyes, he searched the faces peering down at him. "Emeline?"

"She's in the bathroom getting your medicine. She'll be right back," Lucian said.

"Can you give us some privacy?" Emeline asked when she returned with a handful of pills and a tumbler of water.

The two men joined Grimshaw and Weil, who were repacking the painting in the living room. The EMS team arrived less than five minutes later, and Lucian showed the medics into the bedroom. While they worked on the old man, he returned to discover that everyone from the museum had left. Even with the heavy sun beating in through the windows, and despite the painting's pathetic state, with it gone, some of the light in the room seemed to have gone away. He dropped into a seat at the antique card table and stared out at the same view he'd been mesmerized by twenty years before. The Upper West Side skyline stood proudly above thousands of trees. It was June, and the trees formed a solid green canopy made up of a hundred different shades. He spent the next fifteen minutes dissecting their nuances, mixing the colors in his mind on an imaginary palette. Ultramarine blue and lemon yellow for a dark green. A touch of alizarin crimson to make it olive. Cerulean blue and permanent yellow blue for a forest green. It was a silly exercise, and it failed totally to keep his mind off what had happened earlier in Dr. Bellmer's office. Only Andre Jacobs identifying the Matisse had managed that feat.

Lucian didn't believe in reincarnation. He'd studied it exten-sively the year he'd been on the Malachai Samuels case. Regres-sions were only proof of our ability to make up stories, to manufacture dreams. Yes, there was a sense of inevitability to the young sculptor's pain that seemed to mesh with Lucian's, but wouldn't there be? Wasn't it logical? The drama was a mani-festation of his own mind.

When Emeline finally walked the medics, with their empty stretcher, to the door, Lucian was still sitting by the window, mixing colors in his mind.

After seeing them out, she sat down opposite him. "His vitals are stabilized. They didn't need to hospitalize him," she said wearily. "It was probably just the shock of seeing the painting." Without looking down at the cordovan-leather tabletop, she found the fancy gold scrollwork along the edges and traced the design with her forefinger. Her hands were so small.

"You must be relieved."

"Yes, we've had enough of hospitals for a while."

"Does he have a history of passing out?"

She nodded. "He has very low blood pressure."

Lucian was sure that the gin he'd smelled on Andre Jacobs's breath had contributed to the incident, too.

"I have some information for you," he offered.

"About the e-mail?"

"I spoke to Broderick before I came over. He had the department put a rush on the trace yesterday, and—"

"Let me guess. He told you they hadn't been able to figure out where the e-mail was coming from?"

"Did he call you?" Lucian asked.

"No, but I've read about how easy it is to send untraceable e-mails."

"Just because they haven't figured it out yet doesn't mean they won't be able to get a lead."

She looked at him skeptically.

"They're really good at this, Emeline. Broderick told me two more letters came in that they haven't even started working with yet. They could yield different results. The sender only has to make one mistake."

She shivered.

"You read them?"

She shrugged. "I know you both told me not to, but I couldn't help it. There's someone out there. It's impossible to see the e-mail there and ignore it."

"We don't expect you to ignore it, but the police are monitoring your e-mail now. You don't have to put yourself through that."

"Could you stop yourself from reading them if it was happening to you?"

"No, probably not. Broderick said the message was the same."

"I'll kill you and your father, too." Her voice trembled.

"It's normal for it to get to you."

"It's not that."

"What?"

"I'm sure it's nothing…"

"Okay, but it's clearly bothering you. What is it?"

When she didn't respond, he repeated his request. "Tell me," he insisted.

"I think someone was following me today."

"When?"

"This afternoon when I left the store to come here."

"Why don't you tell me what happened? Whatever you re-member. Even something you might think is insignificant can be crucial."

"I was walking on Madison, from the store here. And I just got this crazy feeling."

When she hesitated, Lucian nodded and said, "People say that about being followed. They often sense it first. Go on."

"I turned around, but everything looked normal. I figured I was being paranoid."

"What else happened?"

"I kept walking and then, as I passed by a store, I noticed a man reflected in the windows. I walked a little more. The street's all stores there, so I kept watching. He stayed behind me for another block and a half. I got spooked and stopped in E.A.T, a restaurant on Eightieth Street, to get away from him."

Lucian nodded. "I've been there. Expensive." He smiled. "What did the man do? Could you see from inside?"

"He walked by."

"Did he look in?"

"No."

"Could you see his face?"

"He was moving too fast." She stopped to think, to try to picture the scene. "No, there was a woman blocking my view."

"Do you remember any details at all? Color of his hair?" Lucian had taken out his Moleskine notebook and had a pencil ready.

"No."

"What was he wearing?"

"He had a baseball cap on. Dark. Blue or black." She seemed surprised to have remembered.

"Was he tall? Short?"

"I don't know. Tall. This is crazy. Could anyone really think that even if I was…reincarnated…that I would…that Solange would remember?" She sounded contrite, as if she were blaming herself. "Some man was coincidentally walking in the same direction I was. That's all. I'm overreacting."

While she was talking she'd started running her finger up and down on the fluted edge of her chair. Lucian wanted to reach out and still her hand. She was scared, and he didn't blame her. It didn't matter if reincarnation were possible or not, only that some lunatic out there believed it was. All these years he'd wanted nothing more than a chance to find out who had stolen the Matisse and murdered Solange. Was that possibility finally presenting itself? Was there a way to scare the perp and smoke him out? Was Emeline brave enough to help them if it came down to that?

"It's probably nothing. Those e-mails would make anyone nervous. But I'm going to ask Broderick to give you a security detail for a few days, anyway."

"That's not necessary."

"I think it is. Where do you live?"

"I have an apartment on the west side, but I've been living here for the past four weeks, since Dad got home from his last trip to Mount Sinai."

"Is your apartment in a doorman building?"

"No, in a brownstone."

"Don't go back there until we get to the bottom of this."

"I wouldn't anyway—Dad's not ready for me to leave yet."
She paused, then asked, "Will you do me a favor?"

"If I can."

"Ever cautious." She managed a smile.

"Okay, I will. What is it?"

"Don't tell my father about this. He doesn't need anything else
to worry about."

"I won't."

She looked away from him then and out the window as if
there were a message somewhere beyond this place and this
moment. She was as still as one of the marble sculptures across
the street in the Greek and Roman galleries, and her expression
was just as indecipherable. So why did he feel as if he knew
what she was thinking?

"You believe your job is to protect him the way he's always
protected you, but it's not."

She jerked her head around. "You don't know me well
enough to know what I believe my job is."

"You're right," he said apologetically.

"He's sick. He's so sick. And his drinking makes it worse, but
he doesn't seem to care. He usually holds back during the day,
but as soon as the sun starts to set, it's as if it pulls his resolve
down with it."

Telling him that much seemed to have broken the seal of
secrecy on her life with Andre Jacobs, and now that she'd gone
this far, she shrugged her shoulders as if she didn't care how
much further she went. In a long river of words, she told Lucian
what had happened to her as a girl after her accident, out of
her coma but still recovering.

"I overheard my aunt and uncle talking to the social worker
about me when they thought I was sleeping. The hospital had

assumed Andre and Martha were going to take me home with them when I was released, but they were saying they didn't think they could. I pretended to stay asleep and listened to the whole conversation. They said they were still grieving for their daughter, that they didn't think they could cope. It was too soon, Andre said.

"My mother and father and my brother had died. I was all alone except for my aunt and uncle. I didn't understand everything that had happened, but I knew there was no one else. I had to make them take me home with them. But how?

"When the doctors had taken my bandages off and my aunt had seen the scar on my forehead, she'd started to cry because Solange had had a scar a lot like it in almost the same place. Martha couldn't look at it at first. Andre had to take her out of the room.

"I don't know now how I came up with my pathetic little plan, but after the social worker left, I pretended to wake up and I told my aunt and uncle I'd had a dream that Solange had come to visit me and told me the scar on my head was a mark to show everyone that she was part of me now. It was all make-believe—inspired fiction from a scared kid with an overactive imagination. But it worked. I lied, and my lie worked. Too well. It's what started the whole craziness with them thinking I was reincarnated."

"You can't blame—"

Emeline interrupted him. "I can. Martha believed me without reservation. I don't think Andre did, but he wanted to. He tried to. It was too much for him, though. Too strange. Too incomprehensible. I think that's when his drinking became a problem. He'd come home from the framing store drunk, and he and my aunt would argue. They didn't scream when they fought. Their voices got really low. I'd hide in the hallway and listen to them, but I was always on the other side of the door. I should have told them the truth once they took me to the Phoenix Foundation. I should have. But it was too late. It had grown into something much bigger than me. And I was still afraid they'd send me away."

"I'm so sorry. You must have been very lonely," Lucian said.

Emeline started to respond, then twisted around and looked toward the bedroom. "I think he's up. Let me go check."

Lucian waited at the table where he'd sat so often with Solange the summer they'd lived in this apartment. There was a spot on the cordovan, oblong and irregular, where the leather had bleached out. He hadn't noticed it before but now he remembered a night when Solange had been joking around, using a French accent and mimicking a waiter pouring wine, and had overfilled his glass so that the liquid had spilled all over the tabletop.

"If you want to come in for a few minutes, my father's awake."

Lucian turned in the direction of the voice. She was bathed in a dusty glow from the setting sun. Emeline was light to Solange's dark—cool to her warm, closed to her open, but for a moment he'd seen Solange standing there so vividly he had to catch his breath and focus on what he knew instead of what he imagined.

"What is it?" Her voice was low and urgent.

"The light—this is the kind of light painters kill for." He hadn't expected to say anything, least of all this.

Back in the bedroom, where the thick ivory damask drapes were drawn against the sunset, Lucian found Andre Jacobs propped up against the pillows, wearing a navy silk bathrobe and looking very frail. Emeline lowered herself into a big armchair in the shadows on the other side of the bed, and Lucian remained standing. "I'm glad you're all right, Mr. Jacobs."

"No thanks to you."

Lucian bowed his head slightly, accepting all blame. "There

wasn't anyone else who would know about the mark on the back of the canvas. You're integral to helping us in this case."

Jacobs let his left hand rise and fall, like a dried leaf buffeted by the wind. "So the old man is all you have left. I'm not the best, but I'm the last. Is the painting still here?"

"No. It's back at the museum."

Jacobs nodded.

"You do believe it was the Matisse that was stolen from your framing gallery? You recognized the mark?"

"It's been twenty years. That's a long time to remember the painting so exactly."

"Yes. It has been a long time."

"A lifetime ago. A ruined lifetime ago," Jacobs said, and turned to Emeline. "I'm sorry. I'm not thinking clearly. That was a cruel thing to say."

"No," Emeline said, reaching out and taking her father's hand.

"Let me talk to the agent alone, Emeline."

"You're sure?"

He nodded and then watched her leave the room. Only then did he glance back at Lucian with faded green eyes that once had been the same vibrant jade as Solange's.

"I'm all the family she has. So pathetically little for someone who lost so much."

"You both lost so much."

Jacobs didn't respond except to close his eyes and lean back even farther on the pillows. He didn't say anything at all for a moment and then, with his eyes still shut, he started talking, as if he were telling a story.

"The Matisse only had one owner. Aaron Flaxman bought it from the artist and kept it. Cherished it. Got it out of Paris before Hitler arrived. Flaxman was one of the lucky ones who heard the rumors, believed them and arranged to have his collection shipped out of France before that monster looted the city. He paid an American businessman half his fortune to do it. Thousands who tried the same thing weren't as lucky.

"The mark is on most of the paintings he smuggled out. Like a brand. Usually it's hidden on a part of the canvas that wraps around the stretcher. He put them there in case they were lost and he needed to prove they were his. I don't think he told many people about it…not sure he would have told me either…but on the Matisse it was slightly more obvious. He never needed to rely on the marks, though. His courier was honest and didn't disappear with the collection when he reached the States.

"The Flaxman family made it to America, too. That cost Aaron the other half of his fortune, but as far as he was concerned he had all that really mattered—the people and the paintings he loved. And with those things my friend rebuilt his life in New York, becoming a dealer once again, this time buying and selling paintings on Madison Avenue and Sixty-Sixth Street instead of the rue de la Boétie. The ten paintings he'd smuggled out of France, the ones he left in his will to the Metropolitan Museum, were the cornerstone of his collection and the only ones he never traded or upgraded. The survivors, he called them—more special for what had happened to them, more beautiful after the war than before, as if what they had gone through had imbued them with something magical. He donated them restored and framed. I'm guessing the Met never took them apart and found the marks. But they're there." Jacobs sighed and closed his eyes. For a moment Lucian thought he might have fallen asleep, but then, with his eyes still shut, he continued talking about his old friend and customer.

"He was a romantic. Hitler's army had decimated the German side of his family, he'd seen the worst things man could do to man, and yet he believed that his paintings had grown more beautiful for their ordeal. That Matisse survived the Gestapo and the gas chambers and a fate that felled six million Jews, and then because of me…"

The confirmation was complete. Lucian knew what he needed to know from the one man who could tell him. He stood to go and had started for the door when the thin voice reached out and stopped him. Jacobs, it appeared, wasn't finished.

"You know what I've never forgotten? He never blamed me. Never said one word to me in recrimination. He came to Solange's funeral and sat shiva with me every day and night of that week. Sitting shiva for his painting, I think now. He cried with me and offered me solace even though there was no comforting me. I'd left her there that day. I…left…her…there…I did! Can you imagine living with that?"

I can, Lucian wanted to say.

Jacobs opened his eyes and looked at him, his expression changing to one of surprise. "You almost died, too, that day, didn't you?" He said it as if he was just now remembering that part of the story.

Lucian nodded.

"I wish you had. I wish you had died instead of my daughter."

Lucian turned, walked the last few steps, opened the door and walked out. Sometimes, probably too many times, he'd wished the same thing.

"Would you like some wine?" Emeline was sitting at the table in front of the windows. She held out a glass to him as if it held something much more precious that wine. Like her, caught in the sunset, it glowed.

"It's way past five o'clock," she said, as if reading his mind. "You've put in a full day. And there are some things I'd like to ask you. About my father. About Solange. About who she was. No one else would ever tell me. It's been like living in the shadow of a ghost. Please, Lucian?"

"I wish I could, but I have to go back to the office. This is an ongoing investigation," he said. Then he added, perhaps more curtly than necessary, "I can let myself out."

Chapter
TWENTY-SEVEN

Nina Keyes sat beside her granddaughter on one of the wooden benches in the lobby of the Metropolitan Museum. The little girl was rocking back and forth, her arms wrapped around her chest, tracks of tears on her cheeks.

Malachai Samuels sat on Veronica's other side, whispering to her softly, telling her over and over again that she was safe, that she wasn't alone, and that she didn't need to be frightened anymore.

Even though it was Saturday, he'd been in his office when the call had come through and he heard Nina Keyes's hysterical voice asking him to come to the Met right away. Her granddaughter needed help. He'd been here for at least ten minutes, but nothing he said was having an effect on her. Veronica was deep in her own drama and couldn't seem to hear him.

"We should move her away from all these people," Nina said in a frantic voice.

"Not while she's having a spontaneous regression."

"You need to stop it."

"That's not wise. This could be a breakthrough for her."

"But she's in pain."

"Yes, but she can't get hurt. I promise you that. We're here with her." He returned his focus to Veronica. "Tell me what's wrong. What are you seeing?"

The little girl didn't seem to be able to hear him.

"Veronica, you're safe. Your grandmother is safe. I want you to know that. Nothing can hurt you. Nothing."

Veronica's tears continued to fall, and she emitted small moans, cries of mental or physical distress; there was no way to tell.

"We were walking over to the main stairs when Veronica reached out for my hand and just started crying," Nina said. "She kept saying it was dark and that she didn't want me to go. Nothing I said calmed her down."

"Did you notice anything that could have triggered this attack?"

Nina shook her head and then looked around the great, grand space. Malachai followed her gaze and took in the over-size flower arrangements, the crowds of people, the museum guards dressed in navy blue, and the four flags flying over the entranceway, one for each of the special exhibitions: Vuillard Interiors, Egyptian Jewels, Illusion in Contemporary Photography and Persian Tile Treasures.

"Nothing that I can think of, I'm sorry. Can't you help her?"

"You're safe now, Veronica. You're here in New York with your grandmother. No one is going to let anything happen to you."

"It's not me," she whispered in a tremulous voice. "It's Hosh."

"Who is Hosh?"

"It's not me. It's Hosh. I have to save Hosh."

Chapter

TWENTY-EIGHT

Shush, Persia, 1885

Bibi watched her husband pull his knife from his sheath. His hand shook—not with fear, she knew, but with age. The lamp-light played on the edge of the blade like the devil dancing on the edge of hell, and the woman who was not a witch and had never had a premonition before in her life suddenly felt as if the very air she was breathing tasted of death.

Inching closer to her husband, she grabbed his wrist, digging into his paper-thin skin with her sharp nails. "They are just things…useless coins, pots. Who cares about them? We don't pray to idols, and yet you are willing to risk your life to protect one?"

"They've belonged to my family for centuries." He tried to pry her fingers away. "Let go of me."

"Not until you agree not to go down into the cellar until help comes."

"This is not your decision, woman," he said so harshly she let go and stepped back and away from him as if he had become a stranger.

She waved her hand at the area to the right of the hearth.

"Fine. Go. Protect your legacy." Her voice was tough and weathered, but her dark eyes were glassy with tears.

"This is the one thing I have to leave our sons, and they to theirs," Hosh said as he reached up and brushed her hair with his fingertips. He was old and sickly, spoiling from the inside out, but he smiled at her the same way he had when she was new to marriage and worried every time he'd left the house to go to the temple or to trade in the market. "Go back to bed, Bibi. No one is dying tonight. I promise you."

Lifting the lantern off the hook on the wall, he turned and limped across the room, his elongated shadow following him. Bibi stepped on it, thinking for one crazy second that she could hold him back by keeping his shadow there with her.

Hosh walked past the warped wooden shelves where foodstuffs were stored and stopped at the edge of a small, tattered rug that had been woven with threads of deep red and royal blue but now was a memory of that glory. Faded or not, it still did the job of hiding what lay beneath it. After rolling it up, Hosh pushed it aside and exposed the trapdoor.

"Please," Bibi whispered, reaching out again to hold him back, unable to stop herself.

Ignoring his wife, Hosh opened the door and shone his lantern on the staircase rough-hewn out of rock and dirt. Bibi shrank back. She hated everything about the cavern. Pitch-black and smelling of rotten eggs, it went so deep into the earth it was supposed to reach the sea, but no one was sure because at its farthest end was a thick wall of boulders.

She'd heard the legend about that wall four times because Hosh had told it to each of her sons on the day of his bar mitzvah, and he always began it the same way: *This story has been retold by every father to every son in our family for the past three centuries.*

The wall, he said, hadn't always been there but appeared overnight after the treasures were hidden in the crypt. His ancestors claimed God himself had caused the avalanche to safeguard and protect the legacy from anyone discovering it via the outside entrance. Over time, whenever a family member became curious and started digging out the rocks, whatever they managed to move during the day caused even more stones to cave in during the night and the wall grew thicker than it had been before.

When he was thirteen and heard the story, Hosh had argued that it must be a fable. His grandfather had smiled and invited him to disprove it. The next day Hosh and his two brothers removed twenty-two rocks, and the following morning when they returned to the crypt there'd been a new cave-in and the barrier encroached two feet deeper into the cave than it had been the night before.

But Hosh's grandfather was long gone, and the wall had finally been breached from the other side by a French archaeologist. He'd come to their front door three days ago and, in surprisingly good Farsi, requested that Hosh give him access to the crypt through the house because it would be easier to remove the antiquities that way.

Allow him entry so he could steal their treasures? Hosh had refused. The cave and its contents belonged to his family. The archaeologist was trespassing.

The Frenchman had a declaration on thick vellum from the Minister of Culture granting him the right to excavate the cave and stipulating that he could keep fifty percent of whatever he found for himself as payment. Hosh ripped up the sheets and threw the shreds in the man's face.

"I don't care about the partage system," he shouted. "The cavern doesn't belong to the government, so the government can't give away anything in it."

Hosh and his sons spent the following days and nights reinforcing the stone wall, but this afternoon, while they were observing the Sabbath at schul, the archaeologist and his workers had broken through once again.

Now their sons were out, rounding up men from the shtetl to fight off the looters. All Bibi wanted was for Hosh to wait until their help arrived, even if it meant that while they waited, the archaeologist and his workers carried off one or two of the treasures. What did a bowl or a bracelet matter compared to Hosh's life? But her husband was a stubborn man.

Despite her pleas, he put his knife between his teeth, grabbed hold of a lantern and descended into the earth via a ladder that his ancestors had used before him. The rungs creaked with his weight. Once he'd disappeared from her sight, Bibi counted to ten, gathered her skirts, tucked them into her waistband and followed him into the darkness.

Hugging the sharp, rocky walls, hiding in the heavy shadows, Bibi watched Hosh confront the archaeologist. He wasn't alone. She counted ten young Persians. Filthy from climbing through the rubble and shining with sweat, each was armed with a knife that glittered in the low light. The weapons were redundant. Every one of them was strong enough to take Hosh with his bare hands. Why couldn't her husband see that? Why was he willing to risk so much for these *things?*

"You're on my property." Hosh shook his fist. It was a futile, childish gesture, and Bibi's heart broke for him. "Leave or you will be arrested for looting. My sons are on their way with help. They're bringing the whole ghetto with them. If you don't go, you'll get hurt."

The archaeologist held out another sheaf of official-looking documents that looked similar to the one Hosh had ripped up earlier that week. "These give me the right to excavate here."

Hosh knocked them out of the intruder's hand, and they landed in a crazy mosaic pattern on the dirt floor.

"It's you who is the thief," the Frenchman said, each word spoken with righteous indignation. "You who are hiding ancient treasures here that belong to Persia, to history and to mankind."

Hosh laughed bitterly. "Is that what you are going to do with them? Give them to mankind? Or are you going to sell them to collectors in Europe and America? Don't think I'm a fool because I'm old. We all know what happens to the antiquities that are dug up in our land."

Bibi's mouth was dry, and her heart was like a small animal running fast, trying to escape the cage of her chest. None of this would be happening—her husband would not be in danger and her sons would not be rounding up their neighbors—if Hosh had listened to her and sold these things a long time ago. What good were pots, jugs, jewelry and graven images doing anyone sitting underground?

She was sure the wooden man with wings on either side of his forehead, holding poppies in one hand and a drinking horn in the other, was an evil thing. But her husband had argued that whatever the religion of the men who'd created the treasures, they were important in the same way that the Torah in the synagogue was important—not just for the words they read from it every Shabbat but for the past that the scroll carried into present and would one day carry into the future.

"Get out of my way, old man!" the archaeologist shouted. He was out of patience.

Hosh didn't move. Not a single muscle in his hand or his neck twitched. Not even his eyes blinked.

"For the last time, get out of my way."

Hosh pulled his knife from its sheath.

"Is your life so worthless to you that you would throw it away on these objects?" the archaeologist asked less aggressively, as if he were talking to a child now.

When Hosh didn't reply, Bibi guessed he was trying to stall, hoping his sons would arrive soon with help. But the archaeologist was impatient. He gestured to two of his workers, who stepped forward with the assuredness of the very young and very strong. Bibi thought she heard laughter as they approached her husband. She knew that unless help arrived right away, he was doomed.

Hosh continued to hold his ground.

"Get out of our way," the younger of the two Persians said and pushed Hosh back toward the wall. Falling, he landed on his side and winced. Bibi had to hold herself back. Was he hurt? She hoped that he was. Then he'd stay there out of their way. A small injury could keep him safe.

Hosh got back on his feet, shaky at first but then, rebounding, he lashed out with his knife, surprising his assailant and nicking him on the arm. The man looked down, saw the trickle of blood, and without any hesitation, shoved his knife into Hosh's ribs.

Bibi didn't see the expression on her husband's face change, but she heard him express a small, surprised *Oh*. She'd never heard such a weak sound come from his lips or seen him so defeated. Forgetting the danger she'd be in, thinking only that Hosh was hurt and needed her, she ran out from the shadows and toward him.

No. She wailed as she saw the blood oozing out of him. *No.* His face was slack. There was no flicker of life left in his eyes. *No.* A long, drawn-out note of disbelief. *No!*

When their sons arrived with the men from the ghetto, all the treasures were gone. The crypt was empty except for the tableau of two bodies: Hosh on his back in the dust and dirt with his frail wife on top of him, her blood mixing with his in a red-black stain beneath them.

Chapter

TWENTY-NINE

"It appears to me impossible that I should cease to exist, or that this active, restless spirit, equally alive to joy and sorrow, should be only organized dust—ready to fly abroad the moment the spring snaps, or the spark goes out, which kept it together. Surely something resides in this heart that is not perishable—and life is more than a dream."
—Mary Wollstonecraft

"I always think it helps to fill up your eyes with the real thing before you go off into battle," Marie Grimshaw said as she and Lucian walked toward the suite of Impressionism galleries. Lucian was aware how carefully the curator kept out of his personal space, despite the Sunday crowds pressing in on them.

"Battle?" he asked.

"Authentication is the one arena where the paintings are the enemy. You have to fight them and force them to reveal themselves to you. Take charge of them. Never allow them to overpower you. Subdue them, make them surrender their secrets." She laughed nervously. "I must sound crazy."

"Not at all. It's an interesting way to approach it. I like it,"

Lucian said in what he hoped was a reassuring tone. Marie never seemed able to relax around him, and it was disconcerting.

Lucian had been upstairs with the director. According to the note that arrived with the destroyed Matisse, the man who wanted to exchange Hypnos for the four masterpieces would be contacting Weil sometime Monday between nine and noon. If the museum was willing to make the trade, arrangements would be made on this call. The FBI wanted Weil to insist that a representative from the museum see the paintings before any negotiations took place. Lucian, posing as James Ryan, a Sotheby's appraiser, would play that role. Done with the prep work for the call, Lucian told Weil he wanted to spend some time downstairs looking at the Van Goghs, Renoirs, Klimts and Monets, refreshing himself with the artists' nuances and styles. It was possible that he'd have to leave quickly once the call came. Despite Lucian's insistence that he didn't need a guide, Weil called Marie Grimshaw at home and asked if she'd come in for a few hours and work with Lucian.

When she had arrived and seen him in the director's office, she'd acted almost afraid. Weil had been aware of it, too, and made a joke about the FBI being on *their* side. Marie had forced a smile, folded her arms across her chest and asked Lucian if he was ready.

He wished he were visiting the paintings on his own. Other than Solange, he'd never liked going through a museum with anyone…he had his own pacing…pacing only she had matched.

In the first gallery of the Annenberg collection, Marie stopped in front of a medium-size still life. "There was no flower Renoir loved as much as roses…and none he painted as often as red roses. While his early work had delicate, nuanced characteristics, by the time he painted the canvas in the photograph and this one, he had given up on subtlety and was trying to evoke the tangible rose itself in an expressive, expansive way. You can see that in the circular brushstrokes and—"

Lucian massaged either side of his forehead forcefully. The headache that had been under control all day seemed to have suddenly burst into life inside his skull. Reaching into his pocket, he found the painkillers, shook out three tablets, threw them in his mouth and swallowed them without water.

"Are you all right?" Marie asked with concern. How could she be so uncomfortable around him, almost wary of him, and yet be worried for him, too?

"Thanks. Yes, let's move on."

Walking just slightly ahead, Marie led him through rooms he knew well. Lucian often came to visit with these paintings for their beauty and the grace he felt in their presence. He was almost sorry when she stopped in front of Van Gogh's *First Steps*. He wasn't sure he wanted to look at one of his favorite paintings with her. The soft colors of the painter's Arles palette always soothed Lucian; the aquas, blues and pastel lemons were serene compared to the colors in his darker, more turbulent works. Despite the subject matter's potential for sentiment—a father holding his arms open as his child takes her first steps toward him, the baby's mother letting go of her child—the master had rendered the moment honestly.

Beside him, Marie talked about Van Gogh painting this in 1890, while he was staying in the asylum at Saint-Rémy. "He based it on an engraving of Jean-François Millet's painting. He wrote to his brother, Theo, that he felt justified in trying to re-produce the drawing into oils. It was more like translating the impressions of light and shade in black and white into another language—the language of color."

While she talked, Lucian's mind turned the father into Andre Jacobs, the woman into Andre's deceased wife and the child into Solange.

Forty minutes later, having spent time with paintings from all four artists, Lucian left the museum. Outside, he stood on the granite steps and peered down Fifth Avenue. There was a long vista of uninterrupted cityscape on one side and the verdant park on the other. There were people lounging on the steps, some smoking, others talking on cell phones or listening to music.

The pills Lucian had taken hadn't offered any relief today, and he still had a brutal headache. Sometimes fresh air helped when the painkillers didn't, so instead of hailing a cab and heading home, he decided to walk downtown through the park.

Legions of New Yorkers were taking advantage of the warm afternoon and the city's lush playground, and Lucian strolled among them. His headache started to lift almost right away, and he felt grateful for the familiar environs. The air smelled green and fecund, the way it did only in early June, when summer was still a hope instead of an actuality. It didn't matter which way he went; there wasn't a path that he didn't know. Lucian had grown up in Manhattan and, as it was for most city kids, Central Park was his backyard. His school brought students here to play softball in the spring and football into the fall and to ice-skate in the winter. Lucian had smoked his first joint on the hill overlooking Bethesda Fountain and kissed a girl for the first time in the Belvedere Castle, during a rainstorm.

When he reached the sailboat pond, he stopped to watch. He used to come here with his father, envious of the elaborate boats the richer kids had. Lucian's was homemade. His father had helped him to build it and then encouraged him to decorate it however he wanted and he'd painted it in dozens of crazy colors. Lucian couldn't remember any of those boats he'd coveted back then, but he could still picture his messy, rainbow-striped vessel gliding proudly on the water, the only one of its kind.

With a loud splash, a little boy with auburn hair dropped his boat into the water, held his breath and watched as it bobbed, tilted side to side, then balanced out and righted itself. "Dad? Dad? Are you watching?" he shouted, and looked back for a second in Lucian's direction.

Turning to look for the boy's father, Lucian instead saw Emeline Jacobs.

She was about ten feet away, wearing faded blue jeans and a big white shirt with the sleeves rolled up exposing her fragile wrists. She hadn't seen him yet. Lucian was struck by how young she looked, how vulnerable. It was an odd coincidence—her being here. Or was it? She lived just across the street. It was a beautiful day. She was taking a walk in the park.

"Daddy, are you watching?"

"Yes, I'm watching!" a man answered. At the same time, Emeline noticed Lucian and called out his name.

Right there, in the sunshine, by the pond, with who knew how many people around, the sight of her mouth forming that one word set off a reaction that surprised him—a physical craving that was different from what he experienced with most women. This was edged with memory and melancholy—and fear. His arms ached to hold her, hold on to her and keep her with him, to keep her safe.

As he went to her he worried that something was wrong, that she'd come to find him, except no one knew where he was.

"Are you all right?" he asked when he reached her side.

"It was too beautiful out to stay inside all day."

He concentrated on what she was actually saying, trying to let go of the crazy things he was thinking. There were dark circles under her eyes that hadn't been there two days ago when he'd last seen her.

"Have you gotten any e-mails today?"

Her eyes clouded. "One."

"Was it the same message?"

"More or less. Warning me not to talk to the police or he'd come after Andre and me."

"Are you being careful?"

"Yes, but between Broderick's instructions about using a car service to go everywhere and being there for my father, I feel trapped."

"That's why you came here, to the park, by yourself?"

"On a Sunday with a million people out. What could happen?"

"You can't take chances, Emeline. It's not smart."

"I really am being careful."

"Not careful enough. You're here. I don't want anything to happen."

The words *to you* were unsaid, but they were implied. Emeline held his glance.

"Did you see anyone following you?"

"Not today. Yesterday, I got that same sensation. But I didn't see anything."

They'd started walking and were making a slow circle around the pond.

"When? Where were you?"

"I just left the store to go across the street and get a sandwich. I can't take a car across the street."

"No, but you can order in."

"Are you sure I'm not just getting paranoid?"

"It's not paranoid when you're getting threatening e-mails. I know you're having a tough time, but give me a few more days. I haven't given up putting pressure on Broderick to give you a security detail. He's fighting a slashed budget, but he should know tomorrow."

"Can't they just find him?"

"They're trying." Lucian's hands turned to fists. He wanted Emeline safe, and he wanted Solange's killer. "How is your father?" he asked.

"He's never well anymore, but better today than he was on Friday. I think he's energized by the idea that whoever was behind the robbery might finally be found. Sometimes I think that's all that's been keeping him alive, wanting to see someone caught."

"You said you didn't want him to know about the e-mails."

"I don't. I didn't tell him. He thinks you're going to find whoever stole the painting by tracking down the person who destroyed it."

"So do I."

"That makes it my turn to tell you to be careful." She put her hand out and touched his arm, and he felt her fingers through his jacket sleeve.

They'd come full circle. There were several paths radiating away from the pond, and Emeline took the one that led west. Lucian didn't notice where they were headed at first. They were just strolling. One direction was as good as the next.

"You should know that Andre doesn't hold you responsible for what happened to Solange," she said, her voice even softer than usual, so that he had to strain to hear her, as if even saying Solange's name was verboten.

"Thanks for telling me."

"You still do, don't you?"

He shrugged.

"How could it be your fault?"

"I was late getting to the store. If I'd been there a half hour earlier like I was supposed to be, we would have been gone before your father's clerk closed up. Solange wouldn't have been there alone, waiting for me, and this bastard would have just taken the damn painting and left."

She'd veered off the path, and they walked up a grassy incline. The noise of the park around them struck a discordant note. *This conversation should be taking place in a somber, windowless room,* Lucian thought, *not in daylight, not interrupted by the sounds of kids and dogs and bicycle bells.*

"How long did it take for you to get over Solange? For you to find someone else?"

"I was nineteen…I don't know…eventually…" The truth was, he felt incapable of describing how he had and hadn't recovered after the accident. Lucian didn't know how to talk about Solange, to anyone, but especially not to this woman who was also inextricably tied to her. His feelings were twisted strands of so many conflicted emotions, tucked away where they were out of sight and he didn't have to get tangled up in them.

"It's easy to mythologize a relationship that ends like that," Emeline said. "Especially when you're so young and new at being with someone. Andre put her on a pedestal, too." She sighed. "To him she's forever nineteen and beautiful, with so much potential and so much promise."

"That you couldn't live up to? That you couldn't fulfill?"

She glanced at him sideways and smiled sadly. "Could anyone? You probably can give me the answer to that better than anyone. Can anyone live up to your memories?"

They were meandering through a grove of magnolias now with gnarled trunks, shiny, dark green leaves and a few late, pale pink blossoms. The trees in the Met's Van Gogh would have smelled like this, sweet with just a hint of citrus.

By the time they reached the top of the hillock, Lucian still hadn't answered her question. Emeline stopped beside one of the trees, put her hand on its trunk for balance and reached up to pluck a blossom. Her fingers rested on a weathered emblem cut into the bark: a twisting line snaking around a straight line dug out with a penknife years before.

Lucian flinched at the sudden recollection. He and Solange had come to the park for a picnic with a bottle of wine, a baguette, some apples and cheese and found this very spot to spread out their feast. She'd had this romantic notion of the überpicnic inspired by some movie she'd seen and had brought a book of poetry along that she asked him to read. He'd laughed at her and teased her, but he'd done it. The poem was about ill-fated lovers and time that flies too fast and had depressed her. He'd tried to coax her out of her unhappiness, but she wasn't letting go.

What if something happens to us like that? she'd asked. *No one will know we ever existed. There has to be some permanent proof we've been together.*

Lucian had pulled out his Swiss Army knife and scratched their initials in the bark, an *L* with an *S* twisted around it.

Now Emeline's polished fingernail was tracing those letters, the pale oval touching the curves of the *S* and the straight lines of the *L*. As he watched, mesmerized by the repetitive movement, he wondered just how they had wound up here, at this spot. He hadn't led Emeline here, he was sure of that.

"I put those initials there." As he told Emeline about that afternoon he watched her face. Was she surprised by the story? Had she known? He tried, but failed, to glean a telltale reaction.

There must be a logical explanation for how she knew about this spot. Maybe Solange had drawn it in one of her journals and Emeline had recognized it.

"It sounds like an idyllic afternoon," she mused. "Young lovers at a picnic in the park." Her tone had started out sympathetic but turned caustic. "But you erased all the smudges. Come on, Lucian, try to remember. Didn't the cheese have mold? Didn't a kid come along with a ball and knock over the wine? Maybe Solange had allergies and had a sneezing fit?"

"What are you doing?"

"You turned that afternoon into a painting, Lucian. You can't see it for what it was anymore. Everything about those days is idealized, bathed in sunshine."

The most frequent arguments he'd had with the last woman he'd lived with were about his being a workaholic. But the most damaging argument had been about Solange. Gilly had come across some old and very bad paintings of Solange in one of Lucian's closets and suggested he get rid of them. He'd over-reacted, and she'd accused him of practically the same thing as Emeline had.

What do you think it's like to compete with the ghost of a nineteen-year-old sexpot?

He'd argued that she was wrong, that he never compared her, or any woman, to Solange. But that was what he was doing now, wasn't he? Looking at Emeline, who had brought him here, to this one tree in the park that only he and Solange had known about, and comparing her to a dead girl, noticing not the things, the many things that were different, but what about her was familiar. Except wouldn't it make sense for Emeline to be familiar? She'd been raised in the same home by the same parents. There had to be similarities and shared knowledge.

The sun was filtering through the canopy of leaves, and a breeze was blowing a rain of petals down around her. It should have been a lovely image, but in her amber eyes he saw a fero-cious loneliness. It was her own loneliness, not Solange's. Solange had never been abandoned and—until her death—had never really suffered. She had only just grown up, and hadn't yet started to grow old.

What happened next was automatic, instinctive. Lucian

moved closer, put his hands on Emeline's slight shoulders and leaned down. The pressure of the kiss pushed her backward, up against the tree. The whole of his body was pressing against hers, and he could smell the grass and the liquor of the blooming flowers mixing suddenly with another scent, of lilies of the valley mixed with turpentine and linseed oil—a memory scent of Solange, something he couldn't understand and something he stopped thinking about as Emeline opened her mouth to him. He felt her long, thin fingers grip his shoulders with surprising strength as she pulled him impossibly closer into her body, erasing the space between them until he was lost in a new dimension made of the past and the present and a hint of something so tenuous and fragile he'd forgotten how it could flavor the taste of someone's kiss...a promise of the future.

And then she pulled away with a fierce jerk, as if he'd been holding her there against her will. She gave him a look that was more accusation than question. "I'm not her," she said.

"That's not why I want you—"

"It is. I can feel it in the way you touch me—you're searching for her with your fingers and your tongue. You're trying to smell her and taste her. But you can't, can you? I became what they wanted, to please them, and it's going to haunt me forever."

Emeline was crying now, and Lucian had to hold himself back from reaching out for her. "I don't know who I might have become without her shadow hanging over me." Her voice was brittle and angry as she threw her words at him so hard he imagined they were breaking. "But that doesn't make me her, Lucian. I can't be her so you can assuage your guilt. Don't you do that to me, too." And then Emeline turned and ran through the grove of trees, up the rise of the hill, and disappeared over the other side.

Chapter

THIRTY

When Elgin Barindra returned from taking a walk during his lunch hour on Monday, even though it was seventy-five degrees outside, as soon as he got back to his desk he put on a brown wool cardigan sweater. It was always just a little too cool in the suite of library rooms in the subbasement of the Phoenix Foundation.

Seated at the stainless steel table, he studied an elaborate Egyptian stamp postmarked 1881 affixed to a thick, cream-colored envelope. This was the tenth letter he'd examined today, one of the hundreds written during the second half of the nineteenth century, none of which had been properly archived. The paper had yellowed, and the corners and edges flaked off so easily there was antique confetti left on the tabletop every night when he was done.

The envelope was addressed only to Davenport Talmage at the Phoenix Club, New York City, New York, in an old-fashioned spidery script, written by someone who'd studied penmanship. There was no street name or number or zip code on the envelope, which was something to marvel at in itself— to think that once Manhattan had been that small a town.

Dear Davenport,

I am writing to let you know about papers I will soon be publishing that should create some controversy. Here in Egypt, I have seen accounts of objects including amulets, ornaments and stones, which suggest that the ancient Memory Tools you are so interested in are indeed fact, not legend. I believe I have found proof they were smuggled out of India and brought into Egypt well before 1500 BC, which, you realize, suggests that present-day historians are incorrect about when the trade routes opened. This is going to create quite a bit of debate among the professors at my alma mater and yours when I publish my findings—but I do love a good fight, as I know you do.

I will be in New York at the end of the month upon my return to the States and will stop by the club and give you a preview of what I've discovered. I think you'll be very interested.

Best Wishes,

John Macgregor

Luxor, Egypt, 1881

Tantalizing but nonspecific. Barindra made notes on a legal pad, then logged the letter in and filed it away. Moving on, he repeated the process with six more letters over the next hour. Most of the correspondence was addressed to either Trevor Talmage or his brother, Davenport, who were both prolific writers and communicated with scientists, philosophers, historians, explorers, archaeologists and theologians all over the world. Elgin had made his way through five boxes so far, and there were at least fifteen more to go.

Halfway into the next post, he heard the door open and then Malachai Samuels's cultured voice. "Good afternoon, Elgin. How are we doing?"

Pulling up a chair, Malachai sat beside the librarian and pored over the last letter Elgin had logged in. "I would love to know how this news was received." He paused, glanced at the shelves of still-untouched ephemera and smiled enigmatically. "It will be amazing to see what treasures you find. There could be extremely important information in here. Perhaps real proof..." His voice slipped into a sigh. "Can you imagine what that would be like—how the world would respond to the knowledge?"

"But isn't that what you've been doing here all these years? Collecting proof?"

"We've documented and researched the past-life memories of over three thousand children. Extremely carefully, I might add. We've discovered coincidences too amazing to be anything but evidence and confirmation of past lives. But there's always a way to cast suspicion on our results. My aunt and I thought we were collecting proof, but the scientific community hasn't regarded it as such."

"That must be frustrating."

Malachai's eyes narrowed. "We've accomplished more than any other scientists and still are not given the respect we deserve. I thought Vienna was going to change all that..." His words drifted off as he again scrutinized the letter in front of him. "I'll be damned if anyone gets to the next tool before me." In his lap, Malachai's hands tightened.

"How many of your own past lives have you accessed?" Elgin asked.

Malachai pushed his chair back and stood up too quickly. "You, my friend, have very important work to do, and I don't want to detain you. There is much resting on what you can find. So very, very much." With a forced, enigmatic smile, he gave Elgin a formal little bow and left.

None. The word hung in the air like a miasma even though it had not been uttered out loud. *None.* Why else wouldn't he have answered? *None.* Was that what motivated Malachai Samuels and pushed him so far into desperation that he'd embraced malevolence? *None.*

Chapter
THIRTY-ONE

Los Angeles, California

Expecting the Matisse Monster's call sometime after nine o'clock, Lucian Glass was showered, shaved and dressed and had ordered a breakfast of orange juice, black coffee, whole-wheat toast and honey by eight. The woman from room service told him his order would arrive within a half hour, but after only eighteen minutes he heard a knock on the door. Looking though the peephole, he saw the waiter.

A young man wheeled the cart into the room, closing the door halfway behind him. "Mr. Ryan, would you sign here?" He held out a black leatherette folder opened to reveal a charge slip.

After signing it and adding a gratuity, Lucian handed it back and watched the waiter walk out. Just as he'd closed the door behind him, right before the lock clicked shut, the door was pushed opened again.

"You can't walk into a guest's room," the waiter shouted from the hall.

"I'm his business partner," a voice snapped back, and a man stepped inside, slamming the door and drowning out the waiter's objections.

Lucian looked around for his cell phone, an advanced pocket Taser the local FBI had outfitted him with that could fire two probes up to a distance of fifteen feet, transmitting pulsed energy into the central nervous system of the target, causing him to become immediately incapacitated and immobilized. Unlike a gun, it was legal to carry and something that an art appraiser like James Ryan would have no trouble explaining. But the device was clear across the room on the desk. He couldn't get to it without being obvious. More important, James Ryan wouldn't run for a weapon if a stranger walked into his room; he was a civilian and he'd be confused but not worried. Not right away.

"Mr. Ryan, I'm Bill Weller. I'm representing the owner of the paintings you're here to see." He was about five foot ten inches tall, dressed casually in khakis and a polo shirt. He had tightly curled black hair, tinted eyeglasses that were too large for his face and a thick mustache. Lucian assessed his features, clothing and appearance, filing the information away, but even as he did he knew it was an exercise in futility: the man was wearing a wig and a false mustache and probably had lifts in his shoes. If Lucian ran into him the next day in the elevator he doubted he'd even recognize him. "Would you come with me?" Weller said, more of a command than a question.

"Where?" Lucian asked with more concern than he was experiencing. To an FBI agent this situation wasn't at all stressful, but as an art appraiser it should have been making him extremely anxious.

"Just across the hall."

"I need my phone." He started to turn.

"Actually, the last thing you need is your phone."

Weller waited until Lucian had crossed the threshold, followed him out and motioned to room 715, on the opposite side of the corridor, one door up. "It's a short walk."

Damn. They'd planned for every contingency but this. All the backup FBI agents were either in the lobby or parked outside ready to follow Lucian to the assignation point. Then, when he was certain the paintings were authentic and that he was with the architect of the plan, he'd give a signal and his team would step in and arrest the Matisse Monster for buying stolen artwork. Once he was in custody they planned to use him to track the men responsible for stealing the five paintings—the criminals they wanted the most.

If Lucian didn't give a signal, his team would know he was only with an envoy whom they'd need to tail in the hope that he would lead them to the Monster.

If anything went wrong, Lucian would insist on making a phone call to Tyler Weil to report on the paintings. Based on which coded message Lucian used, the FBI, who were monitoring Weil's calls, would know what kind of help he was requesting.

But if Lucian called now—from up here—they'd step in and blow his cover. That wouldn't have mattered much if the man with him in the hotel room had been the lynchpin of the operation. But he wasn't.

It didn't matter anyway. Lucian didn't have his phone.

The suite was almost identical to his own. Despite the fact that the curtains were drawn against the daylight and the light was low, it was like seeing the sun after spending days in a dark, dank dungeon. His instinct was to shield his eyes, but he knew from experience the gesture wouldn't help. This wasn't sunshine—it was the stunning impact of the artwork.

"These are the paintings," Weller said unnecessarily.

Lucian knew his immediate visceral impression was as critical as any other test and so, slowly, one by one, he focused on each canvas, concentrating, making a slight clucking sound with his tongue against the roof of his mouth.

The small Renoir of lush pink roses was so evocative he almost sniffed the air for their fragrance. Approaching it, Lucian examined the brushstrokes closely. On Sunday, when he'd been studying these artists' work, he'd focused on each one's distinctive patterns and palettes.

Lucian didn't need to take a sample from the Renoir; he had no doubt who'd painted it. Moving on, he focused on the *View of the Sea at Scheveningen* by Vincent Van Gogh. In addition to looking closely at the gray-green, stormy sea and shore, Lucian ran his fingertips over it. A Van Gogh's impasto was part of its identity, Marie Grimshaw had said and told him there were supposed to be actual grains of sand mixed in with the paint in this seascape as well as several others.

Lucian could feel them, grit on his flesh.

Every art student identified with Van Gogh's yearning and longing—and his madness and failure were their nightmare. He remembered how Solange had been angry with one of their teachers who'd said dying young would be worth it if your work would live on for so long after your death. *That's anti-life,* she'd said in retort. *How could it be worth it to reach the greatest peak of renown if you're not alive to experience it?*

The *Beach at Pourville,* painted by Claude Monet, was as peaceful a seascape as the Van Gogh was violent and Lucian reacted to the exuberance of the scene, despite his circumstances.

The contemplative Gustav Klimt portrait was disturbing and dark. One of the artist's less decorative works, it had no shining gold or silver, only a mysterious black-haired woman in a yellow dress, standing against a forest-green-blue background.

After only ten minutes, Lucian was willing to stake his reputation that all of these paintings were authentic. It was an astonishing treasure trove, a find to rock the art world. The Renoir and Klimt were each worth at least five million, the Monet approximately forty and the Van Gogh could go for over one hundred million. Why would anyone want to exchange close to two hundred million dollars' worth of paintings for a minor sculpture of the Greek god of sleep?

"Do you need cotton swabs and cleaning solution? Magnifying glass? Black light?" Weller asked, waving his arm at a table covered with paraphernalia.

"No, that won't be necessary. I'm doing okay." Lucian hoped he sounded apprehensive; this would be a strange position for a man like Ryan to be in. He wouldn't quite know what to make of it.

"You don't need any supplies?"

"No, just a phone," Lucian said. "I need to call the museum."

"Not yet." Weller gestured to the gray-and-white couch. "Have a seat. There's some business we have to discuss first." The words might have been polite, but the tone was threatening. Lucian was about to insist he either be allowed to make the call from here or return to his room to make it when the suite's inner door opened and a second man strode in. He had long, greasy brown hair and a scraggly beard and wore stained blue jeans and a tight, ripped, black T-shirt. Lucian figured that only the man's muscles were real.

Without acknowledging that there was anyone in the room, the grubby man lifted the Van Gogh off its easel and took it into the bedroom.

"I want to make my call now," Lucian insisted.

"I told you, not yet."

"Are you holding me hostage here?"

The second man returned and this time took the Klimt.

Lucian never should have left his room without his cell, but they'd caught him off guard…and these headaches had him off his game. If he slipped up now and Comley thought he was under too much pressure he could force him to take a leave of absence. And Lucian couldn't let that happen. Not now. Not while Malachai was still a free man and Solange's killer was on the prowl.

"It's imperative I make that call now."

"I know, you told me, twice. Just sit tight." Pulling out his own cell, Weller turned his back on Lucian and punched in a number. "Mr. Ryan's here," he said when the call went through. While he listened to whoever was on the other end, the muscle-bound mover returned, took the Monet in one hand and the Renoir in the other and left again, shutting the door behind him.

Weller's conversation was innocuous. Obviously stalling, he was describing the hotel to the man on the other end. "Yeah, you'd like it. Very simple. They have Internet, but you have to pay for it."

Lucian strained to hear noise coming from the room beyond this one, where the paintings were being deposited, but he couldn't hear over Weller's inane conversation. Was anyone else in there? How long would they keep the paintings there before trying to leave the hotel with them? How would they pack them? Would anyone in the lobby spot them? Did they have a car waiting downstairs? There were too many unknowns. He desperately needed to get back to his own room so he could alert his team.

He stood. "This is silly. I did what I came to do. If your boss needs to reach me he has my number."

Weller moved in front of him, blocking him from the exit. "Mr. Ryan, I asked you nicely. Now I'm telling you to sit the fuck back down, you understand?"

Lucian, thinking like Ryan, shook his head and raised his hands in the air.

"Hey, take it easy. What's going on? I'm just an appraiser. I've done my job. I authenticated the paintings, so why are you holding me here?"

"I have to go," Weller said into the phone, and clicked off. "I'm not holding you here. Sorry, man, I didn't mean to give you that impression. Now, what paintings are you talking about?"

"The paintings I came here to look at."

Weller frowned. "I don't know what you're talking about."

Lucian spun around, took three steps toward the suite's inner door, flung it open and peered into a semidark room. A bed, a bureau, a chair, lamps. No personal accoutrements and certainly no paintings. He flung open the closet. Checked the bathroom. There was no point in looking under the bed. Lucian knew what had happened without having to ask. During the time he'd been sitting on the couch, waiting for Weller to get off the phone, the paintings had been packed up and taken out of the hotel, each one probably inside its own suitcase, and whisked through the front doors right under the watchful gaze of the FBI agents.

"Where are the paintings?"

"Mr. Ryan, I don't know what the hell you're talking about. There are no paintings here."

Chapter
THIRTY-TWO

Victor Keither couldn't hear what the man on the other end of the phone was saying with the sounds of construction all around. "Hold on, let me find someplace I can hear myself think." The foreman of the renovation of the Metropolitan's Islamic wing moved away from the activity and stepped into the partially constructed sleep temple. Keither was always drawn to one area on a job. So far this structure was only a skeleton of what it would become, but it already felt like a sacred space. Once it had stood in Greece and been used by the sick and infirm who came to pray and be healed. Now, block by block, it was being reconstructed from hundreds of those original stones. The first time Victor had seen the rough, chipped granite he'd imagined the man who, over two thousand years before, had built it.

It was things like that, like wondering about that ancient builder, that made Victor appreciate his job. His buddies who worked regular sites didn't get what was so different about the Met, and he'd long since stopped trying to explain. Your religion was a private thing, wasn't it?

"Okay, I can hear myself think now," Victor said as he leaned against the plaster wall and rested his eyes on the circle of stones. "Who is this?"

"It's Mac. Mac Wyman—"

Victor didn't need to hear anything else. This was the third time Wyman had called and tried to recruit him for the firm that had stolen so many of Phillips's crew. Victor knew he was a good foreman, but there were other qualified men in New York. He wasn't that special.

Taking off his helmet, he ran his hand through his orange hair. "I told you before, I'm not interested. I have to get back to work, so—"

"I'm offering a very serious signing bonus here."

"Even if I was looking for a new job, I wouldn't want to work for someone who does business your way."

"What do you mean? We do business the old-fashioned way, Vic. We pay for the best craftsmen and workers we can find."

"No, you overpay for them."

"You may think so, but to us they're worth it. And you'd be worth it to us, too. What if I told you the signing bonus would pay for your son's first two years of med school?"

For a second Victor was caught off guard. How did Mac Wyman know about any of that? Maybe one of the guys who used to work for him who had gone over to Wyman had told him, but…

"Vic? Are you still there?"

"Victor." No one called him Vic.

"So what do you say, Victor? You interested in coming down and talking to us?"

He wished he could say yes. It would make his life a damn sight easier to screw his principles and his loyalty to Phillips—except it wasn't really about principles or loyalty, was it? It was about where he went to work and what he did when he got there. He wasn't stuck building apartment buildings or banks;

he'd spent his career helping rebuild the Metropolitan Museum of Art, doing something that mattered to him, something that made him proud. *Pride goeth before a fall,* he thought, smiling, remembering his father's habit of quoting homilies whenever he had an important decision to make.

"I'm not interested."

"I'm very sorry to hear that, Victor."

"Hey, Keither, we have a problem with some wiring that isn't on the plans." His chief engineer had found him and was in the doorway with a scowl on his face and a sheaf of blueprints in his hand.

"I have to get back to work, Mr. Wyman."

At the end of the day, as usual, Victor stayed behind after the crew left and walked the exhibition area, slowly and methodically inspecting the site. Yellow pad and pencil in hand, he took notes, stopping sometimes to mark an area on the wall with a piece of blue chalk. For the past few weeks, the inspections had taken longer than usual. This was something else he could blame on the turnover. It was to be expected, but that didn't mean he accepted or appreciated it. He'd always put his crews together carefully, balancing each man's strengths against another's weaknesses, but with so many men leaving there were gaps.

Finally he reached the room he saved for last each night, the room where he'd escaped earlier to take Wyman's call. He sat down on the wooden crate in the center of the round building that would bridge the Islamic and Cypriot exhibition spaces.

Victor put his hand on one of the cold granite blocks. He'd never heard of a sleep temple before this job, but he'd looked them up.

Ruins of these early hospitals had been found in ancient Egypt, the Middle East and Greece. Some dated back as far as four thousand years ago. According to ancient texts, ill and troubled people came here to be healed. Instead of doctors, priests worked with the sick using chants, prayers and mesmerizing objects to focus attention. Once the patients fell into a deep, meditative sleep, the holy men gave them subliminal suggestions. When they awoke, the priests analyzed their dreams and prescribed treatments for ailments—both physical and psychological. It was the earliest known use of hypnosis.

In Greece most of these structures were built in honor of the god of medicine, Asclepius, but there had been a few built to honor Hypnos, the god of sleep. The stones didn't reveal which god this temple had been dedicated to, but the museum planned on installing a sculpture of Hypnos from its own collection.

When Deborah Mitchell, one of the Islamic department's curators, had needed measurements for the statue's base, Victor had been given the rare chance to see the colossal god dating back to the fifth century BCE.

Hypnos was incomplete and stripped of most of his decoration, but Victor was astonished by his power and mesmerized by his still-intact eye, the obsidian orb veneered with ivory and inlaid with moss-green chalcedony. It wasn't quite human, but it seemed alive. Or was it that he felt more alive looking at it?

Deborah had told him that although Hypnos had most likely been created for a sleep temple, it was improbable it had been made for the actual temple they were re-creating. "It would be too much of a coincidence," she had mused, "for them to be reunited two thousand years later, so many thousands of miles from where their journeys began."

But working on the rotunda, Victor had a lot of time to study its proportions and had come to believe the sculpture *might* have been made for this temple. He'd taken measurements to prove his theory and discovered that the stone edifice and the statue were proportionately perfect for each other based on the golden mean—the equation created by the Greek philosopher and mathematician Pythagoras. He hadn't told Miss Mitchell yet, but he planned to soon.

Victor had grown up in a religious household and had been an altar boy, but it wasn't until he started working at the Met that he realized what he loved about going to church wasn't the liturgy or the service or the idea of God. It was the building that made his spirit soar—the towering ceilings, the astonishing stained-glass windows that threw jewel-colored reflections on his hands if he held them out at the right angle, the elegantly chiseled stone ornamentation. He'd never built a church, but he often felt that working at the Met was as good. The galleries here held art created in the name of not just one God, but all gods, both ancient and modern. There was as much that was holy here as in any cathedral.

Out on the street, Victor stopped to light a cigarette. It was a bad habit but one he couldn't quit. Just as he stepped off the curb, a bus pulled out. He didn't see it coming—his eyes had been on the flame igniting the tobacco. As he watched the bus that had come so close to hitting him drive off, he took a deep drag on the smoke, felt the first rush of nicotine surge through him and headed for the subway.

Descending into the subterranean station, Victor pulled his headphones out of his pocket and pushed the buds in his ears. He was listening to a suspense novel by Steve Berry, and he picked up where he'd left off that morning, with the narrator reading a tense scene in a tight voice: *Malone gripped the automatic and waited. He risked one glance around the niche where he and Pam were hiding.*

Walking down the platform, he passed a short woman with strawberry-blond hair who was wearing tight-fitting blue jeans and carrying a designer purse. He stopped a few feet away, where it was empty and quiet.

The shadow continued to expand as the gunman drew closer.

A twentysomething guy was heading Victor's way. There was nothing exceptional about him—baggy jeans, running shoes, laces untied, oversize green T-shirt, some gold chains around his neck, a baseball hat and a knapsack. He stopped near Victor and examined a movie poster on the wall that featured a man standing at a window, holding a gun trained on the viewer. The kid pulled a quarter out of his pocket and started tossing it in the air.

As Victor watched the coin glint in the station's lights, he sensed a slight trembling coming up through the soles of his shoes. He always felt the oncoming train a full minute before he saw its lights.

The kid tossed the coin again, higher this time, and took a small step back to catch it.

In Victor's ears the narrator's voice continued, tense and anxious. *He wondered if his attacker knew there was no exit. He assumed the man did not. Why else would he be advancing? Simply wait out in the gallery.*

Ten feet away, a middle-aged man wearing filthy chinos and a dirty white shirt that had sweat stains in triple rings under the arms ambled toward the end of the platform.

Victor peered into the dark tunnel, watching for that first shimmer from the train's headlights, knowing from the increasing ground tremor that it was imminent.

The kid with the backpack tossed the coin higher this time and almost missed catching it.

The unkempt man who looked as hungry as he looked strung out stopped near the woman wearing the tight jeans.

The glimmer of ambient light far down the tracks appeared. The voice in Victor's ear stressed the hero's tension as he tried to evaluate the danger he was in.

But he'd learned long ago that people who killed for a living were plagued with impatience. Do the job and get out. Waiting only increased the chances of failure.

The train sped closer. Victor leaned forward slightly to see if it was a local or an express, the way he always did.

The kid tossed the coin again just as the man in the khakis lunged for the strawberry-blonde's bag, grabbed it and took off with surprising agility and speed—more like a professional athlete than a mugger.

The kid had thrown the quarter way too high this time. As he stepped back, estimating where it would come down, he wound up in the path of the mugger who, determined to get away, used both of his arms to push through the space between Victor, on the edge of the tracks, and the coin-tossing kid.

Victor felt a sudden, strong push and tried to keep his balance, tried to grab out for something to hold on to, but there was nothing to reach for but darkness. He slipped off the edge of the platform just in time for the train's blunt nose to slam into him. He flew up, still conscious as he rose above the train, and then gravity grabbed hold of him.

The conductor felt the impact and braked immediately. The train had been slowing and came to a full stop just a few feet too late for Victor, who was crushed to death on the tracks while the voice of the narrator continued playing in the dead man's ears.

Witnesses questioned by the transit police that evening were in conflict over what they had seen. The blonde whose bag had been pulled off her shoulder said that she'd been watching the man who took her purse and that he'd slammed into the deceased, clearly by accident.

A businessman wearing a bow tie said that there had been a

third person involved, a kid with a knapsack who had shoved the mugger away and in doing so had pushed him into the man on the edge of the tracks.

There were three other people who had slightly different versions of what had occurred, but none who suggested that the unfortunate incident had been anything but an accident.

The next-day stories in the papers mentioned that Victor Keither left behind a wife of twenty-four years and two sons: a twenty-one-year-old who was going to NYU medical school in the fall and a sixteen-year-old who had always said that when he grew up he wanted to build museums like his father.

They didn't mention that his death now left open the position of foreman on the renovation of the Islamic wing at the Metropolitan Museum of Art.

Chapter

THIRTY-THREE

On Wednesday morning the museum's board of directors were assembled in the conference room around a large oval table made of rare zebrawood and ebony, being briefed by the FBI. At each setting was a Lalique tumbler and water pitcher, an Egyptian cotton napkin, a Limoges plate and Puiforcat silverware. Down the middle of the table were platters of miniature buttery croissants, golden-brown *pains au chocolat* and salvers of fat strawberries, shiny apples and glistening green grapes in arrangements borrowed from the Henri Fantin-Latour still lifes in the galleries below. None of the dozen men and women who comprised the august body of policymakers had yet taken anything to eat—they were all too astonished by what they were hearing.

Tyler Weil, who'd called this emergency meeting, the first of his tenure and the first in the museum's last decade, sat at the head of the table explaining the situation. Doug Comley, in a pressed navy suit, crisp white shirt and carefully knotted striped tie, was on his left, and Lucian Glass, who was unshaven and wearing his usual black jeans and T-shirt and looked even more haggard and exhausted than usual, sat on his right.

"This is going to be an extremely sensitive negotiation, and I wanted you all to understand what we're planning."

"Before we go there, are you saying you haven't even figured out why on earth this lunatic wants to exchange these four masterpieces for a sculpture?" Jim Rand interrupted. He was an impatient man in his seventies who was the CEO of a holding company that owned one of the largest advertising agencies in the world and had donated enough money to the Met in the past five years to have a gallery named after him.

"No one will fault us for making the exchange. The Van Gogh alone is worth a dozen Greek sculptures," Nina Keyes said. The five-carat diamond earrings she wore bounced in sync to the vehemence of her response. "Just give them the sculpture."

"It's not that simple, Nina. If it gets out that we negotiated or capitulated we leave ourselves open and vulnerable to who knows how many more criminals." Hitch Oster was chairman of the board. His father, a real-estate mogul, had been on the board, as had his father before him. There were half-a-dozen old masters that had discreet plaques beneath them that read, "A Gift of Milton Oster." But Hitch wasn't just fulfilling a family tradition. He was passionate about the museum and its holdings and the importance of the institution. "Museums of our caliber—the Louvre, the British Museum, the Uffizi—we're all encyclopedias of art and humanity. We're the crown jewels of civilized nations. We afford everyone of every socioeconomic level the chance to engage with, learn from and be elevated by the objects on display. We do not negotiate."

"Rules will cripple you every time," Nina responded.

"We will get the paintings back without the museum being compromised in any way," Comley said. "And we'd like to fill you in on how we're planning to do that."

"Can't you just legally confiscate them?" Rand asked.

"Why didn't you do that already?" Nina asked. "You said you were with the paintings for twenty minutes."

Lucian stopped himself from massaging his temples. He'd taken some pain pills a few hours ago, but they were wearing off. The headaches were always worse when he was stressed. Or hungry. The fruit looked good, but none of the platters were near him. "We don't just want the paintings. We want the man who spearheaded this effort." He was furious when he thought about what had happened yesterday…*they* should have—no, *he* should have—expected that a man smart enough to get this far would have every contingency covered.

"Are you saying he was able to get the paintings away from a whole team of FBI agents without being followed?" Rand asked dubiously. "How did he do that?"

Lucian explained as succinctly as he could: as he had feared, the agents in the parking garage, in front of the hotel and in the lobby who were waiting for a signal noticed the hotel guest who left, carrying two ordinary suitcases, four-and-a-half minutes before Lucian got back to his room and called to alert them, but they had no reason to be suspicious. Later, on the hotel's video-tape, they were able to watch the muscle man from the upstairs hallway, the elevator, the lobby and out front where the door-man helped him into a taxi. With the suitcases in the trunk, the cab drove off.

"So you didn't get the paintings or a lead on who's behind this?" Rand asked.

"Did this guy just take a chance that there'd be a taxi waiting downstairs?" Hitch asked.

"Probably not. On the tapes we examined there was a car idling in front of the hotel that drove off about sixty seconds after the taxi pulled out. If there hadn't been a taxi just dropping someone off, our suspect would have probably jumped in that car."

"What about that car?" Nina asked.

"The plates were stolen the day before from a Jeep belonging to a lawyer who lives in Santa Monica."

"So basically—" Nina's voice was strained "—you don't know anything really?"

Victims got angry; Lucian was used to it. "We know the paintings are real and that whoever owns them bought them to trade them, which means the owner is probably not a typical collector. We know the governments of Iran and Greece both have requested the return of this same sculpture to their respective countries, making it possible that one of them is behind this. The law firm of Weil, Weston and Young has been engaged by the government of Iran to ensure that the exchange happens, and we have—"

"What the hell?" Rand turned the full force of his ire on the museum's director. "Why didn't we know about that?"

Weil folded his hands on the table as if needing to feel the wood under them. "My office sent each of you a letter to that effect, which you should have received last week. My father and I are not on speaking terms now and haven't been for fifteen years. I only just found out about this myself from the museum's law firm." He spoke with his usual calm, but when he moved his hands, Lucian noticed that there were impressions of moisture where they'd rested.

"Your father's law firm is working for the Iranian government, which is trying to take a famous piece of sculpture away from us? There's a major conflict of interest here," Rand said.

"No, actually, there isn't," Hitch Oster intervened. "Weil's explained that he doesn't have any dealings with the firm, he is not employed by them and doesn't benefit by association with them, and in no way should this impact us or our faith in him. Now," he said, dismissing Rand, whom he clearly didn't have much respect for, and turning to the three men at the head of the table, "how are you going to get us our paintings?"

"I'd like to bring in someone for you all to meet," Lucian said as he got up and walked out of the room.

Deborah Mitchell looked up when the door to the conference room opened and Lucian stepped out.

"They're ready for you," he said.

Chapter

THIRTY-FOUR

"When the physical organism breaks up, the soul survives. It then takes on another body."

—Paul Gauguin

Using a strip of 600-grade sandpaper, Charlie Danzinger smoothed the underside of the sculpture's thigh-length tunic, enjoying the process of putting the finishing touches on his reproduction. This new Hypnos wasn't an exact replica, since a fair amount of the original sculpture was missing, but he'd based his reconstruction on passages from ancient Greek writings describing chryselephantine sculpture of the day.

Stepping back, he examined the piece. In the past week he'd made a lot of progress. Hypnos was only a few days away from completion, and he shone under the incandescent light. The gold and silver glimmered; the emeralds and rubies sparkled; the onyx, carnelian, lapis and other semiprecious stones gleamed. The Greeks who'd once prayed to this god must have been awestruck by his majesty and opulence.

While he worked, Danzinger listened to classical music, but the two brisk knocks that came one after another were loud enough to hear over the Chopin.

"Come in."

Tyler Weil, Deborah Mitchell and Nicolas Olshling walked in, followed by the FBI agent Danzinger had met last week. The restorer's heartbeat kicked up. Other than Marie, he wasn't used to people coming here and didn't like it. This area of the museum was out of the way and except for the other people in the department, there were so rarely interruptions. And Danzinger liked that. Interruptions made him nervous. So did change. Working on timeless art was soothing. Fixing things and making them whole again made him feel whole. Almost.

"We need your help—" Weil began without preamble, but then stopped to look at the sculpture—not the original, but the reproduction. The other two men with him did the same. Even though they'd seen it the week before, Danzinger could tell they were impressed and was pleased that his work elicited this reaction, especially from the director.

A great majority of ancient Greek and Roman sculptures had originally been highly ornamented and bedecked, but what had survived was stripped by time of its adornments and dulled down by the ages. People who didn't know that were often shocked by the replicas that looked almost garish in comparison to the pale museum pieces. If the original Hypnos was a showpiece, the reproduction was an extravaganza.

"That sure is something," Olshling said, understating the obvious.

"You've done a marvelous job," Weil said and gave a long, deep sigh. "I'm afraid this is going to be a very difficult conversation."

What kind of conversation could Weil possibly have with him that would be difficult? Danzinger listed the possibilities. The most logical would be firing him—but the director of the museum wouldn't be the one to do that. Even if under extraordinary circumstances that was to happen, there was no reason he'd bring Olshling or Mitchell or the FBI agent with him, unless they suspected him of something illegal. Danzinger's heart started to pound again even though he knew he was an exemplary employee.

"Let's sit down, can we?" Lucian asked, nodding at a table covered with books and art supplies in the corner of the large studio.

As Olshling sat he nudged a small box of rubies that fell to the floor. The stones rolled, bloodred against the white tiles.

"I'm sorry," the head of security said with concern as he bent and started to retrieve them.

"It's okay. They're just paste," Danzinger explained as he got on his knees and helped.

"Should have realized you wouldn't have a cup of valuable stones sitting out in the open like that," Olshling said as he dropped them back into their container.

"So how can I help you?" Danzinger was anxious to find out what this was all about.

"What we're going to tell you is highly confidential," Lucian warned.

"I told Agent Glass you've been with the museum for over fifteen years and everyone here has the highest regard for you and your work," Weil said.

"Thanks." Now that he knew he wasn't being fired or worse, Danzinger relaxed a bit.

"We're going to need you to do some more work on the Hypnos." Lucian looked from the reproduction to the original, which stood in the opposite corner of the studio, carefully out of the traffic path. "How long will it take you to make the copy resemble the original?"

"The copy? I'm not sure I understand."

"You know about the four paintings we're being offered in exchange for the sculpture?" Weil asked.

Danzinger nodded. "Of course."

"Well, we're going ahead with the trade. We're going to give the Monster the Hypnos. Those paintings are important masterpieces—we have to do what we can to save them."

Looking from the director to the original sculpture and back to his beautiful reproduction, Danzinger realized what they were asking of him. They wanted to make the copy look like the original and then make the trade with the copy. He felt as if he were hearing about a death in his family.

"I can't destroy it," he blurted out.

Weil looked at him with surprise. "I know how hard you worked on it, Charlie, but we need you to do this."

Danzinger didn't trust himself to talk. Not right away. He concentrated on his breathing and then keeping his emotions in check answered the question. "I'm sorry. I can probably get it to the state you want it in less than a week."

"Good. You have three days," Lucian said. "But it doesn't have to be perfect. From what I understand, other than a half-dozen people who work here at the museum, no one has seen Hypnos since sometime in the 1890s, and there's only one photograph from back then, which is in even worse condition than the sculpture. Right?" He looked at Weil and Mitchell, who both nodded.

Danzinger stood quickly, not taking his eyes off his…off the sculpture he'd been working on for six months. His life was restoration. Even though the Hypnos he'd created was just a copy, it was still going to be the most difficult assignment the museum had ever given him. "If I only have three days…" His voice wavered. He cleared his throat. "I'd better get started."

Of all of them, Lucian was the one who seemed the most

sympathetic to what the restorer was facing. Before he left, he
stopped and put a hand on Danzinger's shoulder. "It's a shame.
You've created something astounding. I wish there was another
way for us to do this."

Chapter

THIRTY-FIVE

As Elgin Barindra unfolded the second to last letter in the box, its left corner flaked off and fell onto his lap. Lifting it carefully with tweezers, he placed it on a felt pad. Even if this letter didn't turn out to be written by anyone of importance, he'd have to catalogue the corner, so before he read the missive he glanced at the lower left quadrant of the one sheet and struggled to make out the signature. At first it was unintelligible squiggles and lines, but he kept at it and slowly was able to make out the individual characters.

Dieter M. Loos

The name didn't mean anything to him, but he slipped the corner between two sheets of plastic, tagged it, then did the same to the letter and proceeded to read it through the protective covering.

My Dear Davenport,
I am pleased to respond to your enquiry. Yes, your colleague
Frederick L. Lennox is correct; our society is in possession of
the artifact in question, a copper sheet of ancient Sanskrit
quite impossible to translate. It was given to our founder by

a group of Indian monks in the Himalayas in 1813. Like you,
we believe it is a list of the legendary Memory Tools. I wish
there was something more I could tell you about it that might
help your colleague, but alas, we only know what it is pur-
ported to be.

Please do write and tell me when you and your lovely wife
are returning to Vienna. It would be a pleasure to have a din-
ner in your honor during your stay.
Yours,
Dieter M. Loos

Elgin's pulse raced as he read the letter for a second time.
This was a clear reference to the list of tools that related to the
robbery in Vienna. The fact that it also named an active
member of the original Phoenix Club who had funded dozens
of digs was important, too. There were threads running
through all of this correspondence connecting people, places
and discoveries, but it was taking a long time to unravel them.
With so many boxes still to go through, Elgin felt a twinge of
impatience.

Putting the letter aside, he stood, stretched and walked up
the stairs. He needed to get some fresh air and report in with
Glass or Richmond.

Upstairs in the wide hallway, illuminated by the art glass that
cast a warm yellow glow on the polished wooden parquet floor,
he slowed as he walked by Dr. Samuels's office, listening for any
stray information he might glean, but it was quiet. He was halfway down the passage when he heard footsteps and saw Dr.
Bellmer turn the corner and head in his direction, with a man
by her side. Under other circumstances the stranger wouldn't
warrant scrutiny—medium height, glasses, slacks, blazer and
briefcase—except that Elgin recognized something in the man's

gait, a relaxed way he had of walking as if lights stopped for him and not the other way around.

"Elgin?"

The voice came from behind him, and he spun around. Malachai Samuels was standing in the doorway to his office.

"How's today's mail?"

"I found a very interesting letter that mentioned a list of Memory Tools engraved on copper sheets from ancient India."

Elgin thought he heard one of the sets of footsteps in the hallway slow.

As Malachai ushered the librarian into his office, chastising him about talking in public, Elgin could still hear the conversation in the hall.

"So how have you been, Mr. Ryan?" Dr. Bellmer asked in a concerned voice. "How are the headaches?"

Chapter

THIRTY-SIX

"The soul is not the body and it may be in one body or in another, and pass from body to body."
—Giordano Bruno, Italian philosopher during the Renaissance, sentenced to be burned at the stake by the Inquisition for his teachings about reincarnation.

Lucian withdrew a sketchpad from his briefcase, opened it to a certain page and handed it to Dr. Bellmer.

The doctor examined the old woman's face. "She looks terribly frightened."

"And I'm the one she's scared of. All of them are."

"How do you know?"

"I don't have the faintest idea."

Lucian had finally admitted to himself that he was no longer coming here just to spy on Malachai Samuels's lair. The agency had Elgin Barindra to do that now—and do it much better than he could. From what he'd just overheard, Elgin was making great progress.

"What the hell is happening to me? Isn't it possible I read a book or saw a movie that's inspiring these regressions? Maybe the accident in Vienna did cause some brain damage?" No matter how hard he fought Bellmer's hypnotic suggestions, he'd succumbed every time, and the realism of the episodes that played out in his mind was very disturbing.

"I know how complicated it is to accept for someone as logical as you are, James. But I can't give you the kind of rationale you want. If you can just stick with it a little longer, for a few more sessions, I believe that what we're doing here will ultimately bring you peace and understanding."

"How? Let's say I believe the unbelievable and every one of the women I'm drawing is someone I knew in a past life and mistreated. Even if we find out who they were, what good will that do me now? From what I've been reading about reincarnation and past-life therapy, don't I have to know these women in this life to work out my karmic responsibilities with them?"

"Basic theory suggests that we come back in each life into a circle of souls we've been with before. We don't have to go searching for them. They're the primary reason we were born into these fragile envelopes in this time and place."

"Envelopes?"

"I think of our physical bodies as envelopes. Poor, fragile holders for our real beings—our souls. When we pass on, it's our envelope that's ripped up and thrown away, not our souls. Those move on, find a new envelope, slip inside and start again."

"You're sounding a lot like a preacher."

"Too spiritual? Okay, let me put in it in more scientific terms. We're made of energy. Energy can't be destroyed, only transformed. So what happens to our energy, our potential, when we die? Isn't it possible that it moves from body to body? Deepak Chopra calls it a creative, quantum nonalgorithmic jump and says life doesn't end, can't end, because it never began."

"You're asking me to adopt a new belief system."

"Chopra uses a wonderful analogy. The *you* in your present life, your last life and your next life are all the same—and that *you* is your soul. He says to think of it as water. A drop of rain and a pond are both water, and water doesn't lose its wateriness no matter its form. If it's an ice cube, a drop of dew or the vapor in a cloud, it's still water, beyond beginnings and endings. It's transformations."

"This is all theory. Dreams I don't understand and can't remember wake me up every night and propel me to draw this crap." He kicked the pad Bellmer had returned to him and that he'd put on the floor. It slid across the room. "You said you could help me."

"I can."

"How? With more hypnosis?"

"Yes."

"Does a soul have to be reborn in an infant?"

Iris looked confused by the non sequitur but answered without hesitation. "No, souls can enter a host body that's already been born and settle there. Usually it's a body in a state of unconsciousness, but there have been cases of drug addicts, alcoholics and attempted suicides who've given over their bodies to another soul, and the new entity has gone on to have a productive life."

"Unconscious as in a coma?"

"Yes."

"Why not be reborn in an infant?"

"Sometimes it's because the soul belonged to someone who died before their time, was in the midst of accomplishing something important and is impatient to come back. Is something about this bothering you, James?"

"Not at all. I read something and was curious." He settled back in his seat and in defeat said, "We might as well do this."

There was a frustrated, plaintive quality to his voice that reached Dr. Bellmer. She reacted to this patient more personally than most, almost as if *she'd* known him in another lifetime and had been one of these women he was drawing. She pointed to the spot between his eyebrows with her fingertip and suggested that he focus on his third eye while she talked to him in a voice that she hoped would be soothing.

Once he appeared to be deeply under, she asked him to think back to a time when he knew the woman he'd drawn that morning. When his forehead creased into a frown, she asked him if he'd found her.

"Yes."

"You see her?"

"She's angry."

"Where are you?"

"In the crypt."

"Where is the crypt?"

"In Shush."

She didn't recognize the name. "Where's Shush?"

"Persia."

Persia? Wasn't he in Greece?

"What year is it?"

"1885."

Bellmer felt a jolt. This was a different lifetime. "Can you tell me your name?"

"Serge Fouquelle."

"And what are you doing in Shush?"

"I've been here for two years on an archaeological excavation being financed by my country."

"What country is that?"

"France." He sounded surprised she didn't know.

"Have you made any discoveries?"

"Many…but this one is the most important because it's the first site that I found on my own."

"You must be proud."

He wasn't; he was angry. "This stupid old woman and her husband are trying to stop me from performing my duties and taking what's mine."

"What have you found?"

"A cache of very rare old pieces—jewelry, pottery, serving pieces made out of silver and gold and the pièce de résistance is a rare sculpture. It must be at least fifteen hundred years old and is quite extraordinary. Wooden sculpture usually rots over time, but this piece is intact. Perhaps being buried down here in this cave, it had more of a chance."

"Where are you now?"

"In the crypt. I broke through several weeks ago and have been making preparations to remove these antiques since." He frowned again.

"What's wrong?"

"The couple who live in the house above this place claim all of these pieces belong to them."

"Do they?"

"Of course not. I am not a robber, madame. The minister of culture said that they have rights to the house but not the land itself, and certainly not what is buried beneath it. His position, which I think is well taken, is that these Jews did not bring these treasures here, did not know they were here when they built their house on top of them and so cannot claim ownership, no matter how long they have lived here."

Serge laughed derisively.

"What is it?" Iris asked.

Chapter
THIRTY-SEVEN

Shush, Persia, 1885

"You're on my property." The old man yelled at Fouquelle and waved his fist in his face. "Leave or you will be arrested for looting. My sons are on their way with help. They're bringing the whole ghetto with them. If you don't go, you'll get hurt."

"These give me the right to excavate here," Fouquelle said, offering the second set of official documents that the minister of culture had given him. Hosh had ripped up the first set; he pushed these away, as well.

"This is my property, and I order you to leave. All of you." He pointed to the nether end of the crypt, where Fouquelle's band of Persian workers stood at alert in the flickering lantern light, all of them armed with knives, all focused on the frantic Jew.

"It's you who is the thief," Fouquelle argued, "you who are hiding ancient treasures here that belong to Persia, to history and to mankind."

"Is that what you are going to do with them? Give them to mankind? Or are you going to sell them to collectors in Europe and America? Don't think I'm a fool because I'm old. We all know what happens to the antiquities that are dug up in our land."

Hosh shook his fist in Fouquelle's face. "Whose law? What law takes away a man's property?"

The Frenchman had had enough. He was going to profit greatly from the find and had no time for this feeble old man's argument. Fouquelle's countrymen had been here for years digging up the ancient cities and benefiting from the partage system, and now it was his turn. He'd been promised half of the half France was getting for all his hard work, and he had a wealthy American collector waiting by the docks for these broken shards of pottery and slivers of history.

"Step away, sir," he said. "I would prefer not to hurt you."

Hosh was as immobile as the giant sculpture.

Fouquelle turned to his men. "Move these pieces out of here. Now. You four take the sculpture and try to keep from breaking it. You two, the pottery. The rest of you take the smaller items. And I know exactly what's down here. So if there's anything missing I'll know one of you has it." He turned back to Hosh. "Get out of my way," he shouted, aware he was running out of time. He didn't doubt that the man's sons were collecting a populist army from the ghetto to come and fight the removal of these works of art. Fouquelle wanted to be gone before they returned.

Hosh didn't move. Not a single muscle in his hand or his neck twitched. Not even his eyes blinked.

"For the last time, get out of my way."

Hosh pulled his knife from its sheath. The blade shone in the archaeologist's lamplight.

"Is your life so worthless to you that you would throw it away on these objects?" the archaeologist asked in a gentler tone.

When Hosh didn't answer, Fouquelle nodded at two of his men, who stepped forward. In their eyes was the assuredness of the very young and very strong.

"Get out of our way," the younger of the two Persians said,

each of them taking Hosh by an arm, lifting him and tossing him to the floor.

Fouquelle watched the foolish man get back on his feet. With a burst of anger he lashed out, surprising the Persian on his right and nicking him on the arm with his blade. The wounded man looked down, noticed the trickle of blood and almost casually shoved his knife into Hosh's ribs.

The man staggered and fell. He put his hand up to this chest as if his frail fingers could stop the flow of blood.

Out of the darkness, a bent and wizened woman came rushing at them, shrieking. She threw herself at Fouquelle, beating his chest with her small fists, cursing at him and crying at the same time.

He brushed her off brusquely and gave orders to his men to begin the removal, but the woman righted herself and threw herself at him again, spitting at him and scratching him with sharp, clawlike nails. First he tried to slap her away, and when that didn't work he kicked her. Finally she collapsed, shrieking atop her husband's body.

"Be quiet!" he yelled.

But her wailing only increased. The sound of sustained agony filled the chamber.

Fouquelle's anger was building. Everything depended on his ability to get these treasures out of here before the neighbors arrived and the woman's screams were paralyzing his men.

With a single sharp tug, the archaeologist yanked the knife from Hosh's chest. Hesitating only a moment, the blood still dripping from its blade, he shoved it deep into the woman's back.

"Hurry now. Hurry," Fouquelle bade his men. In silence they set about removing the giant sculpture, the jewelry and the artifacts. The only things they left behind were the two bodies that lay still in the dust and debris of centuries.

Chapter

THIRTY-EIGHT

Balthazar was a large and noisy bistro that could just as easily have been on the boulevard Saint-Germain in Paris as on Spring Street in SoHo. Ali Samimi watched Deborah Mitchell take in the smoke-stained room, bustling waiters and crowded bar, waiting to see if she was pleased or not with his choice.

"Ali, this place is delightful. I can't believe I didn't know about it. I definitely don't come downtown enough."

Samimi smiled and gave his name to the maître d', who showed them a booth in the corner. They slid in and sat on the worn brown leather facing each other across the white tablecloth.

"There were a lot of people waiting. You must come here often," she said, making him happy that he'd used up his lunch hour to come down here and slip the maître d' forty dollars.

"Mostly for breakfast meetings. Lately it seems as if I have been too busy to go out to dinner as much as I would like to." He didn't want her to think he was a player. "Would you like to have a drink? Or perhaps some wine?"

"Wine would be great."

Samimi perused the list, then motioned to the waiter and, when he approached, ordered the Morgon Lapierre 2006. The waiter recited the specials, then left to get the wine, and while Deborah read the menu, Samimi studied her over the rim of his glass. She caught him looking, and a faint blush rose on her cheeks. He smiled in a way that he hoped suggested he found her charming without it being a come-on.

"How is the renovation of the Islamic wing progressing?" he asked.

She shook her head sadly and he almost regretted the question. The last thing he wanted to do was cast a pall on the evening, but he was supposed to find out what was happening inside the museum from the curator's side, not just what they knew from the workmen.

"Did you read about what happened?"

How to answer? He wasn't sure. If he said he had, would he appear too interested in the doings at the Met? "No. I must have missed it. I hope nothing bad?"

"The head of the construction crew was killed."

"What a terrible thing. May I ask how?"

"He fell onto the subway tracks on his way home from work."

"Could it have been a suicide?"

"The police have been investigating and don't think so. I knew him. He was a wonderful man…"

"Was it possible he was pushed? I have heard of people with mental problems doing things like that to perfect strangers."

She shuddered. "Anything's possible."

"I am so sorry for your sadness and loss. How long had he been working for the museum?"

"Technically, he doesn't—didn't—work for the Met but for Phillips Construction. They've done all the renovations at the museum for the past sixty years. He's worked on eight renovations."

"Did Keither have a family?" he asked just as the waiter

returned with the wine and glasses and set to uncorking the bottle. Samimi was furious with himself. How could he slip up like that, using the man's name before she'd said it? Had she noticed? Would she realize it later?

"Yes. Two sons. A wife. I've met them all. The workmen are bereft. Aside from the tragedy, it's also a problem for the museum. No one wants this to slow down the work on the wing, but it's inevitable that it will."

He appreciated that she'd used the word *bereft*. Her intelligence was part of her appeal.

The waiter poured Samimi a taste of the wine. He took a sip and nodded. As the waiter filled both glasses, Deborah and Samimi were quiet for the moment and ambient noise filled the void. The silence between then was neither forced nor uncomfortable.

Once the waiter was gone Samimi picked up his glass and held it out, suggesting a toast. "To the new wing without any more tragedy," he said, keeping the evening on work terms for now.

"Thank you." She took a sip. "Good choice, it's excellent."

He nodded. "I'm glad that you like it."

She put her hand out, resting her fingers on his arm. "Thank you for tonight. It's so nice. I haven't had much of a social life for a while with the renovation going on." She blushed again.

Samimi was touched by the intimate gesture and the words. "My pleasure. And while I'm sympathetic to you working too hard, I must say that I still envy you your job."

"What do you do at the mission? Don't you enjoy it?"

"I do," he said, answering only half her question. "But it's not as esoteric and interesting as your job. To be able to spend your life in the Metropolitan among treasures, masterpieces. No matter how ugly the world gets, you have your refuge."

She seemed to disappear for a moment, and he let her drift, gave her a moment to deal with her thoughts. He was being *sensitive to her needs.* It was an expression one of his first girl-friends in New York had used when he'd asked her what she wanted most from a man. She'd told him it was even more important than how a man performed as a lover. Samimi tried to pick up at least one lesson from each of the women he dated. He'd started out as an awkward rube when he'd first come to New York three years ago, but the last woman he'd bedded had called him *debonair*. He'd had to look up the word but was inordinately pleased by what it meant. Yes, he wanted to be debonair.

"The museum is a refuge, but sometimes that has its downside. You get tricked into believing that there are people devoted to art who aren't all about commerce and power."

"But there are, aren't there?"

She shrugged. "A small handful. Not enough."

"God said one was enough."

"Quoting the Bible?"

"Are you surprised?"

"A little, but I shouldn't be. Please forgive me…you're very well educated and I should have expected you'd have read the Bible."

"Is it impolite for me to ask you where your ancestors were from?"

She laughed. "No, not impolite, but let's talk about the present, not the past. Tell me more about this mysterious man who wants the Met to put his cup on display."

Samimi's father had once told him that nothing was more appealing than a woman who kept secrets. He'd never understood what he meant, but now, sitting across from Deborah, he had his first "aha" moment. This woman probably had a lifetime of disappointments, interests, frustrations and hopes that Samimi couldn't even guess at, and the idea of them fascinated him as much as her full hips, heavy breasts, her dark hair and shyness.

"Have you decided what to order?" the waiter asked, appearing at the table, pad and pen in hand.

While Samimi listened to Deborah order the French onion soup and then the roasted chicken, he wondered if it was a good thing to allow himself to feel anything for her: if the plan failed and they were forced to set off the explosives, he'd be responsible for her death.

Chapter

THIRTY-NINE

"We've found invitations from Trevor and Davenport Talmage to Frederick Law Olmsted, Bronson Alcott, Walt Whitman and other transcendentalists to come and dine in this very room. There is one box with nothing but handwritten menus prepared by the Creole chef who worked for the family for over twenty-five years and thank-you notes for the meals that include references to spirited discussions on ancient reincarnation beliefs. Elgin even found the bill for our Tiffany wisteria chandelier." Malachai Samuels glanced up at the lavender and green stained-glass lamp. "The entire history of our first hundred years is chronicled in the correspondence."

Once a week the senior staff of the Phoenix Foundation met for lunch to discuss their patients, share insights and keep abreast of developments in the field. Now, as Malachai continued to describe the new librarian's discoveries, Iris Bellmer and Beryl Talmage listened and ate the sesame chicken salad that had been served with soft potato rolls and tall glasses of lemon-and peach-infused iced tea.

"We have the receipts for everything in this room," he said, gesticulating toward the matching stained-glass windows on either side of the fireplace. Also created by Tiffany, the jeweled interpretations of an elaborate trellis intertwined with more wisteria prevented anyone outside from looking in but allowed for soft daylight to filter in, casting the room in a luminous old-world glow. "You know, if not for our clothes we could be sitting here in 1889. It's not only the visible aspects of the room that have changed so little but we lament the same issues that plagued our intellectual ancestors. According to the letters, they also debated how best to present their astounding findings to the public and scientific societies in order to be taken seriously."

Olga, the woman who cooked their lunch every day and kept the kitchen stocked, came in and removed their plates. Malachai was still talking about Elgin's discoveries when Olga returned with a silver coffee service and plate of cookies. As Beryl poured for each of them the conversation moved on to a discussion of their individual caseloads, starting with Iris, who began by talking about James Ryan.

"I'm convinced that each of the women he's drawing is someone he harmed in a previous life."

"How many lives have you touched on?" Beryl asked.

"So far two."

"And how do they relate to his drawings?"

Iris recounted the story James had told her about Telamon and then moved on to Fouquelle. "He discovered a cache of treasures under a home in the Persian ghetto in the late 1880s and was responsible for the death of the man who owned the house and his wife. He killed her himself."

Malachai pushed his coffee cup away and the china clattered noisily. "In Persia?"

"Yes. Shush."

"Are you sure?"

"What is it?" Beryl asked her nephew.

Malachai was leaning toward Iris. "This story that James Ryan told you about the old man and his wife in the crypt. Did he tell you their names?"

"Yes, they were—"

"Wait," Malachai interrupted. From the inside pocket of his jacket, he withdrew a silver and lacquer pen, uncapped it and wrote down two words on a pad by his place setting.

"What are you doing?" Beryl asked.

"I don't want there to be any questions afterward about who said what and when they said it." Tearing off the sheet, Malachai folded it and handed it to his aunt.

Malachai looked back at Iris. "All right. What were their names?"

"Hosh and…"

"Bibi," Beryl read the name Malachai had just written at the same time as Iris said it.

"How did you know?" Beryl asked.

Malachai stood up, walked over to the window and stared into the glass that offered no view. In his calm, elegant voice, he proceeded to tell the two women about Nina Keyes's granddaughter, the seven-year-old who had been coming to see him since Beryl had asked him to take on her case a few weeks before.

"She has a lot of unresolved guilt about what happened to her in her previous life when she was a Jewish woman living in Persia with her husband and four sons. They had a crypt under their house full of ancient treasures her husband's family had safeguarded for centuries."

"Are you saying…" Iris asked, incredulous, "that in a past life your patient was a woman killed by a man who in this life is my patient?" She shook her head. "It's not possible, is it?" She looked over at Beryl.

"Why not? We come back in the same soul circles." Beryl poured herself more coffee. "So you each have patients who were connected in a prior life. This will make for an amazing case study but brings up a few ethical issues."

Malachai glanced over at her warily. "Let's table the ethical issues for the moment. This is an astonishing development. Our patients aren't just connected, Beryl. The archaeologist killed Bibi and was responsible for her husband's death."

No one spoke for a moment. Then Malachai asked, "Do you know his name, Iris?"

"His name is James Ryan."

"His name in his past life. Did he tell you the archaeologist's name?"

Chapter
FORTY

Lucian opened the door. Emeline was wearing jeans and a white boat-necked T-shirt that had slipped off one shoulder, leaving it bare and making her look more vulnerable than sexy. Her eyes seemed bigger than usual, and the circles under them were too deep. Her pale blond hair was pulled back in a ponytail and wisps had escaped, falling around her face, which was even paler than he remembered. She looked as stressed as she'd sounded on the phone a half hour before when she'd called and asked if she could please come over and talk to him, just for a few minutes.

Only after he'd closed the door behind her and she was standing inside did he realize she was carrying a package: a rectangle about eighteen inches wide by two feet long, wrapped in brown paper.

She walked into his large, sparsely decorated loft and gravitated to the table where his sketchpads, cans of pencils and piles of drawings were.

"I didn't know you still painted," she said.

"Still?"

"My father told me he'd read you quit school after the accident."

"I don't paint anymore. Do you want something to drink?"

"A glass of wine?"

"Red or white?"

"Whatever's open."

In the kitchen he poured two glasses of red and when he returned, saw she'd put the package down beside the table and was looking at the drawings he'd done early that morning.

"Here you go," he said, offering her a glass.

She took it, thanked him and then said, "I'm sorry, I didn't mean to snoop."

He smiled, shrugged. "My fault for not putting them away."

"Who are these women?"

"My nightmares."

Emeline searched his eyes. "What do you mean?"

He led her to the couch, where they sat down and he told her about his trip to Vienna, the attack, its aftermath and the dreams that woke him up, surprising himself that he was revealing so much. He'd only shared one part of the story with Dr. Bellmer, and a different part of it with Doug Comley. She was the first person he'd told everything to.

While Emeline listened, she nodded every few minutes and took sips of her wine. When he got to the part about seeing a therapist and trying to access his unconscious to find the women there, she took his hand. He wasn't sure when it happened, but there was a moment when he was a separate individual talking to her and then he was connected to this ethereal woman who was, without even saying a word, offering a level of understanding unlike anything he'd known in too long a time.

"Do you believe what you've found out in the sessions?"

"I've racked my brain thinking about every book I've ever read and every movie I've seen—trying to remember where I first heard the stories my unconscious is offering up."

"You want that badly not to believe it?"

"You've had to deal with the same thing, and you haven't wanted to believe it either, have you?"

"Something has always stopped me. There's a leap of faith I just can't seem to make. The ramifications if it's true…I don't know…" She reached up and brushed her hair off her face. For a moment Lucian could see her scar, and then her hair fell back across her forehead and it was hidden again. "What I did… running away from you in the park the other day…it was very childish. I'm sorry."

"Don't let it bother you."

"But it does. I wanted you to kiss me. I wanted everything that happened. It just seemed as if…I'm not sure…I got scared. I never get scared. But nothing is the same anymore."

"It's all right. You've been bombarded with bullying e-mails, there's a chance someone is following you…you don't have to explain anything to me. I know how stressful and frightening the threat of danger can be. At least Broderick finally okayed the detail and you're under police protection now. They downstairs?"

She nodded. "My shadow army? Yes. And thank you. But none of that is an excuse."

"I think it is."

"Lucian, do you think I'm Solange? That her soul is in me?" Her voice was on the edge of cracking.

"I don't know," he said finally.

"That's the best you can do?" She laughed. But it was a weak sound without any joy. In that moment everything about her looked breakable, and he had to hold back from reaching out for her.

"I've seen the wish for the reincarnation to be real in Andre's eyes so often that I've wanted it to be true so I could bring back whoever he'd been before the accident. I've only seen a shimmer of that man, and only for a few seconds at a time. He rescued me…I wanted to rescue him…him and my aunt—" She broke off.

"But what do you believe?"

"I know things that I can't possibly know. I know about you…" She was whispering, and when he leaned forward so he could hear her better he smelled her scent, vanilla with a twist of amber. Her lower lip was trembling and another lock of hair had fallen into her face. Reaching up, he moved the hair away from her eyes, this time not noticing the scar as he kissed her. He wasn't thinking about who she was or wasn't; only that she was someone he wanted to be with, someone he shared the unknown with.

When Emeline pulled away she was almost smiling. She reached out for the package and handed it to him. "This is for you."

Ripping away the brown paper, Lucian looked down at a painting in a simple black matte wood frame, and the memory came back to him as sharp as a slap. It was the day before Solange had been killed. They'd spent the night together and he'd woken up with her smell all over him to find her standing behind his easel. He'd done a dozen portraits of her, but this was the first time she'd tried to paint a portrait of him. Not at all a realist, Solange created lush, dreamlike landscapes and was struggling to capture him. She had paint on her face and hands and in her hair and was clearly frustrated. He'd laughed at how hard she was trying and she got angry with him. They'd had an argument over him not taking her efforts seriously, and he'd spent a good part of the morning trying to talk his way out of his faux pas.

She'd only gotten it started that morning, and he hadn't realized what she was trying for—but now he understood.

Solange must have gone back to her apartment and worked on it all that night.

It was a portrait of his sleeping face layered with a dreamscape of a dark green-black forest that melded into a blue-black sky illuminated by a crescent moon. A double exposure that was beautiful, disturbing and deeply moving.

"You never saw it finished," Emeline said. Not a question, a statement.

"How do you know that?"

She shrugged and the lamplight danced on her skin. "A guess. It was in her room on an easel. Everything in her room was left the way it was that day. Did you know that? They didn't touch anything. It wasn't until my mother killed herself, in Solange's room, by the way, in her bed, that I finally got Andre to agree to let me have it cleaned out, redecorated."

"But how did you know I never saw it finished?"

She shook her head. "I…I don't know."

He took a long look at the painting and then turned back to her. "Why are you giving me this?"

"You almost died that night, too, didn't you? Andre never told me. I found some old newspaper articles online and read about it."

"For a long time afterward I wished I had."

"I felt like that, too, when I was in the hospital. I didn't understand what death was, but I wanted to stay in that place," she said softly. "You've never really stopped missing Solange, have you?"

He wasn't looking at the painting anymore, but at Emeline. "I'm not sure I knew this before now, but what I thought was missing her has really been missing the part of me that loved her like that."

Leaning forward, he kissed Emeline again. She let the kiss

continue and continue, and after a time he pulled down the shoulder of her T-shirt and kissed her there and then pulled it up and over her head and then he undid her ponytail so that her hair spilled over her shoulders.

She sat naked from the waist up, looking at him with a sad expression in her eyes. "I know what you want and I want it, too, but please, don't do this unless you're sure it's me you want," she said.

"You think I'm looking for someone else inside you, but I'm not, Emeline." He tilted her face up so their eyes met. "I'm just looking for you."

She smiled but he could still see she wasn't sure. Trust took time. He understood that. Lucian picked up her T-shirt and handed it to her. "But we'll wait until that question doesn't even enter your mind."

Chapter

FORTY-ONE

During the flight to Los Angeles, Nicolas Olshling watched movies on one of the portable DVD players the steward handed out while Lucian spent most of the time sketching, not as much because he wanted to as because he felt compelled to. Without his choosing which of the women to draw, it was the old woman from Persia and the young woman from ancient Greece who accompanied him on this trip. It made sense: these two were tied to each other. Across centuries and long distances, both were connected to the statue of Hypnos.

Lucian knew from his extensive reading on the subject and what Dr. Bellmer had reiterated that there are no coincidences in reincarnation. We're given a chance to get our actions right every time we come back, a chance to finally learn our lessons and the lessons of the universe.

If he accepted that, then he'd be able to accept that he was working on a case involving a sculpture that he might have interacted with in two past lives—a piece of art connected to the deaths of two women, Iantha and Bibi. Two deaths he—or whoever he'd once been—had been responsible for.

And if Lucian didn't accept it? Then his unconscious had

creatively used the case he was working as a springboard into fantasy. That was the much more likely scenario; it was both credible and logical. Except that presented a conundrum: if he didn't trust what was happening in Dr. Bellmer's office then he couldn't trust that Emeline was the host for Solange's reincarnated soul. Either regression was possible or it wasn't, and for different reasons he was as desperate to believe it was as he was to believe the opposite.

A little more than five hours after the plane took off from New York's Westchester County Airport, Lucian looked at his watch as the wheels touched down. 8:40 p.m. Eastern Standard Time. He never changed his watch when he traveled out of his time zone.

The Matisse Monster had stipulated a six-o'clock meeting, which gave them twenty minutes to unload the crate. "Not bad timing, despite the traffic delay leaving Manhattan," he said to Olshling as the plane taxied toward an oversize hangar.

Lucian hadn't requested a representative from the museum, but they'd insisted. Someone from the staff always accompanied artwork when it traveled to and from another institution for shows—or, in this case, for use as currency.

There was high security in place inside the hangar, including four fully armed guards, two of whom held lean, muscular German shepherds on short leads.

"Full court press," Lucian said.

"Every shipment from the Met gets this greeting."

As they started to disembark, one of the shepherds growled and his handler said a few sharp words.

"Damn, I told them no dogs," Olshling said under his breath.

"I've known you for a long time, but this is news to me. You have a problem with shepherds or all dogs?" Lucian asked.

"Any dog whose teeth are bigger than mine."

The wooden crate was in midair, on its way down, when Lucian's phone rang at exactly 6:00 p.m., 9:00 Eastern.

"James Ryan here," Lucian answered in a clipped, clear voice.

"Code word Klimt. Where are you?" It sounded like the same man who'd called Tyler Weil in New York to set up the exchange. Lucian knew they'd never get a trace on the call. Not even the Matisse Monster could defeat the location-tracking capability of a cell phone unless he was on a virgin line that had never been used before to accept any incoming calls. And so far that was just what he'd done.

"In the hangar at LAX."

"At VIP courier?"

Lucian had advised Olshling to arrange this delivery the way he arranged any transport—use the same courier service and work with them the same way. Do nothing out of the ordinary. So it was no surprise that the man on the other end of the phone knew the name of the courier.

"Yes."

"In about five minutes two trucks will pull up in front of the hangar. If anyone is standing outside other than you, they'll keep going. Do you understand?"

"Yes."

"Please open the crate. Have the man driving the forklift bring it outside, leave it on the lift, leave the lift running and go back inside. We have someone on one truck who will take care of inspecting and loading the sculpture."

"Not until I've seen the paintings."

"Impatient?"

"No, cautious."

"We'll deliver the paintings to the hangar after we've inspected the sculpture."

"I'm sorry, I can't let you have it before I look at the paintings and ascertain that they are the same ones I saw last week."

"You're going to have to."

"I have strict instructions from the director of the Met. The museum is going against years of policy by negotiating with you at all. If you want the sculpture, I need to see the paintings first. Keep the second truck away. Just send the first—the one with the paintings. If I see two I won't come out."

"Be outside in five minutes, alone, with the forklift and the sculpture with the crate open," the man on the other end of the phone reiterated, and then hung up.

Olshling, who'd picked up most of what was going to transpire from what he could hear of the one-sided conversation, asked, "What do you think he'll do?"

"He'll let see me see the paintings. He wants this sculpture much too badly to risk losing it now."

"As long as he doesn't think to look for the tracking device."

"It would take hours for him to find it and he can't afford to take hours. He's got to get it and get out."

Wasting no more time, Olshling issued orders, and in less than five minutes the open crate was on the forklift and outside. Two minutes after that, all the workmen from VIP and the guards were back inside the building. Six seconds later, the doors to the hangar slammed shut with a metal boom.

Lucian was now standing alone, outside in the late-afternoon Los Angeles sunshine, next to a crate that dwarfed his six-foot-two frame. Almost immediately he spotted a single FedEx van heading his way. When it stopped in front of him, a uniformed driver hopped out.

"Mr. Ryan?" he asked in an easygoing voice as if he were there to pick up an ordinary package.

"Yes."

"Come with me."

Lucian followed him around to the back of the truck, judging which of his bulges were muscle and which might be concealed weapons, so he could be prepared. He knew that Matt Richmond and half-a-dozen local FBI agents were strategically placed on the tarmac with long-range rifles ready to shoot out the truck's tires if Lucian got in and it took off while he was still inside, but ultimately he knew he could rely only on himself.

After opening the double doors, the driver gestured to Lucian, who climbed in, where a second FedEx man sat on a jump seat. Beside him was a stack of four crates.

Behind Lucian, the doors banged shut.

"You have ten minutes," the FedEx agent said gruffly.

"I need more time than that just to open the crates."

"They're already open."

As Lucian pulled out the first painting—the Klimt—and as he began inspection of the painting, he made a slight clucking sound with his tongue against the roof of his mouth, the way James Ryan always did when he scrutinized artwork.

"The light in here is terrible," he said as he held a magnifying glass up to the painting's surface. "Can you open the doors?"

"No can do."

"Well, I can't do my job if I can't see better than this."

"I'm not in charge. Just following orders."

"I'd appreciate it if you would call whoever is in charge and tell them I need more light."

The FedEx agent didn't make a move.

Lucian pulled the second painting out of its crate. It was the Renoir. He was still examining thirty seconds later when the agent said, "We've gone past your time, Mr. Ryan."

"I need more light and I need more time. Call your boss. I'm not going to work against some arbitrary time clock."

This time the FedEx agent did pull out his cell phone. While he made his call, Lucian continued examining the Renoir, slowly, methodically, as if his life depended on his opinion of this painting being correct.

"My boss says it's too bad, but you're out of time," the FedEx man said, still holding the phone up to his ear.

"Let me talk to him," Lucian said tersely, frowning with indignation.

"He wants to talk to you, he says—" Whoever was on the other end must have interrupted, because the man abruptly handed Lucian the phone.

"Hello?"

"Mr. Ryan, I said you could have ten minutes. You've taken fifteen."

"The light in this truck is deplorable. You're asking me to verify that these are the same paintings I saw in the hotel with unlimited time and under much better conditions."

"I'm a man of my word. On my family's honor, those are the same paintings you saw in the hotel."

On my family's honor? That was a phrase you didn't hear often from a criminal, Lucian thought. "I need more time."

"My man has instructions to escort you from the vehicle in five minutes. It's up to you whether you go with or without the paintings. If you aren't sure they are authentic, leave them and take my sculpture back to New York. But understand I'm not going to make this offer again. What is it, Mr. Ryan? Are you going with or without the paintings?"

Chapter
FORTY-TWO

It was late, and Elgin Barindra should have already left the Phoenix Foundation. He only had a few more letters left in this box and was ready for the next discovery. He'd become fascinated by the world unfolding in the missives. New York City at the turn of the century was a rich stage for the spiritualists, philosophers and scientists involved in the Phoenix Club. For someone who loved history as much as Elgin, the hours he'd spent poring over these century-old letters was less like work than an indulgence. He was, in fact, spending so much time down in the subbasement immersed in the correspondence from people long since dead that he often found himself slightly dazed when he left the nineteenth-century Queen Anne–style building and exited into the midst of the bustle and commotion of the present day.

His favorite letters were those Trevor Talmage's wife sent her husband while he was on archaeological digs. Sarah Talmage reported on their children, Esme and Perry, in so much detail and with such love that there were moments Elgin was almost positive he could hear a boy and girl playing in the next room, or thought he'd caught a glimpse of them running down one of the hallways upstairs, *roughhousing*, as their mother referred to it in her letters.

When he came across a black-bordered letter expressing sorrow over the death of Trevor Talmage, Elgin felt grief that turned to anger when he learned, in yet another condolence note, that Trevor had been murdered by an intruder in this very building and found by his wife and children when they came home from seeing a musical. He became first indignant and then suspicious when he read about the scandal that ensued when Trevor's younger brother, Davenport, took over the club and married his brother's widow only eleven months later.

None of today's letters had either progressed the story of the lives of those who lived in the townhouse or shed any more light on the mysterious Memory Tools, and he'd reached the bottom of the box. There were only two envelopes left.

He picked up one, opened it, pulled out a sheet of thick, creamy paper and recognized the by now familiar signature of Frederick L. Lennox, a regular correspondent of both Talmage brothers. There were already two dozen letters from the financier and art collector; this would make the twenty-fifth.

Dear Davenport,

I am fairly certain that I have found the pot of gold at the end of the proverbial rainbow. It turns out to actually be made of gold and silver and ivory and several kinds of precious stones. Serge Fouquelle, an archaeologist who has been working for Marcel and Jeanne Diolafoa in Persia, specifically in Shush, on the ancient site of Susa, has just completed his first excavation on his own and has made a curious discovery; he's found a cache of Greek treasures that date back to the time of Pythagoras and might have connections to the great philosopher. All the signs point to it. As I write this, Fouquelle is travel-

*ing to New York and bringing with him a colossal sculpture
of a Greek god that I am purchasing. Based on all the legends,
this could very well be the receptacle for one of our fabled
Memory Tools.*

*I plan to do something noble with the sculpture itself once
I have rescued what it hides, perhaps offer the giant to the new
museum. Goodness knows, from Fouquelle's description, I
don't have a suitable place for it.*

*But what matters most is that now I may finally be able to
prove reincarnation and by doing so prove that my son Albert's
soul has indeed migrated into the new child my wife and I
have been blessed with.*

Yours,

Frederick L. Lennox

"I didn't know you were still here," Malachai Samuels said.

Elgin was startled and not for the first time. The co-director
of the foundation moved around stealthily, almost slithering,
the agent thought. Raising his left hand, Malachai glanced at
his wrist. "It's already nine."

"I didn't realize it had gotten that late," Elgin said, honestly
surprised.

"That must be very interesting."

"Every letter is…they make the past seem so close."

Malachai nodded as if he understood exactly what his librarian meant as he sat down and began reading the missive.

It was so quiet in the subbasement, Elgin could hear
Malachai's wristwatch ticking. Looking over, he noted that the
square mother-of-pearl face had oversize black Roman nu-
merals and fittings that had to be platinum because it was un-
likely Malachai would wear ordinary stainless steel. This must
have been the seventh or eighth watch he'd seen the reincar-

nationist wear. Nothing about him escaped the librarian's notice. That was his job, to pay attention to everything Malachai said or did and never forget that the man sitting next to him was most probably a ruthless criminal responsible for multiple robberies and the deaths of at least five people.

Malachai let out a long, slow breath.

"Is it something important?" Elgin asked, trying for a believable mixture of professional interest and personal detachment.

"One of the most fascinating aspects of reincarnation theory is the concept of coincidence. Are you familiar with it?"

Elgin said he wasn't and sat back in anticipation of Malachai's explanation. The possibility that this man might be a criminal didn't stop him from being interested in what the reincarnationist knew.

"Nothing is an accident or a coincidence, according to past-life theories that go back though history, through the centuries, circling through cultures. If we were in the East, being skeptical about these moments that seem to be part of a bigger plan would be as unusual as questioning the wetness of water." A look of delightful anticipation sparkled in his dark eyes. "You finding this letter now…" Unlike other people, when Malachai smiled, his expression was always framed by mystery. "You finding this letter now," he repeated, "is nothing short of astonishing, Elgin."

Chapter
FORTY-THREE

The rest of the operation took less than ten minutes. As the first FedEx truck drove off, a second, twice as big, drove up. The courier who climbed out immediately set to inspecting Hypnos. Seventy-four seconds after he started he signaled to his crew. One man jumped up on the forklift. Another opened the van's door.

"We have someone watching," the courier told Lucian. "If you don't want anything to happen to you, you'll wait here until we're out of sight before you go back inside."

Lucian assumed the man was bluffing. Even if the Matisse Monster had positioned someone at the airport, the local FBI agents would have found him by now and would have a long-distance, high-range rifle trained on him.

As soon as the truck was a few hundred feet away, Lucian sprinted back to the hangar. "Let's get going," he shouted to the agents inside as he flung the doors open.

Everyone came to life. Olshling and three agents ran outside to retrieve the crates. A waiting black sedan revved its engine. Matt Richmond opened the car door and Lucian jumped in. As the driver drove out of the hangar and took off, Lucian turned around and watched Olshling supervising the crew loading the paintings into the belly of the cargo plane. Lucian couldn't allow himself any satisfaction; the game wasn't over yet. Retrieving the paintings was certainly important—to the Met it was all that mattered—but the FBI wanted the extortionist, the fences and the actual thieves. Only putting the whole crime ring behind bars would satisfy them. But only finding out who had killed Solange would fully satisfy Lucian.

"The signal is great," said Richmond, pointing to the red blip on the GPS screen that represented the FedEx truck.

"I know it's a long shot, but were they able to pick up anything from all those phone calls?" Lucian asked his partner without taking his eyes off the screen.

"No." Richmond shrugged. "But if this signal holds that won't matter. You did good."

Once Charlie Danzinger had finished destroying the Hypnos reproduction—stripping the gold and silver, ripping out all but a few of the semiprecious stones, artificially aging the wood and turning the gleaming Greek god into a ruined hint of what it had once been—Lucian had spent an hour alone with the sculpture.

Opening the back door, which itself was five feet tall and two-and-a-half feet wide, he'd entered a space big enough for him to stand in. Inspecting the sculpture's guts, he pored over its internal construction, examining the curved wooden ribs that made up the armature. It was an engineering marvel, as beautiful in its own way as the exterior. Running his fingers over the walls, he'd searched for a joint where he might be able to insert the GPS tracking device, a state-of-the-art piece of electronics the size of a pea. A crisscross of wooden slats and supports up near the statue's shoulder proved ideal, and he'd affixed it to the back of one of the slats. Then, using stains, he'd mixed up a mound of putty, matched it to the wood and covered the device with it.

Later, he'd asked his boss to step inside the statue and see if he could find the device. After a half hour, Doug Comley had given up. Not someone who took failure well, for the rest of that day he'd been out of sorts and annoyed. It probably hadn't been Lucian's smartest political maneuver.

The sculpture's signal stayed strong for the next forty-five minutes, and they followed it onto I-405 N toward Santa Monica and then onto US-101 N toward Ventura. At the Ojai exit, the blip veered off the highway. Fifteen minutes later it stopped on what appeared to be a rural road. They were one hour and thirty-eight minutes away from LAX. The Lake Casitas Recreation Area was the closest named location on the navigational system, and it didn't mean anything to any of them.

"Where the hell are we?" Richmond asked as he looked out at the mountainous expanse surrounding them. Born in Brooklyn, Richmond had never lived anywhere but New York City except for the months he spent training at Quantico—which, legend had it, had been an ordeal for him but a bigger ordeal for those around him. He claimed he needed concrete under his soles and bus exhaust in his lungs.

"Nature, Matt. It's called nature," Lucian said.

"Lovely. Now let's collect our friend Hypnos and get back to civilization."

Activating his radio, Lucian checked in with the backup teams. Eight men in three cars were all less than five minutes away. He suggested that they park around the last bend and proceed on foot in case they were being watched. He and Richmond were going ahead. During the call, he never took his eyes off the red dot that identified the position of the transmitting device he'd affixed inside of Hypnos.

Forgoing the open road, Lucian and Richmond trudged through an abutting orange grove and eight minutes later came to a rise. Below them a complex of buildings that seemed to have sprouted out of the rocks, trees, hills and earth spread out over fifteen or twenty acres.

"There's not much activity down there," Richmond said after a minute of observation. "Whatever it is seems shut down for the night."

The area did seem deserted. Lucian counted a dozen buildings, ranging in size from midsize homes to airplane hangars. The stunning architecture incorporated long, low, horizontal lines, strongly projecting eaves and cantilevered balconies. "Let's see how close we can get," he said.

They climbed down the incline and hurried through another grove of orange trees and onto the complex grounds without encountering any kind of gate or fence. Checking his GPS device again, Lucian pointed to a bungalow set off to the side among a copse of eucalyptus trees. "According to St. Christopher here, the statue is in the farthest building to the right, back there."

Years ago Doug Comley had named the first directional signal device he'd used St. Christopher, after the patron saint of travelers, and ever since then his team all used the moniker.

"Hey, Gary, how many people can you see inside?"

Gary Fulton, one of the L.A. team members, studied his P3 mobile remote sensing system. The size of a cell phone, it used microwaves to see through walls. "Looks like there are five people inside."

"When there's a will… Let's go do this," Richmond said in his signature upbeat style. He annoyed some of the other agents with his irrepressible optimism, but never Lucian, who appreciated Matt's energy and relied on this clear-thinking man who believed they were a team of supermen who could overcome any obstacle.

Seven minutes after instructing two of the backup teams to position themselves around the building and the third to prepare to go into the bungalow with them, Lucian and Richmond reached the driveway, where the large FedEx truck was indeed parked. Stealthily, Lucian worked his way around it, his gun drawn, while Richmond and the agents who'd just arrived on the scene provided lookout.

The vehicle was unattended and empty. The GPS had indicated the sculpture was inside the building; now Lucian was certain it was.

He made it back around to Richmond and the rest of the team and cocked his head toward the building. It was time to proceed.

Golden light streamed down from skylights illuminating a reception area with an unattended desk and a half-dozen expensive-looking chairs set against the walls. According to St. Christopher's blinking red dot, they were right on top of the signal. Deep inside the building and to the right, they could hear the murmur of voices and followed them down a wide, carpeted hallway. They'd passed three empty offices by the time they reached an atrium with a double-height ceiling that appeared to be an informal conference room with two exits. The murmurs that had led them here had ceased, and the GPS couldn't zero in any more precisely on the location of the sculpture within the building itself. They were on their own now, working blind. Richmond pointed to first one door and then to himself, and then the other door and then to Lucian, indicating that they should split up.

Behind them a voice boomed out.

"Hands up. You're trespassing."

Chapter

FORTY-FOUR

Even with a gun in hand, the guard didn't have a chance; he was outnumbered and he found out just how outnumbered pretty fast. Lucian and Richmond spun around, Glocks pointed at him while Jeffries came from one side to grab his pistol and Agent O'Hara came at him from the other and wrestled him to the ground.

Just steps behind the first guard, a second guard ran in.

Right into the four FBI agents who were ready for him.

Sellers and Jeffries cuffed both men's hands and feet. O'Hara taped their mouths shut. But what to do with them? Lucian couldn't waste a man to stay with them. He motioned instructions to Sellers. A gun was better at herding than a dog any day, and with incentives at their back, the two men shuffled obediently along.

The first door Lucian tried led to an empty kitchen. The second led to a dimly lit room with dark gray walls and a dozen black leather lounge chairs set up in rows facing a movie screen almost too large for the space. There, two men in FedEx uniforms wielded crowbars and hammers as they worked at prying open the large wooden crate that had come out of the belly of the courier plane a few hours before.

"FBI," Lucian called out. "Drop your weapons. You're under arrest for trafficking in stolen goods."

"We don't have any weapons," one of the FedEx men called out, and then dropped the tools.

The second did the same.

"Down, now. On the floor." Lucian's words shot out like rapid gunfire. "Hands behind your back."

Both FedEx men dropped down and in doing so revealed a third man, who had been standing slightly behind them and out of view. He was well over six feet tall with black hair threaded with silver strands that shone in the indirect light. His eyes were light gray and looked almost like steel as he turned his gaze on the troupe of agents that had just invaded his space. The surprise in his eyes turned to indignation.

"You are trespassing."

The same instincts that enabled Lucian to identify the authenticity of a painting in a few seconds informed him he was looking at the Monster who had defaced the Matisse painting and had been negotiating with Tyler Weil and the Metropolitan Museum.

"Step away, please, sir," Lucian ordered.

The man remained where he was.

"You're under arrest for trafficking in stolen goods. You can make this as easy or as hard as you want. It's up to you."

"Stolen goods? I'm afraid you're wrong." The man glanced back at the partially opened crate and as Lucian approached he could see an emotion in the silver eyes he recognized immediately—longing. "This was a very fair trade."

"Holy shit, Lucian," Richmond said under his breath. "Don't you know who he is?"

Lucian had no idea. "What's your name, sir?"

"Darius Shabaz," he said, pride evident in every syllable.

Shabaz? Lucian pictured a cobalt-blue sky with white clouds, heard a clap of thunder and saw the emerald letters appearing on the movie screen in his mind as, with each flash of lighting, the letters burned and built into the completed logo: Sha... Shabaz... Shabaz Productions.

This was who had devised the exchange of the sculpture for the four paintings? The movie producer?

Lucian pulled out a pair of handcuffs. What was going on? He ran through a dozen scenarios. Could Shabaz have had something to do with Solange's murder? Was he somehow connected to Malachai? The only parts of the puzzle that now made sense were all the professional disguises—the men in the Los Angeles hotel room, the fake FedEx trucks, the choreographed action.

"Darius Shabaz, you are under arrest," Lucian intoned. Shabaz remained still but bowed his head as if in prayer, his posture slumped and his shoulders rounded as if hearing his name had broken something in him.

Lucian was only two feet away from the producer when he felt the floor tremble, saw the walls shake and heard a deep rumbling.

"It's an earthquake!" Shabaz yelled out, as Lucian, Richmond and the three FBI agents fell into a wide crack that had opened up in the floor.

Chapter

FORTY-FIVE

But it wasn't an earthquake at all. The backup teams positioned in the groves of trees just beyond the bungalow heard a rumble, yet the ground they stood on remained still. Just yards away, hundreds of twelve-inch-wide slats of aluminum rose from the ground. In less than twenty seconds, a massive steel fence cut off the building they'd just been staring at. The structure was now hidden from sight. And so was the rest of the compound.

Once the trembling earth had quieted and he could hear the crazy cries of birds reacting to the unnatural occurrence, Special Agent Gary Fulton approached the fence cautiously, gun drawn, aware that if someone had gone to all the trouble of creating a metal moat, they might also have set up booby traps in the ground.

He reached it without incident and inspected the overlapping slats. There were no toeholds. No way they'd be able to scale the smooth wall. Even if they built a ladder of human rungs and they could get an agent to the top, how would he drop down inside?

Running alongside it, Fulton couldn't see an end to the curving metal wall. How much of the compound was cut off?

There was no time to find out. No time to dig under the fence and tunnel in. He and his men needed to reach the

building where Glass and Richmond, Sellers, O'Hara and Jeffries were prisoners.

Fulton got on his radio and called for help. He needed a
chopper and he needed it fast.

Chapter
FORTY-SIX

Lucian smelled earth and mold. He was cold, much colder than he'd been just minutes—or was it hours—before? There was a metal band of pain circling his head. If his eyes were open he could no longer see. The blackness surrounding him was so complete he couldn't tell if he was inside it or it was inside him.

Dazed, he fought through the pain to try to make sense of what had just happened, of where he was, of why he was here, of what he'd been doing. *Remember,* he instructed himself. *Remember.* But he couldn't grasp any thoughts. Pain swept over him in a wave, and all he could see in its inky swells were the faces of the women he had been drawing for the past few weeks. Jeering at him from out of the blackness—one angry, the next shocked, a third weeping. All of them had been wronged, were troubled, were grieving—and all blamed him, demanded something from him. The women stretched out their arms so their fingers were touching, creating an unbreakable chain around him, trapping him not just by their physical strength but by his guilt over what he'd done to them, what he had taken away from them.

Please, he pleaded. *Tell me what I've done. How can I make amends if I don't know what crime I've committed? What do you want from me?*

"Lucian?"

Was one of them finally answering after so many weeks?

"Lucian?"

No, it was a man's voice, calling to him from above the water.

Lucian tried to break the grip of the circle of women and their suffocating demands. He tried to swim up to the surface. He could just see the light filtering down through the murky green water.

"Lucian? Are you okay? Answer me, man. Answer me!"

Lucian concentrated. *Open your eyes,* he screamed at himself. *Open your eyes.* But he couldn't. There was too much pain. Damn, his head hurt in what seemed like a million new ways.

No, not all of it was his head. There was pain ripping across his back, radiating out and down from his right shoulder. He must have hurt himself when he…fell…yes, when he fell. He'd been holding a gun on the Matisse Monster when the floor had opened and he'd fallen.

"Lucian?"

"Yeah, yeah. I'm okay." Forcing his eyelids apart, he looked into a cold white light.

"Hey!" He put his hand up to shield his eyes from Richmond's small but powerful flashlight.

"Sorry." Richmond moved the light so it wasn't shining right in his face anymore. "You scared me there."

"I scared you? You don't scare."

"I do when my partner doesn't respond to me screaming in his ear and slapping his face."

"For how long?"

"A few minutes."

"Damn it." Lucian was taking it all in now, looking around, assessing where he was, peering into the shadows where

O'Hara, Sellers and Jeffries stood behind Richmond. He asked them if they were all right.

"Fine."

"Okay."

"Yeah."

"Are you okay, too, Richmond?" Lucian asked his partner.

"Actually, pretty banged up. We all are. Scratches, bumps, sprains, but nothing we can't cope with. You got the worst of it. Opened your shoulder on some outcropping of rock as you fell."

Lucian was examining the cave. "Where the hell are we?"

"Good a guess as any—hell. We're in hell," Richmond answered as he helped his partner stand.

"What happened?" A wave of dizziness hit Lucian but he fought it, willing it away. There was no time now.

"It felt like an earthquake to me. Not too bad, though. Maybe a two or a three," Sellers said.

"Any idea how to get out of here?"

"O'Hara's working the radios." Richmond looked over at the youngest member of the team. "Any luck?"

"I've gotten through twice but there's too much static. They don't seem to be able to hear me at all, and I can't make out what they're saying. There's a wall of interference between us and the outside."

"Because we're too damn deep," Jeffries said. "We must have slid at least fifteen feet."

"What the fuck is this place? Some kind of museum of natural history?" O'Hara asked.

Lucian looked up into the darkness. "Where'd we come from?"

Richmond aimed the beam skyward, illuminating an inky chute.

"We fell straight, then slid for a while and landed here. It's not a direct plunge. Wherever we came from is out of sight."

With nothing left to glean from above, Lucian scanned the small crypt. He walked the circumference of their trap, inspecting the walls and the floor. When he was three-quarters of the way around he noticed a set of drawings—menacing and primitive black lines on the rocky walls. It was a mural that unfolded like a story, encircling them. It started with naked hunters on horses riding over snakes curled in the grass and finding a herd of bison, and ended with the hunters brutally killing two of the giant beasts and then dancing victoriously around a fire while overhead giant, vulture-like birds circled the sun.

But not any sun Lucian had ever seen. This one had a black center. He stared at it. Something was wrong. He walked up to it. There was a hole in the center of the sun. He shone Richmond's flashlight into the opening and saw an inner chamber half the size of this one, carved out of the same stone. On the floor he could just make out a bone-white skeleton ceremoniously laid out.

Woven baskets surrounded the body. Some were filled with multicolored beads, others with acorns, others overflowed with smaller bones and shells. Bits of fabric lay beneath the skeleton, as if the man's burial shroud had disintegrated. Encircling his head was a headdress of twigs and shreds of brightly colored strings.

The macabre sight looked so familiar that Lucian wondered if this was like the faces of the women he dreamed about, whom he couldn't forget but couldn't remember.

The pain was making it hard to grab hold of a thought and follow it through, but he knew he'd seen this before.

Behind him, he was aware of other men waiting for him to report on what he was seeing. Turning to tell them, Lucian tripped. He wasn't yet that steady after the fall, and as he lost his balance he dropped the flashlight, which rolled away, creating a moving light show on the rocky wall.

"You need to take it easy," Richmond cautioned as he helped his partner up.

"I need to figure out how we're going to get out of here, and you need to help me," Lucian argued.

"How about we try to break a bigger hole in that wall and see if there's an exit through there," Richmond offered.

"There won't be."

"How do you know that?"

Lucian shrugged. "I have no idea." He bent to pick up the flashlight and in the process noticed an irregular rounded stone set into the ground. Even before he looked more closely he knew it had a lion's head carved into it.

The ferocious face stared up at him.

What was happening to him? He didn't know how, but he knew something about this emblematic stone…something that really might help them escape from this dungeon.

Chapter

FORTY-SEVEN

Fulton banged his fist against the aluminum wall. He and his men were as trapped outside as Richmond, Glass and the others were trapped inside.

"What kind of signals are you reading?" Fulton asked Travers, whom he'd put in charge of both the GPS and the MRSS devices while he tried to organize the rescue and continued to monitor the radio.

"The sculpture is the only thing holding steady, and—"

Electronic noise spat out of the radio. Fulton held up his hand to stop Travers, depressed the speak button and shouted, "Come in! Come in!"

Not a single word broke through the angry static.

"Come in. Come in. Are you there?"

The only response was more crackling electricity.

Fulton stared down at the radio, wanting to fling it against the highly polished surface. "Travers, do you have anything new on the MRSS?"

Early on they'd been able to track the first burst of activity when the team entered the building. They'd seen two of the five men already inside show up in the same vicinity as the FBI agents and remain there even after the agents moved in deeper, eventually reaching the area where the three other occupants were. Then all hell broke loose. Now the scanner was having trouble reading inside the high-tech fortress. Travers reported that as far as he could tell it looked as if all but two men inside the building had moved to an area below the first floor.

"Drasner?" Fulton called out to another member of his team. "Any news on the chopper?"

"On the way. ETA less than seven minutes."

There were two ways around the fence. Equipment to rip through the aluminum was on its way by truck but could take as long as forty minutes to reach them. Too much could happen inside the compound in that much time, so Fulton had also requested a helicopter, which could airlift him and his team up and over the wall. They had all the weaponry they needed to storm the building and overwhelm everyone inside—they just couldn't do it from where they were.

"What is taking so long?" Fulton shouted at Drasner, knowing as he did that raising his voice wasn't going to help, but the pressure was getting to him. His job was to think and to act, and he hadn't been able to act on anything for fifteen minutes. There were men in there depending on him, and he wasn't coming through for them, either literally or figuratively.

"We're in the middle of nowhere," Drasner said.

Travers stood up. "Agent Fulton," he shouted, "I'm picking up activity in the building."

Chapter

FORTY-EIGHT

"Help me with this," Lucian shouted. With his shoulder ripped up, he was handicapped, so O'Hara, Jeffries, Richmond and Sellers wedged their fingers under the outer lip of the stone marker and, on the count of three, made an effort to lift it.

It didn't budge.

"Let's try it again," O'Hara said, and started the count.

On three they tried and failed again.

"We need something to slip under there and get some leverage," Richmond said.

"Good idea," Jeffries said. "I'll just jog over to the hardware store."

Lucian pointed to the hole in the wall. "Inside. The body is on top of some kind of wooden platform. If we can get in there we can use pieces of that as a wedge."

"What the fuck is a body doing in there anyway?" Jeffries asked. "What is this place?"

"I told you we're inside some sick museum. Dioramas and all," O'Hara said.

For the next few minutes the four men—with Lucian looking on—struck the wall with rocks, breaking off and loosening large chunks of it, widening the opening. They split their fingernails and scraped their skin, but kept at it, yanking and wrenching and pulling away handfuls of debris until the hole was big enough for the smallest of them—Sellers—to climb through.

Despite the prohibition against disturbing a crime scene, this situation was serious enough to forget about procedure. Pushing the skeleton off the platform where it rested, he broke the wooden gurney apart and handed the planks, one by one, to Richmond and then climbed back through the oculus.

O'Hara placed one end of the first plank under the lip of the lion stone. "Ready?"

Richmond, Sellers and Jeffries said they were.

"On the count of three. One…two…" On three O'Hara stepped down on the plank. A loud, creaking sound echoed in the chamber as the wood snapped in half. The stone hadn't budged.

"Let's go again," Lucian shouted.

O'Hara grabbed the second of four planks.

"One, two and…" Lucian counted. "Three."

O'Hara stepped down.

"You've got it," Richmond shouted as he and the other two agents moved their hands under the stone and lifted.

"It's slipping!" Sellers shouted.

The men let go. The stone fell and crashed back on the ground.

"Jesus H. Christ!" Sellers yelled. "Almost lost my fingers on that one."

"Let's try it again," Lucian ordered.

The plank groaned as O'Hara bore down. The agents got their fingers underneath the opening, grabbed hold of the lip and this time lifted the stone up and rolled it out of the way, exposing a forty-inch hole in the ground. Shining the flashlight down, Lucian saw an iron staircase descending even deeper into the earth.

"How the hell did you know that was here?" Richmond asked.

Up until that moment, Lucian hadn't understood it himself, but now, peering into the escape hatch, he laughed. His memory had nothing to do with the distant past he'd been traveling to in his mind. Nothing to do with the hypnosis sessions. "Didn't any of you see that movie? *The Act of Vanishing?*"

"What are you talking about?" Richmond asked.

"We're on a movie set. I don't know why I didn't realize it before. This place—this whole complex—it's all part of Shabaz's studio. That wasn't a real earthquake. It was a special effects earthquake like the one they used in the movie."

"And in the movie—if you're right and I hope to God you are—does this lead anywhere?" Richmond asked.

"Yes."

"I can hear a *but*. Where did it lead?"

Lucian put his foot on the first rung of the rusted-out ladder that descended down into more darkness. His shoulder throbbed, but he ignored it.

"Where did it lead?" Richmond insisted.

"It was just a movie, Matt."

"Except you're about to go down there, wherever *there* was."

"It led to hell, okay? Ironic enough for you? Still willing to risk it?"

"When there's a will..." Richmond said with a grin, and proceeded to follow his partner deeper down into their very real nightmare.

Chapter

FORTY-NINE

The stone tunnel had an unpaved dirt floor littered with hundreds of rodent skeletons.

"How much of the movie did they shoot down here?" Richmond asked Lucian as they steadily moved forward.

"It wasn't that good a movie. I don't remember the details, Matt. It's amazing the way your mind works."

"My mind? *Amazing* isn't exactly what I was thinking."

"I'm going to have to rent this flick when we get out of here," O'Hara said, his voice echoing in the narrow passageway. "Isn't this place too small to get all that equipment in?"

"They probably shot this part with a handheld," Jeffries said.

"Well, listen to you! When was the last time you shot a movie?" Richmond asked.

"My brother-in-law is a cameraman."

"Here we are," Lucian called out as he reached the end of an S curve and shone his light up to the ceiling, revealing a second iron staircase exactly like the one they'd just used, but this one offered a dozen steps leading up to a hatch. "I'd better change places with one of you. If that's stuck I won't be able to put much strength against it."

Richmond climbed up the stairs and pushed. Nothing budged. He tried again. Wood creaked. "One of you want to get up here and help me? I know there's not much room, but I'm not going to be able to move it on my own."

O'Hara climbed up, and together he and Richmond shoved the hatch open. It fell out with a loud crash. So did the radio that O'Hara had been carrying. Lucian tried to catch it as it whizzed by him, but it was beyond his reach.

They entered. The shack was six feet wide and unfurnished. Just a room with a hole in the floor and a door cut into one wall.

"Okay. Looks like we're almost out of here," Lucian said. "God knows what's on the other side of this door so everybody needs to be on alert." His shoulder and his head were both throbbing, and he knew his voice was sharper than it needed to be. In the flashlight's gleam he could see they had their guns drawn.

Richmond opened the door and Lucian stepped out first, relishing the cool evening air on his face. Twenty feet away was a thicket of trees that would offer camouflage. He pointed to it, dropped to his knees and, gritting his teeth against the pain in his shoulder, crept forward. Was this the same grove they'd seen when they'd scrutinized the area upon arriving almost an hour before? There was no way to tell.

Continuing, careful not to come down hard on anything that might make a crack or rustle, the team members skulked ahead, all of them reaching the edge of the tree line in less than a minute.

"What the hell is that?" Richmond whispered, pointing at the fence in front of them.

"I should have realized…from the movie…everything is the same. That's an aluminum blockade that went up around the building as soon the explosion hit."

"Electrified?" Richmond asked.

"Not in the movie."

"And the building—where Shabaz and the sculpture are—is that on this side or that side? Are we locked in? Are they?"

"If I remember it right, we should be on the outside now, Shabaz and the sculpture on the inside."

O'Hara rounded the curve ahead of everyone else and almost immediately there was a burst of shouts. But Lucian couldn't make out what anyone was saying. The sudden pulse of a helicopter drowned out all the words.

When he rounded the same curve he saw Gary Fulton and the rest of the agents running toward them.

"Good to see you're safe," Fulton screamed over the chopper. "What the hell happened in there?"

Once the agents had been airlifted back over the fence and made their way to the building where their investigation had started they found the FedEx truck still parked in front. According to St. Christopher, the sculpture was also still inside. So were five people.

Richmond and Lucian stood in the doorway for the second time that night, but now they knew who they were looking for. Using a bullhorn he'd grabbed from one of the guys on the chopper, Lucian shouted, "Give it up, Shabaz. We've got a dozen agents outside. A helicopter overhead. Let's cut the games short."

There was no sound and no movement. Lucian repeated his message. When there was still no response, they proceeded inside cautiously, hugging the wall, working their way to the atrium where they found the two guards, still cuffed and secured.

Gun drawn, Lucian flung open the door to the screening room. "FBI. Drop your weapons, Shabaz!"

The guards and the fake FedEx truckers were all there, right where the FBI had left them.

The crate was there, in the same state—partially unpacked—with the sculpture's swaddled head exposed.

And there was a fifth man, his back to the door, who was in the process of turning around. But it wasn't Shabaz. It was a stranger, wearing a baseball cap with an emerald lightning bolt zigzagging across the front.

"Not that I can see."

"Screw that. I still say we're going to get him." Richmond was back on the upswing. "You'll see."

"You have a plan?"

"Not yet, but we'll come up with one. And we do have the paintings."

"You're right. We have the paintings. But I'm never going to be satisfied till we get the guy and find out who he was working with," Lucian insisted as he picked up his pencil and started sketching again.

Chapter

FIFTY-ONE

Samimi opened the envelope that had arrived in that morning's mail. His name was handwritten by a calligrapher on the front and the return address of the Metropolitan Museum of Art was engraved on the back. Running his fingers over the type, he felt the raised letters on the smooth, creamy stock. His hand actually shook a little as he pulled out the invitation and read the date and time of the event, one day short of a week from today. He was elated and nervous at the same time.

> You are cordially invited to attend a private
> showing of Impressionist Masterworks
> Tuesday, June seventeenth,
> at six o'clock in the evening
> The American Wing at
> The Metropolitan Museum of Art

There was a name, and a phone number and a request to RSVP. Yes, he'd respond. He reread the invitation. June 17. Between now and then there were so many things he had to get right and so many things that could go wrong.

Over another dinner two nights before, Deborah had told him about the event, excited because it would be the first time in decades anyone outside of the Met would see any of the paintings or the sculpture.

He'd commented that it sounded like an odd grouping—Impressionist masterpieces and the statue of Hypnos that his country was so intent on having returned—but she didn't explain.

"No one outside the museum has seen Hypnos in over a hundred years," he said wistfully as he signaled the waiter to refill their wineglasses. "What does it look like? What kind of condition is it in?"

She'd smiled and said if he wanted to know, he should come to the reception.

Bingo, he thought, and then smiled. American slang was so expressive.

Now, holding the invitation, he walked across the Persian carpet, headed for Farid Taghinia's office so he could show him what had come in the mail, but at the door, he hesitated. He should go over Nassir's plan once more before he faced his boss. The next set of moves was complex and would require skill, concentration and nerves. Taghinia would question him over and over. Test him. Samimi needed to be prepared three and four steps ahead, plan for each contingency. The outcome of this operation would affect more than where Hypnos wound up and who would own it. The trajectories of many people's lives, his included, were at stake. This was his opportunity to show everyone what he was capable of. If all this worked, he'd be a hero. He'd never have to answer to Taghinia again. But living in New York was an expensive proposition. How long would it take to find another job? He needed…what did they call it? A nest egg, yes, that was it.

Punching a number in on his cell phone, he listened to it ring three times before he heard a man with a gravelly voice answer. Samimi identified himself and exchanged a sentence or two of pleasantries. Then he looked down at the date on the invitation.

"The rugs need to be cleaned, and I think it's time to do those repairs you suggested before any of them get any worse. Would it be convenient for you to come and get them next Wednesday late afternoon, about four? I'd like to have them all done at the same time."

It's not stealing if what you are taking belongs to you, Taghinia had said to him, referring to Hypnos. Did that apply to treason, too? Was it even still treason if those who expected and demanded your loyalty were themselves disloyal?

Chapter

FIFTY-TWO

In the office the Metropolitan Museum had given him to use during the investigation, Lucian fed the shredder and watched strips of paper fall into a basket.

"The detritus of a job well done," Tyler Weil said from the doorway.

Lucian looked up at the director. "There's always a lot to clean up when a case ends."

"You sound melancholy."

"That would be an indulgence."

"Nonetheless, I detect something in your voice and see something in the set of your shoulders."

"If you insist, Mr. Weil. I liked having an office at the museum. It's a special place to me."

Weil nodded. "We'd be happy to keep an office here for you."

"That's something you don't want to wish for—the need for an in-house ACT agent."

"You're quite right." Weil laughed. And then he held out a cream-colored envelope and watched Lucian open the invitation and read it. "If it weren't for you we wouldn't be able to have this little party celebrating the return of the paintings to their rightful home. We do hope you can come."

Lucian smiled gratefully. "Wouldn't miss it."

"It's going to be quite an event, the first time these paintings have been seen in years and the first and only time Hypnos will be on view until the new galleries open."

"You're putting Hypnos on view now? With the paintings? Why?"

"The sculpture was the impetus for the return of the paintings. Marie and I thought it would be fitting, and it will generate great press, which is something our lawyers want us to concentrate on. Build up support now, so when the time comes to argue the provenance of this piece, public opinion is on our side."

The mention of Marie bothered Lucian. He'd had the same reaction every time he met with the curator or heard her name. There was nothing logical about his feeling. It was free-floating anxiety—that inexorable pall that hung over so many of his days now—something he'd never experienced before his trip to Vienna. He shook his head, wishing the movement could dislodge the feeling.

With his eye for detail, Weil noticed the agent's reaction. "Something bothering you?"

Lucian had no intention of attempting to explain what was inexplicable even to him. "Not at all. I'd be honored to come. Thank you very much for thinking of me and for coming down here yourself."

"I wanted to thank you personally. You took on a situation fraught with physical and emotional hazards and did an amazing job. On behalf of the museum, I'm very grateful."

Weil was talking about pigment applied to canvas, about streaks and swaths of colors, about gold and ivory and wood. What was it about these creations, these fragments of imag-

ination, these re-creations of reality, this art that so hypnotized men and women that they devoted their lives to creating it and then preserving it and safeguarding it? Lucian
had come to believe it was because every great work of art
contained the soul of its creator. And by respecting and protecting the art, he believed, we respect and protect not only
the soul of our collective past but our hope for our collective future.

But did any of that really matter when Shabaz had gotten
away? When the men who'd stolen the paintings—at least one
of whom had killed to steal a painting—had gotten away?

"I also brought this." Tyler held out a second envelope. The
calligraphy spelled out Emeline and Andre Jacobs's names and
their address. "My assistant was going to hand-deliver it to
them, but with everything you've all been through, it occurred
to me that there was something fitting about you taking it over,
as if the past and the present were coming full circle. If you want
to, of course."

"I do," Lucian said as he took the proffered envelope. He'd
talked to Emeline late Monday when he got back from Los
Angeles and talked to her again last night. He'd wanted to get
uptown to see her, but Emeline said Andre was too ill for her
to meet him. Lucian was worried about her. The threatening
e-mails had stopped and she hadn't sensed anyone following her
since the police detail had been assigned to her. But now she
was getting menacing phone calls. Sometimes they were quick
hang-ups, other times whispered warnings from a mechanical
voice taunting her, telling her the police wouldn't be able to
keep her safe forever and he'd be waiting for her when they left.

There had been four or five calls every day, each too short
for the police to trace.

The woman who answered the phone at the store said

Emeline wasn't there, so Lucian took a chance that she would be at the Fifth Avenue apartment and walked across the street without calling.

"Nice surprise," she said when she greeted him. A breeze from inside—she must have had the terrace door open—blew her fragrance toward him, inviting him in even before she did.

She was wearing a sleeveless white shirt, white jeans and silver ballet slippers with silver barrettes holding her blond hair off her face. Her eyes were a little more wild and worried looking than the last time he'd seen her, her skin more translucent. It felt as if it had been a long time, but it had only been three days ago. He wasn't surprised by how great a toll the stress she was under had taken. Being hunted was horrifying. He doubted she'd slept at all unless she'd been smart and taken pills.

"I'm so glad everything turned out all right and you're back safe." She hesitated and then added in a lower voice, as if it was a secret, "I very much missed you."

He smiled. "And I missed you, too…" He didn't finish his sentence. She'd used the exact same odd phrase Solange used whenever she saw him after a few days apart.

Emeline was looking at him with a combination of relief and palpable pleasure. He wanted to ask her why she'd used those specific words but at the same time didn't want to question her about it lest it wipe her smile off her face.

"I'm playing messenger." He held out the envelope. She took it, glanced at the return address and then put it on a low bench by the door where there was an assortment of other mail and magazines.

"I'd love to get out of here," she said. "I'm going crazy between Andre and my police escort and staying away from the gallery because of the incessant calls. Could we get a drink somewhere? At least with you I'm safe."

* * *

They sat across from each other at a small table in the Bemelmans Bar in the Carlyle Hotel, and both ordered martinis. As Lucian sipped his he noticed how, in the low light, Emeline looked as if she'd been painted by an old master. Half her face was hidden in deep shadow, the other half illuminated; the chiaroscuro making her expression mysterious and hard to read.

"What are you thinking?" he asked.

She gestured to the fanciful murals of rabbits and dogs, squirrels and schoolchildren all playing in the park. "It never changes here, does it?"

"No, never. That's its charm, isn't it?" He told her how when he was a boy his grandmother brought him and his sister here on Saturday afternoons for hot chocolate. "My sister, who was a huge fan of Ludwig Bemelmans's books, would always make a pilgrimage to that wall when we got here and just stare intently at Madeline for a few minutes, enchanted by the meshing of her fantasy friend and this reality." He took another sip of the icy gin. "That's the power of art."

"Why did you give up on being an artist?"

"I didn't care enough anymore. And you can't do it unless it's the only thing you care about."

She picked up her martini with fingers that looked as delicate as the glass stem. "But you have all your supplies sitting right there where you can always see them. Sometimes the desire must come back?"

He shrugged. "Sometimes."

"And what do you do then?"

He stared at her, unclear about what she was asking, not sure if he was being too naive or too suspicious.

"I give in. And for a while I'm just another poor schlep who will never get what he wants."

"And what would that be?"

"My fantasy was exactly the cliché you'd expect it to be, Emeline."

"But you didn't even give it a chance. That's sad."

"Only if you equate desire—thwarted or otherwise—with happiness. I don't happen to buy into that equation."

"What equation do you buy into?"

"Your glass is empty. I can buy into getting us more drinks."

She shook her head. "I don't think so. I'm already feeling this one."

"Do you want me to take you back to your father's apartment?"

Her no was immediate. "You know what I'd like? To see some of your paintings."

"Why?"

"I'm curious."

Twenty minutes later, Lucian was rifling through the rack of his old canvases. He pulled out three. They were all compositions of people visiting museums, standing in front of and mostly blocking sensuous marble statues of nude Greek goddesses or famous Renaissance masterpieces that he only hinted at with frames and corners of color and style. Looking at them after so many years, he couldn't see talent, only drive.

He lined the paintings up along the wall facing Emeline, who was sitting on the couch.

"Do you have any wine?" she asked without taking her eyes off the paintings.

When he returned with the glasses and the bottle, he found her standing, examining his work up close.

"They're so good, and there's so much promise in them. You were trying to do so much."

"*Trying* being the operative word."

"You shouldn't have stopped."

"It was a kid's dream."

"What do you dream about now? Catching the bad guys?"

He smiled. "That's not such a bad dream. Don't say it like you feel sorry for me."

"Not sorry for you. Sorry for the art you might have made. Beauty matters, too."

"That's why I catch the bad guys."

Now she smiled.

"What do you dream about?" he asked.

"These days? I dream about you catching the bad guys," she said, and then held his gaze in a certain way that made it almost impossible for him to look away.

A feeling of inevitability overwhelmed him. There was no question about why she was here or what she wanted or what he wanted, but as he leaned forward toward her he noticed that the distance between them was greater than he'd imagined it would be, as if his ability to make judgments was off. Not one martini off and a few sips of wine off, but profoundly disturbed.

Lucian fell into the kiss, lingering there on the edge of her mouth for a time that lost measure. He could feel her bony shoulders against his and her small breasts pushing into his chest. At some point he undid her barrettes and loosened her silky hair and her scent, that curious combination of spicy amber and innocent vanilla swirled around him.

Their embrace had an intensity, a wholehearted energy, as if there was nothing else that could matter right then but them being together, now, tonight, this way.

It had been like this with her on Sunday in the park, and like this with Solange years ago. The two sets of experiences merged too easily into one. *No.* He didn't want to remember but just be here in this moment with this woman.

As if she sensed what he was thinking, Emeline pulled back,

turned, walked over to the couch, sat down and picked up her wine. She took a sip, then another. The lamp in the corner of the room cast her shadow across the floor, and it spilled onto the paintings.

Lucian went to her, sat beside her and took her hand. He turned it over, then bent down and kissed her palm. Lifting his head, he looked into her eyes, held her gaze. "I want you." He whispered the answer to the question that this time, for the first time, she hadn't asked.

Emeline leaned forward and answered him by kissing him, full on the mouth. His hands twisted in her hair, his fingertips wrapped in the silk. His lips didn't leave hers and if either of them stopped to breathe they weren't aware of it.

He'd said "want," but he didn't want her. He didn't want to unbutton her blouse and push up her brassiere and feel her breasts and touch her skin—it wasn't want—it was a crazy, desperate hunger, and as he did those things and touched her cool skin and felt her small nipples pucker and as she shuddered in his arms he knew that he was gone, that he'd slipped into another dimension that somehow was and wasn't his past but might be his future. She was breathing his breath, inhaling the air he was exhaling, and he was inhaling hers. And all the while the ghosts of him and his first love sat across the room, watching, because he and Emeline were breathing in each other's air the same way and touching each other the same way and living on the edge of their passion for each other the same way and his heart wanted to break for the awful loveliness of this woman who was alive and the one who wasn't.

"I want you, too," Emeline whispered in his ear with hot breath that was his breath, and the only thing in the world that mattered then was to sink into her and become lost in the time warp that folded around him and held him in a brutally cruel embrace for all that it promised and teased.

Once they were in his bedroom, even before he had a chance to touch her, Emeline was stepping out of her silver shoes and then stripping off her clothes. Not undressing for him, he thought, but proving something to herself.

Naked, she stood before him, staring at him with a brave and brazen look in her eyes, and when she spoke they were the last words he ever expected to hear, the exact words he should have been prepared for even though he didn't know how or why. This woman had been a child when Solange had been killed. There was no way that she could have known what Solange had said to him the first time they were together. Not *make love to me,* not *sleep with me* or *touch me*—but *paint me,* and he had. He'd spent hours standing in front of her naked body and working on that painting.

Emeline's words traveled across the room to embrace him or slap him, he wasn't sure which. As he listened to what she said, under her voice, he heard Solange's voice. How did Emeline know these things that no one could have told her because no one knew about them except for a woman who had been dead for twenty years?

"Paint me, Lucian."

He couldn't fight it—or he didn't want to fight it—he didn't know which and didn't care. Everything was there—the battered beechwood box, the stained palettes, the can of sable brushes and old bottles of linseed oil and turpentine—all there just waiting. Most of the canvases were used, but there was one that had just a few blue brushstrokes in the upper corner, as if he'd started to lay in a background, been distracted and then never gotten back to it.

With the easel set up and the canvas resting on its lip, he

lifted the paint box's lid and with the first whiff of long-trapped
scent that wafted up, Lucian crossed an imaginary threshold
into the dorm room, the only studio he'd ever had.

Oil paints don't dry up or harden as long as the tubes don't
crack, and these hadn't. He looked at the labels, stained with
smears and smudges, and pulled out the colors he needed to
match her skin tones: Titanium White, Cadmium Red Light,
Cadmium Yellow and Burnt Sienna. He squeezed the colors
onto the palette. The brushes, which he'd always been careful
to clean because they were so expensive, felt supple between
his fingers, and he picked out one with a tapered point and a
flat body. Dipping it first into the white, then the red, he mixed
them together. He added a very small hint of yellow and even
less of the sienna.

She was facing him full on, hiding nothing, her body taut,
arms by her sides, palms up, her small chin pointing up, daring
him to look at her.

Lucian stroked the paint onto the canvas, slowly at first,
then working up to a frenzy, not sure which he craved more—
her or this utter abandonment to the act of painting, to something he'd had so much passion for but had given up and
sacrificed to reason. But it didn't matter now. This moment was
beyond logic. His feelings were beyond logic.

How long did he paint? How long did she stand there
naked, the look of wanting him, of wanting this, never
leaving her eyes? How many times did the brush move in a
flurry from palette to canvas in a hot rush of energy, the
conduit of all that he was seeing and feeling? Was he hurrying
to get to her, or just greedy for more of this pleasure? Because
that was what it was: pure pleasure to actually see beyond the
form to what made this woman so utterly beautiful—her fra-
gility and tensile strength, her desires and fears, everything

that made her human, that made her alive—and to translate it onto the canvas with nothing more than a brush, pigment and his ability.

He might have gone on painting for longer, but Emeline chose when he would stop by finally breaking the pose and coming around to where he was standing and looking at what he'd done. She studied it but said nothing. Then she stepped between him and the painting, blocking it from his view, faced him and whispered with a voice that was grateful and excited both at once, as if he'd given her a great gift, "Thank you for seeing me like that."

Lucian sat down on the edge of the bed, put his hands around her waist and pulled her toward him so that his face was level with her stomach. Her skin was smooth and warm, and using his tongue like the brush he'd just put down, he painted her with soft, invisible kisses, there and there and there he kept kissing her, and with every new inch of her that his lips found she arched her back a little more. Her hands reached out and gripped his head, and her fingers tangled in his hair as she pulled him closer still and made small moaning sounds that were anything but fragile. There was no pain in this pleasure for her. Lucian heard laughter mixed with wanting. It was an amazingly joyful noise—this music of their lovemaking—and he kept kissing her so he could keep hearing it. The sound was flowing into all the dark crevices of his soul and lifting him up.

Smiling some secret smile, Emeline straddled him and eased herself down, achingly slowly, onto him, and as he wound his arms tighter around her, she constricted and held him inside her tighter, too. He had one single moment of clarity before he was lost, when he saw her in violent contrasts of light and dark with her head thrown back, an expression on her face that he'd never try to name, and he recognized that he'd painted her in the wrong moment. This was art, this ecstasy; this was what they all tried to capture and express, this moment when the senses take over and there is no thought left, nothing but being.

Chapter
FIFTY-THREE

"What have you got today for lunch, Larry?" the security guard asked the balding construction worker who was carrying the same oversize lunch pail he brought with him every day.

"Two meatball heros. You needing one of them?"

"I sure am," the guard said, smiling, then linking his thumb in his belt. "But I'd better not take you up on your offer."

Larry Talbot gave the guard a grin, swung the lunch pail from one hand to the other and walked on through the entryway and into the museum. He'd shared his lunch with Tommy before, and it wouldn't have been a big deal to share it again if the guard had wanted a sandwich. Larry knew exactly which of the two heros was stuffed with pork and beef meatballs smothered in marinara sauce and which was stuffed with meatballs made of Semtex.

Of the twenty workmen who entered the Metropolitan Museum that morning, five of them were carrying plastic explosives hidden inside sandwiches or cigarette packs or gum.

The security for employees working at the Met was not as tight in the morning as it was at the end of the day. Tommy nodded as each regular arrived, and if he didn't recognize someone he'd stop them and ask to see ID, but since crews from Phillips Construction had been in and out of the museum for decades, Tommy knew most of the men by sight. Incoming employees didn't have to pass through the X-ray system, and the guard didn't need to use his wand. There were only inspections the first few times someone new showed up for work. It was at night that the security was ratcheted up and every briefcase, lunch pail, backpack or shopping bag was inspected to ensure that no one was smuggling out any artwork or artifacts.

Even if the checks had been done, the malleable material wouldn't have set off any alarms or been visible as anything suspect.

Today, for the fifth day in a row, five workers had brought something into the museum that they wouldn't leave with that night, but Don Albertson, the long-time worker who had taken over after Victor Keither died, didn't notice anything about those five that made them stand out. They weren't a clique; they fit in with their coworkers and none of them had ever caused any trouble.

Later it would be noted that they had all been hired over the same three-week period to replace workmen who'd been stolen away by Manhattan Construction. When questioned, Albertson would tell the police that maybe he should have paid more attention to them since they were relative newcomers, but they were good workers who just hadn't drawn any attention to themselves. What he wouldn't tell them about was the cash payment he'd been given by a man who smoked cigars and spoke with a heavy accent in exchange for Albertson not noticing much of anything.

To communicate with his team, Talbot, whose real name would have given away his heritage, used predetermined signs and signals that escaped notice by anyone else. The short, olive-skinned man with hair cropped so close you couldn't tell what texture it was knew at any moment of the day where each of his team members were and what they were doing.

Later, when asked about Talbot specifically, Albertson would shake his head and say that of all his men, Talbot was one of the better carpenters; never the last one to get there in the morning and never the first one out at night. And that was true, but the reason wasn't the man's work ethic. Talbot purposely hung back at the end of each day, taking extra time to clean up and put away his tools, waiting until Albertson left so he could take the Semtex he'd cautiously collected from his men when no one was around or watching and deposit it in a carton that, according to its labels, contained six quarts of Benjamin Moore Bone White #3 paint.

The renovation of the Islamic galleries was at least three months away from the point of needing paint, so while there was no truly safe place for the explosives, this carton was as close as Talbot could get to a secure hiding place. He took every precaution to ensure that the cache remained hidden. So far he'd been lucky, but how long would that last? Talbot wanted his superiors to pull the trigger so they could do the job they'd trained for and get out of there. Despite the suicide belts loaded with explosives that they'd be wearing, Talbot and his men intended to accomplish their task and live to reap their rewards.

That Thursday evening, before Talbot put more Semtex in the carton, he checked to be sure the box hadn't been tampered with and that the stash of explosives hadn't been discovered. Everything looked intact. The tape he'd put down last night hadn't been touched.

And then he heard what sounded like footsteps. He stopped to listen. Someone was heading this way. He stole a second to look at his watch. What was going on? The security patrol for this area wasn't expected for another half hour.

The footsteps echoing on the marble floor were getting closer. He wasn't going to be able to put the rest of the explosives in the box, get it closed up and slide the carton out of the way in time. He was going to have to improvise if—

"You still here?" The guard sounded cautious, but was he also suspicious?

Talbot finished tying his shoelace, then looked up. On his right was the carton filled with over three pounds of Semtex, enough to blow up more artwork than he could even calculate. On his left was his lunch pail. Leaning on the carton, he rose to a standing position, careful to slouch in a nonthreatening way.

"I got all the way downstairs and realized I didn't have my cell phone. I came back up to see if it was here. I'd moved these cartons around this afternoon and the phone must have fallen out of my pocket then." He held it up.

"You leaving now?"

"As soon as I straighten up. Put this stuff back where it was." Talbot's heart pounded as he lifted up a second carton and put it down on top of the one he'd been filling.

"I'm going to have to wait for you," the guard said.

"No problem. You have your job to do and I have mine," Talbot said as he shoved both cartons back into the shadows. "Albertson would be furious if I left anything out of place. He's practically an old lady like that."

The guard smiled.

Talbot purposefully moved a few more boxes around and then glanced up. The guard didn't seem to be paying any attention. Talbot's heart settled down to an almost normal rhythm. Wasn't it time to set this plan into action already? What were they waiting for? Every night he and the other four men met on a private Internet message board at midnight to await orders to proceed.

Once they got the communiqué, on the following day each of them was to create an excuse to stay behind when the first rush of workers left. One would go to the bathroom. Another would get a phone call from his wife. A third would trip and sit down to nurse his ankle for a few minutes. A fourth would stop to help him. A fifth would take longer than was necessary cleaning up a mess. After the construction site cleared out, all members of the team would convene in the storage area and unroll the suicide belts they'd smuggled in. Made of canvas, each had holders for ten two-inch cylinders of Semtex. The men would connect the cylinders with red detonating cords. All it would take to fire the det-cords was the electrical impulse from the ring voltage of a cell phone. Not set to a predetermined time, the plan here was to wear the pretty ornaments for all to see and guarantee that if anyone was thinking of being a hero, they changed their mind. The goal was to get the sculpture out of the museum, not start a holocaust.

Done rearranging the boxes, Talbot stood up. "I'm ready."

The guard looked around, gave a cursory glance to the cartons, the walls, the tarps, the tools, the worktables. "When's all this going to be finished?"

Talbot thought about the two answers he could give. The one the man expected would be the date the museum had set for the renovation to be completed by; the other was his guess of a much closer date that was going to bring this job to a very different and disturbing kind of end.

Chapter

FIFTY-FOUR

Paris, France

After three intense days of negotiating, on Saturday afternoon Darius Shabaz's lawyer contacted the FBI and agreed to their terms: his client was willing talk to them in exchange for leniency, but only if they would come to Paris. Seven hours later, Lucian and Matt Richmond were on the last Air France flight out of Kennedy Airport. They arrived, groggy and needing showers, early Sunday morning and took a taxi to their hotel on the Left Bank.

"Who made these reservations?" Lucian asked as the cab approached 9 rue de l'Université and he saw the hotel's name in brass letters on the marble lintel of the front door.

"Someone in the office, why?"

"Its name…" Lucian pointed to signage that read Hôtel Lenox.

"Yes?"

But the cab had pulled up in front and there was no time to explain.

While Richmond paid the driver, Lucian grabbed their luggage out of the trunk. It wasn't until after they'd checked in, dropped their bags in their rooms and met up again downstairs for coffee that Richmond had a chance to find out why Lucian had been surprised by the hotel's name.

"Frederick L. Lennox was an industrialist and a founding member of the original Phoenix Club. Elgin Barindra has found quite a bit of correspondence from him to Talmage. I think copies are on your desk somewhere."

"I haven't gotten to that stuff yet…"

Lucian laughed. "You never will. Your desk is like a black hole."

The waiter arrived with café au lait and croissants. While Richmond stirred in two heaping teaspoons of sugar, Lucian continued his explanation in between sips of the hot coffee.

"Lennox wanted to examine the Sanskrit list of Memory Tools that the Memorist Society owned and he planned on going to Austria to see it. There's no correspondence confirming whether or not he ever did, but we do know he bought a sculpture found in Persia that he believed contained a Memory Tool. He bequeathed the statue to the Metropolitan Museum of Art."

"Are we talking about the same sculpture Darius Shabaz wanted?"

"Might be. Lennox donated over a hundred pieces to the Met, all of them from the Middle East."

"But there could be a connection between Hypnos and the Phoenix Foundation? Why didn't you tell me that before?"

"It's in the notes—"

"On my desk. I know. I know. Crazy coincidence, isn't it?"

"Yeah, and since no one but Doug and I and your desk know about it, it's just another coincidence that we're booked in here." Lucian broke off a corner of the flaky croissant and ate it. "It really does taste better, doesn't it?"

"The coffee, too. So Lennox thought Hypnos was a Memory

Tool? Do you think that's why Shabaz wanted it? We'll have to find out if he has any connection to Malachai Samuels."

Lucian took another bite of the croissant. He needed to think through how to answer and make sure that his response only referenced facts uncovered by their investigation as opposed to information he had gleaned in the strange regression sessions he'd had with Iris Bellmer. In his memories he couldn't see the treasures in the crypt; he didn't know if Hypnos was there. He only could see the actions he—Fouquelle—took and the terrified faces of the couple who owned the house.

"I don't think Malachai Samuels knew about any of this until Elgin Barindra found the letters from Lennox to Talmage."

"Any details about what that Memory Tool is?"

"Nope, nothing. Malachai must be going crazy." Lucian couldn't help himself; he smiled.

Richmond drained his coffee and observed his partner over the rim of his cup. After a few seconds he asked, "What else is going on with you?"

"No idea what you're talking about."

"I've been working with you for five years. You're always wrapped up in work to the point of distraction. You use it to keep the demons away. I get that. Lots of us do. I don't want to pry. But you're in deeper than usual on this one. Are you all right? Really?"

"Never better."

"You're holding back."

"Don't you know me well enough to know I'd never hold back anything that mattered to a case we're working on?"

"I'm not talking about the case. I'm talking about you. What's wrong with you? Have you looked in a mirror? You look exhausted all the time. Worried. You're always drawing. I know it's a habit, but it's habitual. You're popping painkillers like Tic Tacs. What the hell is wrong?"

"Other than the headaches—it's just work. We're closing in on one, maybe two cases. We're doing our jobs. We're rescuing paintings. It's just work."

"Nah. You've got secrets, man. More than before, and that's saying something. And you're in some kind of trouble because of them."

Lucian was tempted. It would be a relief to talk about the strange dreams and drawings, the regression sessions that had opened up horrifying nightmares, to tell him about Emeline and the crazy idea he was fighting—and at the same time embracing—that she and Solange were connected. Matt was someone he trusted, literally, with his life.

"Let's get going," Lucian said, standing up, brushing croissant crumbs off his hands. Now wasn't the time to update Matt on his personal hell.

Chapter

FIFTY-FIVE

A French maid wearing a simple black-and-white uniform escorted the two agents through the front hall of the apartment on avenue de New York, as if they had come to tea, and brought them into the living room. The purpose of this visit cast all the beauty of the high-ceilinged room with its ornate gilded moldings and floor-to-ceiling windows looking out over the river Seine in a harsh, ironic light. Under his dirty shoes was a yellow, cream and blue Aubusson rug worth more, Lucian knew, than he made in a year. None of the antique furnishings or paintings would have been out of place in a museum.

Darius Shabaz stood when the agents walked in, but it was the overweight, balding man wearing thick glasses who waddled over to them and introduced himself as Eliot Waxman, Mr. Shabaz's lawyer.

There was no preamble, and any pretense that this was an afternoon tea disappeared as soon as all four men were seated in the club chairs set up around a coffee table. Lucian leaned back as if he were relaxed, as if Darius were just another suspect, not the man who might actually give him the information he needed to solve the crime that had changed the trajectory of so many lives—including his own—and was changing them still.

"Mr. Shabaz and I appreciate your coming all this way," Waxman said. "I assure you we have every intention of cooperating and having this move as swiftly as possible to a conclusion we can all live with."

Shabaz, who still had not spoken, nodded in agreement. He appeared concerned but wasn't exhibiting any of the body language of a guilty man.

"You understand that according to French law, Mr. Shabaz can remain here forever without any worry of extradition. But he'd prefer to return home to California and resume his life," Waxman offered.

"I'm sure he would," Richmond said with only a hint of sarcasm.

"And he's prepared to help you in any way he can in order to make that a reality," Waxman continued, as if he hadn't heard Richmond's retort.

"You understand that we are doing you a favor, not the other way around?" Richmond said, this time with more than a hint of sarcasm.

"Mr. Shabaz," Lucian said, directing his next words to the fugitive, not his lawyer, "you're going to have to help us a whole lot if you don't want to come home to a very stiff prison sentence."

"I bought those paintings completely legally," Shabaz said adamantly. "All within the past four years and all of them had—"

Waxman put his hand on his client's arm, interrupting and stopping him from saying anything else.

"Would it be possible for me to get some water?" Richmond asked. He and Lucian had discussed which of them would make the request beforehand.

"Yes, of course," Shabaz said. "Let me call Suzanne."

"Just point me in the direction of the kitchen, that would be fine."

Shabaz reacted at first as if he was going to argue but then seemed to change his mind and gave Richmond instructions.

"What do you want to know, Agent Glass?" Waxman asked.

Lucian noticed that Shabaz seemed distracted. Maybe he didn't like the idea of the FBI agent wandering through his apartment. Well, good; that was the point. He answered the lawyer's question, but looked at Shabaz. "This is very simple. We want to know why you wanted the sculpture so badly. Why go to so much trouble? Why destroy the paintings? Why not just make a clean trade? And we want the names of the people you bought the paintings from. Plus all of your paperwork relating to those sales."

Waxman looked visibly relieved. "And all charges will be dropped if we comply with your requests?"

"Once your client has answered all our questions and we can ascertain that we've been given authentic documents we will discuss leniency."

"No. We need to know what you are offering now," Waxman said.

Every muscle in his body fought back as Lucian stood up. The last thing he wanted to do was leave without answers, but he had no choice. He wouldn't be held hostage to his own personal demons or to this officious lawyer. "My partner and I are staying at the Lenox Hotel if you change your mind."

Lucian had taken only a few steps when Shabaz said, "I'll talk to you now."

He walked back to his seat.

"I'll tell you what you want to know—but I bought the paintings legally," Shabaz insisted.

"It's illegal to buy stolen artwork."

"I didn't know they were stolen when I bought them."

"Do not lie to me. Don't do it," Lucian said, and turned to Waxman. "If you want a deal for your client you'd better tell him that nothing but a one-hundred-percent honest and full disclosure is going to work."

Richmond returned carrying a crystal glass filled with water, and Lucian was annoyed that he hadn't brought him one, too. His head had been pounding since the plane had reached altitude. He resisted putting his hand up to rub his temple. Not only would the gesture make him look weak, he knew by now it was futile. Nothing helped. Not a damn thing.

"I don't have anything to hide," Shabaz said. "I acted in good faith."

"Who did you buy the paintings from?"

"I bought three of the paintings from one man, and two from another," he said and then named them.

Lucian wrote down the names of the two dealers, both of whom had decent reputations. They were now one giant step closer. "And the bills of sale."

"All of the paperwork is in L.A."

"Can you arrange to have it overnighted to our New York office today?"

Waxman looked at his client, who nodded. "We can," the lawyer responded.

"Why destroy the Matisse? Why not just offer the paintings in exchange?" Richmond asked.

"I needed the Met to know how serious I was."

"Why was that?" Lucian asked. "What is so important about Hypnos?"

"I didn't want it going to Iran or to Greece. Its value is so much greater than anyone realizes."

"What right do you have to it?"

Shabaz looked at Lucian as if he was stupid. "It's mine. Hypnos is legally mine. It's my inheritance. It belonged to my ancestors."

Lucian hesitated for just a second, rocked by the implications of the revelation. He saw Richmond glance at his partner as if asking why he hadn't followed up yet. Quickly he threw out the next question.

"Can you explain that?"

"My ancestors were Jewish and lived in Persia. The sculpture, along with two dozen other treasures, was buried under their house until the late 1800s when a French archaeologist stole it. Looted it. Sold it to an American industrialist. Took what belonged to my great-great-grandparents and destroyed everyone's lives."

"Hosh and Bibi?" Lucian's voice came from far away and as he heard the names he was as surprised as everyone else was.

"Yes," Shabaz said, astounded. "How do you know?"

Richmond was staring at his partner.

The words had just slipped out. What had he done? Lucian struggled for a plausible explanation. "The museum's compiled a history of the sculpture," Lucian said, hoping his rationale would pass muster. "Who it belonged to, what its provenance was, that sort of thing." His mouth had gone dry. Without thinking, he reached out and took Richmond's glass and drank half the water down. No one seemed to notice, least of all his partner, who'd never wanted it in the first place. Lucian was almost positive the Met's history only contained the name of the archaeologist who'd sold the piece to Frederick L. Lennox, but he didn't have time to worry about his egregious error now.

"Do you know a man named Malachai Samuels?" Richmond asked.

"I don't think so, no," Shabaz answered.

"You seem pretty sure."

"I don't know the name."

"What about the other objects in the crypt?" Lucian asked. "What about them? Are you trying to get them back, too?"

"The other objects? Four clay pots, two gold bracelets, one pair of gold and rough ruby earrings, two elaborate pearl and gold necklaces, three large oil jugs and a gold pitcher. Every one of them predated Christianity, all from either ancient Rome or Greece and all of them hidden in the ancient crypt under their house in the Persian ghetto. Over the past twenty years I've spent whatever I had to buy them back."

"To what end?" Lucian asked.

"I grew up listening to my grandfather's story of exile from his homeland and his struggle to begin again. At first they were a series of adventures, myths to inspire a young boy to push himself, to fight whatever came his way and never fear the unknown. Over time I became obsessed with the carnage and loss my family suffered, which changed their destiny and ruined them."

"And you wanted to rewrite the story's ending?" Lucian asked.

"I wanted justice."

"And the destruction and carnage you inflicted on the Matisse? Who gave you the right to decide what should be sacrificed and what should be saved?"

"If the Metropolitan Museum returned the statue of Hypnos to Iran or Greece, that would be a travesty far more terrible than the loss of one Impressionist painting. You still don't understand how important Hypnos is. I do."

Lucian stood up. It didn't matter how important Shabaz believed it was. Not now.

The knot that had been coiled deep inside of him for so long tugged. Lucian couldn't think about anything except the names he had written down. Two art dealers. One who might lead him to Solange's killer.

Chapter
FIFTY-SIX

Elgin Barindra had seen Reed Winston at the Phoenix Foundation before. Based on his description, Lucian Glass and Matt Richmond had established that Winston was an ex-operative and instructed Elgin to be especially vigilant about what he and Malachai discussed.

So on Monday, while the broad-shouldered, good-looking man sat next to Malachai, poring over the letters from Frederick L. Lennox to Davenport Talmage, Elgin was on full alert. He attempted to appear uninterested when he was trying to catch every word, even though he knew they weren't going to discuss anything important in front of him.

Malachai Samuels was reading out loud:

"My Dear Davenport,
I've heard about an ancient artifact that might be of interest to us—the Memorist Society in Vienna is in possession of a copper sheet of ancient Sanskrit that so far has been impossible to translate. It originally came from a group of Indian monks in the Himalayas. It was discovered by their founder and brought back to Vienna in 1813. I'm quite sure it's a list

of the legendary Memory Tools, and I'm hoping you can con-
tact your colleagues there and find out if there's any more in-
formation about it we can obtain.
Yours,
Frederick L. Lennox

"And then we found a second letter, dated six months later, also from Frederick Lennox to Davenport Talmage, about a piece of sculpture he'd recently purchased."

As Malachai picked up the next letter, Elgin nudged a pile of books off the edge of his desk. They crashed on the floor. Both men looked up.

"I'm sorry," Elgin said. As he leaned over to pick up the books, his pen fell out of his pocket. He grabbed the pen, put it back on his desk, and then stacked the books and returned them, too. "Unless you need me," he said, "I'm going to get some lunch now."

"Please, feel free. Reed is as interested in the historical significance of these letters as I am, and I want to show him more of the fruit of your labors. Take your time."

Once again Elgin noticed how the reincarnationist's smile never quite reached his eyes. Everything about Malachai was deliberate, he thought as his boss's studied and erudite voice followed him out. It was a letter Elgin had found the week before.

"Dear Davenport,
I am fairly certain that I have found the pot of gold at the end
of the proverbial rainbow. It turns out to actually be made of
gold and silver and ivory and several kinds of precious stones.
Serge Fouquelle, an archaeologist who has been working for
Marcel and Jeanne Diolafoa in Persia, specifically in Shush,
on the ancient site of Susa, has just completed his first exca-

vation on his own and has made a curious discovery; he's found a cache of Greek treasures that date back to the time of Pythagoras and might have connections to the great philosopher. All the signs point to it..."

Chapter

FIFTY-SEVEN

"A Greek god that I am purchasing…"

At ACT headquarters, Matt Richmond and Doug Comley stood at the table listening to Malachai's voice coming over the phone line. Elgin was playing the recording for them on his cell phone. His innocuous pen was one of the agency's most popular recording devices. Even if someone noticed it and took it apart, the high-tech recording device was tucked so high up inside the cylinder, it was impossible to spot.

"Based on all the legends, this could very well be the receptacle for one of our fabled Memory Tools.

"I plan to do something noble with the sculpture itself once I have rescued what it hides, perhaps offer the giant to the new museum. Goodness knows from Fouquelle's description, I don't have a suitable place for it.

"But what matters most is that now I may finally be able to prove reincarnation and by doing so prove that my son Albert's soul has indeed migrated into the new child my wife and I have been blessed with.

"Yours,

"Frederick L. Lennox"

"And have you identified which sculpture the letter refers to?"
The speaker wasn't Malachai—Lucian knew his voice by now.
Based on Elgin's reports, Lucian guessed it was Reed Winston
and mouthed his name to Doug and Matt.

"There's no way to be sure, since Lennox left the museum over
a hundred pieces, all from that same area, but based on what I've
been able to find out I've narrowed it down to about a dozen that
could fit this description."

"I can't work with a dozen pieces, Malachai."

"Don't you think I know that?"

"What are you suggesting?"

"Can you get into the museum's computers?"

"And do what?"

The three FBI agents watched the phone as if looking at it
would give them more facts than they were getting from the
voices. All of them were alert, hoping they were about to get a
break on the Malachai Samuels case, but Lucian was the only
one of them who was sweating. Hearing about yet more information that—if his hypnosis sessions were to be believed—connected to one of his past lives was taking its toll. First there was
what he'd learned in France about Fouquelle. Now this.

"I need you to figure out which piece of sculpture contains the
Memory Tool, Reed. I don't care how you do it or what it costs. Bribe
someone at the Met or hire someone to hack into their computer
system to get the information. It doesn't matter to me what you do
or what it costs. I have to know what piece we're looking for."

"Then what? We can't steal a piece of sculpture from the
goddamn Metropolitan Museum!"

"It's not the sculpture we want but what's inside it," Malachai
said. *"This could be it. Worth more than half the art in the Met.*
Incalculably valuable. This could be a map to our memories from
lives past. Don't you understand?"

Doug glanced over at Lucian and nodded. The look said, *We have him.* And he might be right. The man they'd been following, laying traps for and eavesdropping on had just ordered a hack of the Metropolitan Museum of Art's computer system.

"Can you do it, Reed?" the reincarnationist asked. *"Can you get me the name of the piece of sculpture that Lennox bought from Fouquelle's dig? We don't have a lot of time. The galleries that house these sculptures are being rebuilt. Once the pieces go back on display it will be so much more difficult for us to get to them."*

One thing the recording proved was that Darius Shabaz hadn't lied. Malachai didn't know anything about Hypnos specifically. That meant up until now the reincarnationist hadn't been involved in the scheme to trade the sculpture. While Reed and Malachai continued plotting on the recording, Lucian opened his notebook, flipped past the pages of the women who were always there, waiting, wanting something from him, and with his pencil wrote out the word that Malachai probably would have killed for—might have already killed for—might kill for again. The name that was tied to Lucian's regression sessions, that would give the FBI the break it needed to finally get Malachai Samuels. He passed the notebook to Comley. In the center of the page was just one word.

Hypnos.

Chapter
FIFTY-EIGHT

"I don't agree that it's unethical. It's critical information, and we need it if there's any hope of us obtaining the Memory Tool." Dr. Malachai Samuels was standing in front of the window in Dr. Iris Bellmer's office on Tuesday morning. She was aware of the stress he was under, had heard it over the phone last night when he'd called her and asked her to come in early to discuss something of grave importance. Now, she felt her own level of stress rise as she responded to his emotions.

"Malachai, there's no way I can do what you're asking." She tried to talk soothingly, hoping she could calm him down, but from the way he was repeatedly shuffling the deck of antique playing cards, she clearly wasn't succeeding.

"Yes, there is. Just call James Ryan and tell him that you've been going over his tapes and have found some curious consistencies between his various past-life memories, and you think another session might be beneficial."

The sound of the cards was the only noise in the room. Iris tried to figure out a way to refuse without raising his ire. After all, he was her boss and she loved her job.

Malachai, unaware of her struggle, continued, "Then, when he gets here, hypnotize him."

"And go looking for information he doesn't know I'm searching for? You know I can't do that. It's more than unethical. It could be criminal."

Malachai stopped playing with the cards and looked at her as if he wasn't quite sure he'd heard her correctly. His eyes were cold and unyielding, his face frozen.

Iris hadn't meant to use the word *criminal*. She knew about the FBI's year-and-a-half-long investigation into her boss's life and how much damage it had done to his and the foundation's credibility. It hadn't been smart to remind him of all that now.

"I would never ask you to do anything criminal, Iris." His eyes were boring into her, and she could feel his cold rage. "You do know that, don't you?"

She tried to look away from his gaze. "Malachai, I won't do it to my patient and you can't do it to yours, either. You can't bring in that little girl and push her to give you more information."

"What I do with my patients isn't your concern."

"It is. I work here, too. My reputation is tied to the reputation of the institute. I took an oath to do no harm, and so did you. Our interference would be harmful."

A muscle twitched in Malachai's jaw. "If you don't want to contact your client, then I will."

"Are you threatening me?"

Malachai took a breath. Iris could see he was making an effort, but an effort at what? Reining in a temper she'd never before seen exhibited? Trying to figure out another tactic to convince her to do what he was asking?

"You're right, of course," he said in a soothing, placating tone. Moving away from the window, he sat down at her desk, opposite her, leaned back in his seat and smiled in that odd way he had of moving only his lips without it ever traveling to his eyes. It gave him an inhuman look, she thought.

"I'm sorry, Iris. Did I upset you?"

"A little, yes."

"It's just that this is important to me."

She nodded.

"Forget about asking Ryan to come in again."

She was relieved—until he told her what he wanted her to do instead.

"Why don't you just give me the cassette tapes of your sessions with him and let me listen to his regressions. Let me see if there's anything there that could help us. Then we can discuss this again."

"I didn't get permission from him to actually play his tapes for anyone else."

"You don't have to. I'm the co-director of the foundation, and I supervise you. It's entirely within the code of ethics for me to hear them."

"Is it? I'm not sure."

"You are stubborn, aren't you?" He smiled at her again in that same odd way. Malachai put his hands on the chair's ornate wooden arms and fingered the lion's claws. He studied the carvings for a moment, then glanced up at her. "You know, this chair has been in this building since the Phoenix Club was first convened in the 1840s. Since my great-great-great-uncle decided that reincarnation was worth examining. They were all so fascinated with the idea of past-life regression. Walt Whitman, Bronson Alcott, Ralph Waldo Emerson, Frederick Law Olmsted..." The way he said their names was like music. "Henry Rice Billings, Frederick L. Lennox..." Malachai reached out and picked up one of the snow globes sitting on her desk, the one containing an Egyptian pyramid. Shaking it, he watched the sand—not snow—swirl, float and then start to settle.

"Over four thousand years ago in ancient Egypt," he said, "there was an Egyptian priest named Imhotep who healed people in a sleep temple. Have you ever read the stories of the miraculous cures he was responsible for?"

Malachai shook the snow globe once more, agitating the sand again, then watching as the grains swirled, floated and then started to settle.

"No," Iris said.

"Have you ever been to Egypt?"

"I haven't been, no. My parents brought that back for me. I've always wanted to go."

"When I was there I saw what's left of those sleep temples. Dream temples, they're sometimes called. Priests lulled people who were sick into a trancelike state with a process that's not very different from the process you and I use today to hypnotize our patients." He shook the snow globe again. The grains churned violently, then slowed. "They were priests, we are doctors, but we're all after the same thing—to help people who are in pain and troubled. Four thousand years ago, those priests used hypnosis and religious rituals and kept their patients in a trance for as long as three days while they prayed to their gods to heal them. We work with our patients for a few months and pray our own training will help them. But how different are our jobs from the priests'?"

Once again Malachai repeated the ritual of shaking the globe and watching the disturbed sands calm. "Those ancient priests claimed they succeeded in casting bad spirits from the mind and body. I'm sure they were telling the truth as they saw it. But what really happened? Was it just the power of suggestion? I don't think so. I've read their writings. You believe, and I do, too, that so much of what causes our pain and suffering are unresolved past-life issues carried over into the present. There are tools,

Iris, tools that can help us do our jobs, that could help us help our patients. Tools we could utilize in order to prove reincarnation is real, to prove that you and I and all of us are part of the past and the present and will forever be part of the future. That our souls are part of each other."

He was shaking the globe more slowly now, back and forth, not allowing the sand to settle at all, keeping it in constant motion. "Did you ever stop to really think about what it would mean to us if we could prove it? Really prove it, Iris. We might end wars, murder and crime… If people truly believed that we are all connected, that karma must be paid back, they might not be so quick to harm and hurt. Think about that. And think about how you and I and Beryl could become the heroes of this revolution. The ones who found the proof. The Marco Polos and Columbuses of our day. Who are we to deny the power that might help people far more than we ever will be able to by ourselves?"

As she watched the to-and-fro movement of the snow globe, as she stared at the way the lamplight glanced off its rounded glass surface and glinted with each half rotation, she felt his passion and excitement stir up inside of her. Yes, it would be amazing if there was a tool, and if they could be the ones to find it—if there was a way to help people slip into past-life memories with even more ease, if she was part of the discovery of that tool.

Malachai rolled the globe to the right, to the left, to the right, to the left. "Iris, please give me James Ryan's tapes."

Slightly swaying to the rhythm of the right, left, right, left spinning, Iris rose and walked to the file cabinet behind her desk. She unlocked it with a small key on a silver ring she withdrew from her pocket.

After closing it and relocking it she walked around the desk and over to the man she worked for, who was still playing with the gift her parents had brought back from Egypt.

"I want to be part of the discovery," she said, and handed two small black cassette tapes to Malachai Samuels.

It wasn't until after he put the sandy pyramid back down and she heard its base knock against her wood desk that she realized what she'd done. "Wait," she called to Malachai as he walked out of her office, but he didn't turn around.

Chapter

FIFTY-NINE

The bulk of the estates on Round Hill Road in Greenwich, Connecticut, were on four- to ten-acre lots and set far back from the road, so few neighbors noticed the unmarked Crown Victoria driving through the iron gates of the Canton property that morning.

The housekeeper who looked at the agents' badges was frightened and scurried off to find her employer.

Seconds later, Oliver Canton blustered down the hall. The red-faced, overweight man was wearing a bad toupee and an old-fashioned silk smoking jacket. "What the hell is going on here?" he shouted as he came toward the agents, who introduced themselves and showed him their search warrant.

"You are not looking through anything in my house until I call my attorney."

"By all means, call your attorney. But make sure you tell him we have this," Richmond instructed, holding up the legal document. "He'll tell you that if you don't cooperate it's within our right to look around on our own."

Not succumbing to the threat without a fight, Canton pulled a cell phone out of his pocket, dialed a number and explained the situation. As he listened, sweat popped out on his upper lip, and after a few seconds he hung up. His face was drained of all color.

"What do you want to see?" he asked.

The agents followed Canton into his library, where he grudgingly offered them seats at a round mahogany table.

"I assume you want to stay in business?" Lucian asked without preamble.

"Is there a reason I wouldn't be able to stay in business?" Canton asked with a false bravado as see-through as cellophane.

Shabaz must have already been in touch with him.

"That all depends on you and your willingness to cooperate," Richmond said. "We know you were involved in selling two paintings to Darius Shabaz. He's given us the bills of sale and all the documentation on their provenance that you gave him. Everything was in order."

Canton looked slightly relieved, then confused, and Lucian imagined he was wondering why they were here if the paperwork was in order.

"Everything, until we got to the last owner of each painting. At that point the owners had bogus names. Who did you purchase those paintings from? What are their real names? Did they come to you to fence the paintings, or did you put out the word that you were looking for works from those artists?"

"Those were the names the sellers gave me. I had no idea they weren't their real names. How can I be responsible for people lying to me? The paintings were authentic, and that's all that mattered."

"Bullshit," Lucian spat out. "You knew exactly what you were doing. Who did you buy the Matisse and the Van Gogh from? Real names. Now." He banged his fist down on the table. Lucian was tired and jetlagged, his head hurt and he was absolutely certain this man was lying through his teeth. Canton not only knew he'd bought stolen artwork, but had probably orchestrated the thefts.

"My lawyer said you have a search warrant but that doesn't mean I have to answer your questions. I was just trying to help out."

Lucian stood up. Richmond followed, and together they started pulling out file cabinet drawers and piling stacks of paperwork on the table.

"What are you doing?" Canton screamed.

"We're taking your records and getting out of here since you've stopped cooperating."

Canton's hand shook as he reached for the glass of soda already on the table and spilled some of it bringing it up to his lips. He took a long gulp and then asked, "What do you want?"

"The men you worked with," Lucian said. "Who stole the paintings for you? Were you looking for those specific paintings? Did you put the word out? What the hell happened, Canton?" He knew he was bullying the dealer, but he didn't care anymore.

Canton was hyperventilating, and his skin had turned even redder. Richmond glanced over at Lucian and raised his eyebrows as if to question the man's reaction—was it a performance or for real?

"I need…" Canton whispered and then stopped. "I need…" Reaching into his jacket pocket, he pulled out an amber pill bottle, thumbed the cap off, shook out a pill and, with trembling fingers, managed to get it into his mouth.

"You all right, Mr. Canton?" Richmond asked.

"It's my heart."

Lucian had been able to read the label. The dealer wasn't in cardiac distress; the pills were anti-anxiety medication. "Then we'll just take what we need and leave you to rest," Lucian said as he started dumping the files into garbage bags he and Richmond had brought with them.

Yesterday afternoon the agents had visited Andrew Moreno's art gallery in Chelsea, and the paperwork they'd confiscated from his office was enough to keep them busy for days. With this load added to it, Lucian figured he'd be working nights and weekends for a while. He'd need to call Emeline from the car and tell her he might not make it to the Met's reception tonight. They'd talked twice earlier today, and both times her voice had been tight and twisted with fear. The longer the threats continued, the more distraught she became. Lucian knew from cases he'd worked on how incessant worry and fear frayed your nerves. At a certain point you stopped being able to push the anxiety aside. No one survived attacks like the one Emeline was enduring without scars. She'd told him that she'd gone back to work that morning, and so far had gotten two calls, both in the same mechanical voice: *Tell anyone what I look like and I'll kill you before they find me. You and your father, too.*

"And he repeated it," Emeline had said, her voice tight with the effort of holding back tears. "Three times. Just like in the e-mails."

Lucian reassured her that Broderick and his men were getting close to making an arrest but it was a lie. They hadn't made any progress. This guy had to be smart to go this long without once slipping up. Did that mean he was smart enough to elude them and get to Emeline? Lucian prayed not. One accident was all they needed. If he just stayed on the phone a few seconds too long or walked by the gallery and lingered an extra second peering in the windows.

"This drawer's empty," Richmond said to Lucian as he dropped another five files into a black plastic garbage back and nodded to another file cabinet. "I'll grab that, you get the rest of the stuff."

The color in Canton's face intensified as he watched Lucian move to the desk and pick up the laptop computer. With a tortured *"NO"* the dealer leaped forward with teeth bared and bit Lucian's hand.

Richmond jumped Canton, wrestled him to the ground and had him cuffed in less than thirty seconds. Lucian, excruciating pain radiating up his arm, read him his rights then listed the offenses he was going to charge him with.

"I'll drop the last three and you'll have a chance at spending at least some of the rest of your life outside a prison, but I want the name of the man or the men you worked with to get the Van Gogh and the Matisse."

Twenty minutes later, as Richmond drove away, with the dealer handcuffed and whimpering in the backseat, Lucian kept looking down at his hand as if it had betrayed him by being so close to the dealer's mouth.

Chapter

SIXTY

Iris Bellmer was bewildered and overcome with remorse. She'd let Malachai hypnotize her with his soft, smooth voice, using her own damn snow globe. Sitting at her desk, trying to make sense of what she'd done and calculate its ramifications, she stared out the window at the tree that filtered the view of the street. The wind was blowing, and one branch kept tapping on the glass almost as if agreeing that what she'd done was unforgivable.

Closing her eyes, she practiced deep breathing for five minutes, inhaling to the count of five, holding the breath to the count of five, then following the same pattern of exhaling, holding and then starting all over again until finally she felt calmer.

When Iris opened her eyes again she knew what she had to do: stop Malachai Samuels from doing anything illegal with the information she'd given him and let James Ryan know that she'd released information about his past-life memories without his approval.

She called her patient first. Ryan's phone rang three times before his voice mail picked up. Iris had prepared what she was going to say, but to him, not a machine. She just identified herself and asked him to call her at his earliest convenience.

What she had to do next would be more difficult. How could she convince Malachai of anything? What could she say to him that would stop him from interfering with their patients' lives?

Opening her door, she took a step out into the hallway, surprised to see Malachai and Beryl standing close together talking at the far end. Should she confront him with Beryl there, or wait? Before Iris had a chance to decide, Malachai turned and walked in the opposite direction as Beryl started toward Iris. Should she go after Malachai? He was almost at the staircase that led to lower-level library.

"Are you all right?" Beryl asked.

If Malachai heard his aunt, he didn't turn around. How many more steps till she could be sure he wouldn't be able to hear her?

"Iris?"

"Yes?"

"Is something wrong?"

Iris heard a door shut in the distance—the door to the library. She nodded. "Yes." It came out in a whisper.

Chapter
SIXTY-ONE

As he walked up the museum's grand marble staircase, the pull of the palace reached out to Lucian, but it wasn't a night for sentiment. Passing through the medieval galleries, heading for the American Wing, he was blind to the artwork for the first time that he could remember. Tonight he was going to solve more than one mystery, and as much as it might cause him personal pain, there'd be relief to finally get to the truth. Hard, cold knowledge was the only thing he could trust. The past few weeks had all been a game, and he'd been played. He clenched his teeth against the thought of that and his unremitting headache.

Golden light flooded the Charles Engelhard Court, a glassed-in garden on the park that was home to large-scale sculptures, leaded-glass windows and architectural elements from the nineteenth and early twentieth centuries. There were already at least a hundred guests milling about the three-story atrium, but the space was far from crowded. Lucian recognized and nodded to members of the board of directors. Top-tier museum patrons were there, as well as descendants of the families who had bequeathed the paintings to the Met.

In the center of the room an area was cordoned off by a

twelve-foot opaque screen. Behind it, Lucian found Marie Grimshaw repositioning five empty easels. When she saw him she forced a smile. He had the sudden urge to tell her he was sorry—but for what? Everything had turned out the way she and Tyler Weil wanted it to—the paintings rescued, Hypnos safe.

"Congratulations, Agent Glass. In a career dedicated to protecting art, to keeping the treasures of the centuries safe, tonight should be a major celebration for you. Thank you."

She was right. He should be reveling in what he and Matt had accomplished, but the surprise he'd suffered earlier this afternoon when Oliver Canton finally gave him the name of his accomplices had ruined that. One name meant nothing. The other meant far too much.

Afterward, Matt had tried to convince Lucian to have a drink with him. To talk about what had happened. Lucian had refused and sat in his office on the computer ostensibly working but just staring at the screen trying to figure out how to deal with the information and its ramifications. He'd been made a fool of. He'd wanted to believe something so badly he'd risked his credibility, his job and his fucking sanity.

He'd forced himself here, not for the celebration, but for the confrontation. He'd even dressed for the magnitude of the event, wearing black slacks, not jeans, a jacket made in Italy and suede loafers that replaced his everyday boots. The only item that was the same was the Glock in his shoulder holster.

There were two bars set up at opposite ends of the gallery. The one with the smaller crowd backed up to a Frank Lloyd Wright living room that had been transplanted to the Met in 1982. Since Lucian was officially off duty, he ordered vodka on the rocks and, while the bartender made it, he stared out the windows into the park's lush green backdrop. A familiar sense of loneliness overtook him as he remembered someone who was gone, whom he'd almost been able to reach out and touch. Emeline had raised the specter of Solange's ghost, put flesh on her bones and blood in her veins. It was a mean trick. She should have stayed a memory. Even if he'd mythologized her, as a myth she'd done him no harm.

He could smell her, as if she were right there. It was the curious mixture it seemed he'd been smelling all his adult life, either in reality or in his imagination—that particular mingling of lilies of the valley with turpentine and linseed oil. Solange's scent.

But it was Emeline approaching, leaning on her father's arm. More sickly looking than ever, Jacobs was probably leaning on her but disguising it well. The man's navy suit hung on his frame, his illness all the more obvious for the excess fabric.

Lucian's hand gripped his glass as he fought the urge to throw it in the man's face, battled with the overwhelming desire to beat him to a bloody pulp right here, right now. And Emeline? He had to force himself not to turn away.

Emeline and her father had reached the bar. Her scent was so pervasive. She'd never used Solange's perfume before. Why tonight? To continue the farce?

As she smiled at him, a faint blush rose in her cheeks. She was wearing cream-colored, wide-legged silk pants with a narrow, fitted blouse of the same fabric. On her feet were flat ballet slippers in the same shade of cream with gold strings tied in a bow. Her hair was sleeked back and pulled into a chignon, almost as if she was showing off her scar. In her ears were round diamonds that caught the light and reflected back the sunset's glow.

Reaching up, she brushed Lucian's cheek with a kiss that would appear innocuous to anyone watching—including her father—but wasn't, and then whispered that signature line

Solange had always used on greeting. "I very much missed you."

Lucian couldn't help noticing the swell of her small breasts. Despite everything he knew and all the emotions roiling in him, he was still overwhelmed by an urgent need to touch her skin—to make sure it was warm, not cold—to reassure himself that she was real, that she was still here, that she was not about to evaporate into the past. His heart hadn't caught up to his head yet.

Coming here had been a mistake. He suddenly knew how the men he had put in prison felt. This wasn't the place to pose the questions he needed to ask or to hear the answers he was almost afraid to learn. He needed to get out.

"Good evening, Lucian," Jacobs said formally.

"Good evening, Mr. Jacobs, Emeline," Lucian responded. His own voice sounded forced. He wasn't managing this very well. "Would you like drinks?"

Emeline told the bartender she'd take champagne and Jacobs asked for gin. "No rocks," he muttered, and Lucian noticed Emeline stiffen.

He knew, because she had told him, that Jacobs's daily promises to stop drinking never lasted long past each evening's cocktail hour, despite the fact that the liquor was killing him.

Around them, as more and more people poured into the luminous stone-and-glass gallery, the sounds of tinkling crystal and excited voices rose and hovered in the air along with the mixed scents of flowers, burning candles and perfumes. Satins and silks shimmered in the twinkling light from the votives scattered around the room on the cocktail tables. Diamonds hanging from earlobes, necks and fingers glinted; sequined jackets and beaded handbags shone.

The festivity was an affront to what he knew about the two

people standing beside him. Lucian wanted to climb up on a bar and scream at them all to be quiet, to honor the memory of a dead girl and take revenge on the man who was responsible for her death.

The bartender delivered the Jacobses' drinks just as the string quartet stopped playing and the museum's director, Tyler Weil, stepped onto a platform to the right of the screened-off area.

Weil scanned the audience, found who he was looking for and motioned for Marie Grimshaw to join him. Then, picking up the microphone, he welcomed everyone.

Beside Lucian, Emeline took his arm and pressed close to him. She smiled up at him, and he was struck by her enigmatic expression. She looked as if she was trying to be happy but at the same time was struggling with where she was, with who she was, with trying to assimilate it all. The stress was no doubt real but its source was not what she'd led him to believe. Before tonight he would have been empathetic about her dilemma. Now he knew it was a lie.

Chapter
SIXTY-TWO

The lights in his office were off except for a table lamp, and so Beryl's face was in shadow, but Malachai could read her expression from the way she was gripping her cane—not for support but like a weapon.

"How dare you laugh at me?" Her voice strained with rage.

"But what you're saying is surely a joke, isn't it? What can you think I'm planning? Betraying our patients? Relax, Beryl, please. I'd never do anything to risk the reputation of the foundation."

"You wouldn't? But you have. I can't allow you to do it again. I can't take a chance you'll put us back in the news and harm us further. I've called our lawyers, Malachai. As of an hour ago your name has been removed from the deed of the building, I've stopped your salary and you are no longer co-director of the institute. You're on a temporary leave of absence."

He stood up quickly, his hands clenched at his sides, a muscle twitching in his neck. "You can't do that."

"I most certainly can. I'm the chairman of the board, and I have the unanimous support of the other board members."

"I'm a member of that board."

"You've been outvoted."

"Whatever it is, you owe it to me to listen to what—"

"Here's what I'm offering you," she said, not waiting for him to explain. "If you stay away from Veronica Keyes and James Ryan and make no attempt to use therapy or hypnosis to delve into their psyches to find out more about this sculpture you're obsessed with, then six months from now you can come back to work and start receiving your salary again. Six months after that, your name can go back on the lease. And six months after that, if everything is still status quo, you can resume your duties as co-director. I'm serious, Malachai. I've put up with more than I can stand—and I can't stand that well anymore."

"You bitch." He said it low and deep, and the single word rushed out of his mouth so quickly and came at her so hard she flinched as if it were a physical blow.

"I want you to understand something else. If anything happens to me, or to Iris Bellmer, the directors have instructions to tell the police you are the prime suspect. You're ill, Malachai. You're obsessed to the point that it's threatening your own mental health. My last stipulation is for you to see a therapist. Not a past-life therapist, but a psychiatrist. You need help, even if you can't see it. You are a world-renowned reincarnationist and have everything a man could want in terms of prestige and money. It should be enough, but it's not, and—"

"Don't tell me what should be enough," he interrupted. "You do not have any idea what is enough for me." In one very smooth move, as if what he was doing was of no importance, Malachai opened his desk drawer and pulled out a silver and mother-of-pearl handgun that gleamed in the light cast from the torchiere.

Beryl watched her nephew, holding her breath, an expression of disbelief on her face.

Malachai studied her and then laughed. "Nerves of steel."

"Don't play with me, Malachai. There's a policeman outside

in a squad car. You can kill me, but you won't get away with it. I did you the courtesy of waiting until everyone was gone for the day so you could leave without embarrassment. Against advice I chose not to have you escorted from your own office. I can see now that I was still naive. I always underestimate you, even when I cast you as the devil."

"The devil? Please, Aunt Beryl. I'm not going to harm you. I'm collecting my belongings to take with me. You don't mind if I do that, do you? Or has the board voted that I have to leave my personal effects behind?"

"Take what you need and get the hell out."

One by one he picked up other items from his desk: a deck of antique playing cards, a small tape recorder, three manila files, a leather-bound address book. When he reached for the two small black cassette tapes, Beryl anticipated the move, and her hand was there before his. He reached forward to wrest them from her arthritic fingers, fingers that were like the carved claws on the antique chairs.

"You are hurting me. It's not a wise move, Malachai."

For thirty seconds they stood, frozen in mid-action, hands clasped in animosity, standing on either side of the desk that had belonged to Trevor Talmage when he founded the Phoenix Club over a hundred and fifty years before—where he had been found murdered.

Malachai felt his aunt's grip tighten, and before he even guessed what she was going to do, Beryl lifted her cane and brought it down on his hand, smashing his wrist. He couldn't stop himself. He let go of her, grabbed his own hand…the pain was excruciating…and while he reeled from its intensity, he watched her pocket the tapes and limp to the door. She left leaning on the ebony stick as if the past few minutes had drained her of all her strength.

When she had the space of the room between them, she stopped and turned back. "A few other housekeeping issues. I called Nina Keyes. She knows everything and won't allow you to see her granddaughter again. We've alerted James Ryan not to take your calls, either. Your bulldog, Reed Winston, has been paid off, and our lawyer has warned him that if anything happens we'll give the police his name. I'm not sure what we're going to do about the librarian you hired. He doesn't seem to have figured into this insanity, but our lawyer is checking his references. If he's legitimate I'm thinking of offering him a full-time job." And then she walked out.

Malachai didn't realize he'd bitten the inside of his cheek until he tasted blood. He'd only done that once before, the night his father had told him what a disappointment he was and that of his two sons, the wrong one had died. Spitting into his handkerchief, Malachai fought his rising panic.

This could not happen. It was unthinkable. He was the co-director of the Phoenix Foundation. Reaching down, he ran his finger down the mother-of-pearl pistol sitting on his open briefcase. The lamplight gleamed off the opalescent surface, illuminating the nacre's subtle blue and yellow highlights. As he lifted the antique gun his right wrist throbbed, but he didn't move it to his left hand. The pain was at least a distraction from the greater, more ruthless pain. Malachai put the gun up to his temple and felt the cool metal like a caress.

This gun had belonged to Davenport Talmage, and there was a rumor that he'd used it to kill his brother, Trevor, so he could take over the club, marry his brother's wife and inherit the fortune that had gone to the eldest son.

Malachai teased the trigger. He realized the gun wasn't loaded and, feeling like a fool, sank back into his chair, letting the weapon clatter to the floor. How could Beryl dismiss him? He was her blood, her only family. Malachai shut his eyes and looked into a galaxy of blackness. He wouldn't give up his position…or his quest. He'd talk Beryl out of this. He'd give her a day or two. He'd done it before, talked her in and out of all sorts of things over the years. He had that ability. Always had. Would again.

Snapping the briefcase closed, he stood and was surprised to feel his legs trembling. He couldn't allow that. He was stronger than she was, stronger than all of them. Taking a deep breath, he refocused his energy.

He didn't stop to turn and take a last look at his office because he wasn't leaving for more than a few days. A week. Beryl would change her mind. He'd come too far to give up now; he had made too many sacrifices to give up…taken too many risks. He'd been shot, for God's sake, and was still recovering! Yes, that was it. The painkillers. The perfect way out of this. Everyone knew how easy it was to get addicted to painkillers and act irrationally. Malachai had no doubt he could coerce his doctor to diagnose him and then convince Beryl it was just the painkillers that had clouded his reason and that he'd take a few weeks off and get straightened out. She'd want to believe that. She always wanted to believe that he wasn't as evil as he really was. But he was. He knew it and he could live with it. Like Davenport. The youngest son had no choice but to do what he had to do to survive.

Chapter
SIXTY-THREE

"Tonight I want to welcome you to a very special event," Tyler Weil said into the microphone. "A private showing of paintings that on paper have belonged to our illustrious institution for decades but have never been exhibited. Each was a bequest never received, a gift we never catalogued, studied or learned from. These paintings were stolen before we ever received them. And have been lost to the world until tonight."

There was an audible reaction from the assembled guests as people in the crowd asked each other if they'd ever heard anything about these newly found paintings.

The news had covered the story of Darius Shabaz, the billionaire Hollywood producer/writer/director pleading guilty in a Los Angeles courthouse to extortion and buying stolen artwork, but no details linking his transgression to the museum or these paintings had yet leaked out.

"Ladies and gentlemen, before we reveal the paintings I need to warn you that one of the five paintings we've just added to our holdings has been vandalized, and we hope to be able to restore it to some semblance of its former glory. We've included it tonight because, despite how brutally it's been violated, it's

still a masterpiece. As is the sculpture on display. The story of
this rescue and recovery is nothing less than astonishing, and
although I wish I could share it with you tonight, I've been
asked to hold off until the people responsible are all captured
and brought to justice. But I can and do want to thank those
who have worked so bravely and tirelessly on our behalf to
make it happen. So if you will all join me in a toast—to the Art
Crime Team of the Federal Bureau of Investigation—with our
heartfelt thanks."

While the guests raised their glasses and echoed the director's "Hear, hear!" the screen was pushed back, revealing the
paintings and the colossal statue.

There was a sudden cessation of noise and the large room
became eerily quiet. One pair of clapping hands broke the silence and then others joined in until the room echoed with the
roar of applause.

The Renoir, Klimt, Monet and Van Gogh had been cleaned.
Hypnos was stately and tall, and though only a remnant of
what he had once been, was still commanding. But more
powerful than any of those masterworks was the Matisse in all
its horrific destruction.

"You saved those paintings," Emeline whispered to Lucian.

He looked into her shining eyes and fought the urge to accept
the kindness he saw there. "It's my job," he said, turning his attention back to the paintings. At least they were safe now. Even
the murdered Matisse had a chance of resurrection. Treated by
the best restorers in the world it would regain some semblance
of its former glory.

This was the only reincarnation he would ever believe in, he
told himself. It's only art that keeps us immortal.

From the corner of his eye he saw Nicolas Olshling walking

toward the stage. The stunned expression on the head of security's face made Lucian's blood run cold.

"Take your father and sit down at one of the tables. Get him out of the crowd," Lucian said to Emeline.

"Why?"

"I'm not exactly sure, but something's wrong."

Lucian ran across the room, reaching the stage just as Weil stepped away from the microphone.

"What is it, Nicolas?" Weil asked.

"We just received a bomb threat." He was holding his cell phone as if it were a snake about to strike. "If what I heard is legit, we're under attack. We are under attack."

Chapter

SIXTY-FOUR

As Olshling explained the instructions he'd received, Lucian listened, and at the same time became aware of a commotion across the room as three—no, four—men pushed their way through the crowd. Each wore a hood and black mask.

Instinctively Lucian reached for his gun but instead pulled out his cell phone. There were too many of them. Just one of him. He needed backup. Before he could hit the key to connect him to headquarters a fifth hooded man came up beside him, knocked his phone out of his hand and kicked it away. From behind, one of the others knocked Lucian to the ground. As he scrambled to his feet, Lucian saw around each attacker's waist a wide belt decorated with a half-dozen metal cylinders connected with red detonation cords.

The shortest of the human bombs grabbed the microphone from Weil and started shouting out instructions to the crowd. His voice had a flat, distinct Midwest twang.

"Do as I say and no one will be hurt. Stop moving. Just stop moving and stand still. The doors are sealed. The only way you're getting out is if we let you go."

At first he was shouting over the crowd's panic but they grew quiet quickly.

"Any movement and we'll set off our fireworks." The lead terrorist patted his belt. Neoprene gloves made his thick fingers look like fat sausages. "No calls."

Petrified and panicked, the guests stilled. There was no sound from any of them for a few seconds, and then a cry broke the stillness. It was a child. A little girl's wail, high-pitched and plaintive. Lucian scanned the room trying to pinpoint its source.

Larry Talbot, the ringleader, turned away from the microphone and spoke directly to Olshling. "Get on your radio and instruct your security force to leave the building. Once they're outside, they can call the police or the FBI or God and tell them what's going on. But if anyone even attempts to approach this museum we'll light it up like a kid's birthday cake. We have men on every corner outside and at strategic points in the park and in your garage. If my team spots a single cop car or fire engine or ambulance in the vicinity, we'll blow this space to kingdom come."

Olshling nodded.

"Do it, then." The leader turned back to the microphone and barked out more instructions to the frightened crowd.

"Cooperate and nobody gets hurt. But if you don't…" He gestured emphatically to his corset of explosives.

From some corner, the little girl continued to cry, the sound rising above all the others.

"Now, take out your cell phones. Slowly. We're going to collect them. Needless to say, any attempt at heroics will be plain stupid. Like signing a death warrant. Understand?"

No one spoke, or even moved.

"Excellent…now take out your phones."

The leader was wearing blue jeans and sturdy work boots.

Lucian filed away these small identifying aspects so he'd be able to describe him later. Assuming there would be a later.

After checking on Olshling, who was doing as ordered in a voice he was working hard to keep steady, the terrorist turned to Tyler Weil. "The only way to protect this place and these people is to do exactly what we tell you to do. You're in charge, so this is up to you. Do you understand?"

"What do you want?" Weil asked. There was a touch of defiance in his voice.

"Do you understand?"

Lucian answered for Weil. "Yes, he understands."

Talbot focused on Lucian, who looked right into the man's brown eyes. They gave away nothing. Lucian pressed his arm against his Glock. There were too many people in the gallery to use the gun, too many terrorists, too many unknowns. But there would come a moment when it would be time to act. And he'd be ready.

Olshling switched off his radio.

"You done?" the leader asked.

"Yes."

"They understood?"

"Yes, but if you—" Olshling said nervously.

"Just answer the fucking question that I'm asking. They understood everything?"

"Yes."

From out of the crowd one of the other hooded men struggled toward the podium dragging Nina Keyes with him. A little girl was holding her hand but Nina was trying to break the child's grip and push her away.

"Veronica, don't stay with me. Let go. Run."

"No." The little girl shook her head, and the brown curls bobbed violently.

"Baby, I want you to go." Nina was frantic.

"I won't...I won't leave you," she cried.

This had to be the child Lucian had heard crying. Her little face was filled with fear but with determination, too.

Nina was still trying to pull her hand out of the child's viselike grip, but Veronica held tight to her grandmother and wouldn't leave her side.

It's as if she thinks she can save the older woman's life, Lucian thought.

The man dragging Nina took the suicide belt off his own waist and strapped it around hers.

"What are you doing?" She tried to resist.

"Shut up!" he shouted.

The brute was putting explosives on Nina? Lucian's insides tightened as he realized what these men were planning.

Just then the largest of the masked men arrived at the staging area hauling two women with him as if they were garbage: Deborah Mitchell, with tears streaming down her cheeks, and Marie Grimshaw, whose lips were set into a slash of anger as she cursed her handler with a string of invectives. The man spat. She screeched more foul language. Letting go of her for a moment, the man slapped Marie so hard she fell into Deborah, who tumbled onto the hard floor. When the younger woman started audibly crying, the terrorist kicked her, shouting at her to shut up. When she didn't, the bully kicked Deborah again, and then kicked at Marie. "Get up, both of you. Now."

Lucian found the abuse impossible to watch without taking action but he had to hold back until he could have an effect.

Taking off his suicide belt, the brute buckled it around Marie's waist. The lead terrorist removed his and strapped it on Deborah. A fourth terrorist delivered two more hostages. Unbuckling his belt, he wrapped it around Emeline Jacobs's middle. It was too big and he had to tie it, violently pulling it tighter than necessary, so it would stay. The diamonds in her ears glinted with each tremble of her slim body as she withstood his ministrations without making a sound. Andre Jacobs just stood there, by her side, weeping silent tears from his rheumy eyes as he watched, helpless and frail.

A rush of conflicting emotions broke over Lucian, too complicated for the time and the place.

"Don't any of you know how to count, for fuck's sake? Five belts. Five hostages." The ringleader screamed at his men. "Why drag this old man up here?"

Up till now everything had been brilliantly executed, but here was a snafu. An innocuous mistake for sure, but maybe, Lucian thought, there was a way to take advantage of the momentary distraction. Thinking, planning, he looked from each of the hooded men to each of the women who'd been transformed into a human bomb. From Marie Grimshaw, to Nina Keyes, to Veronica and to Deborah Mitchell, all he saw in their eyes was terror.

Emeline alone looked strong. She was looking at him, and in her eyes he saw determination and faith—faith in him.

"Now—" Talbot turned to Weil "—you're going to help us take what we came for out of here. Or else we'll step outside—" he pointed to the exit doors "—and before you can say boo or unbuckle a single belt, we'll detonate the explosives…" He pointed at the women and the child. "One lovely lady at a time."

Chapter

SIXTY-FIVE

Lucian stepped forward and spoke directly to the ringleader. "No hostages," he said with an air of authority. "We'll help you but only after you get those belts off all these women, now."

The blue-jeaned man laughed, turned his back on Lucian, motioned to his men and carved a slash mark in the air. One of the team stayed with the group of captive women. The other three marauders approached the exhibition.

So they were going to steal the paintings. The thought infuriated Lucian. So many people had worked so hard and risked so much to bring them here, only to have them taken, now, like this.

But none of them touched the paintings. The men surrounded Hypnos and were manipulating the sculpture onto a ready dolly.

Hypnos? Was it possible? Who was behind this? Malachai? Wouldn't Elgin Barindra have picked up on something about this? Wasn't it too fast for Malachai to have planned it? The answers mattered but not now, not as much as the more crucial issue: how to get the suicide belts off the hostages and get all these people out of here before anything went wrong. Because things always did go wrong, even when no one wanted them to. Situations like this escalated. The police wouldn't wait on the perimeter for long. Someone would get anxious and push too far, too fast. And it was going to happen any second. He had to do something now.

"There's a problem," Lucian said, trying not to taunt the leader as much as engage him.

"Your only problem is that you need to shut the fuck up."

"How do you know that's the sculpture you want?" Lucian asked.

Marie Grimshaw held back a gasp. Deborah Mitchell looked up, startled. Tyler Weil clenched his fists.

"What the fuck?" Talbot asked, his mouth twisted into a mean, angry snarl.

"There are two identical pieces of that sculpture in the museum. One is the original. The other is an almost perfect copy. And there's no guarantee which one this is. How do you know the museum didn't put the copy on display, since it was the copy that was instrumental in recapturing the paintings?"

"This is the sculpture I want, and you know it."

"I don't, and you can't. And no one is going tell you which is which unless you take the explosives off those women and get these people out of here." He gestured to the crowd behind him.

Talbot looked at Weil. "Is this sculpture the real deal?"

"It is."

"Can you be sure he's not lying to you?" Lucian asked earnestly. "Don't you think the director of the museum would lie to you if he could so that you'd take the wrong piece? His priority isn't these people. He only wants to protect his art," Lucian said derisively. "I can prove which is the real Hypnos."

Weil cursed under his breath.

Lucian ignored him and continued. "Think about what your boss will do to you if you bring them the wrong sculpture."

The terrorist was fully engaged now—angry, confused and focused on Lucian, which was just how the agent wanted it. "Take off the belts." Lucian gestured at Emeline and the others. "And I'll tell you if this is the right piece or not."

"I'm not bargaining with you," Talbot said. "I'll take all of you out if I want to."

"It's a known fact the original has ivory hands and feet. The copy doesn't, because it's now illegal to buy ivory."

"Is this ivory?" The ringleader reached out and touched the god's left hand.

"I don't know but there's a simple test we can do to see if it is."

"Do it, and fast."

"Take off the belts."

"I told you, no bargaining."

Lucian knew the man was feeling the stress; he could see a flicker of worry in his eyes.

"To find out if the ivory is real..." Lucian pulled out the lighter that he still carried to prove his willpower was stronger than his desire, and flicked it on. "Take off the belts and I'll show you how you can tell if this is the original or the fake."

Chapter

SIXTY-SIX

Marie Grimshaw's jaw hurt where her captor had slapped her, and her hip throbbed where he'd kicked her. Her heart was beating so hard and so fast she didn't think it could keep going for much longer. She watched as the FBI agent flicked his lighter and wasn't sure she could tolerate the flood of tension that rose in her. When the blue-orange flame flared, Nina felt Veronica's whole body spasm as if the fire had reached out and burned her.

"What is it, baby?" Nina asked, bending over, whispering in her granddaughter's ear.

"What is taking them so long? Where are they?" Veronica groaned.

"Who, darling? Who?"

"Hosh. Our sons! The people from the shtetl?"

Nina shook her head in frustration and looked back at the FBI agent.

Beside them, Andre Jacobs hung on to Emeline's arm and she struggled to support him and keep him upright. "I won't let anything happen to you," he muttered, a fool's promise, a drunk's ranting, even as his knees buckled for the third time.

Samimi's panic was escalating as he watched the scene play

out. Everything had been timed. He needed the men to move Hypnos out of there and get it down to the warehouse before Taghinia met them there. All of Samimi's plans depended on that small window of time he'd built into the schedule, but they were fast using up every one of those extra seconds, and the way things were going he was going to lose his opportunity. There was nothing to do now but go take over, even though he was supposed to stay in the background. Samimi allowed himself a glance at Deborah. He didn't want her to see this. Wished there was some way to avoid it. But he knew there wasn't.

Her eyes met his. Her terror was so intense it pained him. But he had only minutes to spare. If everything went all right, it wouldn't matter that he'd exposed himself, and if it didn't…well, Taghinia would take it out on him anyway, and nothing he did now would make that punishment any more merciful.

"Where is the other sculpture?" Samimi shouted. "Get it down here immediately. As soon as we see it, we'll remove the belts."

Lucian shouted at Weil. "Do it. Now."

Weil looked at Olshling and nodded.

"I can get it here in ten minutes," Olshling said.

"You have three," Samimi said. He nodded to two of his men. "Go with him."

As soon as the men were gone he pulled out his cell phone and punched in a number. "Stand by," Samimi said to the man on the other end of the phone. "We'll be ready to move out in five to six minutes."

Across the room he felt Deborah's eyes still on him, but this time he didn't look.

Chapter

SIXTY-SEVEN

Olshling returned in four minutes and ten seconds wheeling a second sculpture that looked identical to the Hypnos already standing in the center of the room.

"Which one is real?" Samimi demanded.

"Take off the belts," Lucian insisted.

Samimi nodded to the lead terrorist, who untied the belt around Nina's waist and then moved on to Veronica.

Once her granddaughter's belt was removed, Nina started to pull the little girl away from the podium.

"I can't go," Veronica screamed. "I can't leave Hosh."

"Shut her up," Samimi's number-one man shouted.

"I won't go!" the child cried.

"If you don't shut her up, I will."

This was how tragedies happened, Lucian thought as he rushed over and knelt down in front of the child. The tension was too high. He had to get the little girl to calm down. He spoke in a low, desperate whisper. "This time," he said, not sure how he knew what to say, not caring as long as it made sense to her, "this time you have to leave. You have to go, now. None of what happened before was your fault, do you understand?"

She was crying, not like a child, but with the dry, choking sobs of an old woman who had no tears left.

"You couldn't have saved him. But this time you can save yourself, and your grandmother."

Veronica's mouth relaxed and her eyes softened and she was just a seven-year-old kid, standing there, terrified but turning, moving, pulling at her grandmother's hands, hurrying to get away from the center of activity.

As each belt came off each hostage, one of the other terrorists took it and strategically placed it somewhere else in the atrium. One at the base of a Tiffany window. Another around the feet of a bronze sculpture of Diana. They were rigging the room with the explosives.

Lucian calculated the threat and tried to figure out the intruders' strategy. How were they planning to escape? How were they going to get the sculpture out of here? And once they were gone, how much time would he and the staff have to empty out the room before the explosives were detonated?

"We met your demands, now tell us," Samimi demanded of Lucian after all the belts had been removed and the hostages, no longer isolated at the podium, had returned to the group of other terrified guests. "Which of these two sculptures is the original?"

"I don't know, but…" Lucian spoke slowly, trying to buy time and anticipate what their next step was, watching their faces, looking for a sign. "When you burn ivory," he said, "its surface will go black, but you can wipe the carbon off and the ivory remains unhurt." He flicked his lighter and held the flame up to the broken thumb on the right hand of one of the statues.

Tyler Weil didn't utter a sound or make a move to stop Lucian as a film blackened the god's finger. A few seconds went by, and then the material started to bubble. An acrid smell filled the air.

"If that was the real Hypnos, if that was what happens to real ivory—" Lucian pointed to Weil "—he never would have let me do that."

Lucian moved a few feet to the left and flicked the lighter again, this time holding the orange-blue flame up to the second statue's broken right thumb.

Everyone watched, mesmerized, as the hypnotist's finger blackened. And then, not thinking about how hot the ivory would be, not caring that he'd burn his skin, Lucian wiped the carbon off.

Hypnos's thumb was intact and unharmed. "This is the piece you want," Lucian said.

At that moment, almost on cue, Lucian heard the sound of acoustic waves.

He looked up.

Hovering over the Charles Engelhard Court of the American Wing was a red-and-white helicopter with the words Sight-SeeNY stenciled on its side in blue. In a city that monitored its airspace so vigilantly, it was absurd that small planes and choppers flying under 1,100 feet weren't required to file flight plans. But they weren't, and so dozens of companies flew tourists around the island on sightseeing tours. But none of those companies would have needed an external sling capable of lifting thousands of pounds. There was only one reason such a sling was hanging off this chopper.

It was a foolproof escape plan. Almost.

Chapter

SIXTY-EIGHT

The west wall of the American Wing faced Central Park and, like the ceiling, was made entirely of glass panes. Dead center were two wide glass emergency doors.

"Open the doors," the lead terrorist shouted at Olshling. "Now."

The head of security looked over at Lucian for instructions.

As the agent most closely involved with the Met for the past eight years, Lucian knew the details of all the security systems in place. To open those doors required both a biometric fingerprint scan and retina scan. He felt a kick of something that was almost hope. Now that he knew how the intruders planned on getting away, Lucian didn't think they planned on detonating the explosives. The goal was to take the sculpture and get away.

Damn if Lucian was going to let that happen.

He was going to need Olshling to be listening and thinking, and not just reacting. Normally Lucian would have bet on him. But knowing someone in peacetime didn't always prepare you for how they would react in war.

"Do it all, Nick. Everything. Open all the systems. Fast," Lucian instructed, and then he stepped to the side. He was standing to the left of the sculpture now. On the right, closer to the door, was one of the terrorists—the brutish one who had wheeled the statue down from upstairs was watching Olshling, who was still in front of the glass doors. They were all watching him. Lucian took a half step back. Then another. He was behind Hypnos now. No one was paying attention to him.

Olshling entered a PIN number and then put his finger on the biometric reader. A red light flashed. Then he looked up. The retina scanner blinked green. A single second later a screaming alarm went off, the ear-shattering noise filling the great hall and overpowering the chopper's whirring.

Talbot rushed Olshling, grabbed him around the neck and screamed in his ear. "Shut it off! Shut it off! No tricks, damn you. What the hell are you trying?"

It took Olshling three seconds to punch in the cancellation code.

The siren came to a dead halt.

"What the fuck are you doing?" Talbot yelled.

"Forget it," Samimi screamed as he shoved the man aside and pushed open the door. "We have to get out of here now. Fast. Move. Everyone out!"

Behind them, the partygoers who saw the doors open surged forward—they wanted to get out—and fast.

Three of the terrorists held the crowd back, pushing and shoving the hysterical crowd back out of the way, while the other two ushered Hypnos out and into the net hanging off the extension sling connected to the helicopter, and then all of the men jumped on beside him. The exodus had taken less than forty-five seconds to accomplish.

As the chopper rose up above the Beaux Arts building, six men and an ancient chryselephantine sculpture swung back and forth above the tree line while, below, the museum's guests stampeded the doors, desperate to escape the building even though the threat was gone.

In the mad rush, Jim Rand, one of the Met's board members, who was holding his wife's arm, was thrown to the ground. Her hysterical screams for help went unheard. Hitch Oster assisted two elderly women, both in tears, through the door. Not far behind him Marie Grimshaw stumbled and found herself being helped by a stranger. Olshling was caught up in their wake, unable to fight the push of the crowd, and wound up outside. He hadn't taken his eyes off the chopper and the swaying bounty it carried. He prayed Lucian Glass knew what he was doing.

Chapter

SIXTY-NINE

Less than a quarter of a mile away, west of the Met, deep in the park, the helicopter hovered above a white panel truck parked in the otherwise deserted loading area behind the Belvedere Castle.

Nassir's master plan had allowed three-and-a-half minutes for the chopper to lower the sling and for the men to hop off and get the sculpture loaded on the waiting truck. They all made it with fifteen seconds to spare.

Ali Samimi jumped in beside the driver, who took off, speeding through the park, heading for a secure location just a mile and a half away.

Above them the aircraft flew off in the opposite direction. To anyone watching from a distance, the delivery, which had been made below the tree line, would have been invisible. Even if the authorities were able to pinpoint the exact location where the chopper hovered, by the time they reached it, the truck would be long gone.

Glancing at his watch, Samimi cursed the minutes he'd lost inside the Met. There was only a slim chance he'd now have enough time to accomplish his own goal tonight. If nothing else went wrong, he might be okay. But it would be close. He soothed himself with the thought that as good as the police and FBI were, if no one knew what they were looking for, they wouldn't be able to find it. And no one knew anything about this truck.

Activating a switch on the dashboard, Samimi listened to the panels on the outside of the van slide forward. A white rig that had no lettering or identification on its side panels when it left the castle's loading dock was decorated with a bakery's logo when it exited the transverse.

With the cookies and milk slats in place, the driver proceeded without incident across town to Seventh Avenue, then south, then west again to Ninth Avenue and then downtown until finally pulling into a warehouse on Twenty-First Street, beating their best practice time by three minutes.

Earlier that day, Samimi had inspected the site one last time, checking the electronic garage door opener and secreting a shoe box–size parcel, wrapped in plain brown paper, in an out-of-the-way dark corner.

Now, while the movers opened the truck doors and started to unload the statue, Samimi retrieved his package and, after checking that no one was paying attention to him, unwrapped it and put its contents in his pocket.

Feeling slightly more secure, he returned his attention to the movers. "Be careful," he admonished from across the room.

A few seconds later, he repeated the warning. Based on the glances they shot him, the movers didn't appreciate his prompts. Finally Larry Talbot, the terrorist who'd led the operation inside the Met and who now had his mask off, let loose. "We got it here in one piece, didn't we? Back off, Samimi, and let us do our goddamned job."

Talbot was right. Samimi knew he was just making it worse, but he was nervous. There was so little time. He needed to get everyone out of here before Taghinia showed up so he could make his phone call and set the final part of the attack in motion.

"Hurry," he said, ignoring Talbot's fury.

Finally, after minutes that seemed like hours, the men piled back into the truck. Samimi opened the warehouse doors and watched the van drive out onto the street and into the night. In less than three hours the vehicle would be crushed and compacted in a plant in New Jersey, reduced to nothing more than a rectangle of useless rusted steel and rubber.

Alone in the warehouse, Samimi looked at his partner in crime. Hypnos sat dead center of the large, otherwise empty space. With the lights of the truck gone, the interior was tomblike. Only one of the dozen fluorescents that hung from the rafters of the old carriage house still worked, casting the sculpture's long shadow across the wide wood-planked floor and up onto the wall. Turning his back on the treasure that had been at the heart of so much turmoil and death, Samimi pulled out his cell phone and started to punch in the number he'd memorized that would connect him to the office of the director of the New York office of the FBI—

"Who are you calling?" Farid Taghinia's voice boomed out as he shut the door behind him and pocketed his set of keys.

Samimi's pulse quickened as he spun around. His boss was three minutes early. "You," Samimi said quickly. Too quickly? "I was calling to tell you everything had worked out and that we were here."

"Excellent job." Taghinia, unlit cigar clamped between his lips, was walking around Hypnos, inspecting it. Reaching out, he touched an ivory hand. "So this is the god of sleep, the brother of the god of death." He touched a broken foot. "We're almost done with this unsavory job, and I for one will be happy when this—" he groped for the right word "—this monstrosity is out of here and on his way back to our country."

While Taghinia still had his back to him, Samimi had to move fast. "I'm not sure that's going happen," he said as he pulled out the Kimber M1911 pistol that he'd secreted away earlier that afternoon.

"What nonsense are you talking?" Taghinia turned around. The cigar was gone. In his right hand he held a SA Sig Sauer P226. Laughing, he said, "Put the gun down."

Samimi's hand shook but he didn't lower his weapon.

"You understand that if you kill me our government will avenge my death with the execution of your entire family," Taghinia said. "Are you willing to risk the life of everyone you care about for that?" He nodded at the sculpture. "I've already alerted them that I have been worried about your loyalty."

"I don't believe you," Samimi said. And he didn't. This was exactly the kind of convenient lie he'd seen his boss come up with dozens of times before.

Taghinia's finger tensed on the trigger. "You don't have to believe me. You just have to have doubt."

There was no reason Taghinia would have been suspicious of him, Samimi thought. He hadn't left a single clue anywhere, hadn't spoken to anyone about his plans. Taghinia couldn't have known, could he?

A second of worried hesitation was all that his boss needed.

The blast echoed through the empty space and, in the rafters, a pigeon that had been nesting flew up, flapping its wings wildly, sending two feathers floating down, slowly, through the air.

Chapter

SEVENTY

In the confusion that ensued after Nicolas Olshling unlocked the doors and set off the alarm, Lucian had opened the wooden panel in Hypnos's back and slipped inside the sculpture. He couldn't know if any of the terrorist team had noticed his action. It was a risk. But that was his job.

As the piece was hoisted up, Lucian put his arms out to steady himself. Twilight streamed through the cracks in the wood, illuminating the coffinlike interior. He'd been inside the copy of Hypnos when he'd put in the GPS tracking device before his trip to L.A., but this was the original, two millennia more ancient and much more precious.

He struggled to stay upright as the sling swung in the air but the wind was strong and a sudden gust threw him off balance. At least the noise of the chopper drowned out the sounds he made when he fell. As long as they remained in the air, Lucian decided it would be smarter to stay down.

He was staring up into the head of the Greek god when he noticed how the wooden supports crisscrossed each other and formed a square in the center. At first, it seemed to just be the result of the way the supports had been constructed, but the longer he peered at it the more curious its position became. There was something about it…something about this hidden area deep in what would have been Hypnos's brain if he'd been a mortal man.

The strange configuration looked so familiar. He and Iris Bellmer had talked about…what was it? Then, he remembered.

Telamon had said Pythagoras's priest had given him treasures to hide inside the piece he'd commissioned.

Slowly and carefully, Lucian stood up and reached behind Hypnos's eyes. The enclosure was sealed. Working his fingers around its edges, Lucian found a small latch. But years of exposure to moisture had resulted in rot and ruin. Finally, after scraping and scratching his skin, he managed to pry it open and lift up the lid. Inside he felt something brittle and leathery.

The pouch was made of cracked and frayed animal hide. Inside was something small and round. Lucian put two fingers into the pouch and pulled out a single bead, slightly larger than a marble.

In the pale evening light that seeped through the cracks in the ancient wooden sculpture, Lucian examined the smooth, finely carved orb made of lapis lazuli, onyx and chalcedony. It looked as if it might be one of Hypnos's eyes.

The sculpture lurched. Lucian struggled to stay upright. He slid to one side and put out his hand to stop from smashing into the wall. The orb slipped out of his fingers.

The sculpture was dropping. Fast. Then it leveled off and landed with a soft thud. Wood on metal, Lucian thought from the sound. The sound of the chopper became less intense. Loud metal doors banged shut. Then everything went black.

Where was he? Lucian couldn't see anything. Could only hear muffled conversation. Then an engine revved, loud and almost angry. They were moving. He tried to figure out what

had happened. Pictured it. The chopper had flown to a rendez-
vous point somewhere close by, probably in the park, and
lowered them down to a waiting vehicle. How far away was the
next destination? How much longer until they arrived? He
couldn't waste a second. Dropping to his hands and knees,
Lucian felt for the object. What if there was a crack in the base?
What if the sphere had fallen out? What if he'd found it, only
to lose it?

When he finally retrieved it, he wrapped his fingers around
it. Lucian couldn't see the jewellike object anymore, but he
knew exactly what he was holding: an orb created by a master
sculptor to represent the hypnotist's third eye.

Dr. Bellmer had described it as the entry point for our unconscious, the portal through which we can access memories
of lives lived long ago. Was this third eye the Memory Tool that
Frederick L. Lennox had been searching for? Was this the
magical talisman the priest from the school of Pythagoras had
wanted secreted away inside of Hypnos?

Lucian replaced the object in its leather pouch. What should
he do with it now? He didn't know where the truck was headed
or who was going to be on the other end to greet it. Reaching
up, he started to put the pouch back in the wooden compart-
ment where he'd found it. The orb had been there for more than
twenty centuries; it would certainly be safe there during the rest
of what Lucian anticipated was going to be a long and dangerous night. But what if he didn't get another chance to salvage it?

Lucian pocketed the treasure as once again Hypnos was
moving, accompanied by grunts and moans and the urging of
a man who spoke with a Middle Eastern accent. This time
when the sculpture was set down, Lucian assumed they'd
reached their final destination—final, at least, for a while.
Standing in the dark interior, he waited, for what he wasn't sure.

After another few minutes, the man who had been urging everyone to hurry dismissed his workers. Footsteps echoed on a wooden floor. Hinges creaked. The truck's engine revved.

Lucian pulled his gun out of his shoulder holster. There was no sound outside of this tomb anymore. Had anyone stayed behind? Then he heard a slight noise…a human footstep? Or a rat scurrying across the deserted building? It wouldn't hurt to wait and be sure before he climbed out of his hiding place. The silence persisted. Finally he figured it was safe. And then, just as Lucian started to push open the door, he heard the electronic click of someone punching in a number on a cell phone and a deep voice echoing in the cavernous space.

"Who are you calling?"

"You," the more familiar voice responded. "I was calling to tell you everything had worked out and that we were here."

"Excellent job."

Footsteps circled around the sculpture as the voice continued. "So this is the god of sleep, the brother of the god of death. We're almost done with this unsavory job, and I for one will be happy when this…this monstrosity is out of here and on his way back to our country."

Now Lucian knew. Shabaz wasn't behind this kidnapping. Nor was Malachai. He pictured the wall in his office, saw all the disparate pieces. The clue was the American-Iranian lawyer, Vartan Reza, who had been killed in Central Park, who'd been working for the government of Iran, going through all the right channels to facilitate the return of this piece of sculpture. The Iranians had hired an even more prestigious law firm to continue that fight after Reza died. That had been done only for appearances. They'd already decided to steal the sculpture. Why? As a political statement? To prove they could infiltrate the museum?

"I'm not sure that's going to happen." This was the younger man Lucian had heard before, his words flung out with nervous bravado.

"What nonsense are you talking?" There was a pause. Then a laugh. "Put the gun down." Another pause. "You understand that if you kill me our government will avenge my death with the execution of your entire family. Are you willing to risk your life and the lives of everyone you care about for that? I've already alerted them that I have been worried about your loyalty."

"I don't believe you," the young man said, but the bravado was gone now and the words quivered with uncertainty.

"You don't have to believe me. You just have to have doubt."

Very slowly and carefully, Lucian pushed open the door and took in the scene. In the low light he could make out two men, both with drawn pistols. In the silence the first metallic click was a deafening warning. Two bullets flew, one less than a second after the other. Both hit their marks.

A pigeon squawked and flew wildly as Lucian raced over to his prey. The man had dropped his gun and was bleeding profusely from the wound in his hand.

The younger victim was leaning against the wall, his eyes open but not seeing, as a wide stain seeped through the fabric of an expensive sports coat that Samimi must have worn that day because he was going to a private showing at the museum.

Chapter

SEVENTY-ONE

"I feel my immortality over sweep all pains, all tears, all time, all fears,—and peal, like the eternal thunders of the deep, into my ears, this truth,—thou livest forever!"
—George Gordon, Lord Byron

Lucian was at the office at seven the next morning. The first thing he did was tag the ancient orb he'd taken from the sculpture the night before, log it in and lock it up. It wasn't evidence of a crime. Not one that had been committed in this century. Not yet, anyway. Whatever it was, whatever anyone thought it might be, Lucian wanted it safe and protected. He had little doubt Malachai Samuels would kill for it.

At his desk, Lucian sat down at his computer and checked through the reports that had come in during the night in preparation for the briefing Comley had scheduled for nine-thirty. Making notes, he added information to the list of events, excluding remarks and suppositions that defied logic. They went on a private list of mysteries the agency would never be able to help solve.

Was Veronica Keyes the reincarnation of Bibi, the woman Serge Fouquelle had killed in Persia over a hundred years ago because she was in the way of his looting of an ancient crypt? Who had Marie Grimshaw been? Iantha, the young sculptor's wife who died because of his hubris? Was Deborah Mitchell one of the soul survivors from the past, too? Someone whose story he and Iris Bellmer hadn't yet found? It didn't matter now. Still, he wondered who he'd see if he looked into Andre Jacobs's eyes. Emeline's eyes. The ghost of Solange?

Had everything come full circle? Had he failed the first time he'd tried to protect each of these souls? Had last night been his second chance?

No. That was the thinking of a crazy man. He was logical, and rational reasoning dictated there was no before, only now. Solange's soul was not alive in Emeline. She'd made that up just like she'd made up her stalker, to deceive Lucian and distract him and protect her father's transgressions from being discovered, to keep Lucian so preoccupied he wouldn't think to explore the obvious solution to the puzzle that had been plaguing him all these years.

Who had been responsible for stealing the Matisse? Now he knew. Jacobs. The framer had hired someone to break into the gallery. He'd planned for everything, except for one contingency—that the teenage boy who had a date with his daughter would be late getting uptown.

Lucian checked his watch again. It was 8:07 a.m. He picked up his phone and dialed Eric Broderick's direct line. The chief of police was always there early.

"Busy night you had. I was just reading about it in the paper," Broderick said. "You all right?"

"Never better," Lucian answered even though his voice belied his words. "Listen, I wanted to let you know you can save the taxpayers some money and call off Emeline Jacobs's security detail."

Broderick had some questions and for the next ten minutes

Lucian filled him in, offering as much information as was necessary but nothing extra.

At 8:20, Lucian called the Phoenix Foundation's legal counsel. The lawyer wasn't in. Lucian did some more paperwork and tried him twice more. He reached him at 8:59 and was on the phone with him for the next twenty minutes getting the information he needed. Next he checked in with Nina Keyes, who said her granddaughter was doing surprisingly well. "Almost as if the incident was healing."

When Lucian walked into his boss's office, Matt Richmond and Elgin Barindra were already seated at the scarred table. Everyone was subdued. Hypnos had been returned to the Met and the head of the Iranian mission to the UN, Farid Taghinia, had been arrested and booked on multiple charges for more than five heinous crimes, but a man had died, and that cast a pall over the meeting. Lucian had shot the gun out of Taghinia's hand only seconds too late. Ali Samimi was dead before he made it to the hospital.

There was a lot to cover, and the meeting had been going on for over two hours when they finally moved away from the incident at the Met and over to Elgin's report on what had happened at the Phoenix Foundation the day before.

"Dr. Talmage called me last night." Elgin almost sounded disappointed. "She said she couldn't keep me on."

"She explained what was going on?" Comley asked.

"All she said was that Dr. Samuels was taking a medical leave of absence and it didn't make sense to have me there without him. I tried to find out more, but she wasn't very forthcoming."

"That's okay. Everything Beryl and Malachai said is on the tapes on our equipment at the apartment," Lucian said. He had his sketchbook open, and he was drawing the little girl who had been held hostage the night before.

"When did you listen to the tapes?" Comley asked.

"I went over them before work this morning."

"Don't you ever sleep?" Elgin asked.

"No," Richmond answered. "He never does."

Lucian ignored the comment. "I was also able to reach the foundation's lawyer, who confirmed that the co-director of the Phoenix Foundation is on a temporary medical leave of absence. He assured me that Dr. Talmage will cooperate if we need to talk to her about anything, including Vienna."

"But we still don't have any proof Malachai was involved in that, do we?" Comley asked Elgin. "You didn't hear anything else about Vienna, did you?"

"Just what I already told you," Elgin said. "Malachai said that the Memorist Society's historian gave him the list of Memory Tools."

"Knowing there was no way we could ever disprove that, since the historian is dead." Lucian practically spat the words out as he slammed down his pencil. "I know Malachai is guilty."

"And we'll figure out a way to prove it," Comley said in a calming voice.

"When?" Lucian challenged. "Here we are, still talking about him…and he's still not behind bars. Not even arrested."

"No, he's not. But you saved the lives of I don't know how many people last night, plus several pieces of priceless artwork. We confiscated enough explosives to destroy the American Wing and the Egyptian collection and to kill everyone in the vicinity. Shabaz will be going to prison. The Iranian government will have a lot to answer for. All that, Lucian. Can't you give yourself a break?" Comley was looking at him, frowning, waiting for him to say something.

"Ali Samimi was dialing our phone number last night when Farid Taghinia walked in on him and surprised him. He *was* calling us. And in his wallet was a note with the address and phone number of a garage upstate and an explanation that the car is the one that killed Vartan Reza and that it was being driven by our friend Taghinia. I'll bet it has all the prints and forensic evidence we need to get that murderer, too. Samimi shouldn't have died."

"No. No one ever should die," Richmond said.

"You got that right," Elgin said.

For a few seconds no one spoke. Comley and Richmond exchanged a brief glance. Lucian saw it. "What?"

"Matt and I were talking before you came in. There's still some more paperwork but we should have our warrant by the end of the day. Tomorrow morning we'll be ready to arrest Jacobs."

"Let me take care of it for you," Richmond said with a hint of trepidation, as if he expected an argument from Lucian. "You don't have to deal with them anymore."

"I think that's a brilliant idea—be my guest," Lucian said.

After the meeting ended, Lucian went back to his office. There was paperwork to deal with, but instead of sitting down at his desk, he attacked his wall, ripping down the photographs, articles and bits and pieces of research he'd tacked up. The case was officially over. There were still indictments and trials and plea bargaining ahead, but that was for the lawyers and judges and jury to take care of. His part was done.

He put the stack of photos on his desk. The one on top was of Hypnos, staring at him with eyes that could not see.

Nicolas Olshling and his team had arrived at the warehouse while the police were still working with the crime scene and stayed until two in the morning, when they finally released the sculpture. The head of security and his men carefully and lovingly wrapped Hypnos in thick padding to transport him back to the museum.

Before he left, Olshling walked over to where Lucian was standing and tried to thank him. "It was my job..."

Lucian recognized guilt and failure on his face. "You've protected the museum from every possible outside threat for years. Now you'll figure out how to protect it from inside threats, too."

Olshling shook his head, too embarrassed to meet Lucian's gaze. "I should have known something was going on."

"You can't know everything."

Despite what had happened last night, Lucian believed the museum should have the orb that he'd found exactly where Pythagoras believed the third eye was. The god of sleep had protected the mystical object for 2600 years—he obviously knew how to keep secrets. At some point he'd return it to them, but not quite yet.

Chapter
SEVENTY-TWO

At noon Emeline called. Lucian recognized her number and let the machine answer. She called again at two. He didn't pick up that call, either. At five he sat down and played the messages back.

"Lucian? The police just left," she said. "They said you called off the detail. I tried to reach Captain Broderick, but he's not in. Does this mean you found the man who's been threatening me?"

She sounded excited. *Good little actress,* he thought.

On the second call, concern colored her voice. "Lucian, are you all right? Last night was so terrible. All I can think about is what would have happened if you hadn't been there. I know you're busy…but when you get a break, call me, okay?"

There was always coffee in the agency's kitchenette, but this late in the day it was bitter and thick. Lucian didn't care. He poured it into a foam cup and headed back into his office. He read a few e-mails and took a sip of the disgusting brew without tasting it. At 5:20 p.m. he shut down his computer and left. He was exhausted.

Lucian sat in his car, unsure where to go. He couldn't get Emeline's voice out of his head. She'd lied to him about everything, and he'd believed her. Worse, he'd believed *in* her. And because of her, he'd delegated his responsibility for bringing a job to a close for the first time in his career.

The traffic was heavy, and it took Lucian almost forty minutes to reach Madison Avenue and Eighty-Third Street. He pulled into an illegal spot and then sat there staring at the storefront. He'd avoided this place for the past twenty years. Even during the past few weeks, he'd dropped Emeline off here once but had never gone inside. The framing store was the only ghost left.

She was happy to see him and so relieved the police had caught her stalker.

"We didn't catch him," Lucian told her.

"Then why did you call Broderick and tell him I didn't need protection anymore?" She was frowning and clearly confused.

"Yesterday we arrested an art dealer for trafficking in stolen goods. With very little provocation he told us the names of the men he'd worked with—one who procured a Van Gogh for him, another who'd gotten him a Matisse. A landscape. *View of St. Tropez.* That man was Andre Jacobs."

Lucian stopped, waiting, hoping Emeline would protest, that she'd argue and offer up an explanation, or lash out, indignant, insulted by his accusation. Or insist she had no idea what he was talking about. But she didn't do any of those things. Emeline remained completely silent. As good an admission of guilt as any.

"Your father may be old and he may be sick, but that doesn't preclude him from being the devil. And if he's the devil, what does that make you?" Lucian waited for her to respond, and was infuriated all the more for her silence. "What did you think? That if you pretended you were Solange reincarnated I'd be so blinded and confused that Andre would be safe?" Lucian laughed bitterly. "Well, congratulations. You did an excellent job. What did you use? Solange's journals? Letters? How did you find out about the carving on the tree? Where'd she write about that? The cherry on top was how hard you fought against the idea yourself. That was priceless. All that protesting about how you wanted me to see you for who you were, about how hard it was for you to live with Andre's and Martha's desperation."

There were clues to what she was thinking in her pale, pale face and in her sad eyes, but he didn't trust himself to read them.

"Tell me how you knew about the tree, Emeline."

"It was in her journal."

"And that she'd asked me to paint her?"

She nodded.

"Did he ask you to set me up like this?"

"You don't understand. It was the tragedy of his life," she said, throwing the words out at him as if he should be able to understand this. "An accident that shouldn't have happened. He never thought the theft would result in murder. It was supposed to be a simple robbery."

"He was a greedy bastard, responsible for his own daughter's death."

"Don't you think he knows that?" she shouted.

Lucian walked over to the door. He put his hand out, about to leave. "Your father's going to be arrested tomorrow morning." He stood there for a moment longer looking across the room at her, at the storefront, at the whole sorry scene, one last time. "Tell Andre if he turns himself in before we come for him, the courts will be more lenient. At his age, in such poor health, with a good lawyer, he should be able to work out a house arrest agreement."

Lucian opened the door. On the other side was a man just about to ring the bell. Well dressed, he was wearing a light brown suit and carrying a rectangular package wrapped in plain brown paper. He had his head down, but something about him looked familiar. Lucian didn't care who he was. He wanted to get out and get away. He left the door open for the customer and walked to his car.

Lucian put his key in the ignition. He was angry—mostly with himself—for getting so emotional. It had been a mistake to even come here. But at least it was done. He looked at the clock on the dashboard—it read 6:26 p.m. He'd been there for less than twenty minutes. It had felt like years. Twenty years, to be exact. He stared at the storefront.

The gold lettering on the black glass read JACOBS FRAMING—EST.1933. The plate glass window showcased a half-dozen elaborate gilt frames. During the day you could see in though the front door, but the shade was pulled down now. The hours were painted on the glass in more gold lettering. MONDAY TO SATURDAY, 10 a.m. to 5 p.m. CLOSED SUNDAY.

He could see the words from where he sat. The store closed at five o'clock. So why had there been a customer waiting outside when Lucian left?

But it wasn't a customer. Lucian knew who it was. He'd met the man twice. Put his hand on his arm. Consoled him.

Leaping out of the car, Lucian raced up to the storefront. The door wasn't locked. No one was in the front room. Brown wrapping paper and a length of string littered the floor. Voices and the scents of glue and sawdust wafted out from the back.

Lucian pulled his Glock out of its holster.

The hallway was dark. At the far end the light shone, casting the two people in a warm yellow glow. Emeline was standing at a large wooden table, laying frame corners on the edges of a painting, trying out different combinations. The customer stood beside her, looking over her shoulder.

Everything seemed completely ordinary—they were picking out a frame—except the new customer was holding a gun in his right hand. Emeline couldn't see it. But Lucian could.

"Drop it." Lucian assumed a shooting stance, his gun trained on the intruder's chest. A perfect bull's-eye shot.

Charlie Danzinger grabbed Emeline around the waist, jerked her in front of him and shoved the barrel of his gun into her temple. He did it so quickly and smoothly, almost as if he'd expected an intruder—almost as if he welcomed one. The hand holding the weapon shook slightly, but Danzinger didn't look scared. The Met's top restorer looked deranged. And that bothered Lucian more than anything else. A cogent argument didn't work with someone who was lost to logic.

"Why don't you let her go, and you and I can work this out."

Danzinger, who'd killed in this very room so long ago, and looked ready to kill again, shook his head. "Can't." His tongue flicked out, fast like a lizard's, and he licked his lips.

Lucian tasted bile. "Why can't you?"

"She's a witness."

"To what?"

"To what happened. To everything that happened. She saw it, she knows."

"What does she know?"

"I worked for Andre Jacobs. He was like a father to me. I was all alone in the city. Trying to get started. He said nothing would happen. He was like a father to me. But she was here. She was here…" His voice wavered and Lucian wondered if he was going to cry. "I've never meant to hurt anyone. Never. Never told anyone. But if she knows…" He nodded to Emeline. "If she knows and if she tells…I'll go to jail. And I can't go to jail. Can't be away from my work. I do important work. I restore things."

Emeline was as still as if she were painted there—not real at all.

Danzinger licked his lips again.

"You don't really believe all that stuff about reincarnation, do you?" Lucian asked him. "It's just some hocus-pocus the papers printed because they needed to sell copies. There's no such thing as reincarnation. She has no idea who you are. She lied about being reincarnated to get sympathy. She doesn't know anything."

"I can't go to jail. I can't be away from my work."

"Charlie, she doesn't know anything. Tell him, Emeline. Tell him how you lied about being reincarnated."

The gold, L-shaped frame corner flashed as Emeline swung it around and up and into the man's face. Its sharp edge sank into his right eye. Danzinger let go of her as he put his hand up to the source of the excruciating pain.

The restorer's scream was endless, a long note of pure, unending anguish, and it echoed in Lucian's ears as he jumped him, grabbed Danzinger's gun out of his hand and threw him down on the ground. Cuffing him, Lucian kept him there on the floor with his knee shoved into Danzinger's back, watching the man's blood pool on the wooden floor as his wound bled out.

It was nine-thirty by the time the police finished taking statements, collecting evidence and closing out the murder scene. After they left, Lucian locked the front door, found a bottle of Scotch and some coffee mugs and poured drinks.

"I don't want it," Emeline said when he put one down on the desk in front of her.

"Drink it anyway." He crossed the room and leaned against the door, as far away from her as he could get. He didn't want to smell her damned perfume or see her pulse beating in her neck.

Like a child, she took the mug in both hands and sipped obediently. His own first gulp went down like barbed wire, but the next wasn't as rough and the one after that was almost smooth.

"Thank you," Emeline said. "You saved my life."

"This time I knew what to do."

"What do you mean?"

He shook his head. "Nothing."

"You mean you didn't know what to do to save Solange?"

"No. I didn't." Lucian drank more of the Scotch.

"How did you know to come back inside?" Emeline asked.

"I saw Danzinger as I walked out. He was there by the door waiting. Just another customer. No reason to pay attention to him. I went back to my car, and then it hit me that if he had been just another customer, why was he waiting outside like that? Why would it matter if there was someone else inside? And it was too late. The store was closed. It was a hunch. Not nearly as clever as you reading old journals to figure things out."

The gibe stung, and she blinked twice. She started to say something, then stopped. Finally, "Lucian, please, I want to at least explain something about that, about Andre and why—"

"I know. He's all the family you have. You love him. I get it. Let's not rehash this."

"But you just saved my life." Her voice cracked.

"That's my job. To save things."

"Things?"

"Just don't ask me to forgive you for what you did. What's so damn ironic about all this is…" Now he was shouting, yelling at her, or at himself, he wasn't sure. "You made me see Solange again. Really see her. And I finally understood how I'd idealized her. Turned her into an impossible, perfect memory. The terrible irony is that I'd stopped wanting her. Do you understand? It was you I wanted—it was you. You! Isn't that something?"

She bent her head and lowered her face into her hands. Her blond hair fell forward like a curtain, making the distance between them even greater.

Lucian ached to get out of there finally and for good, but he couldn't leave while she was like that. The seconds went by. Her weeping was silent, but her back shuddered with each new sob.

"You did it for him? For a man who…" He couldn't finish. He wanted to say something to hurt her, but he didn't. He felt sorry for her, for her misguided effort. Lucian put his hand up to his temple to massage the pain. The gesture had become a habit.

But despite all the confusion, sadness and exhaustion, he didn't have any pain. He hadn't since yesterday evening. He just hadn't realized it until now. It had disappeared at some point during the ambush, and in the ensuing hours it hadn't returned.

No nightmares had woken him up that morning, either. No ghostlike women had haunted his dreams.

Finally, Emeline lowered her hands. Her face was blotchy, her eyes red and bloodshot. Her hair was disheveled. The familiar and very real scar above her eyebrow stood out in relief. In the framed mirror opposite the desk, she saw her own reflection and reacted, wiping away the tears, trying to smooth down her hair, and then attempted a laugh that sounded like a sob.

"Promise," she said, "you won't paint me like this…"

Her whisper reached out and grabbed hold of him. Words that no one but he had ever heard, words that could not have been written down in a diary or a journal or in a letter or repeated to anyone because they had been said only seconds before the woman who'd whispered them had died.

He didn't move. Didn't say a word. Tried to absorb what had just occurred. Attempted to reason it out. Reason all of it out. It was too much for now. Okay then. He just needed to reason part of it out. *If…if there is reincarnation,* he thought, *it's about forward motion. It has to be, or else we would all be forever stuck in the past.*

"Please promise," she repeated, "you won't paint me like this."

They were Solange's last words coming from Emeline, but she was waiting for an answer, something Solange hadn't been able do.

He was looking at her across the room and the distance between them did not seem as great as it had only seconds before. Lucian took a step closer. Both of them had been damaged, like the Matisse, like the sculpture of the god of sleep, but they were survivors, too, maybe more special for what had happened to them, as if what they had gone through had imbued them with something magical. And then the gap was closed.

* * * *

AUTHOR'S NOTE

As with the first two novels in this series, *The Reincarnationist* and *The Memorist,* there is a lot of fact mixed in with my fiction.

The Metropolitan Museum of Art certainly exists—I've been lucky to live in its orbit for my whole life and been able to spend thousands of hours there. While the facts about the museum's history are a matter of public record, their security measures are not. But security experts have assured me the scenario in *The Hypnotist* is plausible (although I certainly hope not possible).

The American Wing exists as do the Islamic Art galleries, which were closed for renovation during the writing of this novel. Many of the paintings I've written about are either real or based on actual paintings, the names of which I've changed.

There is no record of Hypnos, the statue at the heart of this novel, but chryselephantine sculpture is well documented even though only fragments of these colossal works of art have survived. My thanks to Kenneth D. S. Lapatin for his help regarding these works.

Sadly, there is a billion-dollar industry in stolen art, all too often related to drug cartels and illicit arms deals. Cultural heritage concerns and lawsuits are rampant, and they're fraught with the same issues I've written about.

Former special agent Robert K. Wittman, who changed the way the FBI treated stolen art, helped me craft this book's version of the real Art Crime Team with his advice, but he's not to be blamed for the places where I took artistic license.

Whenever possible, dates and descriptions of historical events are accurate as are most of the locales in New York City, my hometown. There is no actual Phoenix Foundation. The work done there is, however, inspired by the work done at the

University of Virginia Health System by the real-life Dr. Ian Stevenson who studied children with past-life memories for over thirty years. Dr. Bruce Greyson and Dr. Jim Tucker, a child psychiatrist, continue Ian Stevenson's work today. (These fine doctors are not to be blamed for any of Dr. Malachai Samuels's personality defects.)

Hypnosis does date back to ancient times, and sleep temples did in fact exist. There is a lot of fascinating evidence that hypnosis is a portal into reincarnation memories, and I've worked with several therapists who've used it with patients to help them discover their past lives.

ACKNOWLEDGMENTS

To Lou Pitt, who certainly proved to me that reincarnation exists by helping this series find a new incarnation as the television series *Past Life*.

To everyone at MIRA Books—especially my wonderful editor, Margaret O'Neill Marbury, and Adam Wilson.

As always the thought of writing any book without Lisa Tucker and Douglas Clegg seems impossible—I hope the impossible never happens.

To Jerry Hooten—if there are any factual errors having to do with security issues and investigative techniques they all are mine, not his.

To Susan O'Doherty, who saves me so much time and grief and so much of my sanity.

A huge thank-you to readers, booksellers, librarians everywhere.

To my wonderful family. And to Doug.